SATAN'S SISTER

Who are you? Angelique's lips silently asked.

The girl said, "I was Sister Maria when you knew me."

Angelique was stunned. *You cannot be her. She was—old!*

"We all have our price. They made me seventeen again—eternally—in exchange for renouncing my vows."

But—you were a nun! In God's name, how could you do this?

"You're shocked." Maria shook her head. "*He* has ways to convert anyone. The Dark Man scares people out of their wits, then makes them choose between slow, torturous death, or giving over their souls to the Devil. He has the power. He's got a lock on this island you wouldn't believe—it's like a tropical Nazi Germany. The Dark Man murdered or converted every person working at the Institute.

"It's high tech Satanism—*and it v* Man now owns everybody here. And a lot more."

Look for all these TOR books by Jack L. Chalker

THE MESSIAH CHOICE

JACK L. CHALKER

A TOM DOHERTY ASSOCIATES BOOK

For August Derleth and Bill Crawford.
both gone but not forgotten

THE MESSIAH CHOICE

Copyright © 1985 by Jack L. Chalker
Jacket art copyright © 1985 by David B. Mattingly

Reprinted by arrangement with Bluejay Books, Inc.

First TOR printing: May 1986

A TOR Book

Published by Tom Doherty Associates
49 West 24 Street
New York, N.Y. 10010

ISBN: 0-812-53290-2
CAN. ED.: 0-812-53291-0

Library of Congress Catalog Card Number: 85-6241

Printed in the United States

0 9 8 7 6 5 4 3 2 1

1

SPIDERS AND FLIES

Horrors and monsters are creatures of the night that have no business being up and about on a bright, warm, sunny morning, or so most think. Few stop and think that should evil rest between dawn and dusk it would be a far simpler and less dangerous world.

As was his custom, Sir Robert McKenzie arose at half past six in the morning, showered, dressed, and went down to the Lodge dining area for breakfast. Because he owned the place, and everything that could be seen or heard around it, he could easily have had his breakfast delivered to him privately in his luxurious suite at the Lodge, but he disliked the very idea of it. A sociable man who thought of the Institute as a sort of surrogate family, he would never have dreamed of cutting himself off from that family, so long as he had any chance to spend time with its members.

But as was often the case, there were few about when he entered the dining room, and, seeing no one he really needed to talk to, he took a table by himself. Knowing he was a man of punctuality who insisted on routine, the staff had his two soft-yolk, sunny-side-up eggs, three fat sausages, toast, and strawberry jam ready for him, it being Tuesday. A staffer entered, went to him, and handed him a thick sheaf of computer printouts. It was virtually impossible to get newspapers delivered to this spot until they were long outdated, but his computer link gave him photostatic copies of the relevant sections compiled by his global staff. He lingered over juice and coffee as he read the items one by one. About halfway through the stack of papers he suddenly stiffened, frowned, then hurriedly polished off the last of his coffee and, tucking the papers under his arm, he left the dining room and went immediately out the front entrance of the Lodge.

He was a big man with thick snow white hair and a matching moustache, and he was never inconspicuous. Only Sir Robert would wear a finely tailored tweed suit, long sleeve shirt, and carefully knotted red necktie in this subtropical heat.

He paused to light a cigar and glanced over at two small electric cars that resembled orange-colored golf carts, but then decided to walk. Port Kathleen was about a two mile downhill walk, and either because he was enjoying the fresh air and sun or because he wished to think on some matter he decided that walking was the way to go. He often liked to walk down to the tiny little town that was the island's only harbor, although he joked to friends and associates that he was far better at his age walking down than walking back up. No matter. Both electric cars and horses were available for the trip back if he required them. After all, he owned not only the Institute but also the town and, in fact, the whole damn island, all 1.8 by 2.2 miles of it.

Allenby Island was the remnant of a long extinct volcano, one so old that little in the way of geography would tell the casual visitor its origins and nature. It was shaped somewhat like a teardrop with a ramp-like terrain; Port Kathleen, at the bottom, was virtually at sea level, while the Institute, at the far end, stood at an elevation of almost two thousand feet, making it a bit cooler and breezier than the area below, but not by much.

A lone road snaked back and forth down the vegetation-covered slope formed by an ancient lava flow to keep the trip from having too severe an elevation for the little electric cars to handle, though for those afoot or on horseback, there were all sorts of trails, old and new, and short cuts. Sir Robert kept to the road for almost half the distance down, though occasionally being passed by a cart going up or down and politely nodding to them as they passed while refusing offers of rides.

He stopped for a moment at one worn trail head and then took it, instantly plunging into the dense tropical forest that was the island's true master and owner. The trail eventually reconnected with the road, but was hardly a short cut down; rather, it was occasionally used as a short cut to the beach, it being at the highest point up the mountain where it was possible to get down to the beach without plunging off a rock cliff.

A few hundred yards to the east of the road the trail suddenly broke into the clear, revealing a small, intimate meadow in which grew bright green grasses and flowers but, for some reason, no trees or vines or other large shrubs. Botanists had theorized that some mineral either present or lacking in this particular segment of rock was producing this effect, as there was no climatological reason for it, but it had never been satisfactorily explained. In the center of the meadow was an abrupt outcrop of ancient black lava upon which nothing would grow. It was a huge mass of obsidian or an obsidian-like rock, quick cooled and glassy, and while it was well worn, its persistence over the eons it must have stood there was another meadow mystery.

There were a great many insects in the forest, and tens of thousands of birds, but no land animals, big or small. Over the years some rats had come from ships that called, but those who survived the eradication campaigns and the numerous cats mostly stuck to the more civilized areas of the island; the jungle was not for tough and world-wise rats any more than it was really for people.

The sounds of birds and insects were all around him, lifting his spirits and making him feel truly alive. Not obtrusive, they were simply a comfortable and natural background to this remote little spot. He approached the glassy black mass and walked around it once, studying it, although he'd been here and seen it thousands of times before. It had, of course, acquired the nickname "the altar stone" even before he'd bought the place, although it was clearly a natural formation linked to larger deposits below. Its rough shape and downward slope could, with a bit of imagination, be said to resemble a facsimile of the island, complete with a depression down the center. The entire stone was perhaps eight feet long and three feet wide, a bit too long to be an island model, but that never stopped anybody.

Sir Robert looked at the depression, walked down to the foot of the stone, then knelt for a moment and examined something at the base. He stiffened. "That idiotic fanatical bastard!" he muttered under his breath. "Well, we'll fix him now!"

He got back up and began to walk away from the stone. He was almost at the edge of the meadow when he suddenly stopped again, turned, and looked puzzled. He could sense a *wrongness*, but for a moment he couldn't really place just what was wrong. Then he had it. The birds, the insects, even the distant roar of breakers and the sound of breezes through the treetops had ceased. It was as if he were suddenly covered by some huge and invisible bell jar, allowing sight but nothing else to penetrate. It was the most unnatural thing he'd ever experienced, and he had the good sense to be as frightened of it as he was curious about it.

Suddenly he heard a sound, back from the direction of the altar stone. A sharp, odd sequence that sounded very much like a great door opening, swinging wide, and then being closed again, a sound coming not really from the stone but from somewhere deep beneath it. Again there was silence, then the sudden, unmistakable sound of something coming, something huge, *as if great feet were slowly and methodically climbing a great stairway from beneath to the surface.*

Sir Robert frowned once more and tried to figure out the nature of it. Broadcast, somehow? Some sort of beam striking the meadow and making it, or perhaps the stone, some kind of radio receiver? It made sense. It fit in with all the other known facts. Anger replaced confusion within him. Just as the ancient shamans had carefully sculpted acoustical canals in their idols so as to make the masses believe they spoke, *he* had repeated the trick in a materialistic age using the most modern techniques. Now, he thought, I understand how it works. Now I know it all.

With that thought came the sudden realization that all this would never have been revealed to him unless it no longer mattered. Looking around, he entered the trail and the forest but stopped as the sounds from the meadow made it seem as if some great beast had now reached the top and was out in the open. It was such a convincing illusion that in spite of himself he stopped, turned, and looked back at the meadow and the altar stone. Nothing was visible in the eerie silence, but now, as he looked on, the grass in front of the altar stone bent and twisted as if crushed by an enormous foot, followed by yet another giant imprint a few yards further on.

Sir Robert turned and began to run down the path. He reached a junction of two trails, one well worn and leading back to the road, the other leading away towards the cliff trail down to the beach. He did not hesitate but took the slightly overgrown cliff trail. The road was his logical choice, and even if he'd met other people out there it would not stop that madman from killing them all to get to him. That he would not have. The cliff trail was also the most direct route to the village, although it was almost never used for that.

There were sounds behind him, sounds of some great beast crashing through the dense underbrush. Beamed-in illusion or true monster, it made no difference; the thing was almost certainly death and it was stalking him.

His heart pounding, he broke through the last of the bush and came to the edge of the cliff. It was more than a hundred foot drop and quite sheer, and he was forced to run along for a few hundred yards, fearing that the terrible thing, whatever it was, that chased him would spot him and simply knock him off the cliff. He was determined not to give its controller that satisfaction. If he could not outrun it, he would make bloody well certain that no verdict of death by accident or natural causes was possible.

He reached the trail break where it wound down the cliff to the sea and took it, going as fast as he dared. He was not in top condition, but he was no heart candidate, either. He jumped a few of the switchbacks when he dared to save time, and heard it break from the trees behind and above him. He dared not look back, but made for the beach as fast as he could. He jumped the last six feet into the sand and fell momentarily, then got up and continued to run along the beach towards the town and also out towards the water.

There was a rocky outcrop ahead, and he knew that the town lay not far beyond it. As he moved to the water's edge, he suddenly caught sight of the steeple of the small church and felt encouragement. *He might just make it!* Slowing, he risked a look back, and saw a huge disturbance in the sand near the bottom of the beach trail; now the sand was falling away, as if pressed in by some great weight, a body that had to be twenty feet tall if it existed at all and with a stride to match. He knew in an instant that he could not make it, and made his way out into the water. Even now sounds were damped, and the breakers came at him not in silence but as if far away. He knew the water was quite shallow at this point, but he hoped that the rough water would diffuse any projection if that was what his stalker was.

The great footprints reached the edge of the water and then began to walk along, paralleling his progress. He felt suddenly elated. *Oho! Don't like the rough water, do you?*

Another five minutes and he would be within hailing distance of the town. Another five minutes of wading in waist-deep water and surviving the occasional high wave and there would be plenty of witnesses, probably too many for such as this. With the supply boat due in today, his assassins would miss their chance.

He had nearly reached the outcrop after which the town would be in full view and he was suddenly feeling confident. He risked stopping for a moment, ten feet or more out, and turned. "Got you, you bastard!" he yelled back at the apparently empty beach. "You cut it too fine this time!"

At that moment a huge breaker came in and struck him in the back, propelling him forward, towards the beach. He stumbled and dropped into the water, losing the papers he'd managed to cling to, and then picked himself up as quickly as possible. He had been pushed forward a good four feet!

Suddenly something he could not see grasped him by the head and shoulders and lifted him out of the water. He was flung by some invisible force fifteen feet or more into the air, dangling and struggling as if held by some great hand.

The "hand" shifted and held him suspended now by a hold on his waist, and he found himself lifted still higher, perhaps twenty or twenty-five feet, and brought close over the sands as if whatever had hold of him was studying him for a moment. He yelled and screamed, hoping that some noise, anything, would carry to the town that was so very near.

And then the great hand slowly tightened, more and more,

and his eyes bulged and his mouth opened wide, only now it was incapable of sound.

And then the bloody, mangled carcass of what was now hardly recognizable as human remains dropped to the sands below, out of the reach of the water that might have saved him.

Quite abruptly the area was alive with the screeches of sea birds, the buzz of insects, and the roar of crashing breakers once more.

2

JIGSAW

The entire beach area had been covered with a huge patchwork of tarpaulins so that it resembled a sports stadium field being protected from the rain, though it was in bright sunshine.

Security officers stood at all access points to the beach area, extending from the trail above all the way to the point at which the body had struck the sands. The body itself had been photographed and then removed, but all else was as undisturbed as it could be considering the circumstances.

Two men walked down the beach from town: one a short, burly man built like a barrel with flaming red hair and an unkempt beard to match, the other tall, athletically built, with a long, lean, angular face and sharp nose. His long hair was turning a premature dark gray.

"Lucky you were so close and could get here on short notice," commented Constable Julius "Red" Mathias, the shorter and older of the two men. "I mean, this is the cushiest job in law enforcement up to now—nothing to enforce and plenty of tropical breezes and really good pay to boot—but this thing would drive *anybody* nuts." Mathias had a pronounced Midlands accent tempered only a bit by being away from Britain so long.

Gregory MacDonald chuckled sourly. "Luck had something to do with it all right, Red, but it was all bad and all mine."

"Ain't as unlucky as Sir Robert, you might note," the other quipped, sticking an unlit, half-smoked cigar in his mouth.

MacDonald noted it. "Thought you were going to quit those."

"Y'don't see me smokin', now do you? Call it me pacifier."

They reached the scene and MacDonald was impressed. "Have 'em roll it back a ways, Red," he instructed. "I want to take a look at what we're really dealing with here."

Red gave a sour laugh and spat. "Oh, this is a winner. A classic, lad. The sort of thing that makes up all at once for a century or two of crime-free living here."

At the constable's order, the crew began to slowly but professionally roll up the tarps one at a time, exposing the death scene first.

"Where'd you get all these people, Red?"

"Oh, they's mostly security staff from the Institute. The place is crawlin' with 'em, so why not use 'em? The others doin' the heavy work are mostly men from the town. Those security fellows fought like hell my bringin' in the others, but when you see what we got you'll understand why I didn't feel right just leavin' this all to the Institute boys."

It didn't take long to see what the old cop meant. One look at the tracks with their great stride told anyone that either this was the most elaborate hoax in criminal history or something was loose on the tiny island that couldn't possibly be hidden.

"You made casts of the footprints?"

Red nodded. "Yeah. Wait'll you see 'em, Gregory my boy. If that thing's for real, I for one sure as hell don't want to meet it."

In spite of the sand and the disruptions and, of course, the weight of the tarp, it was clear from just looking at the things that the old boy was right. MacDonald got out his tape measure and discovered that the damned things were more than two feet long. He measured the stride, not once but at almost every point back to the cliff and found them very consistent. Whoever or whatever did this was very thorough.

Equally revealing was the impression it had made jumping from the top of the trail to the beach below. MacDonald examined it all and then stood up and shook his head. "Whatever it is, I'd put it at somewhere around fifteen feet tall and weighing maybe two or three tons. How the hell does it stand upright without a tail or some other counterbalance? There weren't any drag marks around, were there, Red?"

"Nope. What you see, allowin' for the necessaries, is what you got. Other than Sir Robert's own footprints goin' first to the beach and then to the water over there, and the footprints of the pair that found it all, there was nothin' whatever on the beach but what you see. Of course, there's a lot of prints now, but they was to lay the tarp and photograph the scene, and it's pretty consistent."

"And one way," MacDonald noted. "This monster—how did it leave? The tracks are clear from here, then they go almost to the water's edge, walk along it for a bit—I assume that area of no prints is a high tide mark—and then . . . what? Sir Robert gets into the water, the thing doesn't enter but tracks him, and then suddenly it gets Sir Robert and flings him a good ten feet inward of the breakers. So we assume that Sir Robert wasn't far enough out, or somehow came in to where this thing could reach, and it plucked him out."

"You're soundin' as if you think it was a real creature."

"For now we'll stick with it, but that leaves me with a real problem. Okay, so the thing gets its claws on Sir Robert, lifts him up, does him in, and drops him on the beach. Now what does it do?"

"Huh? Um, yeah, I see what y'mean. No return footprints."

"It doesn't fly away—some of the prehistoric monsters bigger than that could do it, but they'd take a mile of runway at the minimum and really mess up the beach. If somebody hoisted it out, in broad daylight, such a ship or derrick large enough would be seen by the town or by the whole damn island and sure as hell couldn't be broken down in—what was the gap?"

"No more'n two hours between death and discovery, or so Doc says."

The younger man nodded. "All right, then. So the only place it might go is into the water—its stride and the high tide might mask that. But if it could stomach the water, then why didn't it just wade in after Sir Robert? Why play cat and mouse and then wait to hoist him inland?"

"Maybe it's perverse. Cats like to play with mice and rats a long time before they kill 'em. Who knows what somethin' like this'd be like?"

MacDonald sighed. "I wish I could have seen the body as it was, but I'll look at the pictures. Never as good as the real thing, but it'll have to do."

"Couldn't be helped, lad. What would y'have me do? Leave Sir Robert there? I mean, it's one thing if it'd been some janitor, but this was the boss!"

"I understand. You did what you could. The two that found the body—no chance of complicity in the affair?"

"I'd doubt it. Low-level clerks workin' in the supply system in town, not even Institute folks. Comin' out here on a slow day to enjoy a few hours beach time on the boss and maybe a little nookie. Besides, their only prints, to and from, cross a high tide mark *after* the high tide, so they couldn't have been here until at least ten thirty, and that's too late."

"Just checking. Anybody who notices something like that doesn't need me, though. You're a good cop, Mathias." They stopped at the base of the cliff trail. "Okay, they find the body, run back into town, fetch you and a few others, and you all come running up the beach and see the scene. Then what?''

"I checked the body and ordered everybody back from the scene. It was some time before I could tell whose body it was for sure, although I knew from the clothes who it had to be. I sent me gal Friday, Sandy, back to ring up the Institute and give 'em a tentative I.D. Warned 'em to come only by the main road and then to the beach, too. They didn't listen. The whole place up there erupted with security about five minutes later, but I yelled and cussed a blue streak at 'em and threatened to shoot any one of 'em that came down.''

"You don't carry a gun. Even most of *them* don't.''

"Yeah, but in the shock and all they didn't remember that. Otherwise we'd have had a bloody mess out here instead of a near perfect reconstruction. Those photos, by the way, were done by the Institute but I doubt if there'll be any funny business with 'em. Took 'em in three dee, so they should be good'n gory. Got top shots of the whole scene, too.''

"Uh huh. But—after you'd gotten all you wanted, did any of them make their own investigation? I didn't see much sign, although it's hard to tell around the body site.''

"Nope. Bunch of 'em spouted stuff into their walkie-talkies and the like, but they didn't even act all too curious. Of course, I was doin' all the procedures right and they'll have copies of the photos—probably have sent 'em to every-place in creation by now.''

Together they walked up the trail to the top, trying to retrace the path of the victim. At the top stood a tall, tanned man in a loud shirt, jeans, and dark sunglasses, a walkie-talkie on his belt. MacDonald recognized him. "Really nice operation you've got here, Ross," the younger man said tauntingly. "You're so thorough that nothing less than a fifteen foot prehistoric monster could chase and kill the boss in broad daylight without anyone seeing. Real secure.''

Ross didn't seem pleased. He was an American with a hard New York accent and he looked like a bad tourist loose in the tropics. "All right, can the sarcasm, MacDonald. We were penetrated and we blew it."

"Penetrated! I'd say you were invaded!"

"Oh, you don't believe this horse shit about a monster any more than I do and you know it. I don't know how they did it, but somebody's drinking vodka toasts right now and laughing at us as we run around looking for sea monsters." His tone dropped and sounded icy and threatening. "I *will* know, though. My ass is more on the line than yours."

MacDonald sighed. "Well, let's see what you didn't manage to muck up in your zeal to get here. Want to come along?"

Ross did, and the three of them started back along the trail. "Not my fault we jumped to get here," the security man said defensively. "Hell, man, we get word of a gruesome death on the beach and some preliminary indication that it's Sir Robert. You'd have done the same thing in our place and you know it. Beats me why you're here anyway."

"I spent several years at homicide back home. You know that. As soon as the identity of the victim was confirmed the boys at headquarters ran everybody in the company with any sort of background like that through the computers and came up with a number. Then they matched them to where they were and my name came up, my being at that time somewhat drunk and disorderly as befits a vacation about three hours flying time from here. I'm not happy with this, either, Ross, but the buck got passed to me and I'm it." He stopped and examined the foliage hanging overhead. "Anybody in your organization tall enough to break those limbs?"

Ross looked up and saw what the company man meant. The trail had been cut with a hand saw and was kept open the same way with weekly trims, but the area was otherwise overgrown and the trail had been cleared only to a height of eight or nine feet, the reach of the man with the saw. From all the signs, something a lot taller and wider than any man had come through here.

"If there ain't no monster they sure as hell went all the way," Red noted.

They reached the junction to the road, but MacDonald followed the signs even though the foliage was thinning and those signs were getting fewer and fewer and walked up towards the glen. The ground was hard there, with much exposed rock, and not well suited to footprints.

The glen, however, was a different story. Although the grass had begun to recover, the huge impressions in the ground of the clearing were still evident, even with a horde of security men running through. The men didn't weigh two or three tons.

Ross sighed. "There aren't any prints beyond the altar stone," he told the other two resignedly. "We checked."

MacDonald examined the massive stone carefully, checking all the points where it intersected the ground. He hadn't paid much attention to the place in previous visits, but it was clear that if that stone was hinged or moved in any way it had been covered by experts beyond his ability to expose.

Gregory MacDonald felt quite at ease in what he always thought of as his Sherlock Holmes disguise, but it had been a long time since he'd had any chance to use it on a real crime. In the three years since resigning from the Royal Canadian Mounted Police, his powers of deduction had been mostly put to use in testing and designing corporate security plans for the company's many worldwide enterprises, many of which were security sensitive, and many more of which were exposed to terrorism and other criminal threats beyond the ability of any single nation's law enforcement or security apparatus to thoroughly safeguard. Sir Robert had always suspected and believed that the best policemen were of the same mentality as the best criminals, simply restrained by moral codes, culture, or nature from working the wrong side of the law.

MacDonald enjoyed his job, but he hadn't expected to be on or near Allenby again for some time. Although company owned, the island was well defended by a multinational professional security force. Red was basically the company cop, a retired desk sergeant who had served with Sir Robert in Korea long ago. He took care of white-collar crimes, such as embezzlement, pilferage, fraud, and the like, having jurisdiction over the twelve hundred men and women on the island who were company employees and performed the mundane tasks that kept the operation going. This was really more up Ross's alley than Red's and more in the security force's jurisdiction, and that fact bothered MacDonald. Why had they so meekly allowed Red to control the entire investigation? That wasn't like Ross or Jureau, men who loved to be in charge unless they were ordered otherwise.

Clearly Ross was simmering at being essentially second to MacDonald, whom he hadn't liked since the company man had taken a small team and penetrated all the way to the Lodge almost a year earlier. Clearly, too, there was some resentment that the company thought it necessary to dispatch their own expert to the scene; it suggested that they didn't trust the security force.

MacDonald didn't trust them, either, for it was never clear from whom their orders came or even from what branch of whose security forces. He couldn't help but wonder if their seeming lack of interest in this affair didn't indicate a more sinister role in all this. He certainly dismissed Ross's own idea of the culprit or culprits; Sir Robert, caught alone on that beach, would have been far more valuable alive than dead.

Once the trio walked back to the main road they had no trouble tracing the victim back to the Lodge. Many had seen him and spoken to him, and all had been questioned and their interrogations recorded.

The Institute itself never failed to impress MacDonald, although it was neither pretty nor natural-looking. It sat atop the highest point of the ancient Caribbean volcano, almost two thousand feet above the sea. At the far point was the Lodge, a hotel and restaurant for everyone who worked there, an imposing structure looking much like a British manor house, huge and imposing. Arranged in a semicircle just in front of the Lodge were six identical two-story buildings where much of the actual work went on, three on each side of the circle. These were mostly of red brick with red slate roofs, and all looked rather drab.

The road circled around this complex, forming a center island in front of the Lodge, and here one could see that something extraordinary was going on. There were seven of them, all facing southwest, seven enormous dish-shaped antennae with massive feeder and transmission horns pointed at their cream-colored middles. These were the eyes and ears of the Institute, putting them in instant two-way communication with six major defense agencies in six countries, as well as with the Magellan Corporation's own headquarters and far-flung enterprises. More impressive even than the antennae, though, was what was beneath them.

The town and the Lodge had come first, built by an eccentric British millionaire back in the days when that term meant something. It was technically under the sovereignty of the Mornkay Federation, a tiny group of former British-owned islands that together formed one of the smallest and poorest nations in the world, let alone the Caribbean. Allenby was, in fact, their major tax base and primary source of revenue, and Magellan ran it as if it was an independent little kingdom, which for all intents and purposes it was. No Mornkay citizens even lived on the island, and rather liberal payments that were all that kept the government from complete collapse kept it that way. The Queen, and perhaps the Governor General didn't need permission to set foot on the place, but the Prime Minister did.

In front of the Lodge, which had been renovated and turned into its comfortable hotel-like present existence, there had been a monstrous excavation, and within that hole had been placed a building no less than two hundred feet tall, lead-shielded and practically bomb-proof. In there, too, had been placed the most technologically advanced, state of the art supercomputer, the System for Artificial Intelligence Networking and Telecommunications, or SAINT for short. It was so advanced, so new, so radical, that it was the latest word in artificial intelligence computing. Some said it could think for itself, although that was denied. Certainly it was like nothing else on earth, able not only to sift through enough transmitted data to fill a library as high as the moon every day, but to actually evaluate and flag what its operators considered important enough to warrant human attention.

Access was through the six research buildings and tremendous layers of security and a series of complex, mostly automated booby traps. SAINT was its own master security force, and it was formidable indeed.

MacDonald went immediately to the building just to the right of the Lodge and then back to the small but efficient hospital area. Dr. Brenda Andersen was expecting him.

Andersen was a tough, no nonsense sort of woman, a Dane employed by the company who was, in title, "Resident Surgeon," but was actually a fancy general practitioner, mostly setting an occasional broken bone and giving out pills for a variety of aches and pains. She and two medics, one a trained nurse and the other an x-ray technician, handled the medical chores for the entire island from this small clinic and from a similar one in town. They had provided her with facilities and equipment sufficient to handle even major surgery, but for anything serious she usually had patients airlifted by jet helicopter to far more elaborate facilities in one of the nearby friendly island nations. The doctor was in her mid-forties, no beauty but with strength and character in her face and manner. She was there, as she herself admitted, as "a refugee from socialized medicine."

"So," she said quietly. "I had some feeling that they would send you." She had a thick accent, but her command of the language was absolute.

"Bad pennies always return," he responded lightly. "You've done the preliminary autopsy?"

She shrugged. "As much as can be done. The remains are pretty much of a mess. You want to see them?"

He nodded. "And your conclusion?"

"A wine press could not have done a more complete job," she told him. "Except, of course, it vas no press, but an encirclement or constriction around the whole of the torso." She reached down and picked up a blood pressure pad. "More like one of these things the size of a man's torso that you wrap around and then squeeze until it almost all meets. Or, perhaps, as if crushed to death by two gigantic, powerful hands."

He nodded soberly. "What the hell have some of you people been *experimenting* with up here?" He meant the comment in jest, but she took it seriously.

"Look, you may find that someone here did the job, you may find it was all some sort of fancy trick, but there are no monsters here. This is a think tank, as you would say, not a place for mad scientists to build some sort of Frankenstein. Oh, some of these people might well be mad, and some might even set out to design and build such a thing, but there is no place for them to do it here. From here they would get the blueprints; it would be built elsevere, far away from this island."

He put up a hand. "All right, all right. But they *do* have both a biological laboratory and a robotics lab here, do they not?"

She nodded. "But the bio lab could not create anything of such size and force, and as for—oh, I see! You are thinking perhaps a machine."

"It's a possibility. It might not need to be so tall, it might be designed to make absurd tracks with precision, and it might weigh two or three tons. It also might well be remotely controlled and would not work well in the water."

She walked over to a cabinet and opened a door. "Well, it would have to be one very strange machine to make tracks like this and only this." She took out a huge, heavy plaster cast and laid it on her desk. "One of the first casts from the beach, brought down here at my instruction."

He gaped at the thing. It was one thing to see the impressions in the sand, another to see what was made from them. It was a huge print, rather rough and malformed, but still clearly representative of the shape that made it. It was monstrous, resembling the sort of feet that must have been on *tyrannosaurus Rex* or some other bipedal dinosaur of the primeval past. It was certainly unlike anything either he or the doctor or perhaps anyone else had ever seen before.

"So, what do you think now?" she asked him, sounding a little smug. "Tell me the robot that could make *that*."

"Oh, if it was a robot, I'll know it soon enough. I'm running every supplies list for the last three years past a bunch of clerical assistants. You couldn't hide the physical components needed to build it, and you could hardly smuggle it in in your suitcase." Still, he thought, there *was* a way, a fairly easy way, to have done just that. When one has an experimental prototype computer that's several stories by a couple of square blocks large and always is being fixed, modified, or upgraded, who would even notice a few tons of sheet metal and machinery? Only one man might notice, and he was certainly high on MacDonald's suspect list.

For the moment, though, he put such things aside, and with the doctor went to view the remains.

"Very little has been noticeably disturbed by the autopsy," the doctor assured him. "When your subject is already turned almost inside out it is not difficult to do the examination. The experts that are supposed to be coming in later today will do more to it.''

The sight was not a pleasant one. As Andersen had said, the victim had been crushed to death by persons, mechanisms, or creatures unknown. The lower calves and feet remained reasonably intact, and the torso was a mess, but it was the head that was hardest to look at. The eyes had nearly popped out of their sockets, the veins all at the surface, the tongue nearly bitten through—it was a sight that no one who saw would ever forget. Although he'd seen hundreds of corpses, including strangulations and mutilations, in his career, MacDonald felt his breakfast in his throat. Still, he was undeterred and professional about it, forcing it all back for later nightmares. He was quite well aware that this was the case of a lifetime, the sort of thing that, if solved, would make him an international celebrity and almost a worldwide legend among detectives in his own time. This sort of thing fell into the lap of very few detectives, and he knew it.

He was having the time of his life.

He made a slow, methodical examination of the body. ''Any sign of foreign material on the surface or in the wounds?''

''Quite a bit, although nothing that I can not account for in other ways. After all, the contents of his clothing were also crushed. Still, I assume that the professionals will send everything through the labs. Nothing remotely resembling lizard scales or metal filings from a killer robot, if that's what you mean.''

He sighed. ''Listen, Doc. *Something* killed this man here, on the beach, less than twenty-four hours ago. Every single shred of evidence suggests that it was a great prehistoric sort of beast that suddenly appeared in the meadow, chased Sir Robert down the trail to the beach, then caught and killed him there and vanished. Now, either such a beast exists, which means it should be easy to find considering it roams the existing trails in broad daylight, or someone made it seem as if it exists. If the latter is the case, it would mean that damned near every person on this island had to be in on it or else it involved some high level of technology right out of science fiction. And that kind of technology is just what the folks who come and stay here are in the business of dreaming up. Now, you tell me: which of the three theories would *you* pursue first? Or do you have another?''

"I do not," she admitted, "unless you mix in black magic of some sort. If you find the method you will find the murderer, that is true. But if it is someone who can do this sort of thing, what defense will you or any of us have if you get close to it?''

"Because," he said, "anybody smart enough to do it is also smart enough to realize that if *I* go, an infinite number of replacements will arrive. My main concern is motive. Why do it in such a flashy way, certain to attract a tremendous amount of attention?" He thought a moment. "Magellan is a privately held corporation chartered in the United States. Sir Robert owned about half the existing shares, and as far as I know he never married. I wonder who gets those shares? They're almost certainly worth billions."

The doctor shrugged. "His heirs, I presume, whoever they may be, unless he left it all to some home for stray cats. Whoever they are, I wonder if they even know?" She paused a moment. "You will be here for the funeral?"

"Of course, and beyond that, too. Wouldn't miss it. After all, I'm going to be here for the formal autopsy." He looked one last time at the remains. "Closed casket ceremony, I bet. The mortician who could make *that* even halfway presentable wouldn't be doing cadavers—he'd be painting the Sistine Chapel at the very least.''

3

THE DAMSEL IS DISTRESSED

The two men stood at the edge of the helipad just down from the Institute and watched the helicopter come in. It was the company's fanciest model, with all the luxuries and amenities of the very rich and well connected and jet powered, too.

"Well, here she comes." John Medford Byrne sighed. At fifty-three he was director of the Institute, a post which also placed him on Magellan's board of directors. He more than coped on his U.S. $157,000 annual salary with all the fringes thrown in. Tall, distinguished, gray-haired and tanned, he looked in his fancy tailored brown business suit like he should be on the cover of *Business Week*. In truth, he was by all accounts a genius at administration who earned every dime he made and then some, but he was uncomfortable now. At the moment, Magellan was running smoothly as usual, but eventually, when Sir Robert's will was fully probated, there would have to be a board and stockholders' meeting at which control would be passed.

"She's the eight-thousand-pound gorilla, MacDonald," Byrne added. "Anything she wants she gets, including me dressing up in a suit in this climate. You remember that."

MacDonald, who was less formally dressed and far more comfortable, having not brought a suit or tie or anything resembling them when pulled to the island, nodded. Byrne had been after him on and off for several days on this. He was a little sour on the whole thing himself. *I'm expected to save all their fat corporate asses,* he thought, *and if I do they might give me a thousand dollars bonus for Christmas, if they remember at all.* If not—well, his job, low as it might be, was as vulnerable if not more so than theirs.

The thing that made them all uncomfortable was that not one of them had known that Sir Robert had a daughter or, for that matter, any other immediate living relatives. A long lost brother they might have at least accepted, but Sir Robert was always rather cold in all sexual matters, and those who had known him had considered him sexless or perhaps a self-repressed homosexual. All that anyone really knew about her was that her name was Angelique Montagne, that she was just barely old enough to inherit to the full without a conservator. They also know she was crippled in some way, for the company advance information warned them to provide for a wheelchair and a nurse.

That, and a couple of other things, not the least of which was that Sir Robert had made her sole and unequivocal heir to everything he had, including the controlling interest in Magellan. Lots of attorneys in many nations would be gearing up to contest or otherwise stall that part, but Sir Robert was a great businessman with the best attorneys money could buy. In the end, the will would stand, everyone seemed confident of that, and when it did anyone who contested would be on a particularly nasty enemies list. Nor would she be likely to be simply removed, even for the money at stake. Should she die before making her own arrangements, the will provided for such nasty things that all their jobs would go and it was quite likely that Magellan would be carved up and possibly dissolved.

MacDonald was there at her request, and feeling a bit uncomfortable because of that. His command appearance suggested that, other than burying her father, she had made solving the mystery of his death her only other immediate priority.

The helicopter landed, and several staff members went to it, opened the door, and provided a small set of steps for disembarkation. First off the plane was Derek Meadows, Sir Robert's private solicitor and, like the dead man, a Canadian. Harold McGraw, Magellan's chief counsel and an American, had already arrived and was at the Lodge. Next out was an elderly Anglican clergyman whom they took to be Father Dodds, an old and close friend of the dead man who would, by Sir Robert's written orders, preside over the funeral.

Now two of the ground crew went to the helicopter as a wheelchair appeared at the door, and the two beefy men, aided by those still on board, lifted the chair and its occupant gently to the ground. Next out was a fortyish-looking woman who had to be the nurse, and, by her attire, was also quite obviously a Catholic nun.

MacDonald looked at the girl in the wheelchair and sighed. *Why do the paralyzed ones always seem to be extraordinarily beautiful?* he wondered.

Angelique was in fact a stunner, with lush reddish-brown hair, big green eyes, and the face and body of a very young Brigit Bardot. She was petite, beautiful, and she was, from all appearances, a quadriplegic.

The totality of her disability, particularly when coupled with her radiant, almost charismatic beauty, shocked both men, and for a moment both just stood there, not moving.

The wheelchair, however, was no ordinary wheelchair, as she proved, spotting the two standing at the edge of the tarmac. It had considerable bulk below and behind and might have weighed a ton. Without any assist from anyone, it started up and glided towards the pair.

As she reached them, both men saw that she was wearing some sort of headpiece plugged into the chair which included a tiny microphone. It resembled the communications gear of a modern telephone operator. The helicopter was completely switched off now, and they heard her say softly, *"Arrêt!"* The chair halted immediately. The nurse and Meadows had followed her and now stood behind, although it was Meadows who took the lead.

"Mademoiselle Montagne, let me present Mr. Byrne, the Institute's director, and Company Investigator MacDonald, who is in charge of our own inquiry into the facts of your father's death and is a fellow Canadian, I might add."

She looked at them rather nervously. "How do you do, sirs," she managed, in a pleasant, French accented soprano.

"Welcome to our island," Byrne managed, trying to sound both fatherly and formal at the same time and coming off mostly stuffy. "Actually, it's *your* island now, too, of course. You must be fatigued by your long journey. Would you care to come up to the Lodge right now and get settled in? Weighty matters can wait."

"I am feeling fine, *Monsieur,* and not at all out of sorts. I did little on the journey but sleep and think. I have not as yet had time to get used to all this."

"Well, we understand that it must have been a shock to learn of your father's death—" Byrne began, but she cut him off.

"No, no! You do not yet understand, I fear. Until only four days ago I did not know that he even *was* my father."

That startled them both once again. It was a day for shocks. MacDonald's curiosity broke through the ice.

"Um, you mean that you didn't know Sir Robert at all?"

"Oh, *oui*, I knew him as 'Uncle Robert,' and I knew who he was, but all that I knew, all that my records ever said, was that I was the orphaned child of two people I thought were my parents, and that my father had been killed while serving with Sir Robert in Korea. I was raised mostly in a convent in the Gaspé, with Sir Robert a frequent visitor. I knew he had set up a trust fund for me, and this chair is the product of one of his companies, but that he was actually my real father— *mon Dieu!*—I wish I had known!''

Byrne looked even more uncomfortable. ''I suggest we still go up to the Lodge and get out of the sun. It's air conditioned there, and we can have some tea or whatever and talk more comfortably. We have a small tram over there with a wheelchair lift—a few of the Fellows of the Institute also have need of wheelchairs—and we can be up there in no time at all.''

She nodded. ''Very well.''

She commanded the chair, he noted, with simple commands in French in a very definite and slightly unnatural tone of voice. It was an amazing device to him, and one that, he knew, would be beyond the financial reach of many others who could use it. She could even make very small adjustments in its steering by uttering sharp nonsense syllables or clicks with her tongue.

The ride up was in silence, taking but four minutes. MacDonald kept his eyes on her throughout, drawing what deductions he could from the little he had. For one thing, it was unlikely that she'd been in this condition for a long time—the body was perfect, the muscle tone looked normal, and there was no sign of atrophy in any of the limbs. She looked as if she could get up out of that chair and dance if she only wanted to. And yet, her manner, her clear acceptance of the condition, and her total command over that state of the art chair system suggested years of therapy and practice. There was also something of the child in the way she looked at everything in wonder and took it all in, yet she had seemed quite confident and generally comfortable in her speech and manner. Her demeanor might mask someone who knew far more than she was telling, or it could be an equal disguise for someone scared to death and unadjusted to any of this. He wanted to know more, and quickly.

When they reached the Lodge, he excused himself and promised that he would be back in just a few minutes, hoping that it didn't seem either rude or out of place. Byrne gave him a nasty look, but Angelique simply smiled and nodded understandingly.

He went down to the library section, which had a number of terminals plugged directly into SAINT. He was authorized to use the computer under certain restrictions and had the code and password to do so, but he disliked using it for more than routine tasks. By now, five and a half days since Sir Robert's death, he was more than convinced that it could not have been done without using the computer, and he knew that anything he did, any correspondence, inquiries, or communications he had, would be monitored by not only Ross and his staff but probably by the murderer as well. This, however, was different.

Any questions fed in on Angelique prior to now had been met with what was called a "corporate block"—a required set of codes that no one on the island knew. Taking a guess that the need for such things was now past, he brought up the general information files and requested her profile. He had been correct. This time it came up, photo and all.

She was twenty-one by only a few weeks, but that was important. Born in Charlottetown, Prince Edward Island, Canada, to Adriene Montagne. The mother, from a suburb of Quebec City, had died of complications due to the birth less than twelve days after. Given over to the custody of her father, who was listed as a Pierre Montagne of Montreal. Now *that* was interesting, he thought. Baptized Roman Catholic shortly thereafter in the tiny Gaspé town of Matane on the St. Lawrence River. More interesting. McKenzie had been a lifelong Anglican. After death of father was raised in the Convent de Ste. Jean by special arrangement—with whom it didn't say, as such things were not only rare these days but nearly impossible. She should have been placed in foster care . . . unless Daddy wasn't really dead and was very well connected.

She had been a bright, athletic child who'd taken early to skiing and figure skating and enjoyed summer sailing on the river, which was both wide and rough at that point. In spite of her odd upbringing, she had the freedom of the small town and shared in the town's social life. She was developing into a major athlete and a beautiful young woman when she was tragically and permanently paralyzed in a ski accident shortly before her fourteenth birthday.

MacDonald frowned. More than seven years ago, yet her body showed no signs of debilitation for that long a period.

For the next three years she'd been in an experimental physical and psychological program in Montreal wholly financed and supported by the Magellan-owned Master Therapeutics, Ltd. When released, she had accepted her disability as permanent and had reconciled it as a sign from God that she become a nun and devote her life to working with the disabled. She had not, however, taken final vows and had put them off a couple of times, but she was still a novice and had finally decided and scheduled final vows for May 11 of this year! Now *that* was leading somewhere. Sir Robert dies just before this, but in time for the death to at least slow it down if not stop it outright. The order she was about to join had a vow of absolute poverty. She would have been required to divest, and the only way to divest of something this huge would have been to give it to the Roman Catholic Church. That was motive enough for governments, let alone individuals dependent upon the corporation.

He punched up details of her injury and found it a baffler. She had all the classic symptoms of a spinal column severed just at the neckline. She had no sensation at all much below the neck, although she had some limited control of her shoulder muscles—but not her hands. However, while there had been some bruising there, there was no sign any of the best medical tests and even exploratory surgery could find of any injury there at all. For a long time they went under the theory that the illness was psychosomatic, but extensive psychiatric investigation and hypno and drug therapy couldn't get at it if it was.

He quickly punched up the mysterious Pierre Montagne and was surprised to find that one existed. He had been with Sir Robert in Korea, and he had been employed as an office manager in Quebec City. He had also died in an auto accident when she was but two and a half.

He cleared the screen and closed down, knowing he'd dig more later. Still, he suspected that he already knew what he would find. Sir Robert had had a liaison with the woman, perhaps even loved her. She became pregnant and was almost certainly a good Roman Catholic, so she'd gone through with it, even though she'd probably been warned that she had some condition that made having a child risky and probably fatal. To legitimize the child and make something of her sacrifice he'd married her, probably very late in the pregnancy and in, of course, a Catholic ceremony which would include the pledge that the child be raised Catholic. Sir Robert was a man of the old school to whom giving his word meant quite a bit. Still, he did everything possible to cover it all up, including hauling in Montagne to pose as the child's father and spiriting her away to a remote community.

Possibly he feared for her safety, but more likely he had to make the choice between continuing to build and shape his worldwide empire or raising the child and he'd chosen, perhaps wrongly, empire. Such men as Sir Robert were not saints; he'd inherited the first hundred million, it was true, but building it up into a multinational conglomerate worth billions was the job for a tough, hard man of flexible morality—particularly considering some of the nations he'd done work for, and the nature of that work. MacDonald could see Sir Robert's thinking, although he found it very disagreeable. In his own odd world, with his own rather odd code, Sir Robert the father could not justify surrogates raising his daughter and being responsible for her—nor could he afford to without possibly having a child more loyal to other interests than his within the company. But as her kindly billionaire "uncle" he could excuse spending whatever he wished on her and also easily explain to auditors and questioners why he had such an interest and attachment to this girl. When Montagne, whom he'd trusted and essentially employed from that point to be her father, had died unexpectedly, he was caught in his own prefabricated set-up.

When he went back upstairs and entered the lounge, he found that some of the party, including Angelique, had gone. Ross was there, however, and came over to him. "Some real tragedy, huh?" he noted. "Girl lookin' like that and inherits billions and can't enjoy any of it."

"Sensitive as usual," MacDonald responded dryly. He looked around. "Where'd everybody go?"

"It finally caught up with her and she was taken to her room—V.I.P. One, ground floor. You know the one. It also connects to Sir Robert's suite, so if they want to go in and poke around they can. I assume you were down there doing the run-down on her?"

He nodded. "Yeah, although there's not much even unsealed. I keep feeling that there's a lot more we don't know about her, and maybe some she doesn't know, either. She's definitely his real daughter, though?"

Ross nodded. "Oh, yeah. There are all sorts of documents on it—now. Stuff hidden away for years even from us, although we suspected it before. The old man knew what he was doing, I'll tell you that."

"You knew about her? How? If that's not violating anything."

Ross shrugged. "Nothing special, and before my time, but there was a tremendous investigation of her accident after they found no injuries in the tests to sustain it. She's in a dozen medical books, though. The old boy pulled out all the stops on her. The therapy center she was at was nothing until she got there, then it became a big corporate priority. Bet it gets even more, now. You see how her body looks so normal?"

"Yeah, I noticed it."

"It's a series of drugs they developed at fantastic cost. The stuff can't really be synthesized in bulk—costs a few grand a gram or more—but it works. Even if they could get the costs down, though, they don't think it'd be very commercial unless they can figure a way to get those parts to work again on most people.

The detective nodded. "That explains a little bit, anyway. Even after working for this company for several years, I still can't get used to the very rich and what they can do and get. I guess one day they'll come up with some kind of robot, just stick her inside, and she'll be able to walk and drive a car or whatever."

"They're workin' on it, brother, believe me. We can practically do it now."

MacDonald's mind went off again, as it did whenever new information was added. Sir Robert's daughter was a quadriplegic. Because of that, Magellan had devoted tremendous resources first to curing her, and, when that failed, to doing the next best thing. A robot body for a human. . . .

What would it weigh with an adequate power pack? Could you screw on legs that, perhaps, had three long clawed toes and reptilian features? Even if it were waterproof, you wouldn't want to go into a heavy surf with it. If you toppled over, you'd drown when it filled before you could get it right again. But if you could get out, and get it to walk by itself into that ocean, you'd dispose of it and the tracks would be wiped away by the rising tide. It might even be computer remote controlled, then disposed of by just having it march into the sea. . . . A machine perhaps hidden or sheltered in the area near the meadow, waiting for its quarry to come near, perhaps even baiting the trap.

Sir Robert had received some written notice of which there was no trace now with his morning papers. He'd read it, then gone out, rejected a cart, and walked to the glen.

It was a wild, impossible hypothesis, but it fit all the facts as he had them. In fact, the only thing he really didn't have now was who did it and exactly why, and why the method chosen was actually selected. In other words, he had reduced it to a common premeditated murder with suspects limited to the few dozen on the island capable of carrying it out—or, of course, the several thousand executives and nations with stakes in the corporation who could have it all planned out elsewhere and carried out by any paid employee in any position as an accomplice. Or the few thousand who'd passed through here in the past two years with computer access who could simply command SAINT from any telephone jack in the world.

Angelique lay on the big bed and sighed. Sister Maria, who was checking out the luggage and trying to decide where its contents should go, heard and came over to the bed. "I thought you were going to sleep," the nurse chided gently.

"Oh, I was, but I can not. This has simply been too much too quick! Just a week ago it was so simple. I thought I knew God's will and my own origins and destiny. Then, suddenly, *poof!* It is now all so complicated. Good Uncle Robert is really my father and he has left me more money than there is in the world. Everyone and everything is at my beck and call. A big company of which I know almost nothing is scared I will fire them all or something. You saw how they all looked and acted here."

The nurse nodded sympathetically. "I saw."

"And, the worst is, I am already corrupted by it myself. God forgive me, but I actually had a thrill at the power they feared that has been invested in me. I liked the corporate jets, the suites like this one, all the *attention*."

"And you are enjoying it."

"God help me, but I am! On the plane, even now, I have fantasies. I have had no fantasies in years. No, don't look that way—not *those* kind. That, in fact, just gets in the way. I saw them taking my inventory with their eyes. Sometimes I wish they would invent a way to take that away, just leave my head, my eyes, ears, nose, mouth, brain. Powered like that wheelchair or my little mechanical gadgets. Don't look so shocked! There is nothing to me below the neck. Nothing. It does not exist. I no longer even dream of it, not since coming back from the Center. Even if they give me one day a contrivance so I can walk, I will not *feel* it. Enjoying good food and drink is the only pleasure of the flesh I will ever know. I have my mind and nothing else, so I must use my mind. Now I have a great fortune, and the power to direct some of it to good."

"And those are your fantasies?"

She nodded. "Somewhat. But there is also the opportunity to enjoy life as much as I can. Have a gang of servants to literally do everything for me, be my body. See the whole of the world and meet the important movers and shakers of it."

"All this is true," the nurse agreed. "Why do you hesitate?"

"Would you? In my circumstances?"

Sister Maria shrugged. "I don't know. I could never conceive of it."

"But that's just the trouble! Neither can I! Even now. I feel like a very un-godlike Jesus who upon the mount in the wilderness was offered the entire world by Satan as an alternative to dying on the cross. I was headed towards becoming a bride of Christ and doing His work, aiding the sick and handicapped. Now I am offered the world, and I am a poor sinner and not the Son of God! Will God be better served by my giving it all away, refusing it, or by my taking it and influencing what I can. Who knows what cures are possible with enough money and drive behind it? And what poverty might be cured? And all this while letting those who know what they are doing continue to run the businesses as always!''

"I can pray with you," said Sister Maria, "but I can not guide you."

"All this is for some purpose, some grand design," said the woman on the bed. "My disability prevents much corruption and forever reminds me through my dependency of my own small self. It gives—humility, and, perhaps, perspective." She was suddenly wide awake and excited. "Fix me a cup of coffee, will you? I would like to get started in this."

After the coffee, Sister Maria dressed Angelique once more and strapped her into the chair. They had three fully charged battery packs and a fourth charging, so there was almost no limit to her range. After, they went next door, and looked over Sir Robert's tropical getaway.

It was a suite much like theirs, although appointed differently, giving it less the look and feel of a luxury hotel suite than of a millionaire's rustic hunting lodge, complete with a bear rug on the floor and stuffed animal heads on the walls.

They found his desk, an old, roll-top affair of weathered oak, and the nun set up an easel in front of Angelique, who took an unsharpened pencil in her mouth. She could now read through a stack of papers placed on the easel and, using the eraser, slide one sheet over to read the next. It was quite an art and had taken a great deal of practice, but it worked.

"This is quite enough, Maria," she told the nurse. "Why don't you go next door and lie down yourself? I'll call if I need you for anything. I wish to go through this, and if I need some help some of the people at the Lodge will come in to help me. Just leave the door to the hall open."

"You're sure?"

"I'm sure."

The nun wasn't happy with the idea of leaving her alone, although in truth she was exhausted, but she also knew the value Angelique placed on being as self-sufficient as possible. And, as she said, the Lodge staff would be at her beck and call. "Call out if you need me for *anything*," Maria told her, and then left.

Angelique was well experienced with her disability and quite self confident about it, far more so than she was about meeting and dealing with these strange people and this strange new life and power. A thermos with a long, stiff, curved straw was at one side of her chair, allowing her to sip whatever she had instructed be placed in it—in this case some ice tea—and to the other side was a small holder with a number of devices that could be grabbed by her with her teeth. The chair's sophisticated microprocessor could by voice command raise or lower any part of it or the easel. She had other devices, not currently attached, that allowed her to do far more on her own than most people would believe possible.

Still, she had lied when she'd said she no longer had *those* kinds of fantasies. Indeed, it was just such urges that had caused her to put off taking final vows and truly committing herself to a new life.

She had lied, too, about no longer being attracted to men. She was, and she found them fascinating because they were different from the nearly all-female society in which she'd been raised. MacDonald, now—though she'd seen him little enough—she found attractive and handsome. He was the only one who didn't dress up, nor quake in his boots at her every word. He'd even ducked out on the big meeting! She hoped he wasn't a rotten character underneath. It would be nice to have a male friend who wasn't fifty or sixty and didn't ever wear a clerical collar.

She put such things out of her mind and began sifting

through the stack of papers. MacDonald and the others had, of course, gone through much of this before, but they would have been less sure than she was as to what was or was not important.

It was laborious work, particularly with her handicap, but she had long conditioned herself to patience. Many of the papers had notes in cryptic words and abbreviations, mostly from Sir Robert to himself. Others were reminders of non-routine obligations and appointments, various ideas for expanding or changing things in the Institute—Sir Robert even seemed concerned about the color of the drapes in the library—and lots of other such mundane items. All of it seemed quite routine.

After a while she began to get the strong feeling that someone was watching her. It was a somewhat unnerving feeling, and she periodically glanced furtively up to see the open door to the hall and the equally open interconnect to her own suite, from which Sister Maria's snores were quite evident. She also heard voices dimly down the hall, but there was no one anywhere near. And still the sensation persisted, as if someone were almost behind her, peering over her shoulder. The drapes had been closed and the lights off in the room when they'd entered, but she had turned on a strong lamp on a table beside the desk. Now, though, it seemed as if the dark shadows at the opposite side of the room harbored something or someone.

She knew she was being foolish, that the room and the events and the long trip had simply gotten to her, but still it persisted. Finally she could stand it no longer; taking a deep breath she said, quickly and sharply, *"Demicercle droite!"* The chair immediately pivoted around one hundred eighty degrees to the right.

For a moment she saw nothing. Then, for a second, she thought she saw movement in the shadows: a dark, manlike shape that seemed to move, then shimmer, a greater black against the darkness of the corner, and it was gone. *"Avancer!"* she commanded. *"Lentement!"* The chair crept slowly forward to the corner.

She did not fear that whatever it was was still present. Just as she had sensed its presence, so had she felt its leaving. Still, she had to take a look, if only to reassure herself. The corner was empty save for an old coat rack that contained only an umbrella and a well-worn sweater. There was room for a man and more here, but there was no exit of any kind, no place that such a man could go without coming first into the light.

She turned around once more and went back to the desk area, but she was too shaken to continue. She knew it would be foolish to tell someone. Nerves, they'd say. The coat rack was mistaken for a phantom. No way to prove otherwise, although she *knew* that someone had been there.

She decided that she didn't want to be in the room any more, but she certainly wasn't sleepy. She needed to get outside in the sun, and to talk to somebody—anybody. *Well,* she thought to herself, *if I am to be queen of this place, then perhaps I should learn to act the part.*

She commanded the chair forward, guiding it through the doorway to the hall, and then went down it a ways until she saw a security man standing there at his post. He watched her come, and approached when he sensed she wanted something. "Ma'am?"

"Pardon, if you please—will you remove the contents from this tray and replace it in the room back there?"

He reached over and, with her help, removed the tray/copy holder, took off the papers, and placed the tray in a compartment on the back of the chair. "I'll see to it, Ma'am," he assured her. "Anything else I can do to help?"

"Oui—yes," she responded, catching herself. She was nervous, and whenever she was nervous she thought only in

French. "Will you please use your radio or whatever and see if Monsieur MacDonald is available to talk to me?"

"I think I know where he is right now. Where do you want me to send him?"

"I will wait by the entrance there, where I can look out into the sunlight."

4

THE OCEAN OF MEMORY

Gregory MacDonald was surprised at the summons and even more surprised to find her waiting alone. He had assumed that the nurse, at least, would always be present.

"*Mademoiselle*, Greg MacDonald at your service," he said lightly, not really knowing how to react to her.

She smiled. "Please—not *Mademoiselle*. I'm already a little tired of all the formalities which I'm not used to having, and I am not even certain of my family name any more. Everyone has always called me Angie and I would be pleased if you would do so."

His eyebrows shot up. "Very well—Angie. Most people just call me 'MacDonald' or, sometimes, 'Mac,' but I always insist that lovely ladies who inherit the company I work for call me Greg. Fair enough?"

She laughed a little at that. "May we go outside? I need to feel a little of the sun and breathe the air here. I have never been to a tropical place before."

"You're the boss, but I warn you to go slow. If you're not acclimated to this sort of place you could find it physically very hard on you."

She commanded the chair forward and to the doors, which were electrically opened for her. He followed, wondering just what all this was about. It was humid, and the temperature was in the eighties, as usual. That was one reason he had always liked Celsius, where it was only thirty. It was just as hot, but somehow it *sounded* cooler.

The broad porch had tables and deck chairs, but she wasn't particularly interested in lingering. "If we could—I would like you to show me where my father died."

"I'm not too sure about that. It's a ways and some of the terrain's pretty rough. If anything happened it'd be my neck in a noose."

"If I am, as you say, the boss, even though it will take years to get it all settled through the courts, then you are my employee. You are without power to stop me from going, so are you going to come along to safeguard me or not?"

He sighed. "Well, if you put it that way, I guess so. But let me get a walkie-talkie from one of the security boys first so if we run into trouble or that fancy chair of yours runs out of juice I can call for help."

She permitted him to do that, and they were off down the road and around the antenna array.

"Those things can communicate with just about every place in the world, yes?" she asked him wonderingly.

"Oh, yeah. Actually, they're tied into NATO and a bunch of security telecommunications systems as well as our own home offices."

"They are controlled by the big computer, then?"

"*Everything* is controlled by the big computer—the air conditioning, the lighting, the automatic doors, defense and security systems—you name it. This may look like a nice little resort on a charming tropical island, but it's a high-tech nightmare in some ways."

She nodded. "And—who controls the computer?"

"Theoretically the corporation telecommunications headquarters in Toronto, and that by the corporation's top management in Seattle. They basically tell it what to do and make its priorities.''

"You said theoretically."

He nodded, impressed with her line of questioning. If it hadn't been a cruel joke he would have said she had a real head on her shoulders. "Yes, theoretically. The truth is much closer to home. You see, SAINT isn't your ordinary run-of-the-mill computer. It might well be one of a kind, although it's based partly on Japanese work and they have a similar government controlled operation. It isn't just a collection of data bases and operating interfaces and the like; it actually makes decisions, evaluates information, essentially on its own.''

"You mean—it thinks?"

"It thinks. Oh, not like *we* think, and don't get the idea that it's some movie monster computer plotting to take over the world. It thinks about what it's told to think about. It doesn't have an original idea in its head. Human beings tell it what to think about and just how far it can go. Much of its circuitry has to be kept below freezing just to keep it from burning up its billions of parts with its own speed, and while it can talk it's not self-aware like we are. The only man who can be said to understand and really run SAINT is a Brit with the incredible name of Sir Reginald Truscott-Smythe.''

She giggled. "You're not serious."

"I'm afraid I am. He looks the part, too, complete with moustache and summer whites and a dreadfully uppah clahss accent. He's the highest paid repairman in the world and commands a crew of forty—second only to the security forces in staff number. He and two other men designed and built the creature. The other two are Japanese who worked long and hard on their project but just couldn't resist the kind of money Magellan could offer for the job. They're both back in good old Nippon now, but old Reggie, who worked in Japan and speaks, reads, and writes that and a lot of other languages, is still here, king of the hill. I'll introduce you, when you want." They came to the split-off trail. "*Whoops!* Here we are at the detour. Are you sure you can make it through there with this contraption?"

"I think so. This is a very remarkable vehicle—one of only two or three in the world like it. It is one of my dreams that we will eventually be able to mass produce it so cheaply that even national health insurance plans will be able to buy it for all who need it."

Actually, the trail proved more than wide enough, and the suspension on the chair proved more than merely adequate so long as Angie was strapped in. He admired her confidence and control and couldn't help saying so.

"Part of the key was that I was still young when the accident happened," she told him seriously. "Another was the aid of what I now know was Magellan and Uncle—my father. What could I do? I could lie in some nursing home forever, or I could take advantage of everything that was offered and accept it, knowing what worked would eventually make its way down to everyone in need of it. I have much, and now I will have more. At the Center in Montreal they have voice-activated computers like the one in this chair. It is possible with robot arms to get my dinner and feed myself. I can pick up things and examine them. In special rooms with special equipment sensors can be attached to allow the computers to move my muscles, give me a minimal flexibility. God has been very good to me."

"I don't know if I could be in your place and say that."

"But he has! He has put me here as an example to all those now wasting away or thinking of suicide or going mad in their self-pity! We only got out one step ahead of the newsmen as it was. Eventually I will leave this island and return, and I will be, like it or not, a public figure. I intend to be an example to everyone. I will be—*Oh!* It is so *beautiful!*"

They had come to the meadow with its strange altar stone.

"We believe it started here," MacDonald told her grimly, breaking her mood. "We believe that your father was lured to this spot by some bait we don't yet know, and waiting here was the mechanism to kill him."

"But—he died on the beach! Is it not so?"

"He did, but it started here."

"*What* was here?"

"I don't know, and I don't know if we'll ever find it. Whatever it was, it was made to look as if it appeared at the altar stone—that big rock over there. He saw it, and ran down that trail over there. Even then, they took a big chance, or the . . . thing . . . or whoever did this, was overconfident, because he almost escaped. I'm sure they didn't think he'd make the beach. The trail forks down there, one going to the beach, the other back to the road. If he'd taken the one to the road they would have had him, and it was the most logical route to take. The beach trail isn't used much and it's not in good condition. Whatever was chasing him had more of a problem with it than a man on foot. It slowed it down and also made it expose itself. It was blind chance that nobody was on that beach or in a boat out past the breakers. Would you like to see the beach?"

"Yes, I would." A thought suddenly struck her. "*Monsieur* MacDonald—*pardon*, Greg—you are quite charming and very light and flip and irreverent, if that is the word for it. I think this masks a very serious man below your surface. You acquiesced far too easily to my foolish trip in the heat. You would not, by any chance, be attempting to discover if this chair of mine can make it to the beach?"

He grinned sheepishly. "Unmasked and exposed to the roaring mobs! "Yes, I *will* admit that the thought had crossed my mind. Don't tell the others, though—they think I'm a half-witted has-been."

She laughed, then grew suddenly serious, almost somber.

"You think, then, that some sort of mechanical device was used? A robot or something?"

He was really impressed with her. "You are indeed your father's daughter. You're gonna do just fine, lady. The old boys who run the corporation think they're gonna control and devour you, but I think they've got a real shock coming. Yes, I think it was done that way because it's the only way it *could* be done, and you yourself just told me that the technology's there."

"But that was to *help* people!"

"So was atomic energy, but they made a bomb first. I once investigated a case in which the murder weapon was an egg beater. Old laws of history. First, anything and everything can be misused and perverted. Second, anything that can be misused and perverted someday will be. Somebody had the thing built, either here or somewhere else and then transported here, and then they ordered the computer to do it. Then they ordered it all erased from the computer's memory, so there's no record, while their device is out there in the sea someplace, although that was probably an afterthought or a contingency. End result: Sir Robert killed by unknown monster, another mystery of the islands. We needn't go on now, you know. It's not really necessary."

"Perhaps it is. It is for me, anyway. Please—lead me onward."

He did so, and when they came to the fork in the trail she *did* hesitate, but then ordered the chair onward. It was a *very* tight fit, and several times he had to assist in getting it and her over an obstacle or exactly on line, but ultimately they made it to the cliff edge and the clear trail down to the beach. She had to stop, however, where the trail started down the cliff in a series of short switchbacks. "There is no way that this chair can be maneuvered down *that*," she said flatly.

"I agree, and it's too dangerous to let you try, but it was also not used by your father's killer. It jumped from this point—you can see here where the brush is broken and a small part of the shelf has fallen down—to the beach below. Made a hell of a cavity you can still make out down there.''

''It is out of my possible field of view. Still, it is a long way down there. Nothing human, even inside a machine, would have likely survived it unscathed. I also find a robot walking on legs difficult to accept because it would have to have tremendous balance, yes? You, yourself said that they could not expect to have to chase this far. Would they have built all the little gears and levers and the like to have it right itself so easily after such a leap?''

He frowned, knowing that she had a valid point. ''I can't guess as to the nature of the thing without seeing it,'' he responded a bit lamely. ''However, I'm convinced I'm right. It's either my way or we have to accept that a tremendous monster materialized in the meadow, chased Sir Robert down here, did him in, and then vanished once again. Which one is more plausible no matter what the loose ends, eh?''

But she did not answer him. She was staring out at the beach and at the roaring surf. The salt smell seemed particularly nice and the breeze that brought it and that wonderful roar of crashing breakers felt cool and comfortable. She felt a tremendous urge to run down to that beach and dive into the warm waters.

''Something the matter?'' he asked her, concerned that actually viewing the site of her father's death had been a little too much for her.

She sighed. ''A feeling, one that I have not had or allowed in a long, long time, that is all. You take this beach and this sea for granted, and look down, missing its beauty, seeing only a crime scene. I look at it, and its very beauty beckons to me, and I am reminded exactly of what I have lost.''

He undestood it now, at least in abstract terms, and felt both pity and guilt. ''I guess I shouldn't have brought you here. Come on—let's go back up the trail and over to the road and I'll call for a car to take us back up."

"No!" she said sharply. "Not yet! Please! It is very important, this thing I am feeling. The water and the wind are warm, but it blows like ice in my face. In a small town one knows well with few attractions and fewer distractions, it is easy to fool yourself into thinking that everything is still all right, that you go on and do not look back. That is a lie now, I see, born of my ignorance and isolation. This life, this wider world I am now confronting, will always reflect back this thing, this loss. I will always after wish to do what I can not do. I feel, suddenly, the turtle, wishing to withdraw into her shell and remain there, yet I am no turtle. I know that I can not." She paused a moment, noting that he was looking less at her than out at the sea, and she knew his discomfort.

"Tell me about yourself, Greg MacDonald," she said to him. "You have read up on me, I know. Save me the trouble of reading up on you."

He turned and faced her. "Me? I'm thirty-five, born and raised in Victoria, B.C., My dad was a desk sergeant with the city police, and I never much thought of being anything else, although I envisioned following in my dad's footsteps as a constable. I went over to Vancouver to do it, though, partly because I really wanted to see if I could make it on my own, and I got the job and a rather rough beat and I took courses nights at university. After two years I got a bit bored with the beat and I wanted a degree, and so I applied to the RCMP, mostly on a lark, partly because they would help with grants to finish my degree. They took me on, I got the degree in sociology, and wound up spending another two years in Saskatoon, then two more in Whitehorse, then back to Vancouver where I took more training and then back to the Yukon, only this time certified in homicide work. I worked it in the Yukon, then Calgary, then back in Vancouver again, and I got rather good at it. I finally quit two and a half years ago to take a job as a security consultant with Magellan and, being the closest to the scene with homicide experience, here I am. Did I leave anything out?''

"Only the important details. For instance, are you married?''

"I was once. It didn't work out.''

"Oh. Sorry. I did not mean to pry that much.''

"No problem. It's all in my dossier anyway. I'm sorry it didn't work out, but it wasn't anything ugly. I have few regrets about the way things have gone for me so far.''

"Tell me—why did you leave the RCMP? Whenever you bring it up I can feel your fondness for it. You loved that job and that service. Or is this something too personal I should look it up, too?''

He looked decidedly uncomfortable. "Um, no, well. . . . It's just difficult, that's all. Difficult to talk about, particularly to you.''

Her curiosity was overcoming her sense of propriety, and her mind raced with thoughts of scandal. "If it was something illegal or immoral in their eyes it is all right if you don't tell me.''

He mumbled something she couldn't quite catch. *"Pardon?"*

"I couldn't learn French!'' he snapped irritably and in a very loud tone. He calmed down, looking a bit sheepish. "It's the law. You can't make lieutenant or get any further promotions in government service unless you pass your promotional tests in French, both written and oral. I had the best performance and job rating record in the entire west, but I couldn't get promoted. I tried their classes, I tried Berlitz, I tried *everything*, and no matter what happened I couldn't ever get the right case for a verb or stick a sentence together that made any real sense. Oh, I could have cheated my way through—some do—but what if I were posted to Montreal? We had a few *Québecois* in the office and they knew it and teased me unmercifully, but they were ambitious bastards—

pardon the language. I couldn't stay in when I could be so easily exposed or blackmailed.''

"But they have a language requirement in university, no?''

"Yeah, they do. I took Spanish—don't know why, except that I had a couple of friends who were neighborhood folk, immigrants from someplace in South America, and the Spanish department was small and they were doing double and triple duty with what assistants they could find. Spanish had do-it-yourself exams. I cheated, that's all. Just plain cheated. Oh, I could remember the day's lessons enough to fake it back, but as soon as I didn't need it any more it was gone.''

She laughed, and stifled it only when she saw that it really hurt him to admit all this. "I will tell you what,'' she said, trying to break his mood, "we will trade handicaps, yes?''

He smiled a bit guiltily. She *did* have a way of putting things in perspective, he had to admit. He was, however, quite curious about all this. "Can I ask what this is all about? You wanted more than just to see the scene here, and you trusted a complete stranger. Why?''

She thought a moment before answering. "I must trust strangers all the time. I am totally at the mercy of almost everyone. Don't you see how it is for me? I am more than handicapped—I am a talking, thinking head. The machines can do only so much. I must always have others to be extensions of my will. No, no, that sounds bad and I did not mean it to be. Since I was fourteen my life has been a medical complex, a convent, and a very tiny town. I know a lot of people, but since this—condition—happened I have no social life and my friends are friends out of pity or mercy. I am a burden to everyone, and, down there, I lost the only family and the only true friend I ever really had these past seven years. I am an heiress, true, but everyone here is either fearing for his job or currying favor or seeking advantage. I am not a human being to them, either, and I can't be their friend or they mine. One of them killed my father and may have terrible plans for me.''

He looked up sharply. "Why do you think that? Just nerves?''

She told him about the dark figure in her father's office, and was pleased when he did not immediately dismiss it.

"It was a man-like shape?" he asked her. "Average height and build?''

"I would say. I only saw it briefly. You do not think I am hysterical?'' Her voice was quietly hopeful.

He shook his head. "No, I don't think so. I might if you were the first, but you aren't. A number of people both at the Institute and in town have reported similar things. They're mostly dismissed, but the evidence accumulates. The villagers call him simply the Dark Man. Some of them think he's a ghost or spirit.''

"You mean—my father?''

"No, the sightings predate his death by several months. Some of our scientists have seen him, too. They won't admit it, but you can see it in their faces when the subject comes up. Some references in your father's notes and papers indicate that he, too, had seen it more than once and was trying to track it down. He didn't think it was any spirit, though, and neither do I.''

"But you have not personally seen him?''

"No, but your description tallies with the others, leaving out the fear factor.''

"Yet he vanished where there was no place to run!''

"I didn't say he was actually there, only that you saw him. We don't know all of the experiments going on up there, and we don't know all the equipment the security forces have and use—but I'd say it's a dead certainty they know just where both of us are right now and even odds they're monitoring this whole conversation somehow. What I don't know is if it connects in any way to your father's murder. It may have everything to do with it—or nothing."

"I am feeling more afraid and uncertain every moment. yet—where can I go? You can see now what I was trying to tell you? Right now, you are the only one on this island who was both not here at the time of the murder and who has no vested interest in his death or my future other than Sister Maria, and I really do not know her all that well, either."

"She's not from the convent?"

"Oh, yes, but she has not been there long. She trained at the Center in Montreal with the kind of equipment I need and use, like this chair, but after I was there. I am a patient to her, not a friend, and if I do not give this all up and return and take my vows she will be gone very quick." She sighed. "Don't you see? It is not my affliction but my position that is the occasion for pity. I am alone. *Monsieur* MacDonald— Greg—what I need is a friend, a *confidant*. You are correct—I truly know you not at all. But you are here, and I need someone. If you are that someone, then I must reach out to you."

He stood there a moment, trying to think. *O.K., MacDonald, this is one turn you didn't consider, eh? Beautiful, handicapped daughter of murder victim under investigation who stands to inherit a billion or two pleads for your friendship. Damn it! I didn't even think they'd let me near her without ten bodyguards, twenty nurses, and a security force.*

And yet, in spite of everything, he really liked her. He hadn't expected to, and certainly hadn't expected her to be what she was, but she had one hell of a mind behind that pretty face, and a willingness to gamble. "All right, Angie. I'll be your friend." He said it sincerely and he meant it.

"Greg—thank you. Now, will you be honest with me?"

"I'll try."

"Do you think you will discover who killed my father?"

He nodded. "Yes, Angie, I think so. It's too spectacular

and too messy to cover up forever. Also, I fear, just because of the way it is done it is the beginning of a plot, not the objective of it. But even solving it is not justice, nor even proof. It is quite possible that I may never be able to bring them into a dock. It's even possible that it was done on government orders.''

"I understand. But—what do you mean, it is only the beginning?"

"Someone went to a lot of trouble to kill him in just this way. There are thousands of ways to kill someone, many undetectable, and Sir Robert was wide open to an inside job anywhere on the island. He could have vanished mysteriously, or choked on a bit of food, or had what looked to be a stroke or heart attack. He might have been blown up, for that matter. Yet whoever did this instead went to great lengths to be a magician, to commit the possible murder by an apparent monster in broad daylight. Why do it in such a spectacular and bizarre manner that I'm only the tip of a huge investigative iceberg?"

"I—I don't know. But tell me truthfully—am I next? Am I the idiot for even thinking of coming here?"

"No, I don't think so. If they wanted you out of the way they could have done it far easier where you were and with few questions. There is also a sword hanging over all of this until the full estate is settled and you can write your own will, if you didn't know. It's why I'm certain that every move we've made, every word we've uttered, has been monitored and why they're almost panicked that you're even this close to the cliff edge."

"Oh, what is that?"

"It's a code—a set of codes, actually, that Sir Robert established not only within SAINT but within the entire corporate complex. No one knows who has the codes, or who can give them—his open letter to the Directors in the event of his death went into few details, but it is certain that those who have parts of it need only a keyboard, a modem, and a telephone line to send it. In the event of your death before your full legal rights are determined and your full inheritance is worked out, there is no question that those codes will be sent. None. Truscott-Smythe has been working for days on running them down and can't even verify their existence, yet no one really doubts that they are there. Our Japanese friends that I told you about helped devise the system, but can't really find it themselves. If you die, for any reason, and those codes are sent and received by the company's telecommunications network, every single computer data bank will begin to systematically and quickly erase itself."

She gasped. "But that would collapse the company, yes?"

"More than that. It might collapse a number of weak governments, a huge number of banks and subsidiary and dependent corporations in thirty or more countries, and crash stock markets around the world."

"What men have created they can uncreate, certainly."

"Well, they've started trying, but even the method, which was eventually computer devised, was wiped from the computer's main memory and no single human really knows how he did it. It's risky, but it's brilliant and shows he was thinking of you. He bet that they'd settle all the claims and transfer everything before they could figure out and cancel his codes. And he was smart enough to realize that, with the enormity of the threat, there would be far fewer contests and obstacles in the way of probating. Many governments and much of the western economic community would far prefer you to inherit all than to risk dragging out the proceedings, perhaps for a decade, particularly in your condition."

"It is too—enormous. Again I feel like running back to the Gaspé and hiding."

"It's too late for that, if it ever was time after Sir Robert's death. No, Angie, I'm afraid that the danger to you is real but it isn't death that you must fear. Someone, or some project, was about to be exposed by Sir Robert. They couldn't control him, or outsmart him, so they took him out, betting that the resulting confusion and your inheritance would buy them time. They're betting that you'll take the money and let the experts run the business, which is a good bet. Then they'll either get their own people in top spots to protect themselves or capitalize on your, pardon me, ignorance and naivete and get you to vote them what they need.''

"I am both of those, I admit. But if this is true, why did they use a monster?''

"Angie, why were you in such a hurry to make friends with me? To get me on your side?''

"Why, the Dark Man, of course. I was, as you say, naive and ignorant and already fearful of what had befallen me. Alone, in that room, with that—whatever it was—pushed me quickly. I am afraid, Greg, and I admit that.''

"And that's probably the answer. Fear and boasting at one and the same time. Fear of person or persons unknown who could do this, in this way, in broad daylight—and a warning that it could happen to any of us at any moment in any one of hundreds of ways. It is a giant sign saying that 'we are in control, not you. We can do anything with impunity, even something as open and bizarre as this. Imagine what we can do to you.' And it's not just for us—you and me—but for the whole island, the whole community, perhaps the whole corporation. Its heads are human, and humans fear the unknown.''

"But this puts you in great danger, then! And you are not afraid!''

"Angie,'' he sighed, "I am literally scared to death.''

5

THE SAINT AND THE SINNERS

As MacDonald had predicted, it was a closed coffin affair; a simple burial service for a very complex man. They were all there—not merely the top people at the Institute and Magellan's company men, but also many top corporate leaders from the home office in Seattle including, very briefly and just for the ceremony, the President and Chief Operating Officer, Alan Kimmel Bonner. He was a big, rough-looking man with a huge shock of gray hair that seemed in eternal disarray and a hard, chiseled face. He looked more like the popular perception of a dockworkers' union president or perhaps a Mafia godfather than the shrewd head of one of the world's largest multinational corporations.

Although he didn't lack for toadies, he spoke only briefly and gruffly to most of the people there, having a few longer and softer words only with Angelique. After the service he was whisked up to the Lodge for a brief conference with Director Byrne and then he was gone. The island regulars could not remember him ever having even visited the island before, and, from his manner and speed of departure, it seemed unlikely that he would repeat the occasion.

They laid Sir Robert to rest, as he had stipulated, in the small graveyard by the tiny village church, his grave facing not the Institute but the sea. It had surprised some that he had instructed an island burial at all, but he had a strong feeling for this place, which was created a fair bit out of his own imagination, and no really strong feelings for anywhere else. There was a family crypt just outside of Halifax, but he had never gotten along much with his father and other family members and had in any event outlived all of them except his daughter.

They had found a dark suit that almost fit MacDonald, and he walked back from the burial towards the town anxious to be rid of it. Angelique would be the titular hostess at a reception at the Lodge later and would be too busy; he decided to skip whatever he could. As he walked towards the small main street of the tiny town, constructed in an earlier era to resemble a Tudor village, he spotted Ross. The security man was just standing there, watching him.

As he approached, the security man said, "You know they're pretty pissed off at you for endangering her like that yesterday. Byrne told Bonner he wanted the authority to fire you for it."

MacDonald stopped and shrugged. "And am I fired?"

"You'd know by now if you were. Hell, you gave her a bigger thrill than she's probably had in years, and charmed the shit out of her in the process. It might be in your best long-term interest to stay away from her for a while, you might know."

"I'll bet. I'm just like the rest of them, though, Ross. When she calls, I got to come."

"Yeah. Sergeant MacDonald of the Yukon, off to the service of distressed damsels, out to lock up the villains and take their own whips to them. Come off it, MacDonald. Give it up. You ain't gonna get a dime of her old man's dough no matter what."

Suppressing an urge to punch out the security man, Mac-Donald stared hard into the other's eyes. "Ross—tell me, are you a total and complete incompetent who should be canned yesterday or are you a willing accessory to murder."

Ross's composure was slightly shaken. "What the hell does *that* mean?"

"You got the cliff sides wired, you got an electronic security scan system that even includes the beach, yet at ten in the morning the biggest man under your watchful eye gets turned into tomato juice and you don't know why or by whom. I'll bet you can quote every word she and I said to one another, yet you couldn't pick up and scramble on something fifteen or twenty feet tall. Either you are more of an incompetent than you are an asshole or you helped kill him, at least by looking the other way while it was being done. There's no third possibility."

"You've seen the scan tapes. You know damned well there's only one blip from the meadow to the beach. The tripwire cameras, which are stills, didn't show much, either. One had some of Sir Robert's leg, the other, the beach scan, shows nothing even though it should have shown anything on that beach at just the right moment. There's nothing on the audio, not even birds and ocean, but nothing tests out as erased. I'm good at what I do, but somebody was better and beat the system."

"Well, I'm good at what I do, too, Ross. I've got motive and opportunity. When I get method, I'm going to nail the bastards. After that you can start covering up for them, like a good little boy, but I don't have to be concerned with that. I stand on my original comment, Ross. Either you know or your machinery was so nicely tampered with under your very nose that you should be assigned to guard copper mines in Montana. And, for your information, I wouldn't turn down a billion, but that thought had not even entered my head. Now go find a fireplug and have a good pee, eh?" And, with that, he walked on, leaving the security man fuming and staring at his back as if trying to kill him with willpower alone.

Angelique nodded and smiled and made small talk but it was clear that she was pretty unhappy. Most of the guests put it down to the trauma of the burial and were sympathetic, not knowing, or wanting to think, that it was the guests and not the funeral that was the trouble. It was impossible to explain to these people what was going on in her mind, and so this was simply an ordeal that had to be weathered.

How could she explain to them without seeming cruel and inhuman, she wondered, that she felt virtually nothing at the service today or even at the graveside? Sir Robert had been a kindly and wonderful friend as a sort of honorary rich uncle, but now that she knew who he really was she could feel only bitterness. He had from the start placed her off in a corner, away from the modern world, a distant second in his own life's priorities. How do you love a father who treated you as a minor corporate property, who scheduled meetings when it was convenient for him and paid the bills but who was unwilling even to tell you the truth? Even now she wasn't a person, let alone a daughter; she was a corporate weapon, a bit of nasty black humor exercised by a man beyond the grave. He had left her everything, but prepared her for nothing.

The accident had ended her formal education while still in the eighth grade, and she had never really taken up offers of tutoring. Beyond the religious studies and the fascination with automation and medicine from her years at the Center, she'd mostly gotten what she knew from reading books or watching television, and even there her main interests had been romances and soap operas. Perhaps that was why she hadn't been able to get *him* out of her mind.

She knew it was silly, juvenile, and totally irrational, yet she could not deny it. He was older, yes, but handsome, rugged, intelligent, confident, and kind. She was aware of what sort of a risk he had taken with her yesterday and how much these people probably hated him for it, but that had only cemented her first, admittedly emotional, impressions. She had fantasized about him the previous night, imagining things that she never knew she was capable of imagining before. She wished he were here now, but understood why he was not. Particularly after yesterday, Greg MacDonald would not be welcome or at ease in this crowd.

Byrne acted as host, with his wife, Carla, serving as hostess. She was far younger than Byrne, an Italian who might be quite attractive if she wasn't dressing and acting as the corporate executive's wife. Clearly she enjoyed ruling the social roost and used her husband's authority as her own.

The rest of them seemed to come from many nations and all seemed to be called Doctor something or other. There was the medical doctor, a Dane, and a number of men and women, ranging in age from the thirties to the sixties, from places as diverse as India and Kuwait, West Germany, The Netherlands, Norway, Britain, and Brazil. All seemed pleasant, many seemed preoccupied, and, thankfully, none of them seemed anxious to discuss what their work was here. She was having quite enough trouble without displaying her total ignorance.

Sister Maria, dressed for the day in the old-fashioned black habit, seemed to enjoy herself, and had a long and animated conversation with one of the scientists, a tiny and attractive woman who looked young enough that at first Angelique had thought her one of the wives. Still, overall, Maria kept close to her charge and made certain that Angelique was neither trapped nor left alone.

The most interesting of the batch was Sir Reginald Truscott-Smythe, who was everything Greg had warned. Middle aged and ruddy-complected, with a small moustache and neatly trimmed hair—and buck teeth—he was *very, very* British,

y'know. He was so stereotypical he reminded her of a come-
dian putting on the British upper classes, but "Reggie," as
he insisted he be called, was exactly what he seemed to be, at
least in looks and manner. He was also the one man willing
to discuss his own work that she wanted to hear from, and
this delighted him no end.

"You are the man who really runs the whole business, I
think," she said to him.

"Oh, dear me, no! What I am, you see, is the world's
highest priced mechanic, and SAINT is mostly self-diagnosing
and self-repairing, so it's not much of a job, really. Oh, I
shouldn't say that to you—you're the boss now, after all!"

She laughed. "No, no. it's all right. From what I understand, you are worth every cent."

He seemed more than pleased by that. "It allows me time
to try and see what SAINT can really do. We've barely
scratched the surface."

"This computer—it can really think?"

"Oh, my, yes! Don't think of it as one of those things you
see in all the cinema versions of computers with their anach-
ronistic whirring tape drives."

"But it is *enorme*, no?"

"Oh, no, not really. It's quite small, actually, as the
popular vision of these things go. The basic device is probably no more than four by four meters by about six high, and
not a moving part in the whole sand pile. The old computers
used to perform a few thousand calculations on a small chip;
we increased that to tens of millions and then stacked the
chips, each not much larger than a tea coaster, into massive
interlinked sandwiches. It is capable of thousands of millions
of calculations per second, and is to the old business mainframe computer, the one that took a room, what that computer was to the abacus."

"But if it is so powerful, then why all the space below I
am told it needs?"

"Well, some of it is because we are dealing in silicon here—plain old fused and formed sand. Put those tens of thousands of tiny transistors together, pack them tight, and run them constantly at full throttle, and the bugger gets tremendously hot. It requires a massive power supply and extreme cooling—it must live permanently in a sort of giant meat locker, as it were, constantly chilled to keep its temperature down. And everything is triplicated, at least, so that if any tiny unit fails there are three to seven other paths to get to the same thing. That way we make certain that if one part goes down nothing is noticed in the system except that we're given a notice of what and where and what to do to fix it. The rest of the space is for memory storage, cooling machinery, the telecommunications network, that sort of thing—the stuff SAINT runs and the raw material it uses."

"But—it thinks?"

"Indeed yes. It talks, too. Holds conversations in a decent voice that sounds deceptively human. I like the voice, but most people prefer the usual terminals with text readouts. Still, you can give instructions to it vocally and it will then do what you wish, including put up information on a screen. That might be very convenient for someone like yourself to whom keyboards are a roadblock, if you'll pardon me making the point."

"Please—I have long since gone beyond the stage where I take any offense at others noting my limitations. I, in fact, have less patience with someone who tries very hard not to notice. This robotic chair is what gives me a life. That is why I am so fascinated with your SAINT."

"Indeed yes. We are close to the day when the marriage of human and machine will be direct. Even now many paralyzed folk are walking using their own muscles with the nerves connected to microprocessors. The day is not far off when we can fabricate a human-looking body carrying its own internal power supply and microprocessors of the type and density used in SAINT. Connected to the nervous system above the point of injury, it might well be that those bodies will move at the thought-command of the wearer. Eventually, it might be merely something put on, bridging the gap caused by the injury and thereby restoring the natural body. You'll walk yet, my dear.''

She smiled. "Thank you for the thought. I hardly have the background and skills to take charge of the company even if my father's will goes through, but I do intend to have some input, to insist on investment of time and money and resources into that very sort of thing.''

"Quite so. Well, listen—when you're ready and able, let me know and I'll introduce you to SAINT and show you how to use him.''

"Him? It is now a person?''

Sir Reginald looked a bit sheepish. "The voice is masculine, and I hold so many conversations with him, well, it just seems like a person to me, you see.''

"Um—I apologize for the question, but aren't you sometimes concerned about it?''

"Huh? In what way?''

"I mean, it has more information than a hundred libraries, thinks millions of times faster than we do, and it actually does think and talk. What if it gets—ideas—of its own?''

Sir Reginald chuckled. "My dear, you must forget those hoary old sci fi horror cliches the telly always belches out. First of all, it only does what we tell it to do. It's not off in a silicon corner hatching plots. SAINT serves and amplifies our own abilities, solves *our* questions, just like all the machines of the past once did. And if it still gets uppity, we can always pull its plug. Cut its power or simply cut off its air conditioning and watch it fry. I'd hate that—like doing it to one's child, don't you know—but it's *frightfully* vulnerable.''

Finally the ordeal was over, and just about everyone drifted out. Still there, however, was Father Dobbs, who hadn't said much more than condolences to this point, and Harold McGraw, her father's attorney. Both now seemed interested in talking more and neither seemed to realize until then that the other was of similar mind.

"Father, why don't we go back to my rooms and talk?" she suggested. "Monsieur McGraw, please make yourself comfortable and when we are done I will send for you. Fair enough?"

McGraw nodded and excused himself, and she and the priest went back to the suite. The tall, lean, balding clergyman looked and sounded more like an undertaker than a priest, and seemed to have a dour expression at all times as well. She bade him take a seat on the couch near the windows and waited.

"I hardly know where to begin," Dobbs said uncertainly. "This has been a real shock to me, you know. I've known your father for more than thirty years."

"*Oui*. Go on."

"I—ah—I'm well aware as well that your feelings towards him are, at least, ambivalent."

"No, I can not say that. I am most definite about my feelings at this point," she told him coldly.

He got the message. "Miss McKenzie, the fact is that your father was a great man, a genius, and he did a lot of good. A saint, however, he wasn't, and would never be. He treated you most shabbily, he knew it, he felt guilty about it, but he never changed that. That is one of the great many things in his life that can not be excused save by the mercy of God."

"You came here, then, to ask me to forgive him? That I can do only in the Christian sense, I fear. As you say, forgiveness of his sins is in God's hands. I am one of these sins and I am still here. He can not buy with his money what he did not earn with his deeds, yet I will pray for his soul in Purgatory. And my name is Montagne, *s'il vous plaît*. If my father did not wish me to have his name in life I see no reason to change it now. I can pray for understanding on my part and salvation on his, but more than that—no."

The priest nodded. "That is all that I can ask."

"But you did not take me aside to talk solely of this."

"No, that's true. Miss Mc—Montagne, pardon me. Would it shock you to know that your father believed that he might be killed?"

"I have no reason to know one way or the other, but this interests me. Go on."

"He came to me not long ago—a few weeks at best—and at that time he said that he felt he might be done away with. He didn't know by who as yet, but he was becoming convinced of it. He felt that he was being followed and monitored by those outside his employ, that they were stalking him."

"Who is 'they,' if I may ask?"

"I wish I knew. But while your father never spoke much of theology, it was all he could talk about that time. I put it down to depression or perhaps an illness unknown to me, or even job stress, but he pressed and pressed. He was particularly concerned with interpretations of the Book of Revelations—the *Apocalypse*—and on things having to do with Satanism and paganism. I only knew so much and referred him to an expert in the field who's in England, Bishop Whitely. I don't know, though, if he ever saw the Bishop, who's rumored in poor health and had to retire somewhat prematurely, but he told me that if anything violent or mysterious happened to him I was to convey this to you."

She stared at him. "Do you know why?"

"I'm afraid not, nor do I know why this should be of any importance to you. I merely convey the message as I promised him."

"This Bishop Whitely—who is he?"

"A noted academic and scholar in the church and quite a conservative theologian for an increasingly liberal denomination. He was formerly Bishop of Durham at Yorkminster, although briefly—that gave him a lordship, and he is about the fourth highest ranking cleric in the Church of England. I don't really know him at all beyond that. He's not really connected to the Canadian church. He is, however, an academician—most Bishops of Durham have been—and a former Oxford professor who still does some academic research work. He is also a theological conservative and a mystic, probably more conservative than the average Roman Catholic bishop by some measure. They got into some trouble with that Bishopric the last few times around, with one of them questioning publicly the virgin birth and the divinity of Christ.''

She was shocked. ''And they let this man be Bishop of a supposedly Christian church?''

''We all have our problems, I fear, particularly with the hierarchies. Whitely was appointed ultimately to mollify Church conservatives outraged by many of those elevated to Bishoprics in the past couple of decades. That's all I can tell you about him, except that I only really know him by several books he wrote on the Apocalypse and on prophecy, the occult, and such matters. He is fully as controversial in his own way as his predecessors were in theirs, but he is certainly the world's foremost expert on those matters that so intrigued your father in his final weeks.''

She thought things over for a moment. ''Tell me, Father Dobbs—did my father say anything about a dark man?''

Dobbs looked startled. ''Why, now that you mention it, I believe he did! He mentioned something about there being no privacy from the dark man or something like that. I didn't pay much mind to it, assuming it was a reference to someone in his business that was troubling him. Why? Does this give you more information to go on?''

''I—I do not know. Perhaps. Is there anything else?''

"No, not really, I'm afraid. But—tell me, where do you plan to go from here? Have you given it any thought as yet?"

She shook her head negatively. "I'm afraid not. I think perhaps I will stay here for a while. I have no real home at the moment in any case, and this is a good place to learn what must be learned."

He nodded. "And keep away from the press. I'm afraid that once the news of Sir Robert's death came out they scrambled for any and all information on you and discovered some pictures from someplace. They've run all over Canadian, American, and probably even New Zealand television and in all the newspapers. I'm told that there's a standing offer of thousands of dollars to anyone who gets an interview with you and I know that security patrols have intercepted a raftload of reporters attempting to sneak onto this island. Perhaps it's best you *do* stay here for a while, until you're ready to test the waters, as it were. They're like vultures— ghouls. And they act like you are their property."

That frightened her a bit. "When I go, *if* I go, I will have to have some good protection."

Father Dobbs sighed and got up to leave. "You can certainly afford it, my dear."

Harold McGraw was all smiles and warmth, but it was an act and she knew it. The presence of his briefcase indicated that he was there for business reasons only, and he got the pleasantries out of the way quickly.

"I must tell you that perhaps a million dollars in attorney and research fees to experts all over the world went into your father's will, and it's the best document of its kind ever constructed, I wager. That won't stop it from being contested by every sixteenth cousin thirty times removed who discovers your family somewhere in its genealogy, but I wouldn't worry about it. There is a separate trust fund already established in your name and containing massive amounts of stock and convertible paper. It is beyond the scope of the will and is administered by us directly. I hope we can continue to do so in the future."

"I am content with it for now. May I ask how much it represents?"

"Um, at current values, give or take ten percent for the usual fluctuations, it amounts to about twenty-two million dollars. That's American dollars, by the way. Their laws on such trusts are more liberal than ours, although it's directly held as an international account in the Royal Bank of Canada."

The amount staggered her, even though everyone had been talking in huge terms. "And this is—mine?"

"Regardless of the rest. It's free of taxes and fees, of course, and is entirely yours. Considering the unsteadiness of certain markets, however, I would suggest that, to leave principal untouched, you not spend more than one million a year without first consulting us."

She was reeling from the idea. "A million . . . a year?"

"Yes. The easiest way to do this is, well, whenever you wish to buy something, simply have the bill sent to us. For major purchases—say a hundred thousand or more, such as houses, yachts, planes, and the like—have the seller contact us directly so we can work out payment terms to keep it within the range of self-generating income."

"Uh—excuse me, Monsieur McGraw, but I am not yet recovered from this. The very concept of such wealth is beyond my grasp right now, I fear. But still I must go on. If this is my trust fund, as you call it, what is the whole estate worth?"

McGraw shrugged. "Miss Montagne, Magellan is one of the four largest privately held corporations in the world. By 'privately held,' I mean that its stock is not publicly traded, although many subsidiary corporations that it owns are. The whole of the corporation may be worth fourteen to twenty billion dollars American. I can't be more specific than that.

The estate consists of approximately two hundred and twenty million dollars in liquid assets—those things and properties owned by your late father and his bank accounts and personally held stocks and bonds—and fifty and one-half percent of the stock of Magellan. Taxes and death duties are likely to whittle his personal assets to about a hundred million, I'm afraid, but the stock remains. It's rather complicated, but while they will try and get it, it is not directly convertible to value and is protected by stratagems even I can't fully understand from death duties.''

"And he left me—all of it?"

McGraw sighed. "All of it. I've yet to do the formal reading of the will, but this talk will suffice as there are no other pertinent parties. Oh, he left some considerable sums to various charitable and religious groups and established trusts and annuities for many old friends and business associates, but I've already deducted them from the totals I've given you.''

"And this will take years to clear up?"

"I doubt it. Oh, the court cases could drag on into the twenty-second century but I wouldn't worry about them. Actual title should be a matter of months, certainly no more than a year if the unforseen comes up. For all intents and purposes, you own it all as of now. You see—well, let me read pertinent parts of the will. They're already causing bombshells in Magellan's corporate offices now, I can assure you, and probably in many world capitals as well.''

He reached into his briefcase, fiddled a bit, then came up with a small sheaf of papers stapled together. They were clearly copies, and had been marked up with a red pen.

The early parts of the document were long and formal declarations of thus and so, and he began skipping early. When he got to a particular section, though, McGraw couldn't suppress a slight smile.

"Should anyone named in this last will and testament

contest or question any part of it, that person shall receive nothing. Should anyone in the employ of or connected with Magellan or anyone in any way employed in one of my holdings have any part in said contest, whether as plaintiff or as party or witness, said individual shall have his or her employment immediately terminated and shall not receive any further income or employ from any of said companies and holdings for at least twenty years from the date of contest,'' McGraw read her. ''Likewise any corporation, contractor, or government contesting or being a party to said contest shall have immediately and at the date of contest all dealings with any holdings covered herein suspended and shall not be allowed any further dealings with any said holdings. These conditions remain even if a plaintiff later drops a contest or withdraws its complaint or reverses his or her testimony.''

The attorney noted, ''Magellan's holdings are incredible and extensive and are at the heart of some nations' defense and economic establishments. Possibly one in twenty jobs in the west would be directly or indirectly connected to it. Many folks are going to think twice about any contests.''

She gulped and nodded.

''But the real kicker comes further on,'' he told her. ''It says—ah, here. 'If any contest should succeed against my daughter and heir named above, said contestor should be warned that they will win nothing. Should such a contest be upheld through every available court and means, at that very moment Magellan will become worthless. Also, should my daughter die, by any means, natural or unnatural, within five years of assuming her inheritance free and clear, this will also be true. It will be automatic, absolute, and irrevocable. The means of this I keep to myself and take with me to whatever place I go, but I ask one question of anyone who does not believe this, and provide no answer: what would happen if every single data bank in the entire Magellan network suddenly erased itself?''

She shook her head in wonder. "But—what does it mean?''

"I think it means that he arranged, totally outside Magellan, for something to be built in, something that automatically would trigger such an erasure. The computers, all of them, even the big one here, would suddenly be blank again, all information lost.''

"And this would do what?''

"World panic, I should imagine. The banking and financial records alone would be nearly impossible to track down and claim, let alone use. The value of stock in all publicly held corporations either owned by, controlled by, or doing a lot of business with Magellan, would sink. Years of brilliant research would go down the drain. Some nations' economies would collapse, while others would find things from routine imports and exports to defense simply falling apart.''

"Then they will duplicate and move this quickly, yes?''

"Well, because of the sheer volume and the computer's dominance of international telecommunications it'd be damned near impossible. They will save some of the important stuff, the vital stuff, but hardly all. So, you see what he's done? The international financial community and the governments of many nations will scramble, but also hedge their bets by devoting all their time and resources to getting you clear title to it all as quickly as possible. That's why I say it will be months, not years, and why everyone is treating you so carefully.''

"If what you say is true they will drop troops to keep me safe and insulated, whether I wish it or not.''

"There's little real danger of that, I think. You might think of drawing up your own will, too, to go into effect the moment the last probate hurdle is cleared. That will be your best guarantee.''

"I—I will think on it. *Merci, Monsieur* McGraw. You have been most kind."

"I'll not kid you, Miss. We make a ton of money off handling these sort of things, and we only keep accounts like this by doing the best possible job we can. Now—tell me, is there anything we can do for you directly?"

She thought a moment. Probably hundreds of things would come to her later, but now she forced herself to be practical and pragmatic. "First, make certain that my father's houses and other property is safeguarded and catalogued for me, and that they are maintained."

"Already being done."

"Second—for now, it seems, this is the best place for me to stay. I will need attendants. Servants. Whatever they are called. I—"

At that moment, Sister Maria walked in. "Oh, I'm sorry. I thought you were all through," she said apologetically.

"No, no! Come in!" Angelique called to her. "I would like to know your own plans, Sister. How long can you stay with me?"

"Why, as long as you wish. Dr. Byrne informed me just today that they had made arrangements with my order if you so desired. After all, I am one of the few people who knows and understands all this equipment."

She felt much better. "Oh, yes—please stay on, but as my nurse, not my servant. I was just suggesting to *Monsieur* McGraw here that he arrange for servants for all the basics. This will leave you free to take care of medication, physical therapy, and equipment maintenance and leave other matters to others. One with your qualifications should not change diapers or clean up my messes."

McGraw looked startled at the comment. It had never occurred to him that someone paralyzed as she was would *have* to be in diapers, since she wouldn't even know when she eliminated. For the first time, he realized how demoralizing such a condition could be beyond the obvious, and it made him uncomfortable.

"Um, a few more matters," he said a bit uncomfortably. "First, I'll need a power of attorney from you to handle your affairs. Considering your condition, a fingerprint will suffice for the signature. There are also some other similar documents which I'll leave for you to read. We'll have to print every page and have it witnessed, but that should be no problem."

"Very well. I can sign my name with a pen in my teeth if need be, you know."

"Whatever you prefer. Servants will have to be arranged through the security people here, I'm afraid, since not everyone can be admitted onto the island. I'm sure there'll be no problem, though. Mostly you'll need on-call attendants working shifts—that's three—a personal maid, I would think, for dressing and general cleaning and the like. The rest can be provided by the Institute staff. I assume you want all women?"

She blushed slightly. "Yes. I think I will be more comfortable that way."

"All right, then. I won't be going back until tomorrow evening, so I'll leave these documents here for you to look over. Feel free to consult with anyone here at the Institute or call me if you don't understand or like anything, and I'll go over them before you sign in any event in the presence of witnesses." He got up to leave, then stopped and turned back to her.

"Are you certain you wish to remain here? Something here, after all, *did* kill Sir Robert."

"That is true," she admitted, "and I have thought of it. But from what you have told me, they had far less reason to keep him alive, did they not? And any who could kill him *here*, with this amount of protection, could get me anywhere I went. What could I do? Run away? Fight?"

He shrugged. "It had to be said. All right, but be careful.

Premeditation for gain is something I believe you are insulated against. But if it is insanity we are dealing with, or espionage, I wouldn't count on Sir Robert's protections. There are some unfriendly powers, some not that far from here, who might take great joy in the mess the collapse of Magellan might make."

"I will remember," she assured him, and he left.

Sister Maria looked around. "I suppose we ought to make ourselves at home, then. Come—we'll get you cleaned and looking right. If you ask me, though, he's right. Parts of this place are positively creepy."

"I think I know what you mean. But, no, I have another reason for staying right now."

"Your Mister MacDonald? It's a pretty open secret around here, so don't look so shocked. I think everybody knows you've got a crush on him except him." She sighed, but continued to lift Angelique from the chair and put her on the bed. "I'd tread pretty carefully, though. Get to know him a lot better before you get your hopes too high. Remember, with your money now you'll have your pick, but you've got to be realistic about what they might really be after."

"I know, I know. Don't worry about that, at least not now. After all, he is a divorced man, so it would be no marriage in God's eyes anyway. Nor would the Church marry me, since I can not procreate."

Sister Maria stared at her. "I don't know who told you that, but it's not true. The fact that your body won't listen to your brain's commands doesn't mean it doesn't work. It does, and there is still a major neurological connection there. You breathe unaided, you digest and process food normally and eliminate normally. All your organs function normally. *All* of them. There's no physiological reason why you couldn't have a child, or several, if you really wanted to and if you needed to be stimulated down there to get pregnant there wouldn't be any overpopulation in parts of the world."

She was shocked at the tone but fascinated by the information. "You mean—I am able to produce heirs?"

"And have the bucks to give them the best, too. Your old man knew that and it's clearly spelled out in your medical files. That's why you have to be very careful before committing yourself."

"You seem to know an awful lot about it for one with your vows."

Sister Maria chuckled dryly. "I wasn't always a nun. In fact, I only took my vows seven years ago. It's a long story, but I'm no virgin."

She was shocked. This was something that, even if true, nuns never talked about, at least around her.

"Well, I am," she responded wistfully.

The one thing that always surprised people on their first visit to the library room was that it actually had books in it.

"Oh, yes," Reggie said, proud to be showing off his area, dressed in a white uniform including white shorts and looking like some cartoon British naval captain without insignia, "there are books here, but they're really just trophies."

"Trophies?" Angelique stared at the walls of bound volumes.

"Indeed. One can get the contents of millions of books from SAINT with a simple request, and the fax machines—those things that look like copiers—will print out a deucedly good copy in any size print and type style and format one wishes. These books, however, are special. They are the books, magazines, journals, and papers of our distinguished guests over the past few years which resulted from their work here."

"But—couldn't they access the computer from just anywhere?"

"In point of fact they could, but the island is more than merely the home of the heart of the system. It was envisioned by your father as something of a retreat for the finest scientific and technical minds, a place where they would be protected from the outside world, insulated from all the normal human wants and needs, free to think and create and work on any project they wished, not just those their bosses wanted. Writers and artists have had such colonies for a century or two; there were few, if any, such for scientists and mathematicians because of the hardware they need—the computers, the equipment, and the like. Still, there are few and minor laboratories here. This is a place for the theoretician. Most of the work SAINT handles through the worldwide network is pragmatic and very practical; the work done by those who come here for their sabbaticals is pure research, and may or may not even have any real applications. You mustn't think of this as merely the home of a great computer; actually, its object is to push the human mind, the human genius, to the limit.''

She nodded, although she realy didn't understand what he was talking about and saw no purpose to research without any objectives in mind. She steered the conversation back to the library. All around there were small cubicles, or carrousels, each with a computer terminal, a built-in high resolution color screen that was so thin it hung on the back of the cubicle like a painting, and a small desk used for note-taking. Hard copy could be had quickly if desired, by simply instructing it to be done, although the actual printing was done elsewhere and delivered to the individual involved. Only two large, rather quiet faxes, sitting against a wall, were available to those in the room, and those were generally used for printing out such things as morning newspapers from around the world and the like.

She guided the chair expertly up to and in one of the cubicles as Sir Reginald directed. He stood behind her but didn't try and switch anything on. She looked baffled. ''What do I do now?''

''Simply tell it to turn itself on. Whatever language you

use for the instruction will be the language for all data. It will guide you through the rest if you simply talk to it.''

She looked uncertainly at the console. Finally she said, ''Turn on.''

There was no discernible difference, and she wondered if she'd done it right. Then she saw that the screen showed a small word in its center—''READY!'' When she didn't respond for a few seconds, there was a sudden vanishing of the letter, and a voice from the screen said, ''Good morning, Miss Montagne. I am SAINT. How may I be of service to you?'' The voice was normal, very human, and sounded something like a Shakespearean actor.

''He recognizes you through sensors and has checked you out and decided you are authorized,'' Sir Reginald told her. ''Let's say you want to look up something. Just ask him, and he'll find it and either tell you or put it on the screen or print it out as you instruct. If you're unsure of whether or not he has something, just ask.''

Her mind was blank. ''Uh—do you have a file on me?''

''Of course,'' SAINT replied. ''There is a biographical sketch of you, lots of subordinate files and evaluations, and a complete profile and medical history, among other things. The total length, printed out in standard typewriter, would be approximately four thousand two hundred and sixty single-spaced pages. Would you like a copy or would you rather obtain more specific information?''

''Um—biographical sketch. On the screen, please, if it's not too long.''

''Certainly. Just state when you wish to go to the next page.''

And, just like that, up came a neat, formal-looking report on the large screen looking just like a page from a large typeset book.

''I think you've got it now,'' Sir Reginald told her. ''If you'll pardon me, there's a fellow rather insistently attempting to get my attention for some minor emergency or something. When you're through just tell him so and leave. If I may?"

"Yes, certainly," she said, happy to have him off her back. She proceeded to read the file and found it uncannily accurate, including some incidents and friends she herself had forgotten. Clearly a lot of people were keeping a close eye on her. It went on and on, but it finally finished with, in fact, her coming to the island and attending her father's funeral. It was amazingly up-to-date and she wasn't certain she liked it.

"Uh—SAINT?"

"Yes, Miss?"

"You said my file ran thousands of pages. Is there a table of contents that would let me see the topics in it?"

"Yes. Scrolling on the screen now."

She read off the amazing specifics, but finally halted it. "Give me the Psychological Profile," she instructed. "Summary only."

It made fascinating reading, and somewhat uncomfortable reading as well. It accurately pinpointed her lifelong lack of a sense of roots, of belonging, and suggested she had a strong need for a father or authority figure. Her IQ was above the norm but she was hardly a genius. Reading and language skills far above the norm but mostly within the past three or four years, when they were the only ones available. Able to control or even fool people as to her true feelings. Strong romantic and mystic streaks; emotionally immature. . . . It was strong stuff. It did, however, state that she was highly adaptable, practical about her situation, including her disability, and had a logical and orderly mind about things in which she was not emotionally involved.

Physiologically, she confirmed that Sister Maria had been right. But for the fact that orders from her brain were not transmitted past a certain point in her upper spinal column, her body was perfectly normal. The muscles were weak from disuse, but showed, oddly, no signs of deterioration. All bodily organs and functions were normal. She menstruated normally and was capable of child-bearing, although, with no ability to push, she would require a Caesarean. It concluded, as had the psychological, with the notation that there was nothing that known medical science could find wrong with her, and certainly no signs of dramatic injury anywhere in the spinal area. Both concluded, "Disability almost certainly psychosomatic, but unresponsive to any and all treatment."

Psychosomatic. She'd heard that many times before, but all she found in these reports was more of that mumbo jumbo on how and why it might have developed, none of which made much sense to her or hit any raw nerves. She was *not* willing this on herself, no matter what they said.

She abandoned her own file, and looked up Greg's. She was pleased to discover that he had been honest with her about his past. There was a lot more detail, but nothing he'd told her was false. He was not a Catholic; he was, in fact, a nominal Presbyterian without any real connection to a church at all. His marriage had been a civil one, made in civil court, as was his divorce. Oddly, although the Sisters back at the convent would have been upset, this excited more than depressed her. A civil marriage was no marriage in the eyes of the Church, and while non-Catholics were allegedly the object of pity, there had been so few of them in her life that she found the idea rather exotic. There was a photo of his ex-wife in the file, and she *was* rather pretty, although not much like Angelique herself. It was interesting to her, none the less.

His psychological profile, however, was far more general and shorter than hers, and she had the strong feeling that much of it simply wasn't there, almost as if it had either been excised or not put in the system deliberately. Still, it was instructive. He had a fine, analytical mind, and a rather high IQ, as those things went. He was tenacious, stubborn, and seemed to have little regard for his own safety or well-being when in the course of a project or an investigation. One psychologist noted, "Subconsciously, he either thinks he's Sherlock Holmes or would like to be." He was attracted to pretty women, and had never shown much interest in the acquisition of wealth and material things. He also had a distaste for the upper class, a disrespect for any authority not based upon merit as he saw it, and a strong streak of insubordination.

She wanted very much to ask the computer whether or not someone like him could ever be really interested in someone like her, but she did not. She wasn't sure whether she thought it was too personal and revealing a question to ask the computer or whether she didn't really want to know the answer.

"SAINT, do you have any information on the Dark Man?"

"Which dark man do you mean, Miss Montagne? There are quite a number."

"No, no. The one recently reported by—superstitious people around the island and elsewhere."

"Oh, you mean that one. There are no specific files, although Security might have something, which would require their access codes. I wouldn't know, otherwise. However, it is an old legend in the lower Caribbean, this Dark Man, who inhabits the night and the shadows, has no real substance, but foreshadows disaster. He is connected in legend to *obi* and *voodoo* and other dark rites like devil worship. Some such cults have a belief that when the Dark Man ceases being a spirit and becomes real—that is, tangible—he will be the harbinger of the end of the world. Will that do?"

"That is quite enough, thank you. Um, SAINT—this may be a ridiculous question, but do you have any idea who or what killed my father?"

"Logic suggests that he was either killed by a beast of an unknown type or a mechanism simulating it, certainly to induce fear, possibly to attempt to get this island either closed down or opened up to outside authority. It generates insecurity to those corporations and nations who use these facilities because of the tight security. As to who—disallowing the very real but not very probable motive of insanity or personal grievance—the list of suspects, both individual, group, and institutional, is, I'm afraid, far longer than your report.''

"Do you think it—likely—that they will strike again?''

"That will depend on the motives. If the motive was to impair or close down this installation, then the probability is quite high that when this does not happen they will increase their attempts, perhaps in ever greater and more spectacular ways. If it is a stage in a long-range plan or objective, we can expect new developments to proceed. If, on the other hand, it was personal, probably not. Insanity is, by its nature, unpredictable, since while it proceeds from perfect logic, the frame of reference of the insane individual is not based on reality.''

"What would you recommend for me? Should I remain here or go elsewhere for my own safety?''

"I can make no such recommendation. However, logic suggests that if Sir Robert could be killed under those circumstances in a place like this, there *is* no safe place, merely more vulnerable ones.''

"Am I a likely—target?''

"Unknown, again depending on motivation. If the objective is to destroy Magellan and undermine this installation, you would be the most logical target. However, under any other circumstances, you might be the only really safe person on the island. There is, after all, another motive which is most logical in terms of the actual murder of Sir Robert.''

"Oh? What is that?''

"Someone, for some reason, preferred you to him as the owner of the controlling interest in Magellan.''

6

A BRISK WALK IN THE WOODS

She was in the deep forest, the moon showing only slightly through the dense growth, yet she could see well enough. She was naked, and unadorned in any way, yet she did not realize this or think upon it. She did not, in the human sense, think at all; rather, she felt things, basic things, with an intensity she had never known before. There was caution, and fear as well of potential enemies, but there was, too, a sense of exhilaration, of being alive and one with the forest.

Sight, sound, and smell told her that the way was safe, and she got up and moved swiftly and expertly down the forest trail until it opened into a broad meadow with a big dark rock in its center. Once here, she knew, felt, that she was safe and protected.

One by one the others came as well, to run, and jump, and touch, and play with one another in the meadow that was brightly lit by the moon's glow. They were of her own kind and she knew and loved them all, these sisters of the moon-light. They were wild beasts, sometimes on two legs, some-

*times down on all fours, yet they were shaped like the others,
Those Who Must Be Hidden From and Feared.*

*Sometimes they would scamper through the forest and
reach the places where fruit trees grew. Then one or more
would climb the trees as if it were an easy walk and not
straight up and knock the fruit down for others to scramble
for and stuff into their mouths. She always ate with them, yet
no matter how much she ate it was never enough, never
right. There was a hollow, empty hunger she did not understand, a craving left unfulfilled, but she lacked the reasoning
ability to even guess what it could be.*

*And then, as the mists began to build up and the false
dawn crept into the eastern sky, they scampered back into the
woods, back to the safety of their own territorial places
before the sun came up.*

Angelique awoke to see bright sunlight creeping around
the edges of the curtains, and she frowned, looked over at the
clock, and saw that it was nearly time to get up. She did not
feel like it, though; instead, she felt very tired, as if the
dream had been real, and she quickly settled back into a
deep, seemingly dreamless sleep.

In the following weeks, around the world, several small
countries went to war with each other, the U.S. and the
U.S.S.R. had two tense confrontations, the stock markets
mostly were down, although not dramatically, and hordes of
people in various major cities protested one thing or another.
The business of the world went on, and even Sir Robert's
murder, its grisly and mysterious details rather well sup-
pressed, faded from the public's memory. There was still a
bounty on the first new pictures and interview with Angelique,
now one of the richest women in the world if not *the* richest,
and there were the usual messages from the top network
interviewers in the U.S., Canada, Britain, and France—as
well as a host of hustlers and entrepreneurs—coming in, but

on Allenby Island things seemed to lapse into calm and insulated peace.

A small squad of expert workmen and technicians managed, in a very short time, to combine the VIP quarters with Sir Robert's old suite and remodel and remake it into a complex designed to deal with Angelique's physical problems, and to house the new staff while also redecorating to the new owner's tastes. Such things as lights, full or individual, as well as a satellite-fed television receiver, radio, and stereo gear, could be controlled by her voice in much the same way as she controlled her chair. Any dark corners could be instantly flooded with light at a single command. As with her chair, she kept the commands basically to one or two words in basic French, since English was the usual language of the Institute. It kept her from inadvertently giving orders when having a general conversation.

The staff brought in by the Institute was excellent, at least so far. The shift work, or on-call maid and orderly services, was performed by two Haitian sisters, identical twins, actually, named Marie and Margarete, both seventeen and both illiterate, with virtually no schooling. They were, however, friendly, attentive girls who didn't mind the really dirty work and loved the luxury. The third shift was given to eighteen year old Juanita Hernandez, a half-Indian beauty from Venezuela, who was barely literate but made do in English. The twins also made do in English; their native French was such an odd amalgam of dialects and new and old tongues that it was virtually unintelligible to her.

Added to this was Alice Cowan, a nineteen year old Jamaican who was not merely literate but a very fast reader and a capable personal secretary. She was quite tall and very thin, with straight black hair and a light brown complexion, and while she seemed a bit more reserved than the others, she was no less anxious to please and seemed genuinely glad to have the job.

Greg lived in a small apartment down in the village, where he was among friends and felt most comfortable. Angelique had remained in and around the Institute, partly because helping redo the quarters gave her something creative to occupy her mind and also because Greg was a daily visitor.

They had almost literally taken apart and put back together her father's old suite, then moved her into it while they remade her own. Her opinion of Greg had risen, rather than diminished as some in the Institute had hoped, during these times, heightened by a sense of mystery about just what he was doing. Staff people and even Sister Maria had gently pumped her, apparently also out of curiosity, but she could tell them very little. Convinced that he was constantly being monitored, he discussed almost nothing and used unknown means to get his information in and his reports out. It was not even clear, in fact, exactly to whom he was reporting.

Finally, though, she prevailed on him to take her down to the village, and he gave her the grand tour and some of the island's history.

"Nobody really knows who discovered it, but the Spanish first chartered it, and the British took it from them. It didn't really matter. Just one of the hundreds of little flyspeck islands north of Trinidad and Tobago."

"No one lived here, then?"

"Nope. And a number of the islands you see from the mountaintop from here still have nobody on them, except maybe a lonely lighthouse keeper or something like that. The water's in the wrong places, the thing is hell on agriculture, although with modern methods that cost more than they're worth we're able to grow some of the fresh fruit and vegetables up to the west of the Institute, and the lone harbor is shallow and narrow, with underwater rocks and reefs, and cost a fortune just to create the small channel that allows our twice weekly supply ship to come in at all. It just wasn't worth any trouble."

"Then—all of this is my father's doing?"

"Not quite," he told her. "The Royal Geographic Society kept a research station going near the summit off and on until the 1890s, mostly to keep some British presence here just in case somebody else wanted it. Then, in 1894, the government sold the entire island to Lord Carfax, one of those crusty rich eccentrics they used to have in those days. He built the place as a winter resort and getaway for his own use and the use of his friends. He's the one who built the town in a miniature replica of a Tudor village. The staff was enormous, and was brought in from British holdings and Britain itself. Some of the families here are descended from those earliest servants and workers for the old Lord."

"Then—it has been a resort all this time?"

"Oh, no. Not since World War II, really, but some of the people had been born and raised here and they stuck it out, pretty much forgotten in the backwaters of things. The old manor house, with its tennis courts and such, burned down in forty-two, I think, and its remains are mostly overgrown now."

"But—what did the people do during all that time?"

"Fished, mostly. Applied for every British grant they could. Took the dole. They had housing, the Lord's old water system, bounty from the sea and a little bit of land they farmed for their own consumption. Had a few cows and sheep. It wasn't much—outdoor plumbing that worked half the time, no electricity, no conveniences, but the old timers maintain they were happy times, often likening the period to paradise. Britain tried to give it to Trinidad and Tobago or even Guyana in the sixties, and they successfully fought that, but finally the mother country just gave up and outright pulled out and gave them to the tiny nation they don't like and don't feel a part of. They look upon your father as something of a savior—saving the British from the savages,

as it were. The price, though, was steep—they all became
Magellan employees and workers at the Institute.''

They were, however, a friendly bunch in their own little
town, far, it seemed to them, from the colossus looming high
above them. They reminded Angelique very much of the
small-town folk of the Gaspé in spite of their far different
cultural origins. And these were the folk that made it all
work; who unloaded the twice-weekly supply ships and got
the food and other materials up the mountain to the Institute,
who repaired and drove the carts, who did the cooking,
picked up the trash, and threw out the garbage, buffed the
floors of the Lodge and Institute buildings, and did all the
rest of the routine things that made the Institute possible at
all.

For Greg MacDonald, it had been a time of frustrations
and changes. He found himself thinking of Angelique now
only as a friend and companion and, without really being
aware of it, he no longer even thought about the wheelchair
and her disabilities. Not that he ignored them—that was
impossible—but he now simply took them for granted. There
was something about her own spirit, her own unwillingness
to let her paralysis destroy her or even limit her more than it
absolutely had to that he respected. He didn't regard her as a
nuisance or a hindrance, although he'd started out thinking
that might be the case, and he actually found himself looking
forward to her coming down, and missing her when she
wasn't around. He felt quite guilty that her total dependency
seemed to turn him on, but if he didn't know how idiotic it
was he could almost swear he was falling in love with her.

He was frustrated, too, that he could tell her so very little
of what he was up to and what he'd already pieced together.
On Allenby, it wasn't paranoia to believe that every single
word you spoke was recorded in some security outpost.

They went down the beach, listening to the birds and the
crash of the surf, he walking, she riding, he occasionally

having to push to get her unstuck from the sand. Finally, they stopped, ironically not far from where her father had died, although within sight of the tiny church. It was late in the day, and they had spent the afternoon looking over merchandise sold by the crewmembers of the small supply steamer as a sideline. Most of it was probably stolen, but some if it was quality stuff and nobody on their route, including Allenby, was likely to have the authority to make arrests and make them stick.

"You look a little worried," she noted.

"Huh? Sorry. Yeah, got to stop thinking so much."

"Problems? Is the Institute bothering you again?"

"No," he assured her, "that's all been damped down, at least for now. It's just that something was supposed to come in with the steamer today that I've been expecting for some time now and it just wasn't there."

"Something to do with your case?"

He nodded. "Yes. A crazy hunch, if you want to call it that, triggered by what Dobbs told you. Never mind for now. What about you? You're looking more and more tired and drained. You nodded off on me a few times this afternoon. Maybe you should go back and get some rest."

She shook her head. "I don't know what is wrong with me. I am sleeping more and longer than I ever have, yet I feel very tired, as if I sleep very little."

"The dreams again?"

"Yes, I suppose, but how can a dream tire you so?"

"Depends. The mind can do funny things. Have you talked to the doctor about it?"

"Oh, yes, many times. She gives me pills or portions, but they do no real good. She says that the dreams are a textbook set, for all the time I am whole and running free in the primeval woods. They are not *bad* dreams, just strange ones, but every time I go to sleep and have another I feel there is a *wrongness* to it, that the nightmare it is just around the corner. I am a bit frightened by it.''

He looked seriously at her. ''Well, you've been through a lot lately. Still, I'm not sure this place is good for you. You should go to some south seas island, or at least Montreal, and just get away from anything having to do with Magellan or this place for a while.''

She shook her head slowly from side to side. ''I—I can not. What I fear here is nothing compared to that which I fear beyond here. I could not go out there, into the real world, without some sort of anchor, and the only anchor I have, the only friend, is right here with me.''

He just stared at her for a moment, not really comprehending.

''Greg—you will pardon me, but I really don't know how this is done—will you . . . kiss me? Even if you don't mean it and don't really want to? Just for me?''

Pity welled up in him, along with other feelings he didn't quite understand, but he knew what he had to do. He leaned over her and said, softly, ''I'll give you the kiss of your life.''

He had always been a very good kisser, and he had to repress the urge to do more, but the awkward angle he was forced by the chair's presence to take was a constant reminder that she could feel no where else.

He broke it off when his back and arm couldn't stand the strain of supporting him any longer, and he saw that she was crying.

For himself, he had very mixed emotions about the episode, but he was certainly uncomfortable. Although he'd known that she had a crush of sorts on him, up to now it had been a purely non-physical thing, and, therefore, somewhat abstract. Now, he knew, it could get more than a little awkward for all concerned, and he had enough on his mind as it was. When a cop got emotionally involved in a case, even unwillingly, he lost his objectivity and was more prone to take risks and make mistakes. This was a game in which risks and mistakes were what he couldn't afford. The other side held most of the cards, and he had no large force or laws to back him up.

For Angelique, it was the fulfillment of a fantasy. Still very much an adolescent emotionally and desperately in need of a close companion, the father figure of the psychiatric report, she had seized upon MacDonald from the start. What was strangest and most wonderful during the kiss, though, was that she was sure she felt various other parts of her body tingle and glow as well. She wanted to shout out that she loved him, wanted him, would do anything for him, but she was afraid that she might drive him away. She had nothing really to offer him except money, and he had never shown much liking for it in large amounts. His file had said he'd been a lifelong member of the socialist New Democratic Party back in B.C.

And, of course, that was one of his attractions, at least in reassurance terms. She knew full well she'd never lack for suitors, but he was the only one that she could count on from the start not to be thinking first of the dollar signs.

So she said, "Thank you, Greg. It meant a great deal to me."

"No, no! Any time you like! It's in my job description. Kiss any and all beautiful women who ask me."

She chuckled. "And am I beautiful?"

"You bet you are," he answered playfully. "But now I think we ought to get you home."

"Red can run me up with the dusk patrol."

"Oh, no. I'll run you home. We can always get a cart— they're moving stuff up from the ship all evening. Uh—by the way, are you going to tell me about how you got all scratched up or not?"

"Huh? What do you mean?"

"You've got little scratches on your arms, ankles, and

even one up there just on the side of your face. I noticed them as soon as we met but I figured you'd tell me about them.''

She shook her head in puzzlement. ''I—I did not even know of them.'' She looked down at her arms, held on the arms of the chair by small, loose straps. ''I can not see. Undo one and hold it up.''

He unbuckled a strap and did so, turning the arm slightly and carefully so he wouldn't hurt anything. The scratches *were* there—thin, random, and small, but deep enough and old enough to have formed scabs.

''Bruises I am used to—you get them all the time like this and never really know. But these—these look deep enough that I should have at least known when they happened. You say they are also on my neck?''

''Yes—there, on the left side.''

''Funny. I have had an itch there off and on today, but I did not pay much attention to it. I shall have Sister Maria take a look at them when I get back.''

''I think you should.'' He didn't know why they disturbed him—they certainly weren't anything serious—but their mere existence troubled him. If he'd blocked it out before, he now had no doubts that he was the principal reason that she remained on the island. He resolved that if any of his strong suspicions and hunches could be independently confirmed he'd get her off this place, even if he had to physically carry her.

And then, one night, another came to the meadow, one not like them, yet not like the Others, either. Dark he was, darker than the darkest night, yet even as he sat there upon the glassy rock no features could be determined. It was not a man, but the shadow of a man, yet it moved, and had depth and a form that was like something solid and real.

And they feared him, far more than they feared the Others, for he radiated power and fear and his confidence was absolute, yet such was that power, so hypnotic, so magnetic, that they were held, transfixed, and could not flee.

And he played for them tunes on a pipe, and the naked girl-apes danced for him and around him, a wild, frenzied dance that aroused in them all their most primal emotions, and gave within them a sense of power that overwhelmed their fear and intensified that hunger they had felt but never understood or filled.

And when their dancing had reached a fever pitch, he stopped and pointed, and they were off, no longer playful things but a wild, frenzied pack seeking a release they did not understand. They came to a road and waited, hidden in the trees and bushes, their eyes glazed, mouths foaming, waiting, waiting. . . .

And, soon, there came footsteps along the road, and they saw that it was one of the Others, a small man with a balding head and slight goatee, dressed casually in shirt and shorts and sandals. He walked very confidently and seemed unaware that they were there.

As one they leaped out and were upon him in seconds, and he was pushed to the ground and his throat was slashed by nailed hands and biting teeth. He was dead very quickly, but they did not stop, his blood flowing warm and inviting, and they tore at the corpse and drank the blood and ate of the flesh and it filled their insane hunger.

There was a thunderclap which startled them, and then it began to rain quite heavily, drenching them all. From down the road they could hear the sound of one of the Whining Monsters, and they broke off and dragged the corpse with them, back into the woods, back along the trail in the now driving rain, back to the meadow where the Dark Man waited.

Lightning flashed as they reached the meadow, illuminating the scene briefly as if it were day, yet the Dark Man remained the darkest black of shadows. He stood there, laughing, and gestured, and they placed the corpse on the stone, and they howled their joy and triumph over the Others and danced again around the stone with its grisly burden, danced in the mud and the lightning and the rain. . . .

"*Señorita* Angel, *Señorita* Angel, wake up, *por favor!*"

She groaned and managed to open her eyes and blearily see the face and form of Juanita Hernandez standing there, holding a tray.

"Go away, Juanita, please," she managed, barely getting the words out. Her throat was sore and she was sure she was coming down with something.

"But, *Señorita*, it is well past noon. It is not good for you to sleep all the day. If you wake up I will feed you some breakfast."

She groaned again. "No, nothing, please. Just some coffee to help me wake up. I'm not at all hungry."

They were on the small fishing pier in the village, just watching the sea birds and watching the ocean. It was a rough surf, thanks to the storm the previous night, and that made it dramatic, plumes of waves sometimes striking the pier, rising up and threatening to get them drenched.

She had not been able to get the nightmare out of her mind. "It was a horrible dream, the nightmare that I felt was coming."

"You told nobody else about it?" MacDonald asked her, concerned.

"No. I had enough with psychologists at the Center. They would say that my fears and insecurities were causing it, that my frustration at this handicap was coming out in that wild experience, and that killing the man was in some way the resentment against my father expressing itself. But the man was a total stranger! I can see him now, describe him."

He frowned. "Go ahead. Describe him to me."

"But it was just a nightmare."

"That's all right. Real people show up in dreams all the time. Go ahead."

She did so, hesitantly, not wanting to remember too much. Is it—somebody real?"

"I think so. It sounds a lot like Jureau. He's the NATO security representative here—a Belgian. Even more unpleasant than Ross, but you don't see much of him."

"Then I have met him?"

"You must have, although I didn't know he was back, or even if he was coming back. He's been in Brussels since shortly after your father's death. He's a stiff-necked by-the-book martinet that nobody likes."

"Greg—you will see this Jureau? Find out if he is actually here, yes? Find out if. . . ."

He stared at her in disbelief. "If what?"

"If—he is—still—alive."

He sighed in disgust. "Come on! You're not starting to believe this, are you? That somehow you're turned into a beast-girl every night and go out with the other beast-girls to prowl?"

"I—I don't know what to believe any more. When you consider my father, the way in which he died, what is impossible here? Don't you see? If you see him, talk to him, it will disprove it!"

"All right, all right. I have to go up to the helipad this evening and meet the chopper coming in anyway. Just don't go spooky on me. That's how these cults, these superstitions of fear, get you. If you start believing in it, they got you."

"And that is what this is? Some kind of devil cult?"

"I didn't say that, but now that you've asked, that *is* involved in all this."

"And if this Jureau *is* dead, what then?"

"He's not. If he were dead, or even missing for more than five minutes, there would be a hue and cry around here not seen since your father's death. But even if he was, it wouldn't mean anything. There are all sort of drugs and hallucinogens that can be slipped into food without anybody knowing and would have you believing the sky is pale yellow and horses rule the world. You're particularly vulnerable to that sort of thing, remember, and your money and power are real tempting targets. I think it's time you got away from here. I think maybe it's time I did, too.''

"Go? Where?"

"There's a little coastal fishing town on Bessel Island about forty miles due west of here. It's still in the country, but pretty remote. An American friend of mine named Art Cadell has a place there. Not much, but it's a little white stucco cottage facing the sea with a very nice beach. My hands have been tied here, and I'm thinking of moving over there to get a little breathing room. No bugs that aren't alive and a little freedom to ask questions without Big Brother listening in. We could use that while we make arrangements for a more civilized move, maybe to your father's place on Puget Sound, which I understand is pretty nice. I could arrange for security for you, and then see a few folks I have to see in person to ask a few more questions.''

She stared at him. "Greg—do you know who killed my father?''

"I think so. I've known for some time. The trouble is, I need confirmation of my suspicions and fragments of information to do anything, and even then it'll be hell to prove or even act. In the meantime, I don't want you falling under their control.''

He stood up and gestured back at the mountain, partly shrouded in mist. "Come on," he said as lightly as he could. "Let's get you home for now." *But not home for long*, he added to himself.

*   *   *

He couldn't contact Jureau. In fact, the security boys were adamant that the Belgian had never returned from Brussels and was off on a new assignment somewhere. They didn't know where, and didn't care, as long as it wasn't here.

That bothered him more than any stalling or lame excuses. If Jureau had never returned, then Angelique could not ever have seen him. And if she'd never seen him, how could she describe him so correctly, down to a silly outfit MacDonald knew the Belgian favored?

The hell with the renovations, he decided. No matter what did or did not come in on the chopper tonight, he was getting her out of here as soon as possible. He had the place for a getaway, and he had the means, the first time her crush on him would come in handy. He was going. If she wished, she could come with him. If not, she might be here alone and never see him again. He was pretty sure she'd move, only he wanted it to be as sudden as possible. No company helicopters, which were fast but which couldn't be set up on short notice without tipping his hand. No, in two more days the ship was due back, and it would go from here to Port of Spain, from which transportation would be far more easily, and quietly, arranged.

For now, he could do nothing but go down to the Institute's helipad and wait for the executive chopper to come in and hope that what he was waiting for was on board.

Greg MacDonald used company couriers checked out and approved by his bosses for much of his information-gathering work. His biggest frustration, and largest stumbling block, in the investigation was his inability to use the vast telecommunications power the island represented, nor any means that could be sensed by that network. No matter what else he knew or didn't know, he was certain that anything done through computer or telecommunication lines at any point would, if traced to him, make its way to his quarry through SAINT.

He was in the unique position of being the very real leader of a large investigative team and also the decoy and the bait. So long as he remained on Allenby, they felt reasonably safe and secure, for he was the enemy they knew.

The helicopter was due in at 20:45 Atlantic time, and the fact that it was now very late worried him. He had seen Angelique safely to her quarters, and now all he could do was cross his fingers and wait.

They told him that they'd had only spotty radio communications with the chopper almost since it had started out. The pilot reported something like a large electrical storm with buffeting winds and downdrafts all around, yet the weather report and their own weather radar indicated nothing at all. He had been unable to fly out of it or around it, and by 22:10 they were telling MacDonald that the helicopter had turned back for now. He was just about to give it up when he heard the *Whomp! Whomp! Whomp!* of rotor blades together with the whine of the turbine and saw the landing lights for the chopper just to the south.

"Man must be a damn fool or damned crazy to try it with what he was reportin'," a ground crewman, who was also about to pack it up and leave, noted.

The helicopter seemed a bit wobbly, and as it landed, pretty hard and off the mark, they could see a trail of black smoke coming from the rear and could also see, in the spotlights, places where the aircraft's paint seemed blistered or burnt.

The pilot cut the engines and got went back to get his passengers off as fast as possible, as technicians raced forward with special fire gear. It didn't take long for the pilot and passengers, both of them, to get off and away, but all seemed more than a little shaky. One of them, a slender, small woman in a loose-fitting dress, looked around, spotted MacDonald, and made her way shakily to him. She was carrying a small briefcase handcuffed to her wrist.

"Jesus!" she swore as she reached him, looking a little green and more than a little like she was about to throw up. "I don't care what *anybody's* payin' me. I wait and take the boat back!"

"Rough trip, huh?"

"Rough ain't the word! Lightning and swaying and everything horrible that anybody can imagine in a helicopter and then some! Only reason we made it was that lightning struck the interior electrical system knocking out most of his instruments and all his navigation. Somehow he managed to spot a landmark and made for here, since he knew how to get here blind easier than gettin' back to someplace else. I tell ya, it was *awful*. Weird, too. Soon as we got close to the island here it cleared up like it wasn't doin' nothin' at all. Stars, clear air, everything. Pilot managed to jury rig the landing lights. Only reason I ain't throwin' up on you is 'cause there ain't nothin' left!"

He reached over to the handcuffs, brought up her arm, and placed a thumb on a small metal plate in back of the cuff that was attached to her wrist. The cuff snapped open and he took the case. "I think maybe they wanted to stop *this* from getting to me," he told her grimly. "As usual, they used a cannon to swat a fly and muffed it."

She stared at him. "You mean somebody *caused* all that?"

He nodded. "I expected something of the sort when I found that Martinez hadn't reboarded the ship when it left St. George's."

"He's dead," she told him. "They found his body in the hills. Carved up like a ripe melon from all reports. Ugly." The idea, however, seemed far less unpleasant to her than the storm she'd just gone through. "Cops said it looked almost like a ritual murder."

He nodded. "Well, I think you'll be safe now. You were just brought in for this one trip and don't know enough to make you a target. The ship's just left, so you're either here for three more days or you can take the trip back to Trinidad by chopper tomorrow. I know what your feelings are now, but I think you'll find it much smoother going the other way."

She looked dubiously back at the helicopter, its rear panel off, the technicians having stopped the fire now looking at the mess. "Well, maybe. Can't give me a hint as to what this is about?"

"Sorry. You want to be safe—or dead?"

"Safe every time. But—what about *you*? Aren't you a sitting duck now?"

"I doubt it. If they haven't tried for me by this point, I doubt if they'll do it now. There's the tram for the Lodge. Take it with the pilot and the other passenger."

"Aren't you coming?"

"No, I'll catch one going downhill from here to the village. Say—what's your name?"

She grinned, seeming to have fully recovered now. "Kristy. I'm from San Diego."

"O.K., Kristy of San Diego, you just go up and relax. The doc up there will give you something for the stomach if you need it."

"Thanks. You take care, now."

"I will," he called to her, then watched the tram leave. He knew that there would be a routine late tram from the Lodge in about half an hour, and he decided to wait for it. He didn't want to go up to the Lodge with the contents of the briefcase unread and unstudied, and he didn't feel like making his way back down the hill in the dark, even though it was an easy walk. If they could whip up that kind of reception for the chopper, how hard would it be to have somebody waiting for him with a good, stiff blackjack?

There were bright lights on at the helipad, four techs still working on the chopper, and there seemed no reason not to sit down at the edge of the pad and take a look now at what he had. He took his keyring out of his pocket, found one out of the perhaps twenty or so keys, stuck it in the lock, then opened the clasps. If you didn't open them just so, a fairly loud alarm and a canister of tear gas went off, though he didn't really think that was much of a deterrent.

Some of the files inside, though, were dynamite. He didn't worry that they were mostly computer printouts; he knew that this had not been run through any computer connected up to a master system.

Old Reggie, for example, had quite an interesting background. Second son of the Earl of Halsey, who went broke during the sixties when Labour was attacking the old ancestral seats of wealth. Eaton, Oxford, all the best—but that was before. Older brother hanged himself in a London flat in '76, attributed to depression and heavy drug use, particularly hallucinogens. Reggie theoretically inherited, but there hadn't been much to inherit. In fact, by then he'd been a big wheel in mainframe computers and apparently he and his brother hadn't been close. Reggie could have easily bailed out the family financially and covered his brother's debts—indeed, he could have bought back the ancestral home from the American who had purchased it from the bank—but he hadn't.

Reggie's passion was computers—his knighthood, the only title he didn't refuse or surrender—was for his work in helping set up the British intelligence computer network.

All this, of course, was known and easily available in SAINT's own files. Also not new was the revelation that his brother had gotten rather strongly involved with a London-based cult, and that this cult seemed to be a bunch of devil worshippers. They did the drugs and the Black Mass and the ceremonies and were considered quite round the bend. They were also suspected in a number of grisly murders that had made the tabloids' day off and on for a couple of years, but their link was never proven and they were never brought to trial. The identities of most of the members, however, were known to Scotland Yard and they were always under close watch, which seemed to have stopped the murder spree for the past few years.

What *was* new, however, was the discovery of some old records and the writings of some now dead cult members that indicated that Reggie was just as deep in it as his brother, and might, in fact, have gotten his brother involved as a public shill, masking Reggie's own involvement and acting as his surrogate. The security boys at Cheltenham had thought Reggie might be involved in some sort of cult stuff, but because it was entirely British and seemed apolitical, and because he never attended any rites or got directly involved with them, and, also, because he *knew* they knew of his interests, and therefore was unlikely to be blackmailed over it, they let it pass.

There had also, in fact, been an inheritance from his brother. Tons, it seemed, of ancient and modern books and pamphlets on Satanism, devil cults, anthropological studies of worldwide religious beliefs and ceremonies, and all the rest. Where his brother, who'd made his living at the end as a London tour guide, got the money to accumulate such a massive library was unknown, but Reggie had accepted it and had himself seemed rather taken aback by the sheer volume of material. He had, however, had it moved up to his house and had reviewed and meticulously cataloged it. After three years, he'd turned it over to an auction house to be broken up and sold, the money going to various charities, and that had seemed the end of it.

Reggie, however, had been a co-developer of the fax system of input storage, the parent of the machines now in the library at the Lodge. One just used it like a copier, only instead of giving a print-out, it read data, changed it into digital form, and sent it to computer storage files. He'd had no less than six of them at the house during those three years, and all were connected to large mainframe computers. He had also, during that period, employed no less than a dozen people privately, almost all young men and women who passed security muster, some as gardeners and handymen, others as apprentice technicians.

It had taken weeks to get those names and vital statistics out of British work records, and to track down those people today. All had at one time or another either been connected with some typically British nut cult or another or had at least been patrons of occult bookstops and paraphernalia stores.

Then the shocker. All of them—to a one—now worked for Magellan, either directly or through a subsidiary. And five of them were now on Reggie's staff at the Institute.

Where were the others? Seattle, Montreal, Kingston, Port au Prince, Caracas, Port of Spain. . . . None were really high up, but all worked with computers and all had access to the corporate telecommunications network.

Old Reggie had been both patient and busy. He was the spider, sitting at the center of it all, removed and relaxed here on Allenby, Middle of Nowhere, Caribbean, but with today's computers and satellites he was as good as in the center of London. Better, for he was insulated from outside pressures and prying eyes, and privy to whatever secrets were developed here on "his" computer. How large his network might be was unknown, but it was possible, suggested the report, that it could be in the hundreds, perhaps in the thousands, by now. The man who taught you how to play championship poker never told you quite *everything* he knew. The man who more than any other individual designed and created the latest two generations of super computers might not have told his bosses *everything* about his creations. Who would know? Who could tell?

Only, perhaps, the Japanese geniuses with whom Reggie had studied and upon whose pioneering, Nobel-winning work Reggie based his own creations. Even they might take years to discover the tricks their British protégé had added to their creations, and both of his mentors were old men unlikely to either make the trip or undertake the effort—or survive the undertaking.

Reggie had never gotten the Nobel, mostly because he was quite deliberately anonymous to the world and his work almost entirely with national security systems, but there was no sign he ever resented the fact, partly because there was no question of his receiving one when sufficient time passed to make his work public enough to be recognized by his peers.

It was beginning to fit together very well indeed. Sir Robert's interest in Satanism and the occult shortly before his death was only the final nail in the coffin.

All they lacked was any shred of proof that Reggie was doing anything at all improper. The problem was, he was quite obviously doing it through SAINT, and only through demonstrating that fact could anything be brought out. The classic catch twenty-two, as the Americans liked to say.

The only one who could nail Reggie with hard evidence was Reggie.

Just what *could* Reggie tap from his personal interface with SAINT? The answer was, almost anything. Virtually all of the sophisticated computer network maintained by the United States, Britain, Canada, and even NATO in Brussels was at least supervised by him or based upon his ideas and designs. He could not tap the nuclear fail-safe codes. That, thank God, was on a proprietary system isolated from anyone not directly in the chain. Outside of that, though, his power at the center was almost unlimited. World economics was at his mercy.

International banking and trade were too, no matter what codes of their own they used. Smaller, weaker nations in Latin America, the Middle East, Africa, and Asia were potentially his pawns. He could probably start wars, and stop them. And there were a million subtler things.

MacDonald recalled that someone once suggested that one

could do in New York as effectively as dropping a nuclear device on it by simply turning all the traffic lights in the city green in all directions at the same time and cutting the power to the subways. The wrong weapons could be diverted to the wrong nations. Banks might cancel vital credits to companies while giving them to the wrong ones. Nations dependent on foreign shipments of grain or even pesticide might starve and be driven to desperate measures.

The possibilities for doing mischief were limitless, and the incredible thing was that, simply because of his manner and his background and breeding, no one before had put this all together and discovered how much of an omnipresent figure in today's modern world Reggie had become.

Until, that is, Sir Robert McKenzie had somehow stumbled upon it. What had alerted him at the start would probably never be known. Reggie, perhaps, did something that Sir Robert discovered and traced back to him, perhaps. Whatever happened, Sir Robert had come to the same point that he, MacDonald, was at now. He had the facts but did not yet have anything concrete to act upon. Sacking Reggie wouldn't have done much good. It was a sure bet that, no matter what they did with SAINT after he left, anyplace Reggie was with a telephone and a terminal and modem he could access the special files and special commands that were certainly buried there. At this stage, SAINT couldn't be shut down without bringing Magellan and perhaps a lot more down with it, at least not right away. Sir Robert had sacrificed everything, even his daughter, to Magellan.

But, then, why knock off the old boy at all, let alone in such a spectacular way? Unless, of course, SAINT, aided by the massive files and profiles on practically everyone including Sir Robert, had concluded that it was either the old man or Reggie. . . .

It certainly wasn't anything MacDonald really knew, but he supposed, just supposed, that SAINT discovered evidence that Sir Robert had in the past played the ultimate hardball game. That, at least once, the old boy had taken out a contract and had someone in the way killed when he could remove the obstacle no other way? If so, to anticipate SAINT's way of thinking, there would be but one logical conclusion. Either kill Sir Robert before he gets the chance to set up the hit, or be killed.

As simple, and as basic, as that.

But why kill him in such a showy and elaborate—not to mention risky—manner? A demonstration of power, a fear inducer—all these were part of it, but not the real cause.

A self-aware computer sees its maker in mortal danger. Could it, given its compulsory programs, act on its own? Might it choose a time and method for reasons very logical to it, but not to a human?

Greg MacDonald suddenly felt queasy. SAINT knew, or deduced, what these papers contained and the conclusions he would draw from them. It tried to stop their delivery by conventional means—arranging the murder of Martinez—and that didn't work. It tried by somehow causing that terrible storm-like power to crash that helicopter, or at least turn it back, and it failed. *And now he was sitting here in the shadow of the damned thing reading the material!*

He quickly got up and turned around and saw that he was alone. He had been so deep in his thoughts that he hadn't really noticed. The helicopter was still there, silent now, but everyone else had left for the Lodge. At that moment, somebody turned off the helipad's lights and he was instantly plunged into near darkness. He felt uneasy, unnerved by it, although it was quite natural for the lights to go out when their use was no longer necessary.

There had been no sign of a tram going down to the village. He pressed the light stud on his watch and saw that it was long overdue. He'd been sitting there for close to an hour!

Slowly, his eyes grew accustomed to the dark, which was not total. The moon came out from behind the clouds, and up on the hill the lights of the Institute lit up the night sky. Even the road down was illuminated with small battery powered orange lanterns to guide night walkers and drivers.

A breeze rustled the tops of the trees nearby, and he was engulfed in the sounds of the night, the insects and other creatures of the dark. Far off he could even hear the distant pounding surf. Nothing was abnormal, nothing was out of the ordinary, except that the tram hadn't come.

He debated going up to the Lodge, which was not very far although the climb was steep, but something prevented him from doing so. True, there were friends, even innocents, up there, but Reggie was there as well, and SAINT controlled everything from the lights to the air conditioning and saw and heard practically everything.

Better the village, where between a quarter and a half of the population was native or had been hired by Sir Robert directly and predated SAINT. The village itself was independent of the Institute in power and the like and its construction predated all of them.

Sir Robert, with far more light, had been trying to make the village, too. Well, the old boy had been lured to the meadow by something SAINT had printed out with his morning papers. There was no reason for Greg MacDonald not to stay on the road, and he'd walked it, day and night, hundreds of times.

He got up and started down the switchbacked road, walking at a moderate pace. He was scared and nervous, but he did not want to panic and do the job for them—if they intended to do a job at all. After all, he was as much a prisoner to SAINT and its crazy master as everyone else was.

The first switchback below the helipad took him out of sight of the Institute but within sight of the village that seemed so far away below. Then they both came into view again, and he stopped and stared, sensing a *wrongness* some-how and not being able to put his finger on it. *Nerves?* No, something else. It was quiet. *Too* quiet.

There were no insect sounds, no sound of breeze or surf. It was as if a cone of silence had descended upon him, out in the middle of nowhere, where it couldn't possibly occur.

The moon ducked behind a cloud as he looked back at the Institute, and the hair on the back of his neck began to rise. He could clearly see the road leading all the way back up to the Lodge, outlined by the battery powered orange lanterns.

Now, one by one, those lanterns were going out.

And now there *was* a sound, in the distance but growing closer. It was a hollow sound that seemed to echo, the sound of some great feet coming down, marching in an unearthly cadence, as if hitting not the road but some great snare drum.

He began to walk faster. The pace behind him didn't increase, but clearly it was progressing toward him quicker than he was moving, and he became painfully aware of just how many switchbacks there were in the road and just how close the turn up top was to the road turning back just beneath. What was the reach? Fifteen feet? Twenty feet? Could it survive jumping down between the switchbacks as it had so easily survived jumping from the cliffs to the beach, an even greater height?

Greg MacDonald started running.

He ran as fast and as hard as he could, but the thing kept coming on, coming faster although still at a deliberate pace. If it had any sense at all it would begin jumping to insure capture—or would it? Would it really care if it had to go into town or not to get him? He was running towards a harbor and town that was essentially a *cul de sac*. It had no need to hurry, for there was no place he could run.

He turned a corner and spotted not far below a lone man on horseback. For a moment he feared that they were coming at him to block him in, but then he realized that it was Red.

The chief constable stopped suddenly and his horse began to act up. He shook his head and tapped on his ear, as if wondering if he'd abruptly gone deaf. The horse grew more and more skittish, and he tried to calm and control the animal, and so he was still there when MacDonald rounded the switchback turn and practically ran into him.

"Red!" he shouted, breathing hard and feeling a little dizzy. "Red—get me down from here and fast! Whatever killed Sir Robert's coming right down this road!"

Although the man was shouting, his voice was so muffled it was difficult to hear him, while the sudden sounds of the hollow footsteps of some great beast hit them both. The chief constable stared at him, then looked up at the Institute. Although the road lights seemed out up above and were progressively winking out below that as he watched, he could clearly see the Institute and something of the road in the moonlight. Clearly there was nothing there—nothing large, anyway.

"What the bloody hell is going on here?" he shouted at MacDonald.

"No time for explanations now! Let me get up on the horse with you and get us both back down. That thing'll be here in another minute and a half!"

In the distance, through the eerie muffling of natural sound, the breathing of some great beast could be heard along with the footsteps. Red reached down and almost pulled the younger man up, then turned the horse and started back down as fast as he dared.

"But there's nothing back there!" the old cop protested. "I can see there ain't!"

"The damned thing's invisible!" MacDonald told him. "That's why it didn't care about the beach in the daylight!"

Red didn't much believe in invisible things, but he was too nervous to argue right now. "Where'll we head? Surf's too rough to do us much good in the water, and I'll let it get me before I'll lure that fucker into town!''

MacDonald's mind raced, trying to think. The decision had to be made in a matter of seconds. He peered forward and saw the steeple of the little chaple, removed from the town by about a hundred yards. Not much, but it was something.

''The church!'' the younger man yelled. ''It's not much of a chance, but they're devil worshippers, Red!''

They were there only a minute later, and both men jumped off as quickly as they could, then as Red pushed open the door to the church MacDonald looked back up the mountainside. Red was right—he saw exactly what he expected to see, except for the completely extinguished battery lights outlining the road. Still, he could hear the footsteps, very close now, and almost feel the hot breath on his face. He turned and followed Red into the church.

The lights didn't work, but they managed to find a few things to pile up against the only door, including some of the back pews. The pews were all bolted to the floor but these had come loose years ago and nobody had ever gotten around to fixing them.

Red groped for MacDonald in the dark. ''So *now* what do we do?''

''I wish I knew, Red. This may be it. You haven't got a gun, have you?''

'' 'Course not. What the bloody good would it do against *that* anyway? Listen to it!''

It was clearly right outside now, and had stopped. They could hear its massive body rustle and the snort from its nostrils. They held their breaths and waited for what came next.

The creature or whatever it was seemed equally confused as to that question, almost as if, after confidently tracking its quarry without hurry or worry, it had suddenly and inexplicably lost the scent.

Suddenly the entire chapel shook and the windows rattled as it pounded on the walls, again and again, with tremendous force. The shock waves sent everything loose tumbling, and, after a while, the altar in the rear collapsed with a crash. They could hear the bell in the steeple above start to clang, but it was so muffled by whatever it was that surrounded the thing that it could barely be made out from within the church and certainly would not be heard by anyone in town, although that may have been all to the good. The pounding ceased for a moment, and they heard Red's horse give a terrible, unnatural cry outside and then all was silent once more.

After a minute or so, the pounding resumed.

"Sweet Jesus, forgive me my sins and save our poor souls," Red whispered quietly to himself as he crouched down in the center of the building.

MacDonald, crouching beside him, eyes now accustoming themselves to the greater darkness, huddled and looked around and hoped that nothing was above them that would come tumbling down and do the monster's dirty work for it. The pounding went on and on, like a rhythmic earthquake, and both men wondered just how long it would be before the little building gave in to the brute force being applied to it.

Poor Angelique! MacDonald thought, resigned to fate. *Who is left to save you from them now?*

7

CHANGE OF GAME

Kris Symonds had not expected to spend the night on Allenby, but had every expectation when she'd started out that she'd deliver her goods and then take the chopper back to Port of Spain. The people at the Institute had been quite nice to her, though, and she'd finally recovered from the terrible motion sickness flying through that storm or whatever it was had given her. She was even giving serious thought to flying back if they said it was fixed in the morning, and had managed to keep down a light snack and some tea they had offered. She did not, however, have a change of clothes or even a purse. It just hadn't been the kind of job where she'd needed them, and with a heavy briefcase locked on her wrist you took as little extra as you could.

Much of the Lodge was quiet now, although there was always somebody up and about in a place like this, and she sat in the lounge as instructed and waited while they made up a room for her and found her the basics. She badly needed a shower, she decided, and sleep wouldn't be such a bad idea.

She was thumbing through some old magazine when a young, rather pretty black girl entered. "Miz Symonds?"

"Yes, that's me."

"Come with me, please."

She rose and followed the young woman, noting the thick French accent. Haitian, she guessed, or from French Guiana or whatever they were calling the place these days. They did not go up or down stairs, but went along the rear corridor of the building to an oak door. "Go on in," the girl told her. "De security boys, dey hav' ta ask you some questions. Den we'll get you to your room."

She didn't like the sound of this. "Security?"

"Jus' go in. Dey explain everyt'ing."

She knew this was a top security installation, but she really wasn't prepared for this. Oh, well, she decided, there was nothing to it but to get it over with so she could get some sleep. She opened the door and stepped into a small sitting room, with a few comfortable chairs, a couch, and some reading lamps. There didn't appear to be any other entrance to the room but the door through which she'd entered, and there didn't seem to be anyone in the room. She stopped, turned, and said, "Hey! Wait a minute!" but the door closed and she could hear a lock being turned. She tried it anyway, to no avail, and started to get nervous. What kind of place *was* this, anyway?

She went over and sat on the couch, growing more nervous with every passing moment. She hadn't like that MacDonald's intimation that the storm hadn't been natural, and she remembered the details on Martinez.

This had seemed a glamorous, exciting job when she'd applied for it. International courier. Expense-paid trips to lots of different places all over the world, really good pay and bonuses, plenty of vacation time. Although she knew that she sometimes carried valuable things, even lots of cash, she had never really worried much while doing the job and certainly hadn't worried after delivery was made.

She heard a noise from a far corner, and was suddenly

aware of another presence in the room. "Who are you?" she asked, masking her fear with bravado. "I mean, what the hell *is* all this, anyway?"

The figure stepped from the shadows into the light, but it didn't help at all. He was all black—not his skin or clothing, because you really couldn't tell much about that—but strangely, unnaturally so, like a cut-out figure of a man on TV, a man-shaped blackness that moved.

"Please pardon my appearance," said the Dark Man, "but it is necessary for now for a number of reasons to adopt what you might call a high-tech disguise." The voice was deep and resonant and radiated a strange power. "I wish first to simply ask you some questions. Your answers will determine what happens next."

"W—Who—what *are* you?"

"That is no concern of yours," he replied, walking over and taking one of the chairs facing her. It did no good to be this close. It was like looking at a deep hole that moved and rippled. It was more terrifying than facing a man with a gun. "I wish to know who sent the parcel you delivered tonight."

"I—I don't *know*. I only know when I have to meet the person sending it or I need to get paperwork signed. This was a straight drop, using the coded 'cuffs. I'm not even usually down here! Before this I ain't never been further south than Puerto Rico, honest!"

"Who gave you the package and your instructions?"

"Mrs. Corvas, the head of the Service in Port of Spain. I just got an order from Mr. Sanchez, who runs the shop in Miami, where I was at the time, to fly down to Port of Spain and make a delivery."

"You received triple pay for this delivery. Why?"

"How'd you know that? Yeah, well, they told me the usual guy who did this run was killed. I made 'em run the bonus money up when I heard that."

"And what were your instructions? *Exactly*."

"I was to take the chopper, for which clearance had already been made, and meet this Mr. MacDonald at the pad. He would take the case and I would go back and that's *it*. Honest!"

"And they told you the specific details about Martinez?"

"Huh?"

"Ms. Symonds, you must be honest with me because it is your only choice. I have great power, and my power increases moment by moment. Right now my unaided power is limited to individuals, one at a time, but it is considerable at that level, and it will continue to increase. I could order you to tell me all and you would do so, but I prefer a different approach because it serves more then one purpose and because it pleases me to do so."

"What—what are you going to do? Rape me? Butcher me like you did Martinez?"

"Not here, not on this island. It is unnecessary. You need a demonstration of my power, and I will give it. Did you realize, for example, that even while we have been having this little chat you have systematically removed every bit of your clothing and now sit there, legs apart, feeling yourself up?"

She started, and looked down at herself, and found it was true. Her clothing was in a heap on the floor. She wanted to stop her self-arousal and pick up the clothes, but found she could not.

"You see? Your mind, as well as your body, belong to me. They are my playthings, to do with as I will. Only your soul, for what that is worth, is yours, for it can be surrendered only voluntarily. So, relax. Don't fight it because you can not. I have no cause to harm that which I own. Now, down on your knees before me on the floor. There! See?"

Her terror was now absolute, but she couldn't even faint. She couldn't do a thing he didn't tell her to do.

"Now, I wish to know the consignor of the briefase. I wish to know the true employer of Mr. MacDonald."

"I don't know," she answered truthfully, for she could answer no other way to him now. "I know only that it is a pretty big crowd, at least from money and power. Timmons Courier is mostly owned by them, I think. It's a front for their use. You don't ask questions and you get big bucks."

"It is partly owned by Magellan," the Dark Man told her, "but not entirely, nor is it controlled by Magellan. I wish to know of your past in this company. I want to know where, and to whom, you have delivered things since you joined it two years ago."

She rattled off what names she remembered, and dates, and places, and people. A lot of embassies, a few government agencies in both the U.S., Britain, and western Europe, and several small companies, none apparently connected. The government names were interesting, particularly those of minor nations, but the companies were more intriguing to him, for the majority of them had no connection with Magellan at all and were based in small countries who chartered them for profit with no questions asked.

There could be no question in the mind of anyone listening that the primary purpose of the service was to bypass traditional computer and telecommunications channels, no matter how good today's scramblers were. And there was also no question that all formed some sort of intelligence network outside of normal channels.

"What are you thinking now?" he asked her. "Speak freely."

"I'm thinking you have to do somthing. I'll be missed. You got to kill me, I guess."

The Dark Man sighed. "My dear, you have been thrown deliberately to the wolves, an expendable lamb brought in because you knew the least. Tomorrow that helicopter will return, but it will not make it. It will crash into the sea and be lost from sight. There will be no survivors, and no recovery of your body, although sufficient effects will wash up to make your death credible.'' He got up from the chair and towered over her. ''Now—rise. Rise and come to me.''

She stood up, and found herself walking right into him. She did not meet a human form or any resistance, but seemed suddenly cold and surrounded by darkness, with no form, no solidity. And then, quite suddenly, she was again on solid ground, but outdoors, atop a weird looking rock in the middle of a pretty, moonlit meadow. She was still naked, and walked to the other end, the low end, of the rock and turned to face the Dark Man, who stood on the rounded high point.

They were not alone. She had some limited freedom, and looked around to find that there were figures around the rock. They were all women, ranging in age from the teen to perhaps the thirties or forties. All were naked, and all had a wild, savage look on their faces and in their eyes, and all were looking at her.

''You have a free choice to make,'' said the Dark Man calmly. ''One choice and one only. You are of no use to me unless you are joined with us, freely and of your own will.''

The women took up a chant, and the Dark Man made a pass with his hand. Lines of light seemed to run fluidly across the grass of the meadow, forming an intricate pattern that surrounded the stone. There was the sudden crackle of electricity in the air in the area between the Dark Man and the terrified woman, and the onlookers, the worshippers, fell down and continued to chant some more.

The shape in the center took form, a strange and wondrous form, of a creature that was humanoid but not human. It was an angelic form, with great wings mounted at the shoulders and down the back emerging from flowing robes, and a face that was at once beautiful and wondrous and beyond any description.

''Behold Belial, once an angel and now a prince of Hell,''

the Dark Man said. "Fall down and worship him, and give yourself to him and to his Lord and sovereign. We offer you pleasure. We offer to sponge away all guilt, all worry, all fear, and exchange it for that which is wondrous. We offer life, and beauty, and truth, in exchange for your acceptance of and worship of those who would rule a proper universe against a God gone insane. Few are offered this clear choice with such clear evidence."

The creature in the center was so wonderful, so beautiful, that it almost commanded worship, as it had an ancient days, for the angels were created second only to God, and the rulers of Hell were angels always.

"Now consider a God who would not only permit but encourage war and plague and massive suffering and misery. Consider a God who would not only allow, but *command* the Lord Satan to do his worst to humanity. Fall down and worship now, and give your soul freely to the ones who will end this madness! You know the words, for they have been provided you! Do it now, or die in horrible torment here, piece by piece and bit by bit, so at last in your death your soul will go to your God who will not help you now. He's here! Now! All around you! He sees and hears and knows this, and could stop it in an instant, yet he allows it, as he allowed Hitler and Stalin and Mao, as he ignored the anguished screams of the Holocaust and a thousand other Holocausts over the ages. Fall down now, and give yourself to sanity!"

Her terror had not diminished, but the sight of the great creature and the words of the Dark Man penetrated a level of consciousness beyond the terror. She hadn't been to church since she was fourteen, and she hadn't given anything religious much thought, but now it faced her, and the clock was running out on a decision.

"Do you think a God who would allow His own son to be agonizingly crucified will intervene to save you? Pray now, for now you begin to die. Now you must decide—to join freely with us, or to go to your God!''

The angelic creature changed suddenly, in a moment, into one of terror, a monstrous, misshapen thing that roared and drooled and slobbered and shook its bat wings, and gestured to her with a taloned finger from which came a living stream of electrical fire. It struck her and she was instantly in horrible agony, the most terrible pain she could remember or imagine. She cried out, "No! I will do anything! No!''

The agony stopped, but she could feel its aftermath and smelled in her own nostrils the smell of her own charred flesh. Again the figure was angelic, and it waited.

Her mind cracked, and she fell upon the stone, and the words came as she asked them to. "I worship thee, oh mighty Prince of Hell," she gasped, "and give my immortal soul now and forever to thee and thy Lord Satan, now and forever more to the end of time!'' The words had been placed there by others, but at that moment she meant every word of it.

The creature looked down at her and gave a wondrous smile, and reached out and touched her head, and instantly her wounds were healed, her body made not only whole but better than it was, powerful and beautiful and totally free of blemish. She surrendered utterly and felt tremendous peace and joy, and she would do willingly whatever was commanded of her.

She got up, and faced the creature, and it took her wrist and made a single sharp cut across a vein, but it didn't hurt a bit. She turned and got down from the rock, and saw the other women gather around, and they, too, had identical cuts. And she took each in turn and drank a little of their blood, and they a little of hers, and it burned like fiery liquor in their mouths.

And the creature turned and gave its blessing to them all, and the cuts faded, healed as if they had never been, and then it faded out, like a will o' the wisp in the night, and then the glowing liquid forms of energy on the meadow faded as well, and they were at peace and filled with joy.

The Dark Man chuckled softly to himself and took out his hornpipes and blew a tune, and soon they all were dancing to it, she along with them, without a thought or care in the world.

Angelique had gone to her suite after being dropped off by Greg, and the girls had prepared a light snack at the kitchenette installed in the adjoining converted suite where they now lived. Being constantly tired of late, since the dreams had become so regular and so vivid, she elected to go to bed early, and they made no objection.

Still, lying there in the near-darkness, she didn't immediately go to sleep. She kept thinking of Jureau, of the scratches, of how real the dreams seemed, and she couldn't help wondering and worrying. Perhaps Greg was right, she thought. I am still a stranger here, and far out of my element. Had she simply been overwhelmed by it all, or in truth was she now a key pawn in some great struggle for the heart and soul of a monster corporation? Had she, in fact, delivered herself into the very hands of the enemy and refused to take herself out of harm's way?

She knew almost at once that she would go, particularly now that Greg had indicated that he, too, wished to leave. She resolved, at last, to tell him so the first thing tomorrow, and to move out with all possible speed. That decided, she sank into an increasingly deep sleep, the best sleep she had experienced in perhaps weeks.

She awoke suddenly, her mind clear, although she had a slight headache from the depth of the slumber. There had been no dreams, at least none that she could remember, and she was thankful for that.

It was still dark; she turned her head to the left to see the illuminated face of the clock that was always on the night-stand, but she saw nothing. She was aware now of an odd smell, of damp wood and mustiness that certainly should not be in a place as newly remodeled as this. It was difficult to see, but she sensed something strange and different about the place, and began to imagine phantoms moving in the darkness. The sound of insects seemed abnormally loud, and, now that she thought of it, it seemed pretty sticky and oppressive in the room although it should have been air conditioned and filtered. Either there had been some sort of power failure, or. . . .

She became suddenly frightened as she realized that this was not her bed or her bedroom at the Lodge. *This is not real!* she tried to assure herself. *This is just another one of those realistic dreams.*

But she didn't believe it. This was as real as anything she had ever experienced, without any of the mental fuzziness or odd changes she went through in the dreams.

She lay there for quite some time, unable to move, unsure as to what to do. Finally she tried to call out for help, for assistance, but her throat was sore and her voice could barely manage much above a hoarse whisper.

And then, quite suddenly, she *felt* rather than saw or heard someone enter. She was not, in fact, even sure *how* he entered, for there was no sound of a door opening and closing, but she knew he was there, knew it as certainly as she had known it back in her father's study.

"My apologies for being delayed," said a deep, resonant voice, and she gave a start and an involuntary little cry of terror. "We had not expected to reach this point quite so soon, but you rushed us with your actions and showed great power to overcome the holds designed for you, and we have had to account for some people and baggage we did not expect and would not have had to deal with at all otherwise."

It was an additional shock to realize that he was speaking not English but French, even matching her Gaspé accent.

"Who—who are you?" she rasped weakly.

"You know who I am. They call me the Dark Man, although that's just a descriptive term created by a string of *voodoo* and *obi* cults in the Caribbean and west African areas. It fits rather well, never the less, and will do for now." There was a sudden flash and a dark finger touched an old fashioned kerosene lamp which caught and then grew into a warm, flickering glow. It illuminated the room, but not the Dark Man, whose entire form seemed a seamless shape of the blackest black.

She was, she saw, in some sort of log cabin; a one room affair with a small cast iron wood stove, some cabinetry and pots and pans hanging from wall hooks, and some wicker-style furniture. There was a single solid wooden door with a wood bar for a lock, and that bar was in place. The area just next to the stove had a small window, and there were two more small windows with wooden shutters hooked closed on either side of the door.

"Where is this place?" she asked him. "Where have you taken me?"

"It is a cabin in the woods on the island. It's been here for years. It's to the west of the Institute and down about half-way, about a hundred yards in from the western cliffs. It was built just after your late father purchased the island, and housed the planners and surveyors who came first, to plan the whole thing. There were several, but only this one wound up being kept in good repair, primarily because your father liked coming down here in the early days, when things were just building up top, to spend some time in solitude. The others were dismantled and are long gone, but this one has been here, forgotten by almost everyone, unused for more than seven years, its lone trail pretty well overgrown."

"Have you brought me here, then, to do away with me? If

so, I am ready. I can stand this no longer." It was brave talk and she didn't mean a word of it, and he knew it.

"Do away with you? Certainly not! You are quite special, Angelique, more than you know. Greatness awaits you, a greatness that all will envy and that others will covet, but it is for you alone. You are quite safe here. No one even remembers this place exists, and no one ever comes to this part of the island. It is as virginal as when it was as yet unseen by man. None will harm you, and so charmed are you that not even a mosquito will dare bite you, nor an illness infect you. Unfortunately, it is not yet your time, although that time is soon. It may also be necessary, at times, to produce you or to produce your witnessed prints. So, until such time as all is right and we have need of you, this will be your home. I apologize that it is not as fancy or as comfortable as the Lodge, but it is far more secure."

She was appalled. "You expect me to lie here, doing nothing, going nowhere, for days, weeks, *months*?"

"Only if we have to. I doubt if that will be necessary, so long as you behave." He walked to the foot of the bed, his boots sounding very solid on the old wooden floor, and stretched out a dark hand. "Rise, Angelique!"

And she did so, getting up to a sitting position, shifting over to the side of the bed, then, steadying herself with one hand, getting to a standing position. It was so remarkable, so incredible, that she was overcome with emotion that for a moment blotted out all the other, darker circumstances.

"I—I stand! I walk! *I feel!*" she exclaimed. "I am once again whole!" She flexed her fingers and her toes and almost cried with joy.

"You have never been otherwise," the Dark Man told her. "The doctors were correct in stating that there was no medical reason for your paralysis. They erred only in being men of pure science. They could not know, and if they had known could not have accepted, the effectiveness of a true curse."

Almost instantly, her sheer joy turned to hatred and extreme anger. "You mean *you* did that to me? *You* cost me all those years of my life? *You* made me go through *hell*?" Her throat was still sore and her voice raspy, but so great was her anger that the room almost shook with the words. She moved to attack him physically, all thoughts of well-being gone, but he put up a dark hand and she stopped, frozen, unable to advance.

"It was quite necessary, once we realized who you might be and saw the potential there. It preserved you—innocent, virginal, unattached, and naive. It froze you as you were, a young girl unsullied by the world." He paused a moment, and his tone became more practical. "You will notice that the curse is not lifted, merely suspended at our whim. That suspension can be lifted at any time, for any reason, and you will become as bad as you were or worse than you were. If we wished you could become an automaton, seeing, hearing, smelling, feeling, thinking—but unable to control any part of your body whatever voluntarily, doing only what you were told to do. It's up to you."

"You won't get away with this! I'll be missed at the Institute. Security will search for me. Greg will—"

"Greg is most probably dead by now," he told her bluntly. "I should like to have interrogated him, as I should have liked to talk with your father, but others intervened. I should not count on Security. You *will* have to bear their watching eyes on their little monitors if you stray into habitable territory, I fear, but don't expect any help from that quarter. As for any others, this island is at the moment being placed under a security blanket. In modern, tense times like these, those in power tend to believe what their computers print out, particularly when it is confirmed by people in their own employ. This island has become a tiny independent republic for the duration of this—er, emergency, and will be run as one from this point on, with the aid and support of Magellan and the NATO and Caribbean pacts. No one will get on, or off, this island without our knowledge and permission. No one will be able to communicate in any way with the outside world unless we first approve it."

"But you can not keep this up forever!" she told him. "Sooner or later someone will get suspicious and they will demand to come and see for themselves!"

"By that time, we will be in total control of every living thing here. You would be surprised at how long it could be sustained. You see, *we* control more than you or anyone has dreamed by now. We can access the data banks upon which they rely, make a saint into a KGB spy, order suspicious probers to duty in Greenland or Antarctica from a dozen military forces. We can cause diversions—wars in the Middle East, for example, and other threats to vital areas—that will take their minds off us. And we do not have to do it forever, only for a short while. Three or four months. People believe their computers. They depend upon them and the telecommunications networks that tie them together. You would be shocked at what we can do without any resort to the supernatural."

"What *are* you?" she practically screamed at him. "Are you a man? A demon? The devil himself?"

The Dark Man laughed. "Perhaps I am none of those. Call me John the Baptist, if you will."

"You profane and mock the sacred!"

"Well, it has always been the fashion to do so. Perhaps you have been *too* insulated. The world goes around saying, 'Jesus Christ!' at the slightest provocation, and 'God damn!' is probably the second most popular profanity humanity uses. The world is full of the profane. Hell is rampant, as it always has been. And do you know why? Because that's the way God ordered it to be. He's supposed to be all-seeing, all-knowing, omniscient and omnipresent, yet He's never gotten over the fact that He made humanity in His own image and humanity proceeded to screw itself up. He ordered humanity tested, and humanity failed, so He ordered humanity to be tempted, tormented, and punished, rather than face the fact that He, Himself, was obviously imperfect or mad, in that He created an imperfect thing.''

"It is *you* who are mad! There was war in Heaven before the Fall!''

"A later invention; a rationalization by his more intelligent followers to explain the contradiction. It is not so, and Job proves that Hell served God's will by God's command. Nothing is clearer.''

"You can not judge God by man's standards! It is impossible for any lesser being to understand God's will and ways!''

"I will agree that madness is a relative term. By our lights we are sane and God, and God's followers and defenders and rationalizers, are mad. It is a point of view. Consider the evil that God knows of and allows. Consider that He must know what is going on here, yet does nothing to help, nothing to stop it. His solution to the mess was to crucify Jesus in agony. Since that time, the Christian church has primarily venerated its martyrs and been dominated by the charlatans and the power-mad. He allowed the Holocaust and condemned His chosen people who survived to eternal warfare. His other aspects are as bad. Many have sacrifice, including human sacrifice, and all sorts of cruel rites. The Japanese Shintoists actually looked forward to suicide under certain conditions. The Shi'ites venerate masochism and beat themselves with chains. The Hindus use Him to freeze society in an odd variation of the divine right of kings. The only thing as stupid and wasteful as a Crusade is a Holy War. This is madness. This is a universe based upon madness.''

"And in the name of restoring sanity you reduce people to animals, kill, torture, maim, send monsters to crush people to death, cause wars, do all that you boast of doing! That is *some* sanity!''

"In World War II, millions were sacrificed by much of the world to defeat Hitler, who was the greater evil. We feel that the entire universe is at stake. All of humanity, and countless other races out there among the stars. The innocent will suffer and pay the price as it always has been in wars. As to our methods, we are constrained to use them. God's rules, you know. We must play by the rules, as must you, until the battle is joined. The war against Heaven, you see, has not yet been fought. God will not intervene here on Earth, and for a cold, practical reason. It means nothing to Him. *You* mean nothing to Him. We threaten only the Earth, not Heaven. But it is here that it must start—according to the rules. We must make a move here first in order to attack His seat of power."

"And you will lose! That, too, is the rules!"

"Will we? Would we even attempt it if we didn't believe we could attain victory? John of Patmos warned Christians to shape up because God was returning soon and it would be too late. Yet here we are, two thousand years later, more or less, and 'soon' has lost its meaning. John was a fanatic and a mystic and he was certainly either insincere or wrong on his timetable. There is no reason to believe his outcome, either. We know Him. We know His location and His weaknesses. And even if we lose, which we do not intend, we would rather lose and suffer the true death of oblivion than to live under a God like that."

She was shaken and stunned by his statements. Her initial terror had subsided now, and she felt in control once again. She would still have gone after him if she could, but it was useless. He had far too much power, and had to be fought by ways she did not know. What was most chilling was his matter-of-fact brazen blasphemy and his commitment to Armageddon and beyond even if it meant losing.

He sensed her confusion and despair, and jumped on it. "Think of it this way, my dear. Armageddon is coming, as was prophesied and commanded by God. The time is now truly soon. Is it blasphemy to oppose or prevent it when it is so clearly God's will? It is an interesting point, and one we may debate off and on in the times to come. Now, we must deal with the more immediate and intimate situation. We must deal with you.''

She wasn't sure whether she was gratified or not by that change of subject.

"This island is constraint enough for you. We've tried with your nocturnal sojourns to built up your muscles and restore your coordination and balance, and I think that has succeeded. To keep you at the Lodge we would have to keep you immobile and perhaps also incommunicado. This would take a staff as large or larger than we have used to date, and might result in a contest of your inheritance on the grounds of incapacity. Better that you be somewhere else to everyone here not involved in our business, and that you be here and in control of everyone outside the island. It is most convenient just to stick you over here, with the basic needs, and allow you to get used to being a whole person once again.''

That was yet another shock and surprise. "That's all? Just leave me here?''

"Oh, I know what you're thinking, so we will dispose of those thoughts right now. A few small restrictions—spells, if you like, curses if you don't—to insure a harmonious retreat. First and foremost, you will find it impossible to speak to anyone but me or one in my service. Should you attempt to write something, you will find your hand frozen, unable to do it. It would make little difference, anyway. Everyone knows that you are paralyzed and couldn't write and so would doubt the notes, but it is better to be safe than sorry. Should you think about trying to leave the island, I would think again. First, if we discover it and stop you, you will pay a dear price. Second, even if you somehow evaded everything and made it—and I remind you that you never did learn how to swim—the paralysis of your voluntary actions would not only return, it would be total. You would become a human vegetable, unable to communicate in any way, and your paralysis would last the rest of your life unless I, personally, were to lift it.''

That was sobering. She was still relishing the very fact that she could feel her whole self once more. God help her, she didn't know if she could give up that freedom again willingly. Damn them!

''Finally, we can't have you just walking into town or the Lodge. Too many messy questions. Stretch out your arm, now that you can, and watch.''

She did as instructed, not daring to guess at what he planned to do. There was silence for a moment, as if he were concentrating, and then a dark arm reached out and actually touched hers, although she tried to shrink away. It felt cold as ice and a certain energy seemed to flow from him along her skin. As it did, with a mild, tingling sensation, she saw her arm, lightly tanned, turn much darker. She felt the sensation flow from the arm to all parts of her body, even her hair.

''Not much of a change,'' he told her, ''but now your skin is a deep tan and your eyes brown and your short, fluffy light brown hair is long, straight, and black as night. Mute and like this, no one will recognize you, no one will guess or believe even if they note the physical resemblance, yet it can be reversed as easily as it was done in case we need to produce you. And we will make one last adjustment.''

He gestured with his hand, and the nightgown which she wore was violently jerked from her body with a ripping sound. It flew across the room and struck the wall, where it collapsed in a heap. She had always worn a bra, not only for some control and appearance but to prevent chafing and other problems. Now the bra snapped in the back like a rubber band stretched too tight, and the entire thing flew to the same wall and landed in the same place as the gown. Before she could feel acutely embarrassed, though, the adult-style diaper, which she'd always had to wear because of her lack of bowel control, snapped and followed the rest, leaving her stark naked in the room.

She reached in her embarrassment for the sheet on the bed, musty as it was, to hold it up in front of her, but the moment it was up, it, too, was snatched away.

"It is an elemental force, a prankster, but it is effective. You will wear no clothing. None. Any that you attempt will flee from you. Force it on and it will burn like fire until you remove it. Feel free to go anywhere you like, but if you go into civilized territory you will discover that to them you are an illiterate mute with a paranoid fear of any clothing. Your choice is clear. The freedom of living here, and in the woods, or being locked up in an asylum until we need you, as any sane human being would do for one such as you. You wouldn't like the asylum we would use."

"You *bastard*!" she snarled, and spat at him.

He laughed with the confidence that power brings. "I am being kind to you. Do not test my patience or my kindness. It won't be so bad. In the cabinets you will find a small camper stove with sufficient fuel to cook things one at a time if you like. I realize you've had no real experience cooking, but you might wish to boil water or something. Fruits, vegetables, breads, cold cuts, canned foods, and the like will be regularly provided, and feel free, at night, to supplement with the fruits of the Institute orchards—coconuts, bananas, whatever. There is a well about four meters in back of the house and to the side. It works and the water is good. For bathing, there is a small creek and waterfall due south, about ninety meters or so down and toward the sea. The water is warm and there is a small pool formed at the bottom if you wish to bathe rather than shower. Please be careful, though. It runs due west of another forty meters and then goes over the cliffs to the sea in a sheer drop."

"It would serve you right if that happened!" she taunted, it being the only weapon she had.

"Your firm beliefs will prevent suicide, and forces you will never see will check on you from time to time to help prevent accidents. I believe that is it. I must go now. Oh—no, one more thing. Be cautious and fearful of men, for some have uncontrollable urges. We care not about women, but should you be deflowered by a man your usefulness to us is over. The price of such an act, willing or not, is your mind, for it will drive you mad, yet you will then become a willing slave to our own interests. You can't win. You may as well relax and accept your fate; leave the fight to others."

"Wait!" she called out to him. "Why keep me alive at all? Am I some sort of virgin sacrifice?"

He paused and considered his words. "You will not be sacrificed. You are far more valuable alive than dead. Do not worry. In the end, greatness and freedom await you! But, I must go. Until later, *adieu*." He turned and stared at the lantern, which immediately went dark.

The door did not open, but she knew he was gone. She could feel it, standing there in near total darkness. It was, in fact, too dark to search through and find anything, yet she could not simply go to sleep. No matter what had happened to her, she could *move*, she could *feel* her body and control it. She carefully felt her way across to the front wall, and then along it to the door. The bar was heavy, but she managed to lift it and move it out of the way, then reach down as she had dreamed of being able to do all these years and opened it, then stepped outside.

Although it was quite dark outside, there was far more light than inside the cabin and her eyes, coming from total darkness, had no trouble seeing. It was hot and humid, as always, and there was a mild breeze that caressed her body and made it tingle. For all the trouble she was in, there was something exciting, even erotic, about the situation that she couldn't fight down. She decided she would make use of what night was left, since she couldn't imagine wandering long in daylight—not like this.

Oddly, though, the dreams—no, not dreams, for she now knew they were real—had prepared her to an extent for this. They had planned it from the start, it was clear. She felt confident moving around in the dark and felt no fear of the woods, and she knew she wouldn't hesitate to climb high if need be.

She thought suddenly of Greg, and tears welled up inside her. Poor Greg. She had loved him, and would love him, but she could not help him. Who could fight such a power as this unless it was with the grace of God?

She knelt down and said prayers for his soul, putting them far ahead of prayers for her own sake. It was the least she could do.

There was only one window of any size in the little church, a stained glass affair in a crescent shape just over the door. It suddenly shattered with a crash despite the muffled sounds.

"Red! Watch it! Move back towards the altar!" MacDonald cried, and the constable scrambled up and over the pews and out of the aisle, almost beating the young man to the pulpit.

They turned back to the gaping hole where the window had been and, in spite of the darkness, saw a shape come through. At first it reminded MacDonald of a snake, but then he realized that it was an arm—a massive arm that ended in a huge, clawed hand. It was almost too big for the opening, and wasn't nearly long enough, but it did reach the back few rows and began groping, then ripping up pews and tossing them every which way like so many match sticks in the wind.

"Jesus Christ!" the old constable swore, hardly conscious

of how it sounded from the altar of a church. "You sure can see that bastard now! What in the bloody hell *is* that thing?"

They ducked as a random pew flew and crashed into the rear wall just behind them.

"I don't know, Red, but I'll bet you one or more of those big dishes up on the hill are pointed right at us right now."

"You mean the thing's being *broadcast* here?"

"Nothing else makes sense," he responded, when the crash and din allowed. "Somebody discovered one hell of a weapon up there and they're using the computer to do their dirty work."

"Then why in hell don't he just zap you and be done with it? Them things got to be able to cover anyplace on the island!"

"Partly because he's got a weird mind, and partly because, having finished off Sir Robert this way, he's got to be consistent to keep everybody going crazy."

The great arm withdrew, but the pounding did not resume. The respite allowed them a few moments to catch their breath, although they could hear the creature outside and knew that it was still there, trying in its apparently limited way to figure a different way in.

Greg looked around at the chapel, which was in shambles but still intact, and sighed. "They sure knew how to build 'em in the old days, Red. Thank God!"

The constable nodded. "You said, 'he.' You know who's behind all this, then?"

"Yeah, I know, but I can't prove a damned thing. That's the hell of it." He chuckled and hefted the briefcase, which he'd carried through all of the flight and the ordeal in the church as if it were attached to him. "I got it tonight, which is why they made for me. In one way it's a good sign, since this is so stupid. He must know I can't pin a thing on him, and he's got all the cards up there. He panics too easily for his own good. If we're lucky, that'll be his undoing."

"Who is it, lad?"

"Uh-uh. He probably doesn't know you're involved, Red, and if you get out of this you'll be a witness to the monster. If you know, you'll try something and get yourself splattered or worse."

"I want t'know the name of the slimy bastard who's doing this, boy! I don't take kindly to it!"

"Relax. Let others take care of it. You got a family here, Red. They're not gonna let you off the island, and there's no way you could get away with your wife and youngest."

The older man sighed, knowing it was true enough. "So how do *you* plan to get out of here? They got the damn computer, boy! Even if you get out, they can stick you on the most wanted list of fifty nations as the man who murdered the Queen and stole the Crown Jewels, and the stupid shits in every law enforcement body in the world will shoot first and ask questions later."

He nodded. "I know. One step at a time, Red. John Tussey still have that little sailboat of his over at the fishing pier?"

"Yeah, but it's beached and tied down 'cause of the surf."

"I'll get it in quick enough if I have to carry it out beyond the breakwater on my back. I have to get off, though, that's for sure. Ross is one of those types who'd cheerfully obey a shoot-first order if he had written instructions in hand, particularly if it was me."

"That's right enough. But—say! Listen!"

The air was suddenly alive with sound. A stiff sea breeze blew through the broken window and cracked walls and loosened joints, whistling as it did so. The nearby surf crashed with regularity in the distance, and they didn't have to shout any more. The awful sound-deadening effect was gone, and through the broken window they could see what might be the first light of dawn.

Red looked at MacDonald. "Gone? Or a trick?"

"I don't know. Wait a couple of minutes, though, just to make sure. You might tell me why the night shuttle never came down and why you were riding up on horseback."

"The first was the cause of the second, of course. I didn't like it when Harry never showed, so I checked and found that none of the damned carts they left would start. Nothin' to do but get one of the horses and go on up and find out. I was on my way when I ran into you."

"Uh huh. Bet those carts work now. Hang on. I'm going forward. You keep a look at that window just in case."

He approached slowly, tensely, stepping over debris and ready at any cause to dash back to the altar, but he finally reached the door. Gingerly, he pushed it open with a foot, half expecting something to grab it and pull him out to his death, but nothing happened. He cautiously peered out and saw, looking up the mountain, that all of the orange guide lights were illuminated.

Red was suddenly behind him, carryng a candlestick. Cautiously, they stepped out into the churchyard and beheld the flip side of their own ordeal. The exterior looked in bad shape, with parts of masonry fallen away and roofing tiles all over the place. The walk to the church was paved, and the area immediately around was cinder, so there weren't any tracks as such to see, but almost none of the cinder remained.

There was blood all over, and part of horse scattered this way and that, some in clumps that could not be recognized. The head, however, they spotted over in the cemetery.

"Stuck it right on Sir Robert's grave, the bastard," Red muttered. "Come on. Let's get you away before they realize they failed and send down a few boys with guns."

Although it was crudely chocked on the beach, the two men had no trouble getting the small sailboat into the water, although it took some effort and determination to get it far enough out to keep it from being immediately taken back in. Red was invaluable; MacDonald doubted that he could have managed it alone. Now, though, with it bobbing and under control, it was time for Red to leave. The sun was now up, and back in the village there could be seen lights in some of the windows and could be heard the sounds of many people arising to the new day.

Red looked back uncertainly. "What'll I tell 'em, Greg?"

"Just tell it exactly like it was. Don't leave *anything* out. If anything, it'll confirm what they think I know. Answer all their questions, submit to all their tests, even lie detector or drugs. And turn it over to them. Tell 'em it's too big for you."

"And where'll you head?"

"I'm not going to say that, Red. I'm not out of the woods yet, either. I'm going to be hunted today, I think, and the odds are even they'll find me. If I don't—well, just hang loose. I'll be back."

"You're crazy if you come, lad, just as I'm crazy to stay, but you'd better get goin' before all bloody hell breaks loose." He sat in the boat, soaked through, and stuck out his hand. "God protect you, Mac, as He did last night."

"You too, Red," he responded, taking the hand and clasping it warmly.

With that, Red went over the side and with little effort made it back to the beach. MacDonald hoisted sail and made for the open sea as fast as he could, praying for a stiff wind in the right direction and good weather. Because of the direction of the breeze, he went up along the sheer cliffs on the west side of the island.

He hadn't expected to get this far, and hadn't thought beyond it, but now he realized what a hue and cry there would be and just what a search would be on—and it was going to be a clear, sunny day. There were plenty of islands to hide out on for a few hours and catch some sleep while keeping the small boat under some cover, but he knew they'd think of that.

But he'd studied this island in minute detail when he'd challenged and beaten their old security system. Some things he hadn't included in his reports or plans, and his mind raced now. There were a few jagged inlets on this side, with sheer walls and good cover from both landforms and brush. He picked the second one he came to, and managed to anchor the small boat and cover it with brush and bushes under a rocky outcrop. He settled down then, on board, using the seat for a pillow, and tried to relax.

Let them search all the nearby islands. He'd remain here, right under their noses, until dark. Then he'd make his run. When you've cheated a damned monster, Ross and his ilk didn't seem nearly so threatening.

8

DESCENT INTO HELL

Angelique spent much of the night exploring. Not exploring her surroundings that much, although she located both the pump and the waterfall, but mostly exploring herself, her newfound control of her body which had been remotely built up and finely tuned by the nocturnal sojourns over the past weeks.

When the skies had begun to lighten, she had returned to the cabin and tried as much as possible to get a little of the outside air and light into the place. The bed was no more than a simple cot using a wafer-thin mattress on poorly supported springs and slats with a single sheet wrapped around it and an old feather pillow at its head. She lay down on it, and immediately began to feel a burning sensation on her skin. She jumped back up and stood there a moment, adjusting to the pain, and felt it slowly subside and disappear. She put a hand on the sheet and held it there, and it began to burn and she quickly withdrew it. It was certainly the sheet. She pulled it off and tossed it to one side and tried just the mattress. Before long, the sensation returned. She was not to be permitted even this comfort. She could see a little in the cabin now and spotted a straw mat, looking rather new, on the floor to the far side of the bed. It wasn't comfortable, but it was better than the dirty floor.

She suddenly got an idea, and put the mat atop the mattress on the bed. The rough straw was irritating on its own, but she managed to get used to it, and this didn't burn and *did* help.

She finally lay on her back for a while and with her hands explored her own body. It was a strange and wonderful sensation to caress her own nipples and find them stiffen and rise and produce a pleasurable tingling sensation much like a tickle yet oddly different, too, with results also causing changes elsewhere inside her. She had been barely pubescent when they had taken it all away from her, and she had not until now known the feelings of an adult woman's body except through books and through her imagination.

She had been like a little child all night, running around the cabin, just reaching out and picking things up, tossing a few stones, using the pump just to see it gush—all these were wondrous, magical things to her.

The only damper had been when her body had told her that she now needed a toilet, and a toilet was one thing that hadn't been provided here. Whatever they'd used in the past had either been demolished or buried when the other cabins had been torn down. She'd used the woods, but found one process as messy as the other, and nothing to be done about it. She would have to wash herself off every time, which was an unpleasant prospect.

Now, lying there, feeling herself, she began to think a little on her situation and her future. Even though they had been the cause of her severe handicap, the freedom from that handicap was heady wine indeed. Hanging over her always was the threat of the restoration of that condition, which, she knew, could be done almost with the wave of a hand.

She knew she had to fight them. Not merely for her own

sake, for she was certain that whatever they eventually had planned for her would be very unpleasant indeed, but also for the sake of the world. The Dark Man was right—they could seal off this place in the name of the all-powerful God whose name was Security, and they could probably make it stick for a while, being very convincing to those few outsiders who would come in and out in spite of that security wall. With control of that computer and the kind of casual yet awesome power demonstrated by the Dark Man, it was unlikely that any on this island could stop them.

She thought of that little man, Jureau, whom they had caused her and the others to kill. He had been away, so they hadn't worried about him, but he'd come back unexpectedly, most likely. If most or all of the security forces had been hand-picked—with help from computers, of course—as their people, a Jureau would see through them and move to correct things. Those who could cause them real trouble died. Her father, Jureau, now Greg.

Poor Greg! How she longed to have him with her now, when she was whole and could feel the reciprocate his tender feelings! She would have to fight them for his sake and in his memory, too.

Those with the power to do harm were removed. The rest? The Dark Man's power, and most particularly the fear that power could generate, would keep them in line. A few ugly, or even humiliating, examples would probably suffice. Most of the townspeople had families. When it's your children who are threatened and not just yourself, you are even more likely to go along and take it.

The Institute? They'd probably let some of the Fellows up there stay on, and some of them were so far removed they might not even notice anything else going on. Then, when their term was through, they'd be shipped back to their labs and universities none the wiser. Security could send just about everyone who might cause trouble packing before they knew too much, anyway. And all the time, the day-to-day business of information management would go on; Magellan's corporate books would remain balanced, their business uninterrupted, and the NATO and other branches of the various governments and institutions using it to do business would go on as before, betraying nothing wrong. She could expect little help on the island and no calvary riding to the rescue.

At the moment, she decided, she just didn't know enough to even know if anything was possible. She needed time, time to adjust, time to think, time to test herself and them, to find out if there was anything that could be done. And yet, what could she do, naked, exposed, and alone? What could she do to those who her father and Greg couldn't stand against? She didn't even understand computers and had no idea what they even *did* up there at the Institute or, for that matter, what Magellan did around the world.

Feeling both depressed and inadequate, she finally managed to drift off to sleep.

When she awoke it looked like late afternoon. She was feeling a little sore and nauseous. She wasn't used to such feelings, nor the little aches and pains that everyone suffers and takes for granted. She got up to explore the now illuminated area of the cabin interior.

Someone had clearly been there while she slept. Atop the cabinets were small baskets which contained bread, cheeses, some cold cuts, and other makings for sandwiches. There was also some fresh fruit. A picnic-style cooler had also been brought in, and inside, packed in ice, were two bottles of wine, one red and one white, a liter of beer, and a liter of Coke. In the cabinets she found eating utensiles, some dull bread knives, a large jar of instant coffee, and a box of tea bags. She also located, and took out, a battery-operated single burner electric stove small enough to sit on the table top, and a couple of packs of safety matches. Topping it off were boxes of crackers, cookies, and even some chocolate bars. Clearly they didn't mean for her to starve.

She didn't like the fact that someone, perhaps several people, had been in and carried in all this while she lay asleep and had done so without disturbing her, but as uncomfortable as that idea was, it certainly was something she suspected she'd have to get used to. She wasn't up to doing much immediately, so she made herself a sandwich and washed it down with a Coke. It made her feel a little better, and she looked around the rest of the cabin.

The place was really dirty, and it bothered her. She didn't much relish the idea of parading around *au natural* in the sunlight anyway, so she found a bucket and some cleaning utensils and, with a full water pail from the pump and some of the liquid detergent they'd provided her proceeded to wash the dishes, counters, table top, and much of the rest. As she progressed, she found, unmounted and just leaning against the back wall, a filthy old cracked mirror that must once have been part of a dresser. She washed it with detergent and rags and wiped it off, and as she did she saw herself for the first time.

It was a shock to look into the mirror and see a stranger staring back at her. But for coloration, there had been no changes to her body at all, and her face was still her own face, unaltered save for the color of her eyes and the color and texture of her hair, but it was still a shock to see her whole body, the shape of breasts, waist, hips. For perhaps the first time she looked at herself and saw herself not simply as poor, little Angelique but as others had—as a beautiful woman. It was difficult to grasp that the person she saw was really herself. The changes were such that someone might note the resemblance between her and the heiress from Quebec but would think it only an interesting coincidence. She was not profoundly changed, but what they had done, together with her mobility, was, she knew, *just enough*. Enough to dash any lingering hopes that she could somehow make contact with, and establish her identity to, some friend on the island with guts.

Later, when shadows loomed but there was still some light, she took some rags with her to the small waterfall and bathed, then went down along the small creek all the way to the cliffs.

The creek bank was shaded by vegetation most of the way, but there were places where she could sit out, exposed to the sea and the view, letting the breezes dry her body and hair. It was a drop of at least a kilometer to the sea, but the cliff face wasn't sheer, and that interested her. She wondered if, somehow, she could get down there—and, if so, could she get back up again. Certainly it would have to be done in daylight, which didn't appeal to her at all.

As night fell, she could see in the distance small lights that might have been any number of things. Some were certainly ships of one kind or another, slowly moving across the horizon, and some were buoys or other kinds of navigation markers placed so that those ships could safely make a night passage. It was forty miles, Greg had said, to the next inhabited island. That was more than sixty-four kilometers, if she remembered right. Sixty-four kilometers to the rest of the world.

Over perhaps a two week span—it was difficult for her to really be sure—her self-consciousness at being naked and her fears of attack or exposure subsided, and she had cleaned and ordered her environment. Her skin had toughened to the elements, and she was no longer aware of every little thing her body felt. She almost took for granted the mysterious deliverers of food and supplies, and she grew bolder in her forays.

The Dark Man had not returned and she had been left completely alone, which made her feel immeasureably better.

She didn't know what evil he and his cohorts were up to, but at least it didn't involve her any more.

More than once she'd gone up close to the helipad and even to the Institute itself. She found she retained, and even improved upon, the animal-like instincts of the wild pack, and at night, with her dark skin and ability to remain motionless, crouched and still, she could get so close that she could observe and even overhear without anyone knowing she was there.

Important-looking people came and went on the nearly nightly 'copter shuttles, although their identity was a mystery. They were occasionally addressed by people on the ground as "General So-and-So," and "Doctor Such-and-Such," but the names were meaningless to her. There did seem to be fewer people about the Lodge at night, and those she did see, both there and around the helipad, seemed less talkative among themselves and more somber than she would have expected, but it looked so very *ordinary* in most ways. It was only the joyless faces and near dead silence of staff people riding down the mountain in the electric carts that betrayed hints of what must really be going on.

Only when she began to spy on that meadow, that terrible meadow with its grotesque altar stone, in the hours between midnight and dawn, could she really see.

Each night they held strange, horrible, blasphemous rites there. They were not the same each night, nor did they always involve the same people, but they were frightening and revealing.

The rites usually began with a gathering of several dozen men and women in hooded robes, coming from both town and the Institute. They chanted and prayed to Lucifer, Emperor of Hell, Ruler of Earth, and pleged themselves to him. Sometimes strange things would appear, such as designs of colored lights in the grass or apparitions above the stone, and there would be balls of light shooting up and darting about like living creatures. Quite often the rites would climax with a ritual sacrifice, usually a goat but on two occasions human beings, drugged but alive, were stretched out on the altar stone and horribly butchered to the prayers and chants of the gathering. Although none of the people sacrificed were familiar to her, the sight sickened and repulsed her, and she was amazed to realize that the victims had all been men.

Sometimes there would be blood feasts, and other times the suppliants would offer their own to one another. Occasionally they got so worked up into a frenzy that the robes came off, leaving them naked but often wearing primitive jewelry and occasionally with paint on their bodies. They would have sexual orgies in the grass without regard to which sex was which or who was with whom. She did occasionally recognize some of the worshippers; at one time or another she saw Juanita Hernandez and Alice Cowan there, and another time the Haitian twins were also there, performing perverted sexual acts with one another. There were others, too, and she realized for the first time how surrounded she had been all the time. She felt angry and sick that such things could go on at all, and that such people could become such monstrous practitioners of murder, sadism, masochism, sexual excess, and even beastiality.

The presiding priest wasn't the same person from night to night. The Dark Man, who presided but did not participate, was the usual leader, but sometimes he was not there and another took over. More than once it was a woman who led them, a woman she realized was Carla Byrne, the Director's wife. Whether her husband was one of them, or controlled by his wife, she couldn't say.

She tried to get a grip on herself and some understanding of those people as she continued to spy upon them. The servants she could understand, if their culture and background had raised them in this sort of thing, and people like the Dark Man, whoever he was, and the rest of the top

Institute staff who had to be in on it could also be understood by the oldest of rationalizations—a lust for power. But there were others there, in the middle management levels, the product of Christian culture and yet far down in the power structure, both from the village and from the technocrats of the Institute, that were inexplicable. How did the leaders bind and corrupt so many souls so absolutely and so easily?

She would eventually sicken of the spectacles in the meadow and work her way around them, usually going down the cliff trail to the beach where her father died and sit in the sand and let the warm Caribbean waters come up around her and try and think it all out.

She made her way down to the village after a while, and saw the little church in ruins and the graveyard in disarray, and wondered what could have happened here in so short a time, and how the people down here, no matter what, could accept such unspeakable horrors. Did they just look the other way and pretend to know nothing? Had they all been corrupted or enslaved? Some had boats—motor boats, small fishing vessels and sailing boats. Surely some would have tried to escape by now.

Perhaps, she thought, they had tried. Tried and just not made it.

She adapted quickly to her own situation, no longer embarrassed or worried at the thought that her nudity would be seen by someone, no longer even thinking about it or her other limitations, so minor were they when compared to the seven years of far greater limits she had endured. She began to go out during the daytime and get quite close to human activity. Once in a while she'd been spotted by someone, but she'd managed to duck out of sight and avoid any serious investigation. She even discovered that many of the staff and servant women went topless during the heat of the day when outside. This was something new, and indicated how lax any sense of morality and standards had become, but it made it easier for her. Behind a bush, explosed only from the waist up, she might be mistaken for one of the staff workers herself. The imposed physiological changes made on her by the Dark Man to conceal her identity acted in an odd way as a wall against embarrassment. As Angelique she would have suffered acute embarrassment and upset at being seen topless, let alone nude, but as this stranger—it didn't seem to matter to her at all.

She returned to the cabin one afternoon and immediately sensed that something was different, that someone was there. Her sharpened senses gave her caution, but somehow it just didn't *feel* like the Dark Man. Deciding it must be one of the mysterious ones who dropped off fresh supplies, she took a deep breath and walked boldly up to the cabin and in the door. She hadn't really realized until now just how much she had missed human company, no matter what sort it might be.

She was shocked to find a single young woman there. She was dressed in what was becoming the island fashion—topless, with a colorful print skirt—and she looked lean and tan and somehow familiar, but Angelique couldn't quite place her.

The woman put a finger to her lips and pointed at the door. After first thinking that this was a warning that someone was listening, she realized that the woman was motioning for them to go outside, and she did so, the other following quietly. Realizing that the woman wanted to talk and did not want to be overheard, and desperate for any sort of direct human contact, Angelique led her through the wooded area over to one of the clearings on the side of the cliff.

The woman seemed satisfied. She was white and looked to be no more than in her late teens or early twenties. She sat down beside Angelique and said, softly, "Do you remember me, Angelique? Do you know who I am?"

She stared at the other, and tried to speak, but no sound came out. She shook her head negatively.

"You can't talk to me, for I haven't had the guts to take

the sign upon me, at least not yet. Just look at me and speak slowly, as if you had a voice. I can read lips."

Who are you? Angelique asked her. *What is this all about?*

"I—I was Sister Maria Theresa when you knew me."

Angelique was stunned and stared at the other disbelievingly. *You can not be her. She was—old!*

"I know. You see, we all have our price, don't we? Motion, feeling for you, and for me—from menopause to adolescence, physically speaking. Forty-six is a difficult age. They made me seventeen again—seventeen always, they say—in exchange for renouncing my vows and joining them."

But—you were a nun! In God's name, how could you do such a thing?

Maria smiled a bit wistfully. "It's all so simple for you, isn't it? So cut and dried. Good and evil and that's that. I don't put you down for it. They kept you a child, denied you—experience. Not so with me. I was fairly late coming to the Church. Oh, I was born a Catholic and had the usual pressures as a kid and teen, but I was wild. Nobody's fault, least of all my parents. I fell into a bad crowd in high school—right around seventeen, in fact. I didn't want to work, didn't want to grow up, and I wanted independence right then and there. I liked sex. I *loved* men, and I was in the kind of city that had a lot of them, lots of tourists, too. New Orleans. Wide open. So me and a couple of other girls from good middle class Catholic homes started selling ourselves for pay."

Had Angelique been able to speak she could not have done so. She simply couldn't imagine someone doing what Maria described unless forced to it by economic desperation. It was unheard of in the world Angelique had known.

"I know, I know. Welcome to the grown-up world. It wasn't like you read about it in the books. It was *easy*. Just look through the papers, see what conventions were in town, go to the right hotels, and you made a pretty good amount of money just letting *them* make a pass at *you*. For a while it was fun, but then we got well known to the organized working girls. We were competition. We got threats and they really meant it, and we wound up with a Mac—a pimp—for protection. That's when it stops being fun. You get a quota, and you suffer if you don't make the nut. You turn it all over to the Mac and are totally dependent on him for everything. You stop being a person and start being property. Finally you get older and sick and tired of it and you want to quit and they don't let you. You can't anyway. Try being property for eighteen years and you realize you don't even know how to take care of yourself. You start gettin' bags under your eyes and spotting gray hairs and you know you're in the home stretch, that you're gonna be finished, and it's organized crime and after all that time you know too much and can't run. Well, I figured out a place to run to and I did.''

Angelique stared at her. *You never told me. You never told anyone.*

She reached into a small purse, took out a cigarette, lit it, and inhaled deeply. ''Would you? Oh, I told the Church, sure. And they took me in, and I went through all the training and took my vows, and then went on and became a nurse—on them. I wanted to try and do a little good with the rest of my life. They stuck me in Quebec because it was a different country and I wasn't likely to ever run into anybody familiar, and I took a new name and all that. So eight months after I first met you and took on your job, I wound up back in the fire again. These people knew *everything* about me. They knew things I'd forgotten for years. I put up a fuss at the start, yeah, but when they swore to me that they weren't going to harm you and could cure you, there wasn't much else I could do. I never really could be on my own, you know. I sold myself to the Macs, then I went and found the Church to take care of me, then when they couldn't any more these people made an offer and I sold myself again. I'm not real proud of it, but it's a fact.''

Angelique's mind worked on several levels at once. She had a hard time imagining that a num, *any* nun, could come from such a background, or, even if so, could have belief so shallow that the vows meant nothing except self-interest. Still, she couldn't help but wonder if even Sister Maria hadn't been manipulated so that she would be where she was when Angelique's crisis came.

''You're shocked,'' Maria noted. ''You have this high ideal of why folks become priests and nuns and you don't like it shattered. Well, honey, let me tell you, two-thirds of 'em come into the service for personal rather than religious reasons. Oh, some are real strong and real sincere and stay that way, but most are just people. If I had a buck for every pass ever made at me by some fat, middle-aged priest—and a few nuns, too—I could buy my way out of this. I didn't take 'em up on it, but I never really was much for the religious stuff. It was just one of the prices you paid. I needed the Church as a protector. I guess maybe that's why God dropped me right back in the midst of the worst of 'em.''

Angelique looked her squarely in the eyes. *Why did you come to me today?* she mouthed.

''Oh, I dunno. Guilt, maybe. Maybe I just wanted to make sure you were O.K. I really kind of liked you, you know. Oh, me and the other girls have seen you stretched out dead to the world—we bring that stuff in—but I just wanted to see how you were, that's all.''

Are you a part of all this in the meadow at nights?

''I been there, but not much. They want the true believers there. They got ways, though, to convert most anybody. You scare somebody completely out of their wits, then make them choose between a slow, tortuous death or giving over their soul to the devil and I don't know one that wouldn't take up the chants and offer to sacrifice a pig to old Lucifer. They got it made here, you know. Damndest thing I ever saw. High tech Satanism. I think they fake most of the stuff they do somehow, but they still got the power. They got a lock on this island you can't believe. It's kind of like a tropical Nazi Germany except when some outside bigwig comes along and everybody plays normal. They finished off or converted every big shot working at the Institute. They own everybody here, and they got ambitions to own a lot more."

Yes. They killed Greg.

"Oh, yeah? Who told you that?"

She felt a faint stirring of hope. *The Dark Man. The first night.*

"Well, he's full of shit. They *wish* they caught him. Sent their big, lumbering monster or whatever it is after him and he holed up in the church, outlasted it, then made a run for it stealing somebody's boat. I got that from Red—the town constable. He went through a grilling like you wouldn't believe after that, but they finally let him go. Fired his ass, of course. He's now just a common laborer, which is rough at his age, but they got his teenage daughter in their pocket and he's got to go along. But he was there. Not that they didn't search like hell for him. Gossip is he holed up someplace for the day, then sailed until he met up with a Guyanan fishing trawler that took him home. Where he went from there is anybody's guess. They sent out something that he was a Russian agent or something and he's wanted all over, but if they got him I didn't hear, and they're still a little jittery over him. The only one that got away."

Angelique leaped over and kissed and hugged the surprised woman, and then she broke down in tears. *Greg was alive! He got away!* Once again she had hope.

"Don't get your hopes up too high, honey," Maria said gently. "Don't expect him to come over the horizon with the Navy and Marines to save the day. He's a fugitive on the run, was really working for somebody other than the company, and he can only keep alive by staying buried. Knowing what's going on and convincing anybody else of it is two different things.''

She was right, of course, but Angelique didn't care. He was alive! And he would do what he could against these monsters! She was sure of that. Perhaps, just perhaps, he would keep at it a little for her, too.

"So—how have you been doing? O.K.?"

I have had to deal with far worse than this, as you know, she responded. *Still, I wish I could somehow get away, but it seems impossible. They said I would turn into a vegetable if I left.*

"Oh, bullshit!" Maria responded. "Look, they got lots of power. Just look at the two of us now. But it's not absolute. They got to *be* there to do something. Oh, they have these little dolls and they can cause you all sorts of problems, but even then they got to be right around you. What you are now is what you'd be if you escaped. A vegetable is what they might do to you if they caught you.''

She was fascinated. *You are not fooling me?*

"No. They know I'm here—I had to get permission for this—but they don't care any more what you know. They figure they got it made. So even if you *could* get away, what would it get you? You don't have anybody to hide you like MacDonald did. I mean, beg pardon, but anybody who saw you and didn't know about this stuff would take one look at you and figure you as some poor savage from Haiti or more probably French Guyana. They'd either ship you back there or force you into some kind of labor or domestic service. You can't talk, can't write, and there ain't many lip readers in this part of the world and none but me that would believe you if they could. Even MacDonald wouldn't recognize you— but these guys would, and they'd be out looking.''

Marie was right, of course, and she knew it, but she also felt she had to do *something*, regardless of the risks. She looked at the former nun and mouthed. *Do you know what they plan to do with me?*

"No. Only that you got to be a virgin. Come here. Let me check something. Don't worry. I'm a nurse, remember." She leaned over and felt around the inside the vaginal area. "My God! An intact hymen! Girl, you must be the oldest virgin in the world!"

She felt herself flush in embarrassment.

"*That's* what is important about you. You got control of the company and all and you are a pure virgin. Put that together with these guys who really control the company and believe in this devil worship. Figure on them doing a number on you at some point. Virgins are supposed to have big magical powers. If they can turn you around to their way of thinking—and, believe me, they can be *real* persuasive—you'll be you again, maybe the number two head of the cult or whatever it is. I bet that's what they're doing now, setting it all up. Then on one of their big nights, like Halloween or something, they'll come for you. It might be months, but they'll start to work on you before that. You remember going out like an animal and killing that guy . . . Don't look so surprised, we were all there. Well, they can take you a lot lower than that. Drugs, hypnosis, their other crazy powers— they're like little gods even now." She sighed. "I wish I knew what to tell you, but I don't. One thing sure is that they'll break you. They can break anybody. But if you get away like that, you won't last as a virgin for ten minutes with that body, and if you're not a virgin any more they'll just let you stay like this forever and find another sucker. I mean, remember, if they can change you into *that* they can sure as hell change some other virgin into you—and they'll find one eventually."

That was sombering news. Damned literally if she did nothing, damned to life as someone else with no hope of ever breaking it if she did something, and the clock was most certainly running.

"I got to go," Maria said. "They get real sticky if you're too far off your schedule of duties."

They got up, walked back to the cabin and went inside. Maria went to the supplies and removed an object that almost looked like a dead snake with something tied on to it. "I know this isn't much, but you never had much practice with your hands. It's made from local vines, so that spell or whatever it is should let you wear it. Hang it on those gorgeous hips. This little thing on the side holds a gourd; I've brought one, hollowed out. If you want to take something to drink with you, wear this, pour it in the gourd, and shove this cork in like this. It isn't much, but it's the best I could do."

Angelique could only wipe away the tears and plead, *Please come back soon!*

Marie gave her a sad smile. "If they let me, I will."

She was so grateful to the nurse that she kissed and hugged her, and she watched Maria go back through the jungle with a renewed sense of hope mixed with caution. She didn't hold it against the nurse that she'd been forced to join the enemy; she had no doubt of their persuasive powers, and that was what worried her now.

She tried on the vine belt and experimented with the gourd holder, and was delighted to see that both worked and that no force pulled the vine from her nor did it burn or irritate. Nothing had been flung away since the Dark Man's visit, but every time she'd tried putting on any kind of clothing or cloth it had begun to burn like fire. From the rags and cloths they provided and from the remains of her torn clothes she'd tried things, but they had all started to burn within a few minutes and she'd had to remove them. Now she realized it must be an allergy to all sorts of processed cloths and synthetics.

Partly to clear her mind and give her a chance to think, she went out into the jungle and found large leaves of the right size and some of the common type of vine used in making the belt. Using the kitchen tools and a lot of patience, she fashioned a front and rear leaf loin cloth and tried it. It took a lot of adjustment and fiddling, but it worked and did not burn and she was delighted. She felt like Eve, using a fig leaf to cover her lower parts. She went over to the mirror and looked at herself.

She looked, she thought, like somebody you saw in the back pages of *National Geographic*. Still, her loincloth made her feel better, more human, somehow, and less debased.

That night she went over to the beach, found some shells and some small leafy vines. She took to the long, methodical work of creating something with her own hands as if she'd been doing it forever, although there were many breaks and wrong decisions and steps back to the beginning. Finally, though, by the light of the lanterns, she managed to create a primitive necklace of shells, small, light volcanic stones, and laurel-like leaves, and also a headband which helped control her hair.

She was admiring her handiwork in the mirror when she suddenly felt an unwelcome presence enter the room. She looked into the mirror and could see nothing reflected there, but when she turned, *he* was there. No eyes or other features could be seen in that face of total black, yet she felt his gaze.

"Very attractive," the Dark Man noted approvingly. "Very—primitive. It might start a new fad."

"Very funny," she responded. She felt too much hatred and contempt for the Dark Man to fear him, although she respected his power and knew his danger. "I thought I was rid of you for a while yet."

"Oh, no. The past few weeks have been a bit of seasoning, a period of adjustment for you. We've removed some cumbersome baggage from you. You are tougher now, and far more self confident and self-sufficient. The whimpering, self-pitying cripple has been displaced by a newer woman, and perhaps a better one. In a few weeks the girl who was too shy and too modest and too morally hamstrung to even allow cleavage to show now walks naked with little thought of who is watching. The girl who was so helpless she took an hour to figure out a manual can opener now studies and creates basic clothing and even adornment with those same hands. The little would-be nun has been stripped of some of her civilized veneer. Tell me, what did you think of our—services?"

"You mean those abominations in the cursed meadow? Horrible. Grotesque. Insane. Each day and night I pray for your victims."

"And, no doubt, ask God to intervene and strike us dead— but He does not. He hears, but he does not. By the way, there was a telelink today between Mr. McGraw and you. Settled a lot of matters and got you on the record as desiring to assume all the burdens of the estate. McGraw will continue as your attorney, which pleases him."

She frowned. "I made no such contact and you know it."

"Oh, but you did. Because of your paralyzed condition, it was necessary to do it by conference so you could be seen. It's amazing when you think that such signals are actually made up of little tiny pixels, little dots, each with only a little information, and the sound and video are reduced to digital form. All of this, of course, is handled via SAINT's telecommunications net. The fact is, to him you looked bright and cheerful and quite happy and natural, yet your image and voice existed only within the computer. It's amazing what modern electronics can do these days."

She could hardly believe him, yet she dared not disbelieve him, either. No one was wondering or worried about her in the outside world, because they could produce her, authorizing what they wanted and reassuring anyone who wondered, on demand through electronic wizardry. In many ways, that power was as great as the other more supernatural powers the Dark Man displayed.

"Your existence belies your confidence," she shot back. "If all is going so much your own way, and you control this entire island, why is it still necessary for you to adopt this disguise which alters your voice and makes your features nothing? It seems a lot of trouble for someone without worries."

"Oh, this is for a different reason than that, but it is not one that you have to know right now. I am no one you know or have ever met, yet this is still necessary for now. We will discuss it no more at this point."

"And what do you intend with me now, then?"

"A comparison. Two women. Two possibilities. The world is full of possibilities and biographies are the stuff of possibilities. Let us consider just one."

There was a sudden sense of dizziness and some disorientation, and then she was floating, floating in something but without sight or sound or other sensation. No, wait—images suddenly appeared, very blurry at first, but getting clearer, and distant muffled voices became progressively louder and clearer to her ears.

She was lying in a bed in a room painted light green. A hospital bed, surely, in some modern facility. The pain hit almost immediately, and wracked her body. All parts seemed in pain, the agony forcing her to cry out and beg for help from those in the room, but she could not speak or move.

"Should I administer a sedative, Doctor?" the nurse asked, looking down at her. "There's just something about her eyes, like she can really understand what we're saying."

"Don't read more into her than is there, Jenny," the doctor responded. "It's always tragic to see them when they're young and pretty, but she's a vegetable, with little more feeling than a blade of grass or a tree. It's only damned corporate politics that we don't disconnect the intravenous

tubes and let her starve and die. They are paying a fortune to keep her legally alive for some reasons of their own, but she's gone. Only her shell remains, like Karen Quinlan and the other body-live, brain-dead. Such a tragedy."

"No, no!" she tried to shout to them. "I think! I am in terrible pain! I need help! I am truly alive!" But nothing came out. She had no power to move or communicate in any way.

"But her eyes are partly open some of the time—like now," the nurse pointed out. "I'd swear she knows we're here."

"Yes! Yes! I do know! Oh, help me!"

"We've tried talking to her, getting her to blink if she understands us, but it's no use. Forget it, nurse. Don't let your imagination run away with you. Just maintain the current levels and keep the monitors going." He sighed. "Poor thing. With the size of that annuity for her and even today's medical knowledge, she could be like this, for the next fifty years. . . ."

She was still screaming at them inwardly, unable to control a thing, when she was aware that both the pain and the vision were fading and she was floating once again. The experience was so horrible, the absence of pain so intense a relief, that she almost passed out. She didn't know how long the episode had lasted, but it was the most horrifying experience of her entire life, the stuff of nightmares.

"Choose," came the voice of the Dark Man from all around her. "Now choose, but consider this alternative."

She opened her eyes and gazed deeply into the fire and drew strength and power from the spirit it contained. She crouched there a while, but then stood and raised her arms and beckoned all the spirits and demons to attend her. And they were there, and responded to her call, in every tree, in every blade of grass, in every brief gust of wind that struck her almost naked body, and they let their power flow into her. Her body tingled with a totally erotic sense that none else here could understand, the power begetting power and giving off pleasure as a side effect.

She was a virgin, by their standards, yet the tribe all called her Mother and she saw them all, young and old, male and female, strong and weak, as her children. What could they know, from their few minutes of climax, what the spirits and demons could give to one who was one with them, give eternally and on demand?

She gestured with her right hand, and the fire flared up, a torchlike column that seemed to have a life of its own suspended in air. In its illumination she could see them all, her children, on their knees to her, praying to her, watching with awed eyes and fear in their souls, fear she had placed there and fear they had accepted as the price of her protection.

She gestured with her left hand and a great wind came, like some living thing, and swirled around the column of fire and kissed each of the worshippers in turn, then flowed inward to the small stone idol that sat on a bed of straw between the fire and the crowd.

It was crudely fashioned, but now it seemed to glow and pulse and throb like a living thing, and they all saw and made supplication to it, calling on it by name.

"Dobak! Dobak! Protect us! Dobak! Dobak! God of the Hapharsi! Protect thy children from harm and bless our hunt!"

And the demon flowed from the idol into her body, and took it for use as its own, for certainly it was Dobak's to use and willingly so. And while it performed its magic rites and demanded its sacrifices and its blood, her own self was plunged into a realm of indescribable pleasures and delights, orgasm after orgasm, through her mind and body, and she heard not what was being said or done in her body and cared not. So wondrous were the sensations that although a tiny corner of her saw her hands come up, then descend with the knife and plunge it into the writhing, crying body of the infant girl-child upon the altar, she did not care. And at the moment the sacrifice died, she felt that sensation rise to undreamed-of heights as the youth and energy of the child's soul flowed into her while the agony and pain were absorbed by the demon within.

"The sacrifice is good," she heard the demon say with her lips, "and the hunt will be good, and the women of the tribe will be blessed with many strong and healthy children who will not die too young. This I grant, so long as you worship me!"

And they roared and chanted its unholy name, and buried their faces in the earth. And the sensations slowly subsided as the demon flowed from her body and back to the idol, but she felt the lingering, tingling sensations and would for some time to come, and she knew her power was increased and her body made well of all its ills and younger, too. As the demon prepared to leave its effigy, she, too, sank to her knees and prayed to the great god of the tribe in thanks, and suddenly she was floating once again.

"Now choose and merge," said the Dark Man's voice all around her. "Choose not with your mind but with your inner feelings."

He had shown her two kinds of Hell, and she rejected both choices, yet he would not offer any alternatives. The pain returned, the horrible pain and the quiet and the horror of the hospital room. . . .

And so it went, fading from one sensation, one life, into the other, for what seemed like an eternity. She struggled against it intellectually, but the pain of the girl in the room was too intense and too real, and she found after a while that no matter what the horror of the demon and the ritual sacrifice she could no longer willingly leave that existence, that she fought in her mind to remain there, to not go back to that sterile hospital room filled with pain and no hope at all.

Given a choice of hells, she could no longer bear the hopeless agony contrasted to the power and pleasure of the other, when she was forced to choose.

Her body still tingled with those wondrous sensations, but she felt the hard floor of the cabin and looked up at the Dark Man, not illuminated by the flickering kerosene lantern, from her kneeling position.

"A primitive tribe in any time, remote from civilization even in this modern age," the Dark Man said softly. "They are beset by disease, lack of medicine and sanitation, and the vagaries of the hunt which is their only source of sustenance. Yet they are not ignorant. The missionaries had come, but with independence the missionaries had been foreced to leave, and the corrupt new government cared little about the primitives in the bush. They had prayed to the spirits of nature, and had received nothing. They prayed to this white God of the missionaries, and that God sent them nothing. So they prayed to the power, the elemental forces that were the very agents of their misery, and they received help."

"They sold their souls to your master," she managed.

"Ah, but consider the alternative! Did you not just do the same? A high tech hospital, the wonders of medicine and the arrogance of ignorant doctors. He might have given her the benefit of the doubt and shot massive doses of a strong opiate into her, but that risks complications with the heart, liver, and other organs, and considering the millions of dollars in donations and grants in aid that depend on keeping her alive—perhaps his own job—he does not risk it. You knew he wouldn't. Faced with a life of eternal agony or one of pleasure and power, even if it means the sacrifice of innocents and taking a demon lover, you made the same choices they were forced to make."

"But I had no other choices!"

"Neither did they."

"That girl in pain—that was me, wasn't it? Keeping me alive, indefinitely, to safeguard your precious computer!"

"It might be. That is your choice. It is always your choice. One or the other."

"But even Christ had to suffer on the Cross but three hours!"

"Well, he had connections in high places, didn't he? He had his own choice, but he knew how short its duration, how temporary its agony. You do not have that luxury. Your agony is permanent. God expects such a sacrifice, and tonight you failed Him. He's still there. Renounce at any time, and you will return to that hospital, that bed, that pain and helplessness. I think you have learned much tonight about yourself. You have come a long way, and we will explore further in the times to come."

"I have done nothing but play a game of illusion."

"Oh, really? Go to the mirror. Look at yourself now."

She turned and went over to it, fearful of what she might see or be shown. She looked at her image, and gasped.

Her body was still beautiful, and of the deepest brown, but she had changed. The face staring back at her was an attractive face, a young face. Her ears were pierced, and through them ran smooth rings of reddish bronze about the circumference of golf balls, and from each ring hung another, and yet one more. Her headband had become a true headband made of some grasses so finely and tightly woven they looked machine made, and her crude breechclout had become made of the same stuff, and hung on her hips. Her cheeks and brow and breasts were marked with some sort of chalky paint with odd designs in several light colors, and her necklace had become one of tiny, colorful, brightly polished stones. She had never seen that face, yet she knew it, knew whose reflection she saw, and she gave a small cry and turned away.

"I said I gave you a choice," the Dark Man noted.

"Nothing is permanent except that hospital and the bed and the pain. You chose the Hapharsi Mother, and so lock in those attributes, which you take in commemoration of your choice. As you choose more, those attributes, too, will you acquire, inner as well as outer. At any time you may recant, at any time you may deny it, and at that time you will return, then and there, to the pain and the hopelessness of that hospital room. But if you do, then only your total and sincere surrender of your life and soul and will to great Lucifer will get you out."

"You bastard!" she screamed, and picked up a piece of broken chair leg and tossed it at him. It deflected itself to the left and crashed against the cabin wall. She picked up other things, at random, and threw them at him, but no matter how true the throw she could not strike him. Finally she burst into tears and dropped to her knees. "Please!" she begged. "Please stop this! *Stop this horrible nightmare!*"

But he just chuckled and said, "Enough for tonight. Pleasant dreams and sleep well. You are on the right path and deserve a reward. Perhaps I will let your friend come again. She is a good outlet for you, and I grant you the power of speech with her. I wouldn't want you to go mad."

And, with that, he faded and was gone.

She knelt there, head bowed, for quite some time, and prayed to God, to Mary and Jesus and the saints, to deliver her, even to strike her down, but to end this thing.

But, as usual, there was no answer, no response at all. She understood why. God expected her to take the bed, make the sacrifice, go horribly mad in agony year after year. But she was no saint and she knew it. Not even the saints had been required to endure such a painful, prolonged living death, a state well within the power of those who now ran Magellan.

She knew from this very night that she could not hold out, that they would chip away at her soul as they had marked her body night after night until she was theirs and willingly so.

She could and would fight it, but the Dark Man was right. She was allowed only two choices, and that was which living Hell to join.

She knew that, no matter what the cost, she would have to try and escape, even if it meant living the rest of her life like this. She might, at least, die in the attempt and be saved from all this.

Forty miles of water. Yet, if, somehow, she could make it, she had one thing they didn't know. She had a name and address. Just how difficult it would be, looking like this, mute and prevented from writing, to locate the place and get in and communicate her identity once there, she refused to even think about. The odds were she'd never get there in the first place.

9

A COMPROMISE OF DESPERATION

"They have reduced me to the primitive in appearance, and now, night by night, they are whittling away at my mind and heart," Angelique said with a note of quiet desperation in her voice. "More and more of *her* enters in me each time. And you know—she is long dead? Perhaps hundreds, or thousands of years gone. But not her soul. It creeps from Hell at *His* direction and gnaws at my own."

"I know what they can do," Maria replied sadly.

"Do you? From the jungle and the rocks I fashion this stone spear tip, and mount it expertly. I build this lean-to here, although I do not know how I knew to do it, and prefer sleeping in it on the ground to inside the cabin. I find myself, when alone, thinking in *her* dead and far simpler language and nearly forgetting any other. I go to pray to God and find myself praying in that tongue to the spirits of the earth and air. I find myself in awe of the Moon Goddess, and praying to the great god who is the Sun. These marks on my face and body, they do not come off. They are some kind of primitive tattoo. All the information, it is there, in my head—the both of us. But more and more my own self, my own life and feelings and beliefs, become less important to me. If I did not have you to talk to, I could not have fought it even this long.''

Maria did not really have to be told. The wild, primitive, but still exotically beautiful body was beside the point, for she had seen all sorts of changes in folks on this island. It was, rather, as if the words that were coming from that person were what was wrong. Angelique didn't realize just how much of a change there actually had been. It was in her very movements, the way she carried herself, the way she acted and reacted, that the primitive savagery was evident. It was evident, too, in the remains of a fat seagull, speared on the fly with uncanny accuracy by a weapon that had not been made this true in thousands of years, plucked, cooked slightly on a stick over an open flame, and devoured. Her personal hygiene had deteriorated, and the place was littered with garbage.

"And when they reduce me to the point where I stand naked on their rock and perform a sacrifice to the demons with my own hands, they will have me. Then they can restore me to my old form and merge my old and new self, and I will be in their service. Angelique will be but a cloak, a civilized shell that can be worn to deceive everyone, while underneath and in charge will be the Mother, lover to demons, servant of Hell.''

"I think my turn is coming," Maria told her. "They are pressing me to take the oaths, to take their brand upon my forehead which may be seen only under certain lights or by others with it. Now I scrub and fetch and carry for them—I'm getting very good at carrying large things and even jars on my head—for hours on end, and then I must submit to anyone who desires my body.''

"It is getting too late for both of us, Maria," Angelique warned. "Yet I can not do it alone.''

"I know.''

Angelique had become increasingly frustrated over the

unlikelihood of getting any aid. Maria was as a faithful friend as they allowed her to be, but she wasn't strong-willed. Out of desperation, the last few nights, Angelique had tried something both daring and dangerous.

The *Mu'uhqua*—the Mother—had one thing she did not. She had some of the power and she knew how to use it. Angelique had found that she could tap that power, to a degree, and direct it, although she did not really understand how she did it, and the use of it was dangerous beyond measure. To do it, she had to let herself go, *become* the other, and think as she had thought. To do so was to play into the hands of the Dark Man, although she wondered whether in his vast overconfidence he had considered the possibility of that power. She'd had some success commanding animals, particularly after stealing a couple of the village chickens and sacrificing them on a crude altar. She had drunk of the blood and felt the power enter her, minor though it was. She wasn't yet ready to commit the ultimate act that would surely get her the power she needed, but she was ready to sacrifice a goat, a cow, a horse, whatever it took, and she knew just how to do it. Realizing that Maria lacked the courage to act on her own, a plan had formed in Angelique's desperate mind.

She was invoking no demons, for their price was one she still was unwilling to pay, but the elementals, the spirits of the trees and air and fire and water, demanded less.

She concentrated, knowing how tricky this would be. She would have to remain in control, thinking in that ancient, simple language, but conversing in English. She didn't know if she could do it, but she had to try.

Maria was looking out to sea, trying not to think about their dilemma, and didn't notice Angelique drop to one knee and bow her head. *Unab sequabab ciemi*, she chanted. "Spirits of nature come."

And they came, and flowed within her, and she felt the

power. It was a tangible thing, an invisible substance that flowed from her hand and reached out and touched Maria.

The former nun heard the chant and turned and frowned, and said, "Huh? What?" Then the power was within her. There was some resistance, but the chanting girl broke through in a moment.

"Mother be girl," Angelique tried, knowing it wasn't right and trying to do better. She groped for the right words in the right order, and found them.

"Me be mother of Maria," she said solemnly. "Maria is child of mother. Have no mother but me." She quickly realized that the message did not have to be perfect; the thoughts actually carried through the—magic?

Maria stood there, transfixed, as if in a deep hypnotic trance.

"Maria love mother. Worship mother. Mother god of Maria. Maria no fool mother. Maria no question mother. Maria love no but mother. Maria speak mother of mother."

"You are my mother, my god, my only love," the woman repeated in a flat tone. "I will never lie to you or question you."

"Maria belong mother. Maria do what mother say. Maria no think past, no think now. Maria is obey mother, no happy but obey mother. No fear but mother. Maria wake."

The woman seemed to snap out of it, blinked a few times, then looked at Angelique. The smile on her face at that was indescribable, and she gave a squeal of joy and prostrated herself and began to kiss Angelique's feet.

The old Angelique would have been repulsed by it and overcome with guilt, but this new Angelique felt a rush of power and a feeling of extreme satisfaction. Her whole body seemed to get a charge out of it, but she knew that the power was quite limited, and what she had to do.

"Stop, my daughter, and kneel before me," she commanded,

pushing Angelique to the fore but not letting go of the primitive other completely.

"I obey, my mother, my goddess, my lover and protector."

That surprised the neophyte witch. She hadn't put any of that in there, had she? Or did the subject take it from there?

"Do you know how to sail a boat, child?" She felt language coming more easily as her power surged.

"Oh, yes, mother! Not a sailboat, but ones with motors."

"And are there such boats in the village?"

"There are but two now, my mother, which can run."

"And do you know where they are?"

Maria nodded. "They are in a small shed near the fishing pier. But they are guarded by two men with guns."

She suspected as much. "And do these boats need keys?"

"Yes, my mother. One of the guards has them."

"And the *essence*—the gasoline. Is it there, too?"

"They are used by the security people, my mother. They are always kept ready to go."

"Very well, then. You will at some time today get a pen and a small piece of paper and bring it with you. Now, you will do as I say *exactly*. When I dismiss you, you will forget all this, forget that anything of this sort took place. You will not remember. But at two this morning you will remember, and you will do as I say. . . ."

She didn't often come into the village, even in the dead of night, but only because there was nothing there for her. There was a strict curfew in effect, and professional-looking toughs with nasty-looking sidearms saw to it that it was enforced. There was revelry in the meadow with the Dark Man presiding, so she knew she had at least a little time.

There was a clock atop one of the village's Tudor structures. Greg had pointed it out to her, noting it was always inevitably ten minutes slow, but it gave her the edge she needed to keep appointments.

The patrols didn't bother her, although she hoped Maria was up to bypassing them. She looked at them, swaggering arrogantly, and thought how easy it would be for her to kill them.

There was a small office in the back of the boat shed, and two men sat in it playing cards. She watched, and waited, until she saw one of them say something to the other and the other glanced at his watch. She crept up close, invisible in the darkness, bare feet silent in the sand.

"Time to go check 'em," one man said, sounding very bored. It was clear that he thought it a waste of time, but orders were orders and these days you could get creamed for disobeying those orders.

The man came out, went down the small stairs to the sand, walked over to the padlocked door, then took out a keyring, selected a key, and unlocked it. He opened it and went inside. She checked and saw that the other man was still inside, peeking at the absent man's cards, then moved swiftly and silently to the door and peered inside. The man had turned on a bare bulb and now was looking at the boats.

She moved like an animal, incredibly swift and powerful. The act was instinctive yet professional, and so swift that later on she could not remember what she did or how she did it, but the man fell to the floor, turned, confused, and before he could do or say anything, let alone go for his gun, his throat was torn out.

She drank of his blood and dedicated the kill to the moon goddess, absorbing much of his life force as she did so. The force was heady and strong within her, yet she did not linger. There was another to take care of, and she felt a tingling excitement, even an eagerness for the kill.

She heard a door open in back of the shed, and a man called, "Hey, Jerry? What's the problem?"

Receiving no answer, he grew suddenly cautious and suspicious, and drew his pistol. Quietly, he crept up to the half-open door to the boat shed, and, pistol raised, he put his back to the door, then with a single motion turned and pointed the gun inward, ready to fire.

Somehow, in one motion, the pistol was kicked from his hand and at the same instant a bloody stone spear pierced and ripped out his throat. He looked incredibly confused, then fell backwards, dead before his body hit the ground. She dragged him in, removed the spear, and used it to smash the light bulb. She performed the ritual, dedicating the kill to the spirits of the water through whose domain she still had to travel.

These were proper kills, not sacrifices, but still the power she had absorbed from their dying life forces was tremendous. Her mind worked on several levels, but it was basically a thinking version of the type of women who'd killed Jureau. She was Angelique, and she *knew* she was Angelique, yet nothing that she had done seemed unusual to her or in any way troubled her conscience. It was natural. Good and evil, God and the devil, didn't enter into it. These men were of the tribe of the Dark Man, who was the enemy of her tribe and her people. To kill an enemy was an honorable thing; to kill one of your own was evil.

But she was stuck here, now, until Maria showed up. She went back to the first body, having no difficulty in the near pitch darkness, and got the keys. There were a *lot* of keys, and there was nothing left to do but to try them all when they needed one. She walked forward on narrow beams with perfect balance and reached the double doors to the boat house. There was, as expected, another padlock, this one on the inside. She began trying keys, and finally hit it, unlocking the lock but not yet removing it from the hasp. She went back to the door and checked outside. No sign yet of Maria, and that was trouble. She had to have the girl here before somebody noticed that nobody was back in the little office.

Finally, she saw a small figure creep back and forth in the

shadows and finally approach. She wasn't wearing a stitch of clothing, but she carried something in her hand.

Angelique did not worry now. She had the power to make it stick, and she used it. Maria kneeled before her in the darkness. Maria would be a good girl and obey.

"First, get some sand from outside," Angelique ordered. "There! Good. Now put as much as you can in the gas tank of one of the boats. We will use the other."

Now the doors were open and the chocks were removed, and Maria got inside while Angelique pushed. The boat slid almost silently into the water. Now the wild girl judged her distance and the bobbing of the boat and leaped, spear in hand, and landed in the boat.

Maria had tried the keys and found the right one, but waited for orders to turn the engine over. Angelique had hoped the boat would drift out a little, but instead it slowly turned and looked as if it were going to be carried in. There was nothing to do but try, hope the engine caught quickly, and gun it as the patrols raced to see what was going on.

"Do it!" Angelique commanded. "Do it before we wash ashore or crash into the pier!"

Maria turned the key and pumped the starter, and the connected outboard motors in the back coughed and turned over but didn't start. Twice more she tried it, the noise seeming to echo and reverberate through the village and up the mountain, but to no avail. There was a sudden calling of voices from the town, and the sound of running feet.

Maria tried again as the boat, carried by the water flow, headed toward the pier. The engines coughed, then sputtered into life as the first footsteps hit the pier itself. Angelique found herself thrown down and to the rear of the boat as it suddenly took off.

Now there were great shouts, and spotlights came on all over the beach area. Dull-sounding popping noises came to them, and in and around the boat paint chips flew and small pieces of bullet richocheted.

Maria accelereated straight out, then turned and rounded the point to the west shore, the shore away from the meadow and the looming cliffs.

Angelique picked herself up but couldn't manage more than a sitting position on the boat deck. The two rear seats were covered with vinyl and she didn't even bother to try them; she felt safer and more secure sitting low as possible anyway. She had never realized what speed these boats had; the bow was pointing up, almost out of the water, and every time they cut across the current or the chop of light waves it gave a crunching sound and the entire boat shuddered.

She knew there were security patrol boats about, but if she could endure this discomfort she was not about to put in anywhere near Allenby Island. She managed to crawl up near to the manic, spellbound pilot.

"How long can this boat run?" she shouted over the roar. "How far can it go?"

"Three to four hours my beloved mother," Maria responded.

There was a compass aboard. "Head north, then, away from those cursed antennas, until we can no longer see or feel the island. Then we will come around in a big circle and head west."

She settled back on the floor of the boat, feeling a bit queasy. Now, if the Dark Man were correct, she should begin to feel the numbness return, feel all sensation slip away. She did feel seasick, but there was no sensation of a spell breaking. Rather, it was almost the sensation of a spell *tightening* around her, illusion becoming reality, what was imposed becoming what was.

She knew that there would be other patrols out looking for them, and that they would be easy marks for radar and any other tracking system, but it was a wide sea and there were many things both in and upon it.

She drew upon her inner strength and power to suppress the nausea, and eventually she felt better.

Off in the distance could be seen the lights of ships and various navigation lights as well. She instructed Maria to slow down to half speed and begin turning.

She had never expected to get this far, and now she had to make a series of decisions she hadn't thought much about before. There were rocks and reefs out here that neither she nor Maria knew anything about, and certainly the main route to any nearby settled island would be the most watched. They had a compass, but no charts or other navigation aids to find this place, and she realized with a start that she didn't even know the name of the town they sought. Worse, she was feeling some of the changes within her, some of the hardening, that might be part of the spell but might also be the price she was paying for being too much the ancient warrior witch of a forgotten tribe.

She had come a long way from being that poor, paralyzed, naive girl in the powered wheelchair, but the changes had not been in a direction she particularly liked. When all else had failed, she had won by using some of the same powers and methods that the Dark Man had used on her. She realized she needed time to think, to adjust, to understand herself and to plot her next course. Yet, what was best? To get straight there, before the alarms could be in full cry, was tempting—if they could make it, blind to the route. Or should she try to put in at one of the remote islands along the way, hide the boat and rest knowing that they would have the whole southern Caribbean covered. Greg had used a silent sailboat, and even then had been taken aboard a commercial ship. They didn't have those options.

Greg had said that the village was small and very remote. She decided to instruct Maria to try for it, but not go in to the village. She crept forward to look at the speedometer, but she somehow couldn't see or get a grasp of what it was saying. What else was happening to her?

"How fast are we going?"

"Twelve knots," the pilot answered. "It is possible to do much more than that, my mistress."

"As fast as you can on the right course," she instructed. "May the spirits of sea and air take us there before sunrise."

It was clear after a while, though, that no matter what they did they could not make the complete passage in darkness and they were rather conspicuous and in an open boat. There were boats out now from many nations, and they had been able to ignore them in the dark, making certain they were clear of any trawling nets. They had ignored several hails as it was, and clearly couldn't do so in the light of day. False dawn was already making it easy to see, and the sun would be up any minute.

An island came up on their left; it was not much more than a large pile of rocks covered with thick vegetation, but it seemed possible to land on one side where the trees came right down to the water. The shape was sufficient to offer some disguise from the sea, and the overgrowth of trees made spotting anything by air unlikely. It was as good a place as they could hope for, although it was certainly uncomfortable and not foolproof. They had no rope and no anchor, and had to hope that the tiny inlet between jagged rocks would hold the boat fast.

Angelique left Maria with the boat and clambered up the rocks to the trees and then up onto the island itself. It didn't take much time to explore it and discover it had no usable water and nothing that really looked edible. It did, however, have enough ropelike vines to secure the boat to a tree. After that, she helped Maria up onto the island surface and they walked back just a little.

Angelique was dead tired, and she knew Maria must be in an even worse shape, but she didn't dare allow herself to

sleep just yet. Something within her told her that there was
an urgency to doing the little things, and she didn't hesitate
to believe it.

She stood and faced Maria, and began a small chant,
placing a finger on the controlled woman's forehead. "Maria, Mother free you from spell. Remember all."

The captive girl's body swayed, and then she seemed to
wake up and look around in wonder. "Oh, my *god!*" she
breathed. "It *wasn't* a dream!"

"No dream," Angelique told her, suddenly finding
words difficult again. "We escape. Now my life, you life,
whole plan in you hand."

"Angelique—what's the matter?" Maria was tired and
thirsty, but she was scared most of all. "Why are you talking
so funny?"

"I use power of spirit. On you. On me. That why we here.
More I use, more I am—*her*. Angelique still in head, but
think *her* tongue. Much less words to speak, think. Think in
her tongue, think her way. You see?"

Maria sat down and shook her head. This was much too
much for her at one time. Still, she was aware of their
situation and scared to death, and Angelique was all she had
right now.

"Let me get this straight. You used—magic—to control
me. But now because of that you're finding it hard to think in
English or French?"

"Yes. Old tongue. Plain tongue. Must fight to find words
for you to know my talk. Is curse. No power, no get away,
no live. Power make me not her but like her."

"Then what can I—what are we going to do now?"

"See in hand. Speak totem."

Maria brought up her right hand, and for the first time saw
that she was tightly clenching a ballpoint pen and a piece of
wet and crumpled paper. She had apparently been holding on
to it the entire time. The pen was broken, the paper useless,

coming apart almost as she looked at it. "It's no good. It's broken." She looked at the plastic refill. "Maybe I could write, but there's nothing to write on."

Angelique sighed. "Then you sleep. When night come, you go. Bring help. I wait three moons here for help."

"Go? Where? Get help from who?"

"You—write. Do on skin, Say—Bessel Island. Art Cadell. In white little house looking to water. Speak what happen. All. Come back for me. If not—Greg—or you come, will go. Never see again."

She wrote down the information, with difficulty, on her arm. "But why just me? I mean—I don't have a stitch on! Why not both of us?"

"You speak clear tongue. You say, they know. See me, laugh. Dark Man look for me. You bring Dark Man, we die. Bring friend, we may stop Dark Man. Be brave. Use head."

"I—I'm not very brave. I could never have done this much without your hypnosis or whatever it was."

"You be now. Dark Man, he catch you, he lie sweet but he mad. He put you in living hell. Believe."

"But—what if I'm caught? What if I can't make it in time? What if nobody's there any more?"

"Then Angelique use power. Get to big land. Live in jungle. Be wild thing but not Dark Man thing."

"You're sure? You'll be on this island—alone. No food or drink. No boat, and you can't swim."

"No worry 'bout Angelique. You do?"

"I—I'll try. But I worry about you, even if I *get* back."

"No can stop. Must become like her. Come too far to get power to do this. Had to be price to pay. Angelique know this may be. Not mind. Get arms. Got legs. Am strong."

Maria was genuinely touched by that. Angelique was paying what was, to Maria, an intolerable price, but was it intolerable to Angelique? She would foil, perhaps stop, the Dark Man. She had traded her attractive Canadian self for the body of a young priestess of a Stone Age culture—and perhaps of the Stone Age itself. A quadriplegic heiress becomes a whole Stone Age person, cut off in communication from the world of today and forced to think in a simple, more basic, and probably long dead Stone Age language with few words and much mysticism. The language would in itself force her to think in those terms, make her inside what she appeared to be outside.

Was it worth the price? Was it a better choice? Maria didn't know, but certainly Angelique had decided it was.

Maria had no doubts that the Dark Man's people would be sweet as honey if they caught her, but out for terrible revenge when they recovered Angelique. Being hypnotized or whatever it had been would be no excuse. If they could create a monster out of something or other to do their killing and restore her youth while changing Angelique into—this—they would be very creative when she no longer had value. She'd been too long on the streets of New Orleans with the amoral, the vicious, and the truly evil to think otherwise.

"I will do it. Somehow I will do it," she said, and kissed Angelique.

"I—I not be same when you come back. Be Hapharsi. Look, act, think Hapharsi, but be Angelique in head. No worry. Not all spirits evil. Find good high priest. Break spell. Angelique be like old but no stiff. You see."

And, with that, they slept, huddled in each other's arms.

It was dream-filled, troubled sleep for Angelique, but her dreams were not of anything she could remember. Rather it was something of an inner house cleaning, a rearrangement of her mental furniture. She could fight it while awake, at least slow it down, but asleep she was at its mercy. Still, some corner of her mind held on ferociously, at least until this part was done.

She awoke before it was totally dark, and slipped silently

away from Maria's still form. She went down to check the
boat and saw that it was indeed still there. Reassured, she
went back up and sat, cross-legged, across from the other
woman. She needed to think.

Was she doing the right thing, allowing one who had
betrayed her once to go alone? Still, she knew she had to do
it that way. She was what the Dark Man's magic had de-
creed, and his was the stronger magic. By that magic he had
marked her, making her choose this life, but, no matter what,
she had not lied to Maria. This life *was* better than being a
living statue. She was whole and strong and she knew how to
provide the basics to live, and thanks to the magic she wished
for no more than those basics. But they would be looking
over a tremendous area for two women, and of the two she
was the one they most keenly sought. A warrior priestess is
born, anointed by the spirits, and she does not get captured
by an enemy. She fights and perhaps she dies, willingly, but
she does not fall twice into enemy hands.

The Dark Man had anointed her the Hapharsi Mother for
this time, but he did not want the true spirit of the ancient
Mother to consume her. He wanted to break down Angelique,
to remove all things of her old people and tribal customs and
rituals, to allow her to see the joy of living with power. To
tempt her, so that she would be brought to their altar and, to
get the highest pleasures and the greatest power, she would
willingly wed herself to Dobak or some other great demon
and herself perform the sacrifice.

She knew she craved the power and the indescribable
bodily pleasures that this would bring, that she had experienced second hand through the ancient Mother's spirit. But
were she not to do his bidding, he could not find her any
easier than he could find any other woman, and she could
still have some power and some pleasure, for she had no
children now to be responsible for.

She didn't really believe Maria could make it. She understood the odds, and she knew that even if Maria got all the way to the home of friends it might have been long deserted, or discovered by the Dark Man. There was every reason for the friends not to be there.

She would prepare to use the essence of this little island itself. It would take perhaps two days, and it would complete the process, for she would have to willingly undergo the full initiation of a Hapharsi Mother. She was not afraid. It was the only way. Then she could talk directly to the elemental spirits of the world, and then she could bargain for her journey. She knew still that there was a great land to the south, and that it was not unlike the land the Hapharsi had lived in. Beyond the great cities and power of the tribes of the coast there was still a huge, dense jungle, with all that she needed. With no tribe, no children of her own to care for, she could be absorbed into it, communing directly with its spirit and perhaps becoming one with nature. A soul so purified might be so clean as to rise to Heaven itself.

It was such a wondrous possibility that the only thing that kept her from doing it was her hatred of the Dark Man and what he stood for. He was a demon, certainly, and probably a prince of demons, preparing the way for the Father of Evil to come and swallow the world. She would give up all the glories of the spirit world to be a part of the battle against such a thing. Just to wound him, to spit in his eye and laugh, would be worth any sacrifice.

Maria groaned, rolled over and seemed about to wake up. Angelique suddenly realized that if, by some miraculous intervention of the Heavens, the girl succeeded, she, Angelique, would need some way to speak to them and they to her. She sat back again and let her mind flow free, and asked the advice of the spirits of the island and the air.

There *was* a way, they told her, but only if the girl was willing, and she was of the sort who disbelieved in magic even when it was done to her and in front of her face.

Maria groaned again, awoke, and stretched, and opened her eyes. "Still here," she moaned. "Still no dream. God! Am I thirsty! And hungry!"

Angelique, sitting Buddha-like, did not move, but she fought back her inclinations and forced the words to come. "I can give."

Maria stared at her. "Give what?"

"Drink. Food. But only to Hapharsi."

"Well, that may be, but you're the only Hapharsi or whatever it is here, or maybe in the whole world."

"Can make Hapharsi. Can be Hapharsi, you."

Maria, still waking up and trying not to think of what was ahead, wanted to please the woman she'd felt so sorry for. "Me? You want to make me a member of the tribe?"

"You like? I do." She was well aware that Maria had no idea of the seriousness of what was going on in so far as Angelique was concerned. If she accepted and the ritual was performed, they would be bound together. It would not cause Maria many problems, but it would place tremendous burdens on Angelique, for she would then have a child and responsibility for it. She would be bound to protect her child, Maria, and to honor her requests.

"Yeah, sure. If it makes you happy. What do I do?"

"Let mind go free. Look at me."

Thinking it a hypnotic trick again, Maria was uncertain, but she determined that this time she'd keep control.

"*Unab sequabab ciemi*," Angelique chanted, and almost immediately there seemed to be a breeze through the trees and Maria heard the rushing of wind. An air disturbance formed, apparently between them, and she stared, fascinated, even though she knew it must be some kind of hypnotic trick.

Then there seemed to be a sparkle in the disturbance, as if a hundred tiny fireflies were loosed there and held captive. It was beautiful in its own way.

Now she found herself getting up, although she was fully

awake, and walking towards and then into the whirling, intangible mass. She felt a slight tingling all over her body, and it felt good.

Now she heard Angelique chanting in that strange, dead language, as if from far off and from everywhere around her at once, and she found herself repeating the syllables with the exact same inflection. And the more she chanted, and the more she said the words, the more she seemed to understand them.

"All the spirits hear me, and the gods of heaven and earth, fire and water, Father Sun and Mother Moon, for I will swear my will." It was fascinating. She knew she could back out at any time, call it off, but it seemed both beautiful and fascinating.

"I renounce all ties to other tribes and other ways," she continued. *"I will call no woman mother but the Mother of Hapharsi, and no man father but the Elder of the Hapharsi. I proclaim myself before all a Hapharsi, and a Hapharsi only, and willingly do I become again a child, a girl, respectful of her mother and father, who are wise and powerful and the only guides to the true ways. I will respect all the ways of the Hapharsi, and keep them. So do I promise and swear, and give my blood as seal."*

Angelique touched Maria's left breast, making a scratch with her nail that drew blood, but did not hurt, then she did the same to herself, and then, in turn, they took of each other's blood with their mouths.

And Angelique said, "Girl, I name you First Love, for you are now my flesh of my flesh and blood of my blood, and nothing shall break this bond between us." She paused a moment. "It is done."

The mist and breeze and sparkles faded, and Maria found herself standing still, looking at Angelique. She looked at her breast and at Angelique's and saw that the scratches were real, although hers still didn't hurt and seemed already to be healing.

"You wish food and drink for your journey," said Angelique, and Maria started, realizing that she was understanding that crazy gibberish, not English. If this was hypnosis, she'd somehow been taught an entire language in a matter of minutes, maybe? Who knew? "Cup your hands and face me."

Feeling a bit silly, Maria did as instructed. Suddenly she felt a wetness, and looked down and saw her hands slowly filling with what looked to be clear water. She couldn't hold it for long, and she was so very thirsty, so she brought it to her lips and drank it. It was, in fact, plain water, and it was not enough.

Angelique let her repeat three more times until finally the strange woman with the power said, "Enough. It will take you where you must go." She broke off a nearby leaf and gave it to Maria. "Eat of this leaf."

Uncertain, Maria took a nibble, and was surprised to find that it was soft and somewhat chewy. It was nothing much on taste, but it seemed to have a thickness and consistency that shouldn't have been there, and it went down well. Angelique let her eat two leaves, then provided one more handful of water, and no matter how much more Maria wanted, that was it.

"You must go now," Angelique told her. "Be brave and cautious. The waters, winds, and sands will guide you to your destination, but they can do little against the Father of Evil. Beware and bring help, for the great evil is on the rise. No matter what happens to me, you must get the message through."

Maria didn't know what to say, so they kissed and hugged and Angelique saw her down to the boat. There was some water in it, but it was still more than serviceable.

"Which way do I go?" Maria asked her in that strange tongue.

Angelique pointed. "Just below the setting of the sun. Trust your feelings, for they are the wind and water helping you. Goodbye, and may the spirits favor our side."

Maria was uncertain, scared to leave and make a go of it, unhappy to be leaving this strange girl with her even stranger series of tragedies and afflictions, but more than happy to get out of there and toward civilization. She started the engine, surprised that it caught the first time, and Angelique untied the vines, and watched the small craft back up out of the tiny inlet. It was out of sight when she could hear the engines reverse, and the sound grew loud, then slowly vanished in the night.

Angelique stood there until the last remnants of that noise were gone, then turned and walked back into the miniature jungle. She knew she couldn't stay, half in this world, half in another. It was pulling her apart, and madness served only the Dark Man's ends. But the Dark Man had underestimated her strength, courage, and determination, and he had the modern man's contempt for ancient and more primitive cultures.

Primitive, though, now as ever before, was a relative term, one used by modern man, modern civilization, to judge on the basis of the way a culture looked and what a culture used in relation to their own digital watches and jet planes and computers. It did not measure the soul, nor admit that a different value system might be no less sophisticated than their own.

She removed the belt and the two hanging straw flaps that formed the breech clout, and the headband, and let them drop to the ground. She went to the center of the tiny island, which itself was barely a thousand feet across, then sat, assuming her cross-legged posture. She directed her own power inward, inducing in herself a trance-like state, slowing heartbeat and respiration, clearing her mind of all thoughts, all hopes, all fears. Time, and place, had no more meaning to her.

For a while she existed in this peaceful state, but then she began to float, like a spirit of the wind. She floated upward, out of her body, toward the heavens.

And a great presence came to her, without shape or form, and touched her. It had great power, greater than she had ever known, but it was not stained or tainted and was pure.

"I have had a long sleep," said the presence, *"yet I did not think that I would wake until judgment called, for none were left to my authority. The great, rich plains full of game have turned to sand as humans cut the timbers that preserved it; even the great jungle forests are mostly gone, and what remains is being ravaged by humans or eaten by the encroaching sands. Who is this who calls me from my slumbers?"*

"I am called Angelique, and the evil has forced me to this, yet I do not mind."

"I know you now, Angelique, better than you know yourself. Know me, then. Once I had charge of the tribes of the Earth, those who lived in harmony and peace with nature and were a part of it. The Sioux, the Cherokee, the Delaware, the Iroquois and a thousand more knew me once. So, too, did the tribes of the south, and of Africa and Asia, and the Pacific know me, and lived full lives in harmony with me. They were human, and I had my opponent, but their sins were against one another, not me, and the balance was preserved. Together we built trade routes that spanned continents; together we created great art of the Earth against the canvas nature provided. Together we built civilizations deep in the jungles and along the mighty, free river systems. War, famine, and disease were my enemies and theirs, yet so, too, did we have honor and respect.

"But then the kings and princes of the world lost their honor and respect, bending to the will of evil. They believed that their civilization was so high that many proclaimed

themselves gods and had their people worship them. The altars ran red with human blood as the demons ascended, and they traded honor and respect for power, and went to conquer and enslave the lesser peoples. They descended into the deepest pit of depravity, and mocked nature itself, setting themselves up above the heavens. They fell upon one another and destroyed one another, and so great was my pain and anguish that I destroyed what was left. I reduced their numbers so that they could no longer maintain their civilizations, and confused their minds, and sent their children back to the wild once more.''

''Are you, then, the greatest of spirits, the Father of the Universe?''

''No. I am but a pale reflection of that greatness, a servant. No more. I was a guardian, and an inadequate one. So corrupted were the souls of humanity that in the forests and the jungles they still remembered what they had once been and hungered for it. It is humanity's lot not just to suffer what fate brings, but to triumph over that suffering.

''The Hapharsi are a microcosm of the whole. Once they were a small part of a great civilization that ruled central Africa and built great cities and temples and discovered great things. Then evil corrupted the leaders, and they fell upon one another and ripped their civilization to shreds. Only scattered remnants and no structures remain. The Hapharsi, who followed one of those leaders, were reduced to hunting and gathering in a jungle that could support and sustain them only by their constant working, their constant search for food and the basics. They might have reached for harmony, and so lifted themselves out, but instead they cursed their toil and their lot. They let their groves grow wild, and they depleted their game rather than managing it; they brought themselves to the brink of extinction. And when by their own foolishness they brought this upon themselves, they blamed not them-

selves and their impulses but Heaven, and cursed it, and took the easy path that Hell always offers."

"I am saddened for them, but why must all the choices be so terrible?"

"What is is not what seems to be," it answered. "Life is choices, and most are choices of evil, or misery, or sacrifice. Misery can be a learning experience, as can joy. Evil promises immediate rewards, but an eternity of misery followed by oblivion. Sacrifice promises immediate suffering, but an eternity of joy and reward. Consider the Hapharsi. They prospered for a time in evil's service, but eventually one of the newer civilizations, one from the north, swept in and cut them down, recognizing evil for what it was. Not a man, woman, or child was spared, and the demon who they served did not intervene, but rather rode with the conquerors and ate the souls of the Hapharsi as they fell. The demon now rode with the conqueror, which promised greater rewards for it, abandoning its charges."

She went for the Hapharsi, and for the souls of the conquerors as well.

"But what of today? Evil rules much of the world and wants it all. It prepares for the final battle against Heaven."

"Evil is always with humanity, for without it how can good be determined? Today is no different than yesterday. Humanity is ruled in the main by oppressors who may not even know that they are evil. The demons can whisper words in the ears of people that are so sweet that they can believe that black is white, blue is red, and evil is good. Today there is power greater than that of the rulers of nations. Mighty companies sell weapons to rulers filled with fear of their enemies, and sell the same weapons to their enemies. They build great things for the rulers of nations, yet those things are at the expense of the people who are suffering and oppressed. Such companies take on a life of their own and thrive only in a world of evil."

And she was ashamed, because she knew the corporate symbol on those orders for guns and bombs and planes, ornate palaces and super computers.

"Your father believed that the evil crept in and took control of his great work, but he was wrong," it told her. *"Evil can not exist without human beings who embrace it. It is humans who perform the evil, and when so much evil is concentrated at one point, one focus; the ultimate evils are possible. The Father of Evil himself is drawn to such a place like a magnet, but the magnet, like the woes of the Hapharsi, was created by humans of their own free will. They had the easy choices, the simple choices. But as that evil becomes stronger, the choices of those who would oppose it also become more odious. Your father could recognize this, but not fight it, since he could not see that the conditions were of his own making. He had fashioned the beast of Hell and was content with it so long as it did only his bidding. But like the demon of the Hapharsi, it grew too strong and too ambitious, and consumed him. Now it rules, with a power incomprehensible to those who believe it serves them."*

Reduced to this, the distance between the Hapharsi and Magellan was not that great at all. *"But is there no hope?"* she asked it. *"Is this, then, the way humanity dies?"*

"Perhaps. Perhaps not. They move deliberately to structure events to fulfill a prophecy. Left unchecked, they will force the final war. In this, you are the key. No army can prevail against them. No long-range determination will break them. The choices given to the few who must fight will be increasingly severe, the price extracted for a temporary respite will be high. They can lose a thousand times. Ten times ten thousand times. They will not stop, and they need win only once. It has been thus before and will be until they prevail."

"But this need not be the time?"

"This need not be, but without shedding of innocent blood

*there is no remission. To save yourself is simply to choose
the correct path, though that is hardly simple. To save the
world requires the ultimate choice, the Messiah Choice.
Each in turn will face it, you more than once, but at the right
time and the right place it must be made by another."*

*"But we are humans, not gods! We carry the seeds of our
imperfections within us! We are no Messiahs, who can take
upon ourselves the sins of the world!"* She thought again of
her own private Hell, the hospital, the pain, the total lack of
movement, on and on, year after year. . . . She knew, even
now, that she could not make such a choice as that.

*"To gain strength and inner peace, be one with nature. To
reconcile yourself to your condition, you must accept it and
embrace it. Renounce all but nature, and gain your power
from it alone."*

"The spell can not be broken, then?"

*"Any spell can be broken, and will be. But to break it you
must face its creator, and that time is not yet, and may or
may not be, for choices lie between. It is given only to One to
know, and I am not He. If you are true inside yourself, what
matter who or what you are? Your choices will shape, but
not necessarily determine the outcome. If evil may use the
tools of good, then so the reverse is true. Merge with me
now, and be cleansed."*

And she merged and saw the world with eyes that saw
what no human's could. She saw the beauty of every glistening
dewdrop on every leaf, and the wonders of color in the
ripples of a pond. She saw the beauty in a blade of grass, and
felt the awesome power of a storm at sea. She saw and felt
the joy and wonder in the faces of innocent children of all
races and colors, and shared that wonder herself, becoming
again the child of wonder and so beholding this corner of the
dominion of God.

She walked in wild abandon with the spirits of the elements, and rode their breezes around the world. *The Earth*

was alive and still wonderful, if one but stopped to see. There was nothing that anyone really needed that nature and the spirits could not provide, yet to mask one's humanity built a wall between it and nature that obscured the basic truths. And yet, the ordeal was to come, and she was human and as weak as the others. She could deal with the mystic world, but she no longer had a place in the material one.

Maria had been piloting the boat mostly on instinct and the basic directions that were given to her—west southwest—but now she could see lights in the distance and much closer some navigation markers in the water that could only lead to the harbor in the distance.

She was amazed it was really there, and that she had found it so easily. She began to wonder, just a little, if maybe there was more to this magic stuff than she'd thought.

She got down to where she could make out the darker outline of the small and remote island even against the darkness of the night. She had no intention of coming right into town; they would almost certainly have some people watching there.

Instead, at minimum throttle, she worked her way south of the town, since it looked like there was something of a beach there, while the north edge was rocky and had lots of rocks painted white and a few battery powered warning lights.

About a hundred yards out from the beach she cut her engines entirely and tested the direction of the flow. The tide was coming in, by luck, and she was being taken towards the sandy shore.

The boat was now a liability to her, since it could easily be traced back to its origin and would raise signals all over the southern Caribbean. There were drain plugs in the deck, but they looked like they'd need tools and strength to get out and she had nothing.

She raised the rear hood and looked down at the engines.

They were tandem outboard motors, and they didn't have much gas left in them. The accelerator was a simple chain running under the floorboards to the motor throttles, though, and that gave her an idea. She pulled on the chains, getting a fair amount of slack, then tried to run them a little extra way around the metal fittings so that they kept the throttle out. It didn't hold, and she looked around. There were still some sticks and branches in the boat from their attempt at camouflaging it, and she tried and tested a couple until she got one that she felt, with a twist and a jam in there, would hold out the chains.

She then went forward, took a deep breath, and turned the key, hoping the engines were hot enough to fire with the throttles open.

They were, and did, and the boat took off, away from the beach, throwing her backwards in it. She got up quickly, then jumped overboard, not waiting to think and just praying she'd clear the engines. She went down into the water, then back up, and looked around. She heard the motor sound off in the distance and fading, then looked back at the beach. It was going to be a good half-mile swim, but with the tide.

It still took what little of her strength remained to make it, and when she stood up and walked onto the beach, she collapsed, coughing and breathing hard, and lay there for several minutes recovering, hardly thinking at all.

She knew, though, that she could not remain on the beach all night. This wasn't Allenby with its company and its guards, but it was civilization of a sort never the less.

She looked at her arm in the dark, and brushed away the sand clinging to it. Maybe it was too dark to read anyway, but she could see nothing there but a few faint marks of blue on her deeply tanned skin. The water had washed away the information it contained.

She tried to remember the words, and couldn't quite. She sat up, drew her legs to herself and put her arms around her knees and stared out at the dark sea. *Oh. Angelique! I made it but I blew it!* she thought despairingly.

And suddenly, as if in answer, the information returned. Art Cadell. American. White little house facing the sea with beach. Bessel Island, near little fishing village. . . .

Was *this* Bessel? It *had* to be. And here was the beach. But she was all in, and in no condition to go calling in any event. Sandy, nude woman who even MacDonald wouldn't recognize steps in with this story. She could see it now.

As tired as she was, she looked back up the beach towards the town and knew she had to do a little more than that. She wondered if anyone hung their laundry out to dry overnight. Even a towel would do. Then she would find a secluded spot and get some sleep. Tomorrow she would see if Mr. Cadell was here and was home, and, if so, whether this wasn't just walking back into the lion's den. It didn't matter. She had no choice.

10

A BRUTAL GAME OF CHESS

Too tired and too confused to really do much, Maria had gone up the beach a bit and found a quiet-looking part of the inner beach almost surrounded by large rocks and driftwood, and in there, in a small area of sand, she had settled down to rest and think and soon drifted off. By the time she awoke, the sun was high and very hot and she felt like a refugee from a monster movie in which she was the monster.

Being naked was enough of a handicap in itself, but having been naked and gotten out of salt water, then having salt and sand dry on her, made her skin painful and irritated. Every muscle in her body ached, and she felt like she'd been run over by a truck, while her mouth burned and tasted of acid and bile.

She managed to get to her feet and peer out, hearing the sounds of humans on the beach not far away. She looked out and saw four people, fairly young, two men and two women, frolicking in the surf and along the beach. Both sexes wore skimpy string bikini type suits that were hardly anything at all; the women were topless, which wasn't all that unusual in this area. What *was* unusual was that they were extremely

tanned but still undeniably white, a fact which marked them
as foreigners in this remote part of Bessel. She watched them
for a while with envy, feeling more and more miserable as
time passed, but they eventually grew too hot or too bored
and picked up their things and went inland.

There were some small boats out on the sea, mostly small
fishing boats and one or two tourists' party fishing craft,
but they were well out and of no real concern. She knew she
couldn't find clothing without giving herself away, and looking at the foursome gave her something of a plan, although
her body groaned and burned at the mere thought of it.

She walked out and into the water, steeling herself for the
ordeal, and went out to where it was just above her hips. It
was low tide and the sea was calm, although an occasional
wave would come in and momentarily cover her with water.
It stung at the start, but eased as she got used to it.

She was pretty much at the northern limit of habitation, so
she began to wade back towards the town perhaps a mile
away, studying the houses on the beach. There weren't many
of them, and while all were rather small and plain they were
clearly owned by people with money or influence. They were
painted various colors, but only one was white, a stucco that
had a patio jutting out almost on to the beach, its property
large enough to set it off a bit from its neighbors. She knew
that it might not be the one, that in fact there might be a
dozen more white houses further along, but she was just too
tired and sore to care any more. She felt she had done more
than she could possibly be expected to do, and at this moment she didn't even care if the Dark Man was sitting on the
back porch.

She walked out of the water and across the sands and onto
the patio area. Her only real fear right now was that nobody
would be home. Everything was closed up, but she could
hear the rumble of several window air conditioners and that
boded well. Going up to the back door, she knocked on it,

growing suddenly nervous and feeling both shy and embarrassed. Losing her nerve, even the way she felt, she hesitated to knock again, but suddenly the door opened and she was face to face with a young black woman of slight build whose eyes grew wide at the sight of the naked stranger.

"I—I'm sorry," Maria managed. "I need help. I lost my boat and I've been mostly in the water for hours. Please help me." Her voice sounded like atonal sandpaper.

For a moment, the black woman hesitated, then she opened the screen door and said, "Yes, come in." Her accent was West Indian English, and she was probably a local resident.

The place wasn't fancy, and the kitchen into which she entered wasn't really air conditioned, but it was such a relief to get out of the sun that it felt *wonderful.*

"Come—sit down on the couch in the living room dere and I will get you some water," the black woman said, sounding concerned, and leading her through a small hall to the room. It was a plain little room furnished with musty old furniture, but an ancient window air conditioner provided some circulation and relief. The couch was simply a cane affair, like the other furnishings, but it had soft cushions and backs and two small pillows and she sank into it all with tremendous relief. She felt as if she would pass out at any moment.

The black woman returned with a glass of iced tea and a cool wash cloth, and Maria downed one greedily while allowing her hostess to apply the other gently to her face.

"I am Paula Mochka," her hostess told her.

"Sis—ah, Maria Martine," she responded. "Thank you very much."

"You are burning up with de fever," Mochka told her. "If you can stand for a moment, I t'ink we first get you showered off some, den you take some aspirin and lie down a while."

She did manage somehow to get back to the tiny bathroom

with its peeling paint and cracked porcelain, but she allowed herself to get washed off, grateful beyond measure to this kind woman who could not possibly know anything about her and seemed to be in the house all alone. After, she was taken back to a small bedroom which had another old and noisy air conditioner in the window along with an unmade single bed that looked recently slept in.

Mochka gave her the aspirin with some more tea. She took them, but tried to explain a little more of what was going on, being as cautious as possible. "I was in trouble out there. . . ." she began, but her hostess cut her off.

"No more now. You rest. Beat de fever. When you wake up, den you tell me everyt'ing, O.K.?"

Even though her skin felt on fire, she was fighting off a near comatose state and she just couldn't fight any more under these conditions. She began to say something else, but everything just sort of drifted away.

She did, however, have dreams; dreams she could not fight and which she had to endure, although they faded in and out and often ran into one another.

There was the meadow and that terrible altar stone, and she was stretched out on it, bound hand and foot, naked and helpless. All around were the leering men of the Dark Man's company, and she knew just what they intended to do. She looked around, frantically, and caught sudden sight of a strange figure of a woman dressed in light blue and white.

"Mother Superior! Help me! In the same of Christ save me!" she cried, but the older nun shook her head sadly and had that stern face she always wore.

"No, no, no," responded the Mother Superior as if talking to a kindergarten child. "You've been a very naughty girl, Sister Maria, and you know it. You weren't forced onto the streets of New Orleans; you chose it deliberately instead of honest work or education, and you got what you deserved. Then you came to us to save you, and we gave you every

chance, and at the first opportunity you cast off your new habit and went back to the old ones.''

"But I rescued Angelique!"

"Angelique rescued Angelique. Nope. Sorry. Three strikes and you're out." She turned to the leering, slobbering men who didn't really have faces any more. "O.K., boys," screamed the Mother Superior, "fuck her brains out and then feed her to the devil!"

They all advanced, and the Dark Man laughed and laughed, but the scene faded and for a while she drifted.

And then Angelique's voice whispered to her, in French-accented English, "Art Cadell, Bessel Island, white house on the beach. . . ."

"Hard to believe, but her prints say she's the damned nun!" a strange male voice said casually.

"Well," a woman replied, in a clear American tone that was otherwise accentless, "if they can make a monster, I guess they can do most anything."

"Christ! She's burning up! If she gets through this she might be days coming out of it," the man noted, concerned.

"No, no!" she shouted. "Angelique! Don't have enough time to save her!"

"Hear that?" the woman asked. "I wish we had a doctor we could trust around here."

"In these sticks? Can't risk it. Just keep her cool and keep giving her what you can to break the fever. We lose her, it's all over anyway."

But the voices seemed to fade even as she protested, and in the darkness a leering, looming shape rose.

"You can't save her," taunted the Dark Man. "Why, you can't even save yourself."

It went on and on and on. . . .

It was night when she finally awoke in the same bed. She still felt terribly tired and very weak, but she looked around and saw the black woman there, asleep in a rocking chair and lightly snoring. She couldn't remember the name, but she had to communicate. She didn't even know how long she'd been out.

"Hey!" she croaked, her throat raw and sore. "Hey! Wake up!"

The woman stirred, opened one eye, and then was immediately awake and on her feet. "How do you feel?" she asked Maria.

"Horrible. Can I have some water?"

She was given some, but even the water hurt to swallow. Finally she asked, "How long have I been out?"

"Dis is de second night you've been here. You been ravin' out of your head."

"I—I guess I have. The nightmares were—*horrible*. Not so horrible as what I've seen and what I've come through, but horrible all the same."

"You come from da professor's island, I t'ink by your ravin's. You were held dere or somet'ing?"

"Sort of." She had a sudden sense of urgency. "You know a man named Art Cadell?"

"I know him. He sometime come here. Why? What you got to do wit' Mister Cadell?"

"He—he's a friend of a friend, sort of. That is, he knows somebody I have to get word to."

"Oh? And who's dat?"

"A man named MacDonald. Gregory MacDonald."

"Lot of folks look for Mister MacDonald. He very wanted man. Dey say he some kind of Russian agent, y'know. Dere is big reward for his capture."

She sighed. "I thought as much. Still, this was the only place I had and time's running out. She won't wait for anybody but him or me and I'm in no shape to go anyplace right now."

"We get some soup, maybe some fruit, in you. You'll feel

better real fast." With that, the black woman went out of the bedroom and she could hear her go into the kitchen and start rattling pots and pans. She was still out there when a man walked into the room, looking a little sleepy himself. She had never seen him before. He was black, middle-aged and somewhat distinguished looking, but dressed in a faded plaid shirt and old and worn jeans.

"Good evening, Sister Maria," he said, in a pleasant baritone. His voice was also West Indian, but highly educated and probably Trinidadan or Jamaican.

She started and felt fear rising inside her, but she knew she was too weak to do anything.

"I'm Harold St. Cyr," he said, settling down in the rocking chair. "It's Doctor St. Cyr, but don't let that fool you. It's quite literally in philosophy, not medicine."

She sank down but relaxed a bit, realizing that this house was probably used by a lot of dignitaries as a vacation retreat and he was probably the one using it this week. "I'm sorry to barge in on your vacation, Doctor."

"Oh, don't worry about it. Can you tell me from whom you got Art Cadell's name?"

"Huh? From—a friend in trouble."

"Angelique Montagne?"

She grew suddenly wary again, as Paula Mochka came in with a platter holding a bowl of soup and some sliced fruit. She didn't feel hungry, but she was very weak and knew she had to eat something.

"Yes," she replied, as Paula fed her some soup from a spoon. "How did you know?"

"Art Cadell," the doctor explained, "does not exist. It's one of several hundred names used to identify the origin of anyone just happening on a place like this. We verified that MacDonald gave it in conversation to Miss Montagne, so she must have given it to you. The only question left is whether she gave it voluntarily or involuntarily."

The soup had some effect, and she began to feel a little better inside. She wasn't dumb, either, and the implications of all this were most interesting. If they checked on the origin of Cadell, they had to check with MacDonald himself—and they would hardly use long distance communications, which went by satellite these days, to do it. Not if they were on the other side.

"She gave it to me," Maria told him. "I don't know any way to prove that, though. We escaped together, but she didn't come all the way. She's waiting for a rescue now, I hope, but she won't wait much longer."

"Indeed? Why don't you tell me your story? All the details?"

She managed a slight smile. "How do I know which side *you're* on?"

"Fair enough. You don't. And, the fact is, we've expected company here for some time, but not of your type. We felt the place was compromised, but we wished to see who or what would show up or what sort of surveillance would be placed on it. I've been spending the summer here, just waiting and incidentally finishing up my book on unique south Caribbean value systems. Not, I don't hesitate to say, soon to be a best seller, but it will save my chair at Northwestern. We'd almost given up hope that this would pay off at all, and now here you are. I'd say you should tell us what the whole story is simply because you have no choice. Either we are friends who can help you, or we are enemies in whose power you now are and who can get anything from you we wish by other means, or, if you're no use, we can simply shove you out the door, naked, penniless, on a remote little island with a population of under four thousand and a per capita income of about eight hundred dollars a year. So, let's hear the story."

And she told him, starting with her arrival at the Institute, and she spared nothing in detail, not even her encounters with the Dark Man and her fear-induced conversion to his use. He broke in only occasionally, asking a question or two, but mostly let her speak her piece. He was particularly interested in anything she could give him on the Dark Man himself, which was very little.

Angelique's transformation fascinated him, but he did not question it. He was, however, quite concerned about the thrust of the attack on her core identity.

"They are trying to reduce her to the basic primitive—emotional, not rational, living half or more in the metaphysical realm. Her lack of real life experience makes her very vulnerable to this sort of thing. When they break her, they then plan to slowly build her back up the way they want her to be. I am, however, apprehensive at the ease of her escape when she is so central to them. I fear that this may not be a victory so much as part of the process."

"Ease! I'll tell you, it wasn't easy!"

"But it was. A complex like that would have constant watches on someone so important. Now consider the result. She has been forced more and more into using the metaphysical—*their* way—to survive, and every time she does she becomes more and more like them. She has killed—not only under their control, but of her own free will—and thought nothing of it. After years of powerlessness, she has felt the heady wine of physical and metaphysical power."

"Then—it was all for nothing?" Maria felt crushed by the idea.

"Perhaps. Perhaps they have overplayed their hand. They are quite adept at doing that, believe me. Until now, we have been relatively powerless, helpless onlookers. This is the break we prayed for, but it is a dangerous game. She is the key to their plans, and she is now exposed."

Maria felt a surge of energy. "Then—you'll rescue her?"

"We will try, of course. You see, we still operate under a handicap in that we don't really know their ultimate goals, only that she is a key player in their scheme. Whoever controls her controls something of the game. She will not only have to be gotten, she will have to be removed far from here as quickly as possible. Think of it as a game of chess. Both sides are playing, their side is winning, but there is only one queen. They have elected to jeopardize that queen in the hopes of greater gains. Our highest percentage move is to remove the queen from play, thus making their winning strategy impossible."

"Doctor—can you tell me this? Is this really some kind of black magic, some horrible thing from the supernatural, or is it science gone mad? Are we dealing with men and machines whose power and knowledge is so great that they fool themselves as well as us? Or is this truly the devil's own work?"

"I wish I knew. Both God and the devil have been quite content to work through humans most of the time, so the answer to that question may in fact be irrelevant. Many definitions of magic are based upon the idea that magic is anything the onlookers do not know or understand. The line is not clear, and we argue about it constantly, but the truth is that they can do what they claim to be able to do. They can materialize monsters to kill, they can bewitch and curse, and they can change the aspects and affect the wills of other people. Give me the identity of the Dark Man, and perhaps I can give you an answer. Perhaps." He paused a moment. "How do you feel?"

"Lousy," she told him. "But I am up to whatever is necessary."

He nodded. "Good girl. Now—could you find your way back to where you left her?"

The question startled her. Until now, she had never thought of this not inconsiderable problem. "I—I don't know. I *shouldn't* be able to, but somehow I think I might. I can't explain it, and I can't know if I'm right until I do it."

He nodded again and glanced at his watch. "It's now close

to one in the morning. Dawn is about three hours away. Use the time to gather what strength you can. Paula has found something for you to wear—not much, I fear, and probably not quite the right size, but it's a slip-on dress that will give you a little protection.'' He got up. ''I must go out and make some preparations. We've had something set up on a contingency basis, if only to move you rapidly away, but now we have to activate it. We should leave as soon as possible.''

After he left, she got up, and discovered just how weak she really was. Still, with Paula's help, she made it into the bathroom. She wanted to shower if she could, to wash off the last of the sweat and grime and sand, and she managed it. Standing there, toweling herself off, she looked at herself in the mirror. She was tanned unevenly but quite darkly, and there were spots where flecks of dead skin were peeling off. The spell had held; it was still a young, pretty face that stared back at her, the face of a teen-ager.

If only they could somehow win, the mirror promised a whole new life, a total new chance. For the first time she realized that the spell was more specific, more personal, than a mere gift of youth. This was the face and body that she'd had the day she'd made her terribly wrong choice on what to do with her life. This was Maria just before the Fall.

Neither the doctor nor Paula would be coming. A couple of big, black, musclebound men rowed her out from a point well north of the town and took her in silence to the looming hulk of a good sized fishing trawler. The crew looked native and the dominant language of the decks was Spanish, but she was ushered into the cabin area and came face to face with a big, bearded white man with long hair and weathered skin. A huge black man sat off in a corner drinking coffee. He hardly glanced at her as she entered.

''If you're the nurse, you *have* changed,'' the bearded man said genially. "Please—take a seat at the table here and get comfortable. We've met before. I'm Greg MacDonald."

She stared at him wonderingly, and it took several seconds before she could see that it was indeed the detective. "You're a wanted man," she noted. "Am I supposed to trust you?"

He grinned. "Not any more than any other man." He grew more serious. "Look, here's a chart of the entire area between Allenby and Bessel. I want you to look at it and tell me as much as you can from the point of your escape through all you can remember."

She stared at the map and saw the great number of tiny islands that lay in the way, but her mind seemed oddly clear. "We came around the island here, and then headed away due north until the place was completely out of sight."

He looked and nodded. "Good choice. The big antennas can't turn and see that close in that direction, let alone shoot anything. O.K., so we go north to about *here,* then what?"

"We—we made a sweeping turn to the southwest and headed—*oh!* There are *dozens* of islands along there! But we didn't see or hit any until the one we stopped at!"

"That's O.K. Now, you say you found a sheltered anchorage. Was it right on course when you hit the island, or did you have to go around it a bit?"

She thought a moment. "We went—right, along the coast a little. But it wasn't very big. It was a slip in the rocks, nothing more. We had to grab on to tree limbs and hanging vines to get up on the island itself."

He stared at the map, then beckoned a big black man with a thick moustache dressed in a formal shirt and striped gray pants. Clearly he was an officer of the ship. "Well, Señor Garcia? Think you can pick the spot?"

The man looked at the chart, then reached under it and pulled out a large set of bound maps, each a blowup of part of the area covered by the larger chart. He flipped through, then said, "There, I think." His accent was heavily Spanish, but it was impossible to tell the country. "It almost has to be this tiny one here—San Cristobal. The name is bigger than the island."

"Señor Garcia is the navigator," MacDonald explained to her. "Sorry to be so short with introductions, but we're on a tight schedule here. Look at this and see if it seems right."

She looked. Blown up to the scale of this map, and looking down, it was impossible to tell, but she saw that there was one tiny area that was shaped very much like her tiny slip, and the profile chart indicated a table top topography with rock sides. "It might be. I can't be sure, but it's got everything."

"I will inform the captain," Garcia told them. "We will not be able to lay in close there, so it will have to be done with the dinghy."

"How long until we get there?" MacDonald asked.

"Perhaps two hours, perhaps a little less. After five, certainly."

He whistled. "That's cutting it close. We may wind up doing this in daylight."

"Then I had best get started," Garcia responded, and was gone, leaving them alone in the cabin.

MacDonald sighed and got up. "Want some coffee? I sure need some. A good stiff belt after, but coffee right now."

"No, thank you. I'm still weak and my stomach's upset." She paused, hearing the engines begin to rise in pitch, and feeling as well as hearing the increase in their throbbing speed. The windows rattled rhythmically with the *thrum! thrum! thrum!* of the engines.

He got his and sat back down. "Rook couldn't give me more than the bare outlines. Mind filling me in on the story again?"

She didn't. "Uh—but what's this rook?"

"Chess piece. He's King's Rook. I'm Queen's Knight. I'm afraid you became Queen's Pawn One."

"Who's the king, then?"

He grinned. "That would be telling. They have their Dark Man, we have our King. I wish King had the powers the Dark Man had, but he's strong enough—I hope. Now, I want to know everything, starting with just what happened on that island while I was still there."

She told him, describing the terrible rites in the meadow, the tremendous power of the Dark Man and just how convincing he could be, the whole works.

He took it all in. "Tell me—did you ever see Sir Reginald with the Dark Man?"

"I never saw him at all, except occasionally in the dining hall or the library, going from one place to another. Why? Is *he* the Dark Man?"

"I don't know. He's the instigator, the man who started all this, that's for sure. What we don't know is whether or not he's still in control of it, or whether he just *thinks* he is. Go on. You were about to tell me about Angelique."

And she told him of the nightly forays, the terrible things they were made to do, and of the final transformation of Angelique and the spells that still bound her. And when she finished he pounded his fist on the table in anger, making the whole cabin shake.

"*Damn* them!" he said in anger and frustration. "That poor girl. So we're going after somebody who's forced to look and think like a naked, stone age woman. Great!"

"She still knows it all. She might not be able to find the words for it, but she knows who she is and how she came to be that way and she'll know us, too. She hates the Dark Man. I think she'd do anything to defeat him. And, somehow, I get the feeling that as bad off as she is, she still feels better that way than the way she was. We can't know what kind of hell those seven years without feeling, without being able to move more than her head, but with the heart and mind of a young and smart girl, was like."

That sobered him. "Yeah, maybe you're right." It was trading one sort of hell for another, that was true, but there were always degrees of Hell.

"I'm not proud of my part in all of this," she told him, "but maybe somehow I can help make it right now."

"Yeah, well, don't let your guilt get to you all that much," he told her sympathetically. "I don't see how you could have done much else under the circumstances. This is a rough crowd, the most dangerous maybe that anybody's ever faced, and they're ready to spread out way beyond their current little base."

"And you—what of you during that time? They said you were dead."

"They knew better. I should have been, that's clear. I'll never know if they just built a good strong little building there or whether it was the fact that it was a church that stopped the thing. Others have been working on that question. The only thing I'm sure of is that it was real, at least for the time it was after me, and it almost got me. After they took King's Knight everybody told me to get out of there. I'm surprised they let me go as long as they did. I guess it was because of Angelique. They needed to keep *her* there until they were ready to move, and she stayed because *I* was there."

"You said they took out the other knight?"

He nodded. "Yes. Camille Jureau. He was one of the first to stumble onto a real plot, and he apparently tipped it to Sir Robert, which forced their hand and started the ball rolling. They must have figured Jureau for an obstacle, but at Sir Robert's insistence he was recalled to Brussels for consultation and to help set up an independent organization that could investigate and fight this thing. Why he came back I'll never know. He was a cocky, arrogant little bastard always real full of himself, but who am I to talk, considering how long I stayed with my neck in the guillotine? I guess we all think we're immortal.''

"And you—you know of this when you arrived on the island?''

"Only part of it. I was really ignorant until Sir Robert's murder. Then, when I was contacted by the company to investigate it, they also told me that something was really rotten there, that he and Jureau were investigating it, and so forth. I was given contact names and addresses and a method of getting information in and out using couriers and go-betweens who worked the supply ships. Sir Robert had set up the King's side; the Queen's pieces were added as we went along, starting with me. In a way, it's still Sir Robert's game, played from beyond the grave.''

"And after you escaped?" She was fascinated by it all, even if it still seemed unreal.

"I got lucky running into that trawler. I'm no big shakes as a sailing man and that sea was still rough. They put in at Port of Spain, where I was able to slip off and call one of the emergency numbers. By that time the opposition had a lot of the region well bottled up and had put a price on my head, and I didn't really want to try and run for it anyway, since that'd just take me completely out of the game. So, since that time, I've lived on various boats like this one, shuffling from one to the other before they make any major port. We have a lot of connections and some big money, thanks to Sir Robert's planning. Not that it's done much good. Allenby's been bottled up for weeks now and any time you call you get cheer and a lack of problems from anybody. I guess that damned computer can imitate anybody. Jureau is still making reports— or so it seems—and Angelique even gave a mini press conference on what it felt like to inherit all that money and take over all this. It was very convincing—I've seen a tape of it.''

"You know the doc believes we were allowed to escape," she said nervously. "I find it hard to believe, but. . . .''

"Yeah, well, I don't doubt they made you work hard on it, but he's probably right. That's why this is gonna be hairy—particularly in daylight, if that's what it takes."

"But—they can send orders to the navy to pick us all up and turn us all over to *them!* I know it!"

"Yeah, they can—but I don't think they'll take the chance. Things just might explode. Too many witnesses, too many people to doubt and maybe buck it upstairs. No, if they try anything now it'll be with their own people and as closed as possible. At least, I hope so."

And, with that, Gregory MacDonald got himself that shot of whisky and tried to relax.

The sun was not yet over the horizon, but the sky was rapidly growing light. There were signs of gathering storm clouds to the east that the marine forecasts said were heading in their direction, and the seas were already starting to be choppy as the little dinghy closed on the island. Aside from the rowers, it contained only Maria, Greg, and three submachine guns.

Maria was feeling very weak and nauseous, and the rapidly roughening sea did not help matters any, but she was determined now to see this through. She pointed to the island. "There! In back of those rocks! This is it, I *know* it!"

MacDonald frowned. "Damned if I can even *see* an inlet there. How the hell did you ever find it the first time?"

"I—I don't know. Angelique, she's got some of those crazy powers herself. Oh, I hope she's still here and all right!"

They rounded the rocks with difficulty and found the little safe cut just as Maria had predicted. She was not physically able to manage climbing up there, though.

MacDonald looked at her. "You say you can speak that crazy language?"

"Yes. She—taught it to me, somehow."

"Call to her, then. Tell her she's got to get down to us and fast!"

Maria's mind was awash with differing thoughts and emotions, and she had some trouble concentrating on that strange tongue. Finally she called out, as loud as she could, in Hapharsi, *"Angelique my mother! Come to your daughter and to friends! Come quickly, for the storms blow and the sun rises as we speak!"*

MacDonald looked at her in amazement, and the two rowers looked dubious. Though sheltered, they reached down and picked up the automatic weapons, ready for the unexpected. If somebody else had found her first, they were the fish in the barrel.

There was no response, which made them all even more nervous than they already were. "Try again," MacDonald urged.

"Come, my mother, or we all perish! Come, or we must leave you forever!"

The wind was picking up, making it more difficult to hear anything, but suddenly a voice penetrated the noise. It was a pleasant, woman's voice, saying words in a melodic tongue that was the same one Maria had used but far sweeter and more expert, like one born to it.

"They must put down their metal spears, my daughter," said the voice to Maria. *"Then I will come. They are all friends?"*

"Yes, my mother. One is Greg." She turned to the others. "You must put down your guns," she told them. "She's afraid she'll get shot if she shows herself."

"You're sure it's her?" MacDonald asked worriedly.

"I'm sure."

"No way to tell if she's under her own free will. Still, I'll signal them to put the guns down. We're dead ducks in here anyway." He gave a hand signal. "Wish I could speak Spanish, damn it all," he muttered.

Suddenly the small, dark perfectly proportioned figure of a woman appeared above. She looked at the boat, then scrambled down the side of the rocky wall as if it had a ladder attached and dropped into the boat.

All three men were shocked at her appearance, MacDonald most of all. They had been warned of this, more or less, but seeing it was something else again.

Angelique and Maria hugged one another, and then the strange exotic-looking woman took a seat next to Maria and looked back at MacDonald with recognition in her eyes and a trace of embarrassment as well.

The detective stared at the strange newcomer as the men pushed out and then fought the increasing surf back to open sea and the trawler. He found it impossible to think of her as Angelique, for not a trace really remained. She was certainly exotic looking, and attractively so, but her skin was so dark and shiny it was almost a blue-black, the deepest and darkest coloration he'd ever seen in an area where ninety percent of everybody was "black." Her hair was straight and long and even blacker than her skin. As she held on with the rest of them for dear life against the pitch and toss of the small boat, she betrayed strong muscles in her arms.

But what set her apart the most from others were the markings. Each cheek bore three stripes, each the thickness of a finger, running back nearly to her ears. The top was a deep blue, the second crimson, and the third yellow. They were regular and smooth, and slightly indented in the skin, as if a natural part of her face. Similarly, the nipples on her firm, hard breasts were ringed with the same three colors in the same order, and so, too, was her vagina, around which there seemed to be no pubic hair.

They made it to the trawler, but had some difficulty securing to the side so that they could all climb up the rope trellis let down for that purpose. The sea was getting rough indeed, and it took several tries before they could make it, MacDonald and one of the crewmen having to just about carry Maria while going up the bobbing ship's side. Angelique seemed to have no trouble at all, and helped Maria to the deck. They then made it inside the cabin while the crew tried to lift and stow the dinghy.

Finally they did, and the captain immediately started forward, turning south and west to try and outrun the storm. There were suddenly a great number of voices yelling at once in Spanish, and Garcia came in, looking worried. "Señor Gregory! Two helicopters approach with strong searchlights! We do not like the look of this!"

MacDonald immediately made his way to the door, finding it hard to walk as the boat seemed to want to move in two dimensions at once, but he made it and looked out to where Garcia was pointing. There was no mistaking their nature or their intent.

One of the choppers approached close to the ship, and it was clear that the pilot was a very good one indeed to hold that thing in these winds.

The captain pulled back the sliding window to the left of the stick and looked back and shouted something in Spanish.

"They are ordering us to turn and follow them," Garcia told him. "They want us and them clear of the storm and then we will stand to and be boarded. They say they are outfitted as helicopter gunships and in this weather are in no mood to argue!"

"I don't blame 'em," MacDonald replied. "Have the captain follow their direction for now. Have the men stand by their weapons but they are not to fire. Come on—let's go up to the wheelhouse."

As he said that, one of the helicopters let loose a tremendous but short burst, striking just ahead of the ship. There was no question that they were what they said they were. The captain didn't have to have MacDonald's instructions relayed, and he began to turn as instructed.

MacDonald made the wheelhouse and walked back to the marine radio. "This is a vessel of Panamanian registry in legal commerce in international waters," he said, trying to sound as indignant as possible. "You have no right to order us about or fire on us. This is an act of piracy!"

"So yo ho ho and a bottle of rum," somebody on the radio cracked back, apparently less than intimidated. "Now just don't give me any of that legal shit or I might put a few hundred rounds in that wheelhouse. And nothing funny, see? Each of these choppers got two rockets underneath, any one of which could blow you all to hell. Just shut up and keep off the air waves and do exactly what you're told to do."

"He does not seem surprised to hear a Canadian accent," Garcia noted. "I think we have been had, señor."

"Maybe, maybe not. We expected something like this. Don't think they got it easy up there. If you think *this* is rough, you should feel what they're feeling. Those pilots are fighting a war just to stay up at all right now." He stared at the helicopters at the window. "They got the missiles, all right, but they won't use them. If they kill us, they kill who they're after, too, and this all becomes a waste."

"It seems we could knock them down with the machine guns," Garcia noted, sounding almost wistful.

"No, not those babies. I don't know which division of Magellan they got 'em from, but those are combat choppers. Armor plate, bullet proof glass, the works. We'd need good armor-piercing stuff to get anywhere inside them. Tell the captain not to hurry, though. Go as cautious and slow as they'll allow and safety permits. If that storm comes in faster than we can get out of its way, they'll either have to break off or go for a swim."

The captain, an old hand, was already doing just that.

After several minutes in which the choppers took a real beating, the radio crackled, "Snap it up down there! You get cracking faster than that or we'll put some rounds where they'll do the most good and light a fire on your tail!'' The message was repeated in perfect Spanish, just for emphasis.

"We may have to try and knock 'em down," MacDonald said worriedly. "Let me get back and prepare the women, eh?"

He made his way back, and found them both sitting on the deck, holding on to whatever they could. As quickly as possible, he explained the situation to a very sick looking Maria, who tried to translate as much as she could.

"There are evil men in great metal birds that can shoot thousands of arrows in the blink of an eye," she told Angelique. *"They are making us run from the storm so they can take us back."*

Angelique frowned and got up, then went to the window and looked out. She knew what helicopters and guns were even if there were no words for it, and she saw that all was not perfect with their tormentors. *"How can they still fly in the storm?"* she asked, and Maria translated.

"Not very well," MacDonald replied. "They're having a worse time up there than we are here, but we're going out of the storm's path."

"She asks if they would fall to the sea if caught in the midst of the storm," Maria told him.

"They aren't made to take this kind of beating, yeah. But the storm's on a different track. We're going out of it."

Angelique cast out her mind to the things and felt the evil there, but not evil of the depth she feared. She stepped back, grabbed a rail to keep standing, closed her eyes, concentrated, and began her soft chanting.

"Spirits of nature come to the Mother of Earth. Speak to the great storm. Tell him that his power is great and we are awed by its fury and also by its beauty. Beg for his great presence to come to me."

The men on the ship and the men in the helicopters were suddenly aware of the clouds behind them. One by one, as they noticed, they turned and called to their fellows and pointed as the clouds rumbled and gathered and began to flow towards them at a fantastic speed. They seemed like something alive, something not altogether natural. In less than two minutes the storm had rolled over them like a great wave, and lightning and thunder rumbled all around them and strong rain pelted their frail vessels.

Angelique felt the tremendous power, but she no longer feared the elements. Before Greg could stop her, she opened the door and went out onto the deck and then aft. MacDonald followed her, but could hardly stand in the crash and roar of the storm that tossed the ship like some child's toy in an immense bathtub. She, however, had no such problems, her bare feet sticking to the deck and fixing her firmly.

Both helicopters were in trouble, and clearly would have broken off if they could, but they were stuck in the midst of the ferocity. It was clear that neither would probably make it as it was, but Angelique was not going to let them go that easily. She felt supercharged, a tremendous exhilaration running through every fiber of her being. At last, again, she was not victim but in total control, and she relished the power.

She raised her arms over her head, palms out, oblivious to the wind and rain and the pitch and yaw of the ship. MacDonald and some of the crew watched as a great bolt of electricity seemed to arc down and strike those arms, and the small woman was bathed in an eerie green glow, while around her danced small globes of the same green fire.

Suddenly both hands went out in front of her, index fingers pointing at the two aircraft, and from her there seemed to shoot beams of green fire, leaping from her to the two helicopter gunships and bathing them in the same green glow. There were sounds from the aircraft that carried over even the roar of the storm, moans of protest as their power and electrical systems went out, leaving them helpless, yet suspended for a moment in that green glow.

Angelique dropped her arms to her sides, and the two helicopters crashed into the sea behind the trawler and erupted in tremendous explosions, sending bright fireballs into the sky.

MacDonald was transfixed by the display and not a little scared, but he finally moved towards her, soaked to the skin, pulling himself along on ropes rigged along the trawler for this purpose. The green had faded and vanished and the globes of green fire shot off back into the heart of the storm and disappeared. She turned to him now, and he saw on her face an expression unlike he'd ever seen on a human being before, a wicked, self-satisfied grin and eyes lit with joy. She herself frightened him more at this moment than the enemy did.

Forward, the captain had not seen the full display but he'd seen the helicopters fall and heard their demise and he was taking full advantage of it. He brought the ship around into the wind and prepared to ride out the storm, but before he could do more than take the elementary precautions the storm clouds rolled back in unnatural motion, a reverse wave returning to its original course, and the wind died down and the rain stopped.

MacDonald stared into those strange, large brown eyes not quite daring to think, but he knew he had to snap out of it. With great effort he turned and made his way forward again. She followed him, holding on to the rope now herself but in a more casual manner than he found necessary. He opened the door and she re-entered the cabin, but he then continued on forward and entered the wheelhouse.

Garcia saw him, and saw his expression, but did not press it. "The radar is showing the storm receding rapidly to the northwest," the navigator informed him. "There are several large and small vessels but a few kilometers to the south, though. One or more must be the one they were herding us toward. What should we do? If we can see them, then they can see us."

The very news that they weren't out of danger yet seemed to jolt him out of his daze and bring him back somewhat to reality. "We can't afford to meet them, and they have this ship marked now. We have to—"

At that moment the captain let loose a string of Spanish that even MacDonald knew contained some choice expletives.

"Three small craft have detached themselves from the largest vessel and are headed our way," Garcia told him.

"Probably small gunboats. How close are we to the mainland at this point?"

"About thirty kilometers, señor. Over two hours in this sea. They will catch up to us before that."

He was all business now and thinking fast. This sort of situation was one in which he was at his best, and the pressure and continued danger helped shove the fear of other things back from his mind. "We're already in somebody's territorial waters. Whose?"

"Venezuela, señor."

"Get on the radio. Call the Venezuelan Coast Guard on the emergency frequency. Identify yourself, give your position, and state that you have come under sttack by pirates. Ask for protection if possible."

"But they will hear, too!"

"Yeah, I know. That doesn't matter. *Do it!*"

Reception was poor; there was still a lot of electrical interference from the storm and its aftermath, but Garcia finally got through. A Venezuelan navy destroyer answered, being closest to them, and after an exchange of positions they headed for it.

There were suddenly other voices on the channel, all talking furiously in Spanish.

"They are identifying themselves as Caribean Pact Security Forces and state that they are not pirates but in pursuit of a criminal ship. They ask that the Venezuelan forces stand down and allow them to reach and board us."

They all sweated the next few minutes. MacDonald was counting on the Venezuelan captain, who now had two different versions to contend with and had to make a decision. He did, and it was the only one he could have made under the circumstances.

"*Capitan* Gonsalves has replied," Garcia told him. "He says that this is all in Venezuelan territorial waters, that our registration checks out, and that the Caribbean Security Forces have no jurisdiction here, which is true. He demands that their forces break off and retreat to international waters. They are protesting. They do not like being told what to do." Garcia was grinning.

MacDonald turned to watch the radar screen. For a while, the three small blips continued to close on them, and he began to fear that they were going to take their chances with the destroyer. He knew that on their mother ship they were radioing for instructions and calculating the odds.

"The captain is getting very upset and a little bit nasty," Garcia told him. "National pride is at stake now. He has threatened to call for air support if they do not break off immediately and vacate the area."

For a few more anxious seconds, the blips continued to close, and were now almost certainly within sight of the trawler. Then they peeled off and took a wide circle, and reformed heading back towards the mother ship. The relief and jubilation on the bridge was a tangible thing.

Now they had only the destroyer to worry about.

11

PAST AND FUTURE

Getting off the boat was tricky, but was a well rehearsed routine by now. All along the gulf coastal area were oil platforms, many in this region no longer staffed or supported but run automatically. A few were shut down entirely, either because they had played out or gotten to a low point where they were more economically kept in reserve. They stood in the water like odd prehistoric sentinels, and the trawler entered their silent domain on its way to link up with the destroyer. In the confusion of blips on any observer's radar screen, it was possible to actually stop briefly by one of the derelicts, if only for a minute or two, allowing anyone aboard to jump off. Maria was still in no shape for this sort of thing, but she knew she had to see it out, and she explained to Angelique what had to be done.

As they came up to the small metal dock of a rusting platform, MacDonald shook hands with Garcia and then jumped over to the structure. Angelique did the same, and together they were able to pull Maria across. As soon as they did so, the trawler accelerated and swung away, still keeping close to the line of platforms though and taking it slow and easy.

"What will happen to them now?" Maria asked him.

"They'll be all right. They're a legitimate operation whose main job really is fishing—shrimp trawling, mostly—and they'll link up with the destroyer, be taken into a Venezuelan port, searched, and interrogated, then finally released. They'll head east from here along the coast to Panama, so they should be safe from retribution. Speaking of safe, we ought to get up and in. That thick cloud cover is already starting to break up, and we'll be naked to satellite photography after that."

It was a long, desolate climb up to the top of the platform on a network of ladders and scaffolding, and the thing was covered with rust and not very inviting nor really all that safe. The superstructure had been mostly dismantled and taken away for use elsewhere, leaving only a flat top of rusting metal, but just below, between the platform and the supports, was a small area that still offered some shelter. The corridors and tiny rooms looked like those in a submarine, but a couple still had serviceable cots in them and the tiny galley obviously had been upgraded and cleaned and stocked with a limited amount of canned and dry goods and one small sink actually had water.

"Go easy on that water. It's a little rusty because of the pipes but it's good. Mostly collected rain water and hard as a rock, but it'll do until we can get off this can," MacDonald told Maria.

The place was hot enough to be almost an oven in itself, yet Angelique shivered inside it. It felt cold, dead, lifeless, and the only sign of life were the massive amounts of bird droppings that covered much of the area exposed to the outside.

"What do we do now?" Maria asked him, feeling the desolation of the place herself.

"We wait. I don't know how long. Considering the welcome, they'll be cautious in coming for us, that's for sure.

We could probably go a week or ten days with the stuff that's here, but I'm afraid there's no showers and no change of clothing so it can get pretty raunchy. There's also no electricity, I'm afraid, so except for a couple of flashlights here that we'll have to be real careful using and a few camping style lanterns that are located so they won't show from the outside, that's about it. There are a few navigation lights on the platform connected to a master electrical cable running under the water, but we weren't able to find a good way of tapping them without being detected.''

Angelique said something to Maria, and she translated. "She wishes to know if we must stay inside this thing all the time. It bothers her.''

"No, just keep to the bottom catwalks, and get back in at the first sign of a boat or plane. After dark is best, but be careful. No lights outside, and none until you're well in here and away from any windows.''

It was not a comfortable time for any of them, and least of all for Angelique, who took to spending almost all her time outside, walking the catwalks and just sitting and staring out to sea. She felt very mixed up inside as well as out, and she tried to sort it out as best as possible.

Somehow, she'd always retained the romantic feeling towards Greg, always thought of him as her savior and perhaps eventually her lover, but she'd seen his face when he'd first laid eyes on her as she now was and she'd felt his fear of her, a fear that had only partly diminished. He was still the handsome and confident agent, it was true, but she was no longer of his people, his color, his customs and understanding. She had changed radically, and for the first time now she was feeling what that change really meant.

To make matters worse, it was clear that he and Maria were at least physically attracted to one another, a condition made worse by their close quarters and by the fact that they really had little choice but to go around nude. She felt, somehow, *betrayed* by both of them, the only two people she really had in the world. It was Greg whose affection, whose love, she craved, yet oddly, she knew that even had he been and done what she dreamed of she did not dare go far with him. Her power, her one edge over this modern world, was dependent on her remaining chaste from the pleasures of all men. And in that loneliness and jealousy she cast a spell, without ever really consciously realizing she had done so.

It was a dark, moonless night, their third on the platform, and Maria came to her at the far catwalk. Greg, as he did much of the time, was up listening to the small short wave receiver, getting the news and listening for a pickup cue at one and the same time. They conversed in Hapharsi.

"It hurts me to feel you so troubled, my mother."

Angelique stared out into the darkness, watching the lights of the other platforms and an occasional ship's light in the distance. "I ache with the knowledge that I am the only one of my kind," she responded. "Until now, I had not thought of this truly as a curse."

Maria, unbidden, began to rub Angelique's shoulders and back, and it felt good. "You must not think so. You are whole, and you feel, and you are attractive."

"I repulse the sight. Even the men of the boat reacted to me not as a woman but as some sort of strange thing, an animal."

"You are beautiful to me," Maria whispered, and with that and the sensation of the fingers massaging and caressing the energy flowed from Angelique into Maria, an energy born of tension and desire and feelings she did not understand.

Angelique did not stop it; in fact, she encouraged it, and allowed it to go quite far. But she did stop it, at last, using willpower to stop it short and dampen down the artificially raised ardor, and afterwards she felt even more unclean. It felt—*unnatural* somehow. Deep down, she was still the innocent small town Catholic girl and it just didn't seem right and proper to her, somehow. Perhaps worse than that, it had been artificially induced, not arising out of genuine love or even attraction. It was, however, the shock to her system that she needed.

From here on in, she would be totally chaste. The desires would be there, but those were perhaps God's price for her power and mobility. She would wait, at least until this terrible curse would be broken and she was restored to herself once more. She was certain that such a thing would happen; either that, or she would die in the assault on evil and join the spirit realm herself, beyond such things.

They came for them on the fourth night, shortly after midnight. It was a low profile jet helicopter with security-type engine mufflers that really damped, although they did not eliminate, the telltale sound of the whirlybird. The pilot was good; he landed atop the platform without lights. He was also apparently part of the organization, for although Greg and Maria had re-donned their clothes, such as they were, he didn't bat an eyelash at the sight of Angelique.

Maria in particular had worried that the helicopter might not be in friendly hands, but Greg had no problems. He apparently knew the pilot and the timing was right on the dot.

The only problem they found was in getting Angelique comfortable. The seats were upholstered in fabric, and it stung her after a while. Greg finally figured out a solution by taking a fair number of papers from the cabin—some old newspapers, sheets from the pilot's clipboard, anything—and lining the seat. It seemed to work, and then they were away as fast as possible, the pilot skimming the surface of the sea at or below the level of the oil rigs to avoid any hostile radar.

Greg took the seat next to the pilot, and as he flew they talked.

"Sorry it took so long, but it's been damned complicated,

or so they tell me," the pilot told him. "You all are hotter'n a firecracker in this part of the world. Then they had to figure out a meeting place everybody could get to that was far enough away from here that they'd find it hard to figure, and still met the little lady's special needs."

They were soon over the Venezuelan mainland but still flying, in just about pitch darkness, at close to treetop level.

"How are they going to get us out of here?" Greg asked him.

"Old private airstrip up ahead a few miles. It ain't much and it's mostly dirt. These days it's used for smuggling. Drugs, that kind of thing, you know. The local authorities can be persuaded to look the other way on it once in a while, if you know what I mean. We got an old crate in there waiting. No seven forty-seven, mind, just a hunk of junk, but it'll get you where you got to go."

Within minutes, they set down at the field, a dark and forbidding strip hacked out of the jungle and lying between nasty looking hills.

The plane waiting was what some folks would call an antique flying boat. A war surplus HU-16 seaplane, it was impossible to say during just which war it had seen active duty. Able to land on both land and sea and get in and out of places with short, tight runways, it had the large boat-like body and overhead wings with pontoons so familiar to navy war movies, and its two great prop-driven engines were almost as loud inside the plane as outside, but it was surprisingly roomy inside, if militarily spartan.

The two pilots were both middle aged and looked like retired military, but they were long enough out of it and jaded enough to look like they slept in their clothes and peeled them off anually for showers.

The older and grayer of the two shook hands with Greg. "I'm Mitch Corwin, and that's Bob Romeriz. Welcome aboard Air Nowhere."

"Glad to see anybody," MacDonald assured them. "You know the score?"

"All the way. That her? Wow. . . . O.K., no more comments now. Pile in and let's get the hell out of here. We're cleared from Caracas to Kingston, where we'll take on fuel but nothing else. Then we go up the coast with fuel stops every six hours. There's water in the cask in back and Dixie cups next to it, and there's cold box lunches and beer in the coolers there, and if you got to go there's a porta-potty in the back. Assuming no problems, the whole thing should take forty-four hours give or take, allowing for the fuel stops. These babies don't go real fast and they're not designed for comfort but they'll get you there in one piece."

They got in, but the old fabric seats proved impossible for Angelique, and she wound up sitting on the floor of the aircraft, simply hanging on to the metal seat bases as they took off.

There was, in fact, a great deal of noise and vibration, but the ride itself was fairly smooth and stable. They munched cold chicken, drank a little beer, and mostly otherwise kept to themselves during the trip.

They landed at a general aviation strip outside Kingston while it was still dark, but aside from staying down low inside the plane there was no trouble. The plane had a manifest and flight plan that was proper and provided a stop for refueling but no other purpose in Jamaica. The lone, bored looking customs man was there only to make certain nothing unauthorized got in or out of the plane; he couldn't have cared less what it carried and did not try to look inside.

It was past dawn on a gray, overcast day when they made their second stop, this one in Cancun, on the Yucatan Peninsula in Mexico. Again, with just a refueling and a refiling of some paperwork, there was no hassle. From that point they used small, private airfields, heading northwest across Mexico. For something planned in a hurry, it was certainly well organized.

"Oh, we do this all the time," Corwin told them. "It's the way you make money with a small outfit like this. You prepay the bribes and have a lot of options to move."

"What do you usually carry?" Greg asked him.

"A little bit of everything. Dope of all types, of course, and sometimes wetbacks and other times it might be political refugees from Latin America. We had two trips getting pharmaceuticals to Cuba, if you believe that. Those are hairier than the drug stuff but they pay best of all."

"I'm surprised you haven't gotten caught and strung up by now no matter what your contacts," Greg noted. "You're not in a long-life type of trade here."

"Well, hell, we're equal opportunity, see? I mean, we've run stuff for the CIA, so the U.S. stays off our back or covers for us. We've run stuff for the Reds, so we don't get no flack from the Cubans or Nicaraguans or anybody like that. Almost every government's used us at one time or another, and we're a special favorite of certain Mexican politicians."

"Seems to me you could afford better airplanes," Maria noted.

"Oh, hell, honey, we got any kind of plane you want for anything, and old pilots to fly 'em. This was the best overall for this job, considering that turkey airstrip we started at and where we got to wind up."

"Just where *are* we winding up?" MacDonald asked.

"Well, sir, near as I can tell, they got to thinking. They needed a place with a big international airport so's everybody who needed could get in and out, and they wanted a kind of place folks might go anyway. Now, add to that someplace where they wouldn't give a second glance to your little tattooed lady there, beg pardon—no offense meant. If she was dressed at all, that is."

They flew the entire distance up the California coast well out from shore and low enough to be out of most of the air traffic control radar. They landed on the water for the first time over a hundred and fifty miles out in the Pacific off the California coast, but near a small chartered tanker that was there to give them more gas. From that point, they disappeared from anyone's clear trace, landing in the water again, this time about twenty miles off the coast and in daylight. There they unstowed and assembled and inflated a large orange life raft complete with outboard motor, and all, including the pilots, transferred into it.

Away about a mile, Romeriz took out a small metal box, raised an antenna, then flipped up a cover to reveal a single contact switch. He pulled it down, and two very small muffled explosions could be heard in the distance, panicking some gulls.

"I hate to lose her, but we can't afford to keep her any more," Corwin told them. "She'll be on her way to the bottom now with any luck, if those explosive boys were right, and nobody'll ever know we were here."

They put in at a small, deserted beach of black sand, then deflated the raft and took it back out into the water, letting the motor's weight sink it to the bottom.

Air Nowhere certainly knew its business. They walked over a huge amount of driftwood piled up in back of the beach and then up an almost overgrown trail to a small turnout near a two-lane road. A small camper truck was parked there, but it didn't seem to bother the pilots, and Romeriz went up, selected a key off his key ring, and unlocked the thing. They waited for some general traffic to pass, then got Angelique and the others inside.

"*This* we will not sink or blow up," Corwin told them. "It was rented fair and square in Astoria for a week and it's going back there when we're through. Settle back—we've still got quite a drive. Either of you want to take the wheel, you're welcome to do it. After we drop you off, this gets turned over to an innocent and unsuspecting family that wants to drive north along the coast road in a camper, and they'll check it back in. It's rented in their name, so anybody who wants to trace this will have one hell of a time proving anybody was ever in it that they want.''

And that was how they got Angelique to San Francisco.

"Outside of theaters and espionage circles I don't think there'd be much of a call for this stuff, eh?'' MacDonald commented, applying another batch of a seemingly clear liquid to his hair and beard and then showering it off. It had the effect, over a period of time, of turning dark hair gray and doing so convincingly. Applied to both hair and beard, it had the effect of adding twenty years to his apparent age.

"Rather simple stuff, old boy,'' replied a tall, distinguished-looking man in his sixties or early seventies. He wore an aloha shirt and brown slacks, but somehow he still looked quite the British civil servant which he used to be.

Lord Clarence Frawley, who insisted on being called "Pip'' by everyone unless under formal circumstances, had quite a lot of experience in that end, being, for some eleven years, the real-life counterpart of James Bond's legendary "Q'', the master of gadgetry for spies. His own Ph.D. was in chemistry, but he knew an incredible amount about almost everything in the sciences. He had not, of course, been the one man show of the cinema, but rather the administrative head of a research-and-development wing that employed only the best and the brightest and the most secure. A staunch materialist and top scientist, he'd been one of Sir Reginald's bosses at one time when the renegade computer genius had worked for the British government and he was also familiar, as a prior Fellow of the Institute, with the actual layout of Allenby Island.

For that reason, he was Queen's Rook.

The house itself was quite large and set back from the ocean, but also set apart from any other houses atop a large hill about an hour's drive north of San Francisco. The place itself was actually owned by a Hollywood writer who leased it out for the six months of the year when he had to be in Los Angeles. None of them had ever heard of the writer, who apparently wrote television spy shows for some series or other and had gotten his start as the author of a series of spectacularly successful low-budget hack and slash horror movies, and none knew how the house had been secured, except that it had been done by agents of the King.

Pip fixed himself a whiskey and soda and sank down on the couch. "We've got the tests back on her, and they're quite amazing," he said simply.

Greg MacDonald, equally relaxed but in a bath robe, joined him. "How's that?"

"Well, the fingerprints are certainly hers, and I think it's pretty certain that she is indeed Angelique Montagne."

"Well, I'm certainly glad to hear that. Otherwise this was all one hell of a waste."

"The bone structure, cellular structure, and the like though, is simply amazing. They didn't merely give her a disguise. As near as we can tell, she is *genetically* what you see. That, and our mysteriously youthful nurse, tell us a lot."

"Such as?"

"Well, they can really do it, that's what. Someone, sitting up there, using that marvelous computer, found a tremendous breakthrough. The implications are *enormous!*"

"And scary."

"Well, yes, that too," he agreed, accepting the idea almost as an afterthought. "I can't see any other way to do it but to somehow encode a human body inside a computer, every little bit of it—and then introducing whatever physiological changes the programmer desires and then recreating the person with the changes. It's energy into matter with the most complex organism we know—and it's *alive!*''

"Well, maybe," MacDonald responded. "But if that's the way they do it, why keep the fingerprints? And why worry about Angelique at all? They could just take one of their own, change her into Angelique so absolutely that nobody could prove any difference, and go on from there. All this makes no sense if you're right."

"Exactly so, my boy," came another, deep, melodious British voice behind them. Into the room walked Lord Alfred Whitely, retired Bishop of Burham at Yorkminster, professor emeritus of theology and philosophy at Christ's College, Oxford. "One can never trust a Cambridge man to think things through."

The Bishop was about the same age as Lord Frawley, but round-faced and hawk-nosed with thick white hair and a ruddy complexion. The Bishop was also wearing very unclerical red plaid Bermuda shorts and a tee shirt which read, "I left my cash in San Francisco."

"And I suppose you have a better idea?" Pip asked sarcastically.

"Why of course! Researchers on my end have come up with wonders. But do go on. I would like to hear what you've found—excluding the speculation, of course, on miraculous and vaporous gadgets that don't exist and don't make sense."

The look the Bishop got would have fried an egg.

"Well," Pip went on, "we also discovered a legitimate physiological cause for this aversion to most materials. It's a definite series of allergies, far too severe to be treated without long hospitalization and lots of experimentation, but we tested a number of things after wondering why she didn't come down with problems using the straw and the like. That suggested that there were things she could tolerate, and we found one that works."

"Oh, really?" Greg was very interested. "What?"

"Silk. Real silk, not the synthetic variety. We also discovered a range of non-alkaloid dyes that could be used, and even now we've got folks working on things. We've taken many fittings, and perhaps we can have something this afternoon. The real problem is that we must tailor with silk thread as well. Do you know how bloody difficult it is to get that much natural silk these days?"

"The facial tattoos, I fear, are permanent. We can't figure out even now how they were done. Those long rectangular stripes are actually set into the skin, for example, as if the face was actually molded around them. They're thick and solid, although pliant. They'd have to be removed surgically and the face would be a mess. The scars would never color, either. Still, it's a small price to pay if we can get her dressed and allow her some mobility."

"What about the language? Anything on that?" MacDonald wanted to know.

"Well, whatever hypnotic conditioning techniques they use, they're quite sophisticated and quite probably drug reinforced. All the information, all that she's ever been or known, is still there in her head, but it can't be fully accessed and the conditioning is so deep that she is convinced that nothing can be done about it. It's like the old voodoo thing in Haiti where someone makes a doll of you with some clippings of your hair and the like. Do what you will with the doll and nothing happens. But *show the victim* the doll and do something, and it happens to the victim. Pain, crippling, even death—because the victim knows and believes in the power. She believes. She had a religious, somewhat mystical outlook in her upbringing to begin with, I believe. Raised in a convent and all that. It'll be hell to shake her out of that belief. Best we leave it alone and let it come to the fore in social situations. Once she inadvertently reads a sign or understands a comment in

English or French, such as a danger warning or somesuch, it'll all come back.''

"Perhaps," Bishop Whiteley commented. "If, indeed, that's all it is. I feel very sorry for the poor child, though. Still, she's better off as she is and with us than with them, that's certain.''

"So how has your God Squad been coming along?" Pip asked him. "Any results as yet?"

"Well, the plane with the latest information arrived this morning. Damned nuisance, having to do all this direct and without using long distance lines or direct computer terminals, but it's necessary. We don't wish to tip our hand.''

Greg looked at him quizzically. "Just what *have* you been up to, Lord Bishop?"

"Pip calls them my God Squad. Actually, they're some very talented young people working on a continuing project for me at Oxford. Let us face it, my boy—if *they* have a computer, then *we* must have one, and one which can be cut off, in whole or part, from the international telenet. This project's been ongoing for years, and it's finally starting to pay off.''

"Oh?" Greg was curious. This was, after all, the man Sir Robert was told was the greatest expert on cults and mysticism in the world. That was why, although Sir Robert had never lived to meet him, much less recruit him, he was now Queen's Bishop.

"In many ways, it's the counterpart to Sir Reginald's little project. Um—do you know why I was made Bishop of Durham? And why I was so quickly and somewhat forcibly retired?''

"I admit I don't. I'm afraid the Anglican Church isn't my strong point.''

"Indeed. I don't think it's mine any more, either. You see, lad, it's a state religion, so it must accommodate a tremendous range of religious views. The Durham seat has always gone to an academic, and most of the academics have been, shall we say, on the radical left of theology. Our brothers here, the Episcopals, are called radicals because they ordain women and in some cases even homosexuals of both sexes and because they go all out for radical causes, but they're mild compared to the old mother church. Not one of my three predecessors believed in the virgin birth or the divinity of Christ. My immediate predecessor, in fact, saw religion as an ethical guidance system and believed that whether or not God existed, He was irrelevant."

"Eminently sensible," remarked Lord Frawley.

The Bishop gave him a frown. "Pay no attention to him. He was Labour, of all things."

Greg decided to say nothing. His own political affiliation was with a party at least as leftist as British Labour.

"At any rate," continued the Bishop, "God may install vacuous clerics, but He keeps hold where it counts, with the parishioners. There was finally such a hue and cry and actual mass walkouts from services that the Archbishop finally decided to fill the next Durham bishopric with me. Now, I'm the true radical in the Church. I believe in the holy Catholic Church, in the virgin birth, the divinity of Christ, the resurrection and the existence of both heaven and hell. But, most importantly, I believe in the existence of evil and the reality of sin."

"In other words," Pip injected, "the Bishop isn't Tory, unless you count one who would be at home most in the court of Henry the Seventh a Tory."

"No, no, Henry the Eighth," Whitely retorted. "I picked the correct church. But, you see, they couldn't keep me shut up and on track any more than they could keep those social reformers' mouths shut. I began to speak from the pulpit against the way many of the Church leadership had strayed, and had the temerity to suggest that anyone who professed not to accept the trinity and the resurrection should be excommunicated and told to join the Unitarians. I drew quite a following, and enormous pressure to resign. I did so, not because I was wrong to do it and say it, but because I couldn't get any of it through their thick skulls. They feared I was starting a revolt, a cult within the church, to gain personal power. Never once did they even consider my actual arguments! Their minds were so small and so limited that they simply couldn't believe that someone would act out of Christian faith and devotion; they could only interpret all my actions in the same way *they* thought—as petty power politics. I certainly knew how Henry and Martin Luther both felt in their day. One does not leave the church out of faith. One turns around one day and realizes that the church has left *him*.''

''All this is well and good,'' Lord Frawley said sourly, ''and I'm sure we will all buy and avidly read your autobiography, Alfred. But what is the point?''

''The point, dear boy, is the whimsically named God Squad project at Oxford. There we have our own computer— not as good or as fancy as the one on Allenby, I daresay, but adequate—and some really bright young programmers who are also solid Christians. We've been pouring in, and classifying, and doing comparative analysis, on a tremendous mass of religious writings through the ages—and not just Christian, either. We ask questions, and if the question is valid and the information is sufficient and the program is good enough, we occasionally get an answer. Well, with the debriefings and other information provided us, and what theology we can glean from what we've seen them about on Allenby, we have some answers, including a couple I suspected the moment I first saw that photograph of the Institute.''

Both Greg and Pip were interested now. ''Go on,'' MacDonald urged him.

''All right—let's go back to the beginning. Sir Reginald's brother is caught up in this Satanist thing and perhaps drags his younger brother into it. At any rate, Sir Reginald is left this huge library of cult, occult, and Satanist lore, and because he has this enormous project and this way to feed information in huge doses into a computer and store it in compressed form, he does so with the library. He can then sell the physical library at Sotheby, which he does, and distance himself from it while still having all of it."

"We already had that much," MacDonald told him.

"Well, yes. Now he plays around with it, doing the sort of correlating we're doing at Oxford, but he can only get so far until he's offered the job on the Magellan artificial intelligence project. They build this ironically named SAINT on Allenby—I'm sure they must have worked to get that acronym—using the Japanese technology, and all goes swimmingly until Sir Reginald, on his own, dumps his huge file of occult material into the computer in his own private area. Now, I'm told this computer actually thinks—not in the way *we* do, but the end result is the same."

"That's correct," Lord Frawley told them. "That's exactly correct."

"But the thing's still a machine, and that's all it is. Garbage in is still garbage out, but it has no way of really telling what is and what is not. Now Sir Reginald uses as his hypothesis for his own program that all of the material he's put in it is actual, is real. The computer is told that it contains basic truths, things it is to assume as givens. Do you follow me so far?"

Frawley remained silent, deep in thought, but MacDonald nodded. "I think I see. It was told to believe it, so it did. So what? It's still only going to use it to solve Reggie's arcane little problems with the occult."

"I think it went further than that. Remember, there is one difference between this computer and the one Sir Reginald used originally to compile the information, the same difference that it has with *my* computer. Unlike those, it *thinks*, it *reasons*. But it's a box, an assemblage of silicon locked in a room.'' He reached over to one of the end tables and picked up a red-bound book, opened it, and paged through it to a page near the end.

"I thought about this almost immediately,'' he told them. "Now, listen. 'And I saw a beast rising out of the sea, with ten horns and seven heads, with ten diadems upon its horns and a blasphemous name upon its heads.' '' He paused a moment. "Now let's skip down just a bit. 'Men worshipped the dragon, for he had given his authority to the beast, saying, 'Who is like the beast, and who can fight against it?' '' He sighed, then went on.

" 'And the beast was given a mouth uttering haughty and blasphemous words, and it was allowed to exercise authority for forty-two months. . . . Also it was allowed to make war on the saints and to conquer them. And authority was given it over every tribe and people and tongue and nation, and all who dwell on earth will worship it, every one whose name has not been written before the foundation of the world in the book of life of the Lamb that was slain. If any one has an ear, let him hear: If any one is to be taken captive, to captivity he goes; if any one slays with the sword, with the sword must he be slain. Here is a call for the endurance and faith of the saints.' ''

"Very instructive,'' Pip noted. "Now what's the point of all that mumbo-jumbo? What is that you're reading, anyway?''

"The Bible, old man. Revised Standard Version, which is not as melodious, but it's good enough. *The Revelation to John,* also known as the *Apocalypse*. The final authority even for any Judeo-Christian based occultist. Now consider what I've read. There are a million interpretations possible and ten million have already been made through the ages. Put it together with all that Satanist claptrap, sew it all up, assume it as real, and we have our SAINT looking at itself. I can tell you still don't see at all. Go get that photograph of the Institute.''

Greg got up, went into the study, found it, and brought it back. It was an aerial photo used by the company in some publicity shots. It showed the buildings of the Institute surrounding the great antennas of the computer.

''Behold the seven heads of the Beast,'' the Bishop told them.

''Hmph!'' Frawley snorted. ''And where's the ten horns?''

''Inside the seven heads. All have single feeder horns for sending and receiving, except the ones on each end and the one in the center, which look slightly different and have two apiece. That's ten 'horns,' as I believe they're called sometimes. Now consider what they do. They listen to and talk to most of the world, including the Soviets whether you deny it or not. Our modern world today still has the bulk of its people in subsistence life living as their ancestors did, but even the most primitive of nations is dependent now on the computer and on telecommunications. All international banking, most military work, most diplomatic work, is done that way. News, television, radio, telephone and telegraph—it's all done by computers via satellite. All the nations of the Earth now bow down and worship their keyboards, their disk drives, their terminals and telecommunications programs. We're so dependent on them, and so completely obedient to them, that we follow them as if our very lives depended on it. Computers are taken as best testimony. I'm *still* getting bills from Harrod's for stuff I never ordered and they *agree* I never ordered. But I shall still be hauled into court one of these days for not paying for it. As for the blasphemy, I can think of worse things, but the word SAINT written inside each one of the dishes is good enough I should think.''

''What are you saying?'' MacDonald asked, confused. ''That SAINT is the devil incarnate or something?''

''No, I'm saying that it reached that conclusion on its own.

What few criteria didn't fit it arranged to fit. It believes that it is the Beast of the Bible, the terrible dragon, the serpent of Eden incarnate. Now, tell me—this master telecommunications network, this worldwide super system. How long has *it*, rather than SAINT, been active and operational?"

MacDonald thought a moment. "Well, SAINT's about five years old, but the master network was installed, oh, about three and a half years now."

"Not about. Exactly."

He strained to remember. "Um—operational date was, I think, three years ago last May. Maybe April."

"Could it have been April thirtieth?"

"Uh—yes, now that you mention it, I think it *was* the last day of April. Huh! Three years to the day before Sir Robert was murdered."

"Indeed. Walpurgis. The night of that date is particularly powerful in Satanist lore. And six months later, October 31, is All Hallow's Eve, another important Satanist date, although no more prime than others. Still, the last day of October of this year will mark the forty-second month that the telecommunications network has been in existence. So the Beast will have reigned, and set up, and caused its evil for forty-two months at that time. Then will be the beginning of the end of the world. Then it will delegate its powers, relinquish them to the one who will lead the world to Armageddon, the last war. That person will be the Antichrist."

"You mean it expects to anoint a human being, the Antichrist, on Halloween?" MacDonald felt a little ill. "And that person will lead the world into—atomic war?"

"I fear so. That's why it was so circumspect up to now and why at this stage it is moving much faster."

"And who will this be? The Dark Man, whoever he is?"

"I think not. We've done a good deal of thinking on this, and come up with the usual hundred theories, but we must factor in how this is progressing and with whom. Remember, we're not working so much on what the full literature says, in allegory and symbolism, but on how this literal machine interprets and acts upon it. I believe I have its monstrous scenario, which explains the rest, but I want to check and double-check everything before throwing it on the table.''

"So what we have, then, basically, is a mad computer," MacDonald said, thinking it all over. "But how does this explain invisible monsters and this great power they have over people's bodies and minds?"

"Science," Lord Frawley stated flatly. "Allenby is a think tank for the west's greatest scientists and engineers and theoreticians. All of that work, some of it considered so far out that no government or corporation would finance what would be necessary, went into SAINT, and SAINT has access to the full resources of Magellan. We have no idea what incredible things were worked out on that computer and using graphics models. Most of the great minds involved probably believe the work is still in the theoretical stages, but that's where they have the edge. They can send an apparently valid order to a thousand places, each building and testing small components of a system, all cloaked by national security seals, and then assemble it when and where they wish. I find it difficult to believe that a computer such as SAINT could act as you describe unless told to do so, but, much as I hate to admit it, Alfie's got the basics down. I think you'll find humanity more than capable of providing sufficiently demented brilliant minds to carry it out with tools like SAINT, alas. It's actually an old story—the misuse of breakthrough technology for evil ends—but we have progressed so far in our knowledge and resources that the potential for this dwarfs Hitler.''

"Perhaps," said the Bishop. "Perhaps. But there are inconsistencies, holes in it all, as our young friend here pointed out. There's no room up there for secret laboratories and wide scale experimentation on people. It is a close community and is rather open to all. A think tank, not a place for experimentation. I've seen the blueprints. There is no way such labs could have been added without everyone noticing; they take time to build and expert, specialized staffs to maintain. No, my friends, this is the real thing. This is Satan's work, working through men as he always does. People will regard the Antichrist as a great human being capable of miracles and speaking in God's name. Our materialism, the materialism of our society, leads us to reject the truth when it stares us in the face. Hell has been handed the opportunity and the method and it is taking advantage of it. Do not dismiss their off-handed powers lightly or try rationalization too much, or we shall lose.''

"Oh, Willie, enough of that spiritualistic clap-trap,'' Frawley snorted. ''Next thing you'll say is that since it's in the Bible we shouldn't stop it, that it's our duty to let the world be destroyed or dominated by these madmen.''

"No, we must try and prevent it at all cost. God is not as absolute as all that. Men and women must struggle to the last breath against Satan and retain their trust in the Almighty. God's mercy saved this brave lad in the church from their pet demon. Still, I can not deny that I worry about our role in this.''

"Eh?'' MacDonald felt like an observer at a tennis match.

"The beast shall be delivered a mortal wound by the people of God, and that wound will be healed, or so it says. The beast will be apparently vanquished, then resurrected by the Antichrist. We've come far, gentlemen, and we've accomplished a lot under their very noses, but I worry that this is partly playing into their hands. I can't help but wonder if we are the instruments that are to mortally wound the beast in God's service. We could very well triumph in this and actually advance their own mad cause.''

*   *   *

After so long sleeping on hard straw mats or the harder ground, Angelique found it next to impossible to sleep on a bed even when it was covered with a silk sheet. They had made her slippers which allowed her to walk through the whole of the house, which was mostly carpeted, and that certainly had lifted her spirits, but the clothing was more important to her, as it restored a sense of both freedom and dignity.

She stood there as Maria tied off and put the finishing touches on a beautiful light blue silk dress. It had been designed as a *sari,* and it gave her an exotic, third-world appearance that seemed almost natural in an international and cosmopolitan setting. It took some time to get used to moving in it, feeling something soft against the skin, but it felt almost sensuous. With a little help—some cleaner and polish for her jewelry, which was welded on, and some dark red lipstick, and a touch of exotic Oriental perfume, she hardly knew herself looking in the full-length mirror. The girl that she saw there was yet a third *persona,* not the crippled and defenseless girl from Quebec nor the priestess of some ancient time, but rather an attractive, exotic, even sensuous woman from some far off land, who looked quite foreign but even more mysterious and sensual for all that.

The men of the house, even MacDonald, were equally impressed and affected by it, and by the inner change it seemed to bring in her. She felt human again, part of the human race, and it showed.

With Maria's help in translation, they had quickly worked out a somewhat elaborate sign language for her, so she had a method of communicating even with those she no longer could understand. She was now feeling somewhat irrepressible. She wanted to feel some of that freedom in more than this cloistered setting. She wanted to go out and see this place, this new corner of the world.

At first they were hesitant, but they realized that no one

can be a freak and a specimen but so long without going mad. She needed to reclaim her humanity.

The first few forays were brief and in a lot of company—a walk down the narrow streets of Sausalito, feeding the birds on the pier, eating ice cream bought from a vendor. She drew some stares, it was true, but also a lot of admiring glances from strangers, and after she saw some of the normal denizens of the Bay area in their crazy costumes and painted faces, she realized why the location had been chosen.

Ultimately, one of the staff would drive just her and Maria into the city itself. She liked the feel of San Francisco, and liked browsing in the shops, particularly in the silk shops of Chinatown. Maria was always there, dressed in a curly blonde wig and dark glasses, the worldly-wise guide.

Still, she felt only a visitor here, not a part of things. She could read none of the signs, understand none of the prices, and could make no sense at all out of the ceaseless babble around her.

One evening in late September they were walking back to the car as it was growing rapidly dark. They had limited themselves to the daylight, mostly for safety's sake, but Angelique found she had no sense of time at all and Maria had lost all track of it. The area where they'd parked seemed now full of shadows, dim and deserted.

They didn't even notice a group of four big, young men on a street corner until, when they were actually at the car and Maria was fumbling for the keys, they were suddenly all around them in the otherwise deserted lot.

Strong hands pushed both women with force up against the car and then turned them around. The four stood there, grinning and leering, and there were knives in the hands of two of them.

"Look, you can take the money, the car. Just go and leave us alone," Maria told them, trying to sound brave when she was actually scared to death.

"Yeah, well, maybe we take more than that, babe," said one, obviously the leader. "What's she? Some kind of *Af*-frican princess or somethin'?"

"Y—yes. African. She doesn't speak any English."

"I never had no *Af*-rican meat before," one of the others noted. "Not the genuine article. And you, babe, you look good for the bunch of us yourself."

Angelique could not make out the words, but she felt almost overwhelmed by Maria's terror and there was no mistaking the intent of the men. She repressed her own fear and mentally called for the spirits to attend her, even in this desolate and unnatural jungle.

One man reached out to undo Maria's jeans, while another closed on Angelique with intent clear in his mind, and something snapped inside her.

Feet shot out powerfully into one man's stomach, knocking him back into the one behind. Somehow, in one motion, Angelique had landed on her feet with the knife from the first one in her hand. It was a strange sensation; she was working on instinct and with such speed that the men all seemed to be moving in extreme slow motion.

The knife plunged into the one closest to Maria while Angelique's body knocked the other away. Although tiny, Angelique had tremendous power and speed. Her *sari* unraveled and fell away, and as they were getting up to come at her she was already in their midst. She leaped like an antelope, a foot striking one's Adam's apple while the other came down, maintaining perfect balance. She whirled, and before another could leap on her the knife in her hand whirled, too.

Maria watched, stunned, unable to believe what she was seeing, in spite of knowing that Angelique had taken care of the two guards in the boat house back on the island. This was unnatural, perfect; Angelique was a killing machine and she was enjoying every second of it. The sight of it, the combination of the attack and her friend's response, and the welled-up tension of the past weeks all seemed to gang up on her at once, and she panicked and started running blindly away from the parking lot towards the street and people through an alleyway.

Angelique was on such a high that she didn't even notice, but now, standing over the bodies of her victims, she looked around and saw nobody there. She was suddenly aware once more of where she was and what she had just done, although she could still see no alternative. She knew, though, that this place would not stay deserted for long, and that when the authorities came they would find her and take her in and there would be fingerprinting and descriptions that would go out across the country and would be seen and heard by the ever-present listeners even on their remote island. And the Dark Man had a very long reach.

She looked around, found the crumpled *sari* and hastily moved off into the shadows, clutching it. Only in the safety of the darkness did she pause and retie the thing as well as she could manage. She had had a lot of practice. The whole thing was held in place in the end by one inner safety pin that had given way at her first leap. Fortunately, the pin had remained embedded in the cloth.

She knew she had to get out of there and fast. She couldn't waste time looking for Maria, not now, and she was sufficiently exotic that even if they discounted the idea that such a small woman could have taken and done in all four attackers they would run her in on general principles.

There was, and had always been, a contingency plan in case of any separation. There was a place where far-off people visited, the Place of the Fishers, which was always brightly lit and was right on the water. If anybody was separated, they were to go there—Maria had shown her the exact spot—and wait near the old sailing ship until help came. It was an open area, so someone could observe the spot without actually being there and thus make certain of rescue before exposing yourself. But she was not near the water, but well into town, in the places of business and guest houses rising to the sky, and it was dark, the high buildings and city lights obscuring any view even of the sky and moon.

She turned a corner and found herself on a hilly street filled with pedestrians and horseless wagons with bells and bright, garish lights, and she was alone, with only a rumpled *sari*, hopelessly lost and confused, with no command of any language she might encounter, with no money. She had had no real fear of the four men; they had been evil ones, barbarians who had to be dealt with, and she had the power and the skills to do it. But now, here, alone in this strange city, she began to feel afraid.

12

AND ALONG CAME THE SPIDER . . .

The headline in the paper read, "FOUR THOUSAND DEAD IN MIDEAST SUICIDE ATTACK." The sub-head was "Gunman kills 40 in Chicago Mall." The madman who hacked and slashed nine people to death in Philadelphia, including five children, did not even make the national news.

Three bloody revolutions erupted simultaneously in Africa. No one from outside could get in or out, so it would be some time until the death toll was known, which was still the headline. Nobody much cared which side won.

There were forty-two revolutionary groups in various stages of fighting throughout Latin America, while in Sinkiang, China, a general at the Lop Nor nuclear facility went mad and was stopped just short of launching four atomic missiles into the heart of the Soviet Union. Nor were the Soviets immune, although little of that news leaked outside. In Leningrad, however, police were still baffled by the Canal Slasher, who mutilated and tortured at will despite the best efforts of the police and KGB. It was rumored that he was himself either a top KGB man or perhaps a top party official.

The Secretary of the Air Force was attempting to keep

quiet, while demanding to know the cause, why no fewer than twenty two-man nuclear missile launch teams had had at least one officer go mad during quiet times, so much so that he either shot or had to be shot by the other.

There were two assassinations and five attempted assassinations of world leaders during a forty-eight hour period. No motive or connecting thread could be found. Thirty-seven nations now boasted that they had atomic bombs and delivery systems for them. The others who had them weren't telling.

And Angelique, ignorant of all this, was on the crowded streets of San Francisco, frightened and alone.

It had been easy, up to now, to kid herself into thinking that perhaps her situation wasn't all that bad, that she could find and perhaps cope with a life for herself. Now, surrounded by flashing signs she couldn't read, people who totally ignored her and with whom she could not converse even to get simple directions, enclosed by a strange and spiritless shell of concrete and steel, she understood just how terrible her curse really was.

Everyone seemed her enemy, although she was indeed not only ignored but, after dark, wasn't even particularly odd looking or behaving by her own and others' standards. The sight of so many men being so openly affectionate with other men, and women with other women, shocked her. She had been in a big city downtown only twice, and both times it had been Montreal, which at the time she had felt was bizarre and strange. Now here were men and women dressed in everything from faded jeans to flowing robes, some with shaved heads or bizarre haircuts, mixing in with, and being ignored by, the ordinary-looking folk of middle America.

She climbed to the top of one hill, hoping to spot the harbor, but the fog, while light, was definitely in and illuminated only up to the next hill. She stood there, feeling wet and chilled, and tried to decide what to do. Behind her she could hear a great many sirens and, looking back, saw police cars and ambulances heading to where she'd just come from.

In their eyes, she was now a murderess, and she knew it. She couldn't tell her side of the story, no matter whether it would make any difference. The four had not merely been dealt with, they had been butchered like steers in a slaughterhouse, and she knew that, given the same situation, she'd do it again without thinking.

She was perhaps a third the civilized human being she had been raised to be and two-thirds stone-age survivor. Worse, she knew that after the paralysis, the helplessness, the powerlessness of all those years, she enjoyed power and control— and the power and control that she had came from her Hapharsi self, a part that grew every time it was let out.

In the wheelchair, paralyzed and dependent, she had never really hated anyone, nor had she really blamed anyone. Now, however, looking at these apparently carefree people going about their lives, preoccupied with petty day-to-day problems or in search of a little pleasure as a release from that day to day existence, her envy knew no bounds. She hated them, hated them all. She had never had a chance at what they took for granted, and even now, among them, she could not join in, could not participate.

She idly remembered that the horseless cars that went up and down hills went to the place where she wished to go. True, she didn't know if they all did, or whether *this* line did, but she followed the tracks anyway, down one hill and up the next. It was growing incredibly cool very rapidly, and she was unprepared for it. Still, atop the next hill she could smell the sea and feel the spirits of water and wind, and she knew that she was headed right.

A drunken man lurched out of a doorway and said something to her, coming very close and reaching out. She didn't know what he said or wanted, but she repressed a defensive instinct and merely traced a little sign with one finger. The drunk suddenly lost interest in her and just stood there looking confused, as if he couldn't remember what the hell he was doing there.

Her power and her defensive skills were the only armor she had to defend herself against the forces of civilization and she knew it. They were more than Maria had, it was true, but Maria now could step into the light, could make a phone call, take a cable car to the meeting place. To a large extent this was her element, and freed of the immediate threat she could do quite well on her own here.

The cable car tracks ended at a turntable in the middle of a hotel and light industrial area, not at the harbor, but that didn't bother her. She knew that the harbor could be only a few blocks further on in the same direction. She could hear, feel, *smell* it, now.

Thanks to a light drizzle and a moderate chilly wind off the water, Fisherman's Wharf wasn't as crowded with tourists and locals as it usually was, and the sidewalks and cobblestone areas were slippery, particularly to her bare, chilled feet. She spotted the spot by the sailing ship, but took a position across the street in the shelter of an archway leading back to a hotel and small arcade. It offered some slight relief from the wind and rain. She knew it might be a long wait, and she drew herself up as best she could and tried to think warm thoughts, although this would be balmy for this time of year in Quebec.

It was the waiting that really got to her, because it meant she could only brood about things. It wasn't really the people that she hated, it was herself, this existence, she knew. She wanted out. She wanted it ended. She would even take the paralysis and the chair again, she thought darkly. At least then her body couldn't feel the cold, the discomfort, nor ache for love and closeness. When paralysed, at least she could *communicate,* and in that way she could participate to an extent in this mainstream of human affairs.

She had been wrong. It had not been a fair trade to her advantage. The Dark Man was indeed having a good laugh at this.

She couldn't even have let them kill her, and remove her from all this, for suicide was as repugnant to the Hapharsi as it was to she who had a Catholic upbringing, and she had been obligated in any event to protect Maria.

She waited only about an hour, but it seemed a lifetime, before a familiar car pulled into the pay lot at the Wharf and Greg MacDonald, wearing a raincoat, got out, paid the man, and walked over to the area by the old ship. She spotted him and ran to him, almost slipping once or twice, and when she reached him she flung her arms around him, and he looked down at her in sadness and hugged her back. It felt warm, and good. He led her back to the car and she got in, and found Maria sitting there in the back seat, looking nervous and ashamed.

Maria's emotions and thoughts were a confused unhappy mess. She had felt tremendous guilt when she panicked, and even more when she couldn't locate Angelique at all, but some of her fear inside was directed towards Angelique as well. She had seen her friend's butchery, and seen, far worse, the absolute glee with which her companion had done it, and at that moment she'd had a hard time distinguishing between Angelique and the Dark Man at the altar stone.

They rode back in a tense silence that could be cut with a knife, and Greg wasn't about to get himself involved. He'd heard Maria's account, of course, and blamed himself to a degree for leaving them too independent, but the damage was done now.

The house was ablaze with lights when they pulled up, and several cars and small vans were there, with the staff hurrying back and forth loading things into them.

"We're pulling out?" Maria asked him. "I mean—I thought the car wasn't traceable."

"It's not. Counterfeit plates that match a real registration in New York, car stolen off a used car lot in Dayton and repainted. It's the prints, Maria. Fingerprints in the car, maybe on the keys, you name it. Yours and Angelique's. They'll put it on the wire to Washington and it'll go via satellite. SAINT will intercept the transmission, flag it, and know immediately where we are give or take fifty or a hundred miles. Local, state, federal, and company cops will be swarming over the whole region any time now."

"So where are we going this time?"

"We change cars here. That mini-van over there will have to do. Rook and Bishop are coming with us, so it'll be cozy. The weather's really bad all through the Sierras, so we'll have to move overland at least as far as Carson City. There's a private airstrip just east of there where we can get a small plane to fly us to the boondocks. You both get in over there. Your things, as much as we could manage, are already packed and in the van. Both of you go over and get in. We've got to move pretty quickly before they get bright and beat their roadblocks."

Maria turned to Angelique. *"We must leave this place. Tonight's deeds will draw the Dark Man to us. We are to use that one over there. The two elders will accompany us. Come."*

Angelique complied, feeling even worse about it all.

They sat in silence in the van for several minutes as bedlam continued all around them. Finally Angelique said. *"I am sorry, daughter, that I shocked and offended you. There is a part of me that I did not wish or desire that sometimes takes control."*

Maria sighed, feeling even worse. The more she thought about it, the lousier and more confused she felt. What could she say? Damn you for keeping me from being gang raped and murdered? What could she say, or do, or feel, when both love and hate were paired so directly in her and centered on a single individual?

The two elderly British lords were spry old cusses, walking and acting younger than many of the young people on the staff. Bishop Whitely now wore a black suit with reversed clerical collar and a black porkpie hat and looked for all the world less a retired bishop than an old Catholic parish priest in fine shape. Lord Frawley, on the other hand, now wore a tweed business suit and tie and wore a mackintosh over it as partial protection against the rain. He had an unlit curved pipe clenched between his teeth.

They got in, smiled, and took their own seats. Greg was last, bringing with him a long oblong wooden case. He put it on the front passenger's seat, which was vacant, and opened it, then took out what was inside. It was a gleaming weapon, a cross between a rifle and a machine gun, and he loaded a long clip underneath and then put it on the floor within easy reach, closed his door, started up the van, and backed out of the driveway.

"Oh, dear," Frawley remarked on seeing the weapon. "Do you really think you're going to need that?"

"The name's Bond," MacDonald cracked back. "James Bond. No, sir, I hope I don't have to use it on anyone, and particularly not on some dumb lawmen just doing their jobs and following orders, but I have to be willing to do it."

The van had Utah plates, and he'd picked up a license and registration for it noting the same state as residence. Forgeries, of course, but not phonies, which today's highway patrol could pick up through their computer network. There really was a van of this license and description registered to a real James V. Higgenthorpe of Salt Lake City, Utah. The computers would verify this and would not question such a registration. The computers would not, of course, check and discover that said van was parked in James V. Higgenthorpe's back yard at the time and that he was in fact at home.

MacDonald drove over to U.S. 101, then down to San Rafael and across the bridge to connect with Interstate 80 East. He kept a citizen's band radio on, but very low. It was crowded with jerks and lonesome truckers, but it would tell him if there was a backup or roadblock going up ahead.

"I had an attack of nerves driving past San Quentin Penitentiary back there," he told them, "but I feel a little better now."

"Indeed so," Lord Frawley responded. "This is going to be a close one. Poor things. Don't you ladies blame yourselves for this. Something was bound to crack sooner or later."

Maria translated and Angelique gave a wan smile. It didn't really help to be absolved in a case like this.

Still, the further they got from San Francisco and the closer to Sacramento, the more they relaxed.

"I say, old boy, I think I've worked out the rest of their nasty little plot," said the Bishop almost casually.

"Huh? I'm all ears," MacDonald responded.

"It helped to get into their head, and also to get information on the type of cult Sir Reginald's brother had been involved in back home. What sort of beliefs and practices they had and so on. Pretty unimaginative stuff, it turns out, centering on your basic Black Mass. Still, that was a key. You know, of course, that the Black Mass is a regular mass turned inside out and upside down? Even the cross is there, only inverted, and, of course, they pray to Satan. Cults like that tend to follow the game of opposites to extremes, and that gave me the link."

"Yes, yes, go on," Frawley urged. "Do we always have to get a lesson in superstitious nonsense before you get to the point?"

"Yes, you do," replied the Bishop coolly. "Besides, what else have you got to do? At any rate, the Bible's none too specific on the nature of the Antichrist, which allows both sides a lot of latitude. The initial beast, Satan incarnate, is a water elemental—that is, it rises out of the water. Nice touch for a computer atop a tiny island, eh? The second beast, though, our Antichrist, is an earth elemental, and that means human, since humans were made from the dust of the Earth. It supposedly has two horns like a lamb, but speaks like a dragon. Since the lamb is a recognized symbol of Christ, it stands to reason that this person will be a sort of Christ-like figure, at least to the masses. Pure and without blemish and probably claiming to speak in God's name. The dragon, of course, is Satan, so we're really seeing someone who seems to be divine but is actually the commander of evil. Eventually, says their dogma, everyone will worship the beast under a brutal and absolute totalitarian dictatorship with the Antichrist as its leader, able to perform miracles to get the power and the following. The end result might be a lot of ravings or code to ancient churches as you will, but could also be taken as foretelling an atomic holocaust—and its terrible aftermath.''

"So how does all this tie in with all of us?" Greg wanted to know.

"Well, think on it. They need someone who will serve and be obedient to the beast, yet be a human symbol to the world. This takes a great deal of power. This human must already occupy a place so exalted and be so well recognized that the face and identity will be known to all and they can get all the media coverage they want, and audiences with world leaders. Now, think again of the Black Mass, the opposites, and the requirement to already be in the center of worldwide wealth and power and you will see where they're going."

And Greg MacDonald *did* see. "Angelique! If Christ was male, then the Antichirst will be female. The head of Magellan. A recognized face, but seomone known to be a helpless cripple. She's pure, still somewhat innocent in spite of what's happened, and even still a virgin. Considering Magellan's activities, she could get an invitation to the White House *and* the Kremlin.''

''Indeed,'' interjected Lord Frawley. ''Western intelligence has been trying to prove for years that several great advances in computer science and technology in the Soviet and Chinese blocs were the result of deliberate capitalist espionage. Magellan. They've already built or maintained master computers for defense and international finance in most of the western world, and what they maintain they can modify. Now, if they secretly sold the same sort of thing to the Soviets and the Chinese. . . .''

''Exactly,'' the Bishop agreed. ''At the right moment, when Angelique assumes complete control, so, too, will the Beast be in control, not just of one computer but of almost all the vital ones. A tyranny by computer.''

''But both the Russian and American launch computers aren't on any sort of network like that,'' Frawley pointed out. ''Without the codes, which are changed daily, what can they do to start Armageddon?''

''Even I can answer that,'' Greg responded. ''You don't *need* the codes, if you can create a crisis so intense that you will cause one or the other side to push the button. Starvation, revolution, mutiny—it's all one and the same. That dictatorship isn't national, it's multinational—Magellan. A multinational corporation of slaves. She'll take it, build it, and mold it until it's just right, and then it will cause conditions that will *force* one side or the other to World War III. Oh, my god!''

Whitely turned and looked at Maria. ''Do you think you can get the gist of that through to Angelique, my dear? She should know, after all.''

''I—I'll try. I'm not sure I understand it myself, but I'll try.'' And she did.

''They say that the Dark Man will make you the daughter of the Great Deceiver, the Father of Lies, as the one who

died on the cross was the son of the Supreme God. You will assume the trade of your father and with it control the whole world. You will have miraculous power and people will worship you as a god yourself and do as you command, and you will command them in the future to wage a great, last war against themselves so that they may then wage war against Heaven. Do you understand what they say?"

That was the trouble, Angelique thought sadly. She *did* understand. They would corrupt her utterly and then control her, making her not only better than she was but almost Christ-like. *The Antichrist! They want to make me the Antichrist! God protect and defend me!*

They were through Sacramento now, and going up into the mountains. He had elected to go via the twisting, winding little road leading to the pass at Lake Tahoe, and from there over to Carson City. It wasn't a well used route, particularly in the middle of the week and at this time of year, and it was the road on which they were least likely to encounter trouble.

"Well, she can't be their jolly little Antichrist if we've got her," Lord Frawley pointed out.

"Indeed. But for how long do we have her? A close shave tonight, old boy," the Bishop retorted. "I'm certain that for symmetry's sake they'd like to have it done on October thirty-first of this year, but so long as she is around it can be done almost any time. We can't keep running forever, and their resources are enormous now and getting greater every day. We fed the problem into *our* little computer, with some help at Stanford, and we came up with some answers, although not cheering ones."

"Yes? You mean short of doing her in outright?" Frawley asked, and heard Maria give a little shocked gasp.

"Oh, yes. Put it all together and it's correct. They are quite fanatical in their own way. They require a sexually pure woman. That was the point of the quadriplegia. An impure

Antichrist might fit in well with *our* notion of opposites, but they're playing by their own rules."

Lord Frawley was agog at the idea. He was having trouble rationalizing all this occultism with his nuts and bolts universe as it was, and he accepted it only in terms of the beliefs of madmen—a company in which he included Bishop Whitely. "You mean—all we have to do is get someone to knock her up?"

"Yes, but that's not as easy as it sounds," Whitely reminded him. "I mean, a few hours ago four big men had the motive and the method and the opportunity, and they'll be buried in a couple of days. I suspect that even if you drugged her, there would be something, somewhere, planted as a booby trap to prevent it. They know the stakes as well as we do, and I'm certain they allowed for this eventuality. No, to do it she would have to do it freely, willingly, out of desire and out of love."

Maria had sat in the back in silence, not translating any of this in spite of Angelique's pokes in the side to do so. "She might do it," she told the men. "She might do it for one person. She's got a real, solid thing for you, Greg, and I mean it."

Although, deep down, he knew it, he still was startled by all this and fought to reject it. "What—would it do to *her?*" he asked, not caring who answered.

Whitely, too, felt somewhat uncomfortable with this, but he saw it as the only expedient out of a dangerous situation. "Tell her about it, Maria," he ordered sternly. "Ask *her* that question."

And Maria did so, as best she could.

The very fact that the Dark Man planned to use her as the ultimate instrument of Satan's final war had shaken her, and she'd remembered the Dark Man's comment that the war between Heaven and Hell had yet to be fought. Now, here it was—a choice. A choice she did not wish to face.

"She wants to know if this would cause the ruination and fall of their ultimate plot," Maria told them.

"No. I'm afraid not," responded the Bishop. "It buys time, that's all. Time for us while they frantically search to cover their losses and find another candidate. A few years, perhaps. Perhaps longer. They will create a puppet Angelique to take control and proceed as before, I suspect, but they will not be able to use her. They may have someone in the wings—they certainly seem to plan ahead—but I suspect that their Angelique will become pregnant and bear a daughter who will be a direct heir and will also be totally under their control from the beginning. It might buy us a generation."

Maria told Angelique what Whitely had told her, and the strange young woman nodded sadly. "As I thought. Still, a generation is a long time, and the cup will be passed from my lips. Yet, for a Hapharsi Mother to surrender herself and her office, there is a high price to be paid both for me and for the other."

"What—will happen to you?" Maria asked nervously.

"Me? I do not know what traps the Dark Man laid, if any, for they are beyond my detection. But it is certain that I will lose all my power and all my communion with nature. I will surrender my self and my will. Hapharsi Mothers are supreme because they have all the great attributes of womanhood, yet call no man their master and thus are superior to men, having the highest attributes of both. This is not so of a Hapharsi wife. Wives surrender their own selves to their husbands. A Hapharsi wife is totally loving, and obedient to her husband's will. She becomes an appendage of him. As he has arms and legs, and moves them as he wills, so is it with his wife. There is no choice, no other way. When his essence enters my body of my own free will, I become part of him always."

Maria was appalled. "You talk like you'd be his slave!"

"In a sense, that is true, only it would be voluntary,

willing, and forever. One is not a slave if the choice is a free
one. Still, this much is clear. I will remain in this body, with
these thoughts, with these limits, for the rest of my life, with
no hope of ever being different and no way of even communi-
cating save by sign with anyone else, for I will not have the
power or authority to take on daughters such as you."

Angelique dwelled on the implications as Maria gave what
translation she could to the men. *This way forever.* . . . No,
not this way. Without power, she would be defenseless against
anyone and anything. Her upper body strength would ebb.
She would be weak, and ordinary, but she would remain
looking like this, cut off, allergic or whatever it was, and out
of place in the world no matter where she was. It was not a
nice fate, and the only compensation would be that she would
have Greg, although she would be in a way as dependent on
him as she had been on Maria while in that wheelchair. Still,
if the alternative was to become the *Antichrist*, her duty and
sacrifice was clear. It wasn't the hospital and the vegetative
hell. She would do it—but she had to be honest with Greg
about *all* the consequences.

Maria was startled by Angelique's comment, but she relayed it. "Uh— Greg, she says that when her power leaves
her it will exit through you, binding the two of you. As near
as I can figure it out, if you make it with her you'll never be
able to make it with any woman *but* her again. You just
won't be able to get it up."

"Enforced monogamy. Incredible," breathed the Bishop

"Unmitigated, superstitious bullshit," muttered the Rook.

Greg, however, was not so sure. "Hey! Wait a minute!
Doing it is one thing, but that kind of deal—I have to think
about it!"

"You don't mean you actually believe in that balderdash!"
Frawley exclaimed angrily. "You remember our discussion
of voodoo? It only works on you if you believe it. If you

believe it, then it's true. Get your brain back in the real world where it belongs, boy!''

"Leave him alone, Pip," Whitely said seriously. "I'm sure at one time or another we all would love to live in that wonderfully ordered, totally predictable universe of yours. It must be so nice. Unfortunately, few of us do. I think the young fellow deserves a chance to think it over."

"And the alternative if I don't?" MacDonald asked them, hoping for some easier way out himself.

"I'm afraid, old boy, that there *is* only one alternative," Lord Frawley responded. "We must stop somewhere in a civilized area, then take that fancy little weapon you have there and shoot her to death, after which we will mutilate her so badly that only fingerprints and dental information will be available. She actually retains a crown and two fillings from her old days. Then we call the police, they try and identify the body, the information goes through the telenet and is intercepted by SAINT, and this in turn triggers that nasty little wipe out monster lurking in its system, for while they can fool the world about Angelique, they can not fool themselves, which is all that's really necessary we think. I'm well skilled in how to do it right and proper, if need be."

"Jesus Christ!" said Gregory MacDonald.

Maria said nothing for a few moments, then said, "I thought it would come to this. You have no choice in the end but to kill her. I know people just like you. I knew them in New Orleans. Oh, you've got national security to rationalize your deed and they were in it for the money and power, but you're really the same people."

"Now, wait just a minute!" Greg almost shouted at them. "Nobody's going to be blowing her away! I didn't go through all this just to have that happen. If I did, it would have been easier and better to do it back there in the islands. And don't you dare translate any of this for her or I'll cheerfully kill *you*, Maria!"

"No," Maria responded almost woodenly. "You couldn't have done it back there. In your head, yes, but she wouldn't have permitted it. Now—I'm not so sure she wouldn't welcome it. At least, she wouldn't stop *you*, Greg. You've pretty much ignored her, or treated her as some kind of strange creature, and it's hurt her, but you're the only thing she's got."

A heavy silence fell upon the van, which was all right with Gregory MacDonald. Up until now he'd enjoyed playing the secret agent, but the fact is that this was exactly what he'd been doing—playing. He wasn't any James Bond; just an ex-homicide detective from British Columbia. Until now, he hadn't even minded the danger, or the risk, and after he'd escaped from that creature on the island and then from the island itself, his self-confidence knew no bounds. Part of it was that he lived for the game; his work was his life and beyond that he was more or less an idle bum. He was a thrill seeker, a man who loved to play the dangerous game, and was willing to do so because he generally risked only himself.

Self-centered, egocentric, the Sun Cop—that's what his ex had said when she'd walked out on him. People weren't real to him, they were just props, actors there to support his starring roles. He had a false but convincing bedside manner, it was true—all part of the game—but the truth was that he was good at what he did precisely because he was never in the slightest emotionally involved with his cases. Still, before he'd only had to solve them, perhaps apprehend the criminals, sometimes leaving that to others. Until now, he'd always been a player, not a piece on the board of his own deadly chess games.

And like his father he'd always been a socialist and a realist; his church affiliation was nominal and really amounted to none at all. He'd always voted NDP and touted socialist realism. But he had never before been chased down a mountain by a monstrous thing he could not see, until its arm was forced to solidity when reaching in vain through a church window.

And Angelique. He had gotten emotionally involved with Angelique back on the island, no matter how much he'd tried to deny it to himself, but he now felt detached from her present incarnation. Was it because she was now black? He had to wonder, no matter how much the idea that such a kernel of racism could be inside him troubled him. Or because she'd been transformed, into a strange being with a painted face who could neither speak nor understand? He hated that idea almost as much.

For, inside that head, inhabiting that form, was still Angelique, the vulnerable girl he'd gotten to know on Allenby, an unwitting pawn in a very deadly game. And now, here it was—the cold logic of national interest on one side versus a permanent and bizarre involvement on his part. Homicide from the other side, or Angelique and him in a kind of permanent union—not the Angelique of the island, but *this* Angelique, looking as she did now, cut off from any real communication. Pip Frawley might be certain, as the Bishop had mocked, but Frawley hadn't stood on the deck of a trawler and watched her call a storm to herself and manipulate the lightning as if it were sets of ropes and cables to bring down two helicopters. He did not doubt her power now, whether it was mystical or some kind of ESP or whatever, and he did not doubt she'd lose it the moment her cherry was broken if only because, as Frawley said, she *believed* she would lose it.

But she also believed that such an act would bind him, at least sexually, to her for a lifetime. As she had controlled Maria and as she had manipulated that storm, there wasn't a doubt in his mind that she could do it to him in a last act of power.

Somehow he'd known it would come down to the idea of killing her. His own deductive mind always led to that conclusion, but he'd always rejected it or put it aside in his mind, confident that if no other way could be found, someone else would do the deed, and efficiently, out of sight and mind.

And now, here it was, with only the Bishop standing in the way of Frawley's cold rationalism. Frawley's way was the most efficient, of course, but it did leave several unknowns. Right now, they knew the names and location of the enemy. That enemy wouldn't die just because the computer erased itself. All the data was backed up somewhere, in a thousand different places, and they had the talent and skills to put SAINT back together again by this point, surely, although it might take years. And if Angelique died with no heirs, Magellan might be shaky, but the projects would continue because so many nations and financial institutions depended on it.

The Dark Man might well be the key there, and his importance was doubtless the reason he kept his identity so secret. He would probably become, if need be, a major figure and take managerial control in the crisis. Who would know?

He could think of a half a dozen ways this nasty group could survive either alternative, and both Frawley and Whitely agreed on that themselves. There was, however, the mind set of the leaders on Allenby. He had relied on that for many of his actions, and now the Bishop was doing the same. They had planned for Angelique; they wanted Angelique, and had gone to some risk and great pains to prepare her. To remove her from the game would be as devastating to them as killing her. In fact, the two alternatives were clear. Both would set them back, both would buy a fair amount of time, neither would be fatal to them . . .

. . . but one would be fatal to Angelique.

They stopped for gas and some carry-out food in Lake Tahoe, and were able to find restrooms in the back of a carry out that allowed them all to use the facilities without being seen more than necessary. It was quite cold in late September at this elevation, and there were even some flakes of snow in the predawn air. They had driven long through stiff winds, rain, and fog and it was still no picnic where they were. MacDonald made a call from a pay phone, then came back to them.

"The house in California was raided shortly after we left," he told them gravely. "They got a few of our people, although most of them and all the important stuff got away or was destroyed."

"How could they have known that quickly?" Bishop Whitely asked. "You said the car couldn't be traced."

"Maybe it couldn't. It makes no difference how they found it, the point is that they found it and they found it in time to get some of our people. The fact is, it wasn't a raid by officials. It was clearly a private deal, and they were nasty and well armed and prepared. If our people were in the hands of the cops, they wouldn't crack, but Magellan's not bound by the rules of procedure and the rights of the accused. They may know we're in a blue van, but they don't have a real description or license number or anything like that, so I'm not too worried on that score. They'll have good descriptions of *us*, though, so Carson City's too hot now. Our people want us to lay low for a day or so until they can work something else out. That means we find a couple of motels, split up and stay in more than one so there's no group portrait, and wait."

"That sounds all right to me," said the Bishop, yawning. "I feel as if I could sleep for a week."

They selected two motor inns about a half a mile apart on the highway. One was rather posh and had a small casino attached. This would be for the Bishop and the Rook, who looked the part for such a place and could comfortably go about there. The other was a small motel with two blocks of outside-opening rooms and a small detached coffee shop. It was a budget motel catering to transients. Greg was taking no chances on this one, though; he would stay in the same room there with Angelique and Maria.

The floor was carpeted, but the staff had been on the ball and Angelique's slippers were easily found to help with that. They had also packed two sets of silk bedding—one clean and one dirty—which meant that they could remake one of the twin beds for her.

Maria took a shower and changed clothes, and for the first time in these past busy weeks MacDonald noticed a real change in her. She had been well built but thin on the oil platform; now she was having a lot of trouble getting her jeans on. She had put on a considerable amount of weight in a very short time.

"I'm dead tired but I'm really starved," she told them. "I'm going over to that little coffee shop. Can I bring you anything?" She asked the same of Angelique. Both indicated no, but Greg told her to go ahead, that they'd probably be asleep when she came back.

Maria left, and for the first time since this all began, Greg and Angelique were alone together.

She sat on the side of the bed, completely undressed, and watched him remove his own clothes. He just went down to his jockey shorts, but he felt her gaze and looked back at her. He stared into her big brown eyes and for the first time he saw beyond the shell, and sensed the woman within, the Angelique he'd first seen trapped in a motorized chair. She was a lonely, pleading, tragic figure, and he felt great pity for her and much ashamed of himself. She looked, even *smelled* so very different, yet her spirit, so lacking in the joys of life, still shined there. He thought of that time back on the beach at Allenby, where she'd reached out to him so desperately and asked for a kiss.

He sat down beside her, and put his arm around her and held her close to him. She shivered a bit and responded, then looked up at him. He looked into those big brown eyes and could see no one but Angelique there, and he kissed her, long and passionately.

Maria had told them that Angelique would demand a ceremony, a marriage ritual she respected and considered binding, before she would take the ultimate step, as it were. Since the Hapharsi ritual was out of the question, that meant Catholic, but no Catholic priest would perform this marriage without a lengthy period of time and all sorts of other formalities. Angelique, however, knew that Whitely was a priest, and he certainly looked to be the right kind and she had regarded him as such, using the term Father-Elder to Maria. Whitely could and would perform a simple ceremony, giving a religious if not a legal and civil marriage validity in her eyes. He'd do it to save her life.

But MacDonald had had no doubt, on talking to King's base, that they had finally decided that the pressure was too great to take any more risks. They had Frawley to do the grisly work that had to be done to make her virtually unrecognizable, yet eminently identifiable to a pathologist. The fact that she didn't know this made her sacrifice and her obvious affection for him all the more poignant.

She was a wild, intensely erotic lover, who seemed to know just what he wanted done and where and how to do it, although she could have had no experience whatsoever. She would not allow penetration of her own body, but she brought him pleasure so intense that when they were done he was thoroughly convinced of her true wishes.

There was no spell or supernatural magic—at least, he was pretty sure there wasn't—but there were other ways of communicating than speech and writing. She wanted him to marry her or kill her, but in either way to release her from Hell's bondage, and he had clearly given her his choice.

*   *   *

Maria seemed startled that he would actually marry Angelique, conditions or not, and it seemed as if she was fighting back a tinge of jealousy. She certainly didn't have to tell Angelique of Greg's decision, and she half suspected some sorcery was involved no matter what the protestations. When they'd awakened in mid-evening, they'd called the Bishop at the other motel and told him, and he had been absolutely delighted.

The remnant of the mountain storms had caught up with them as Maria went and picked up Whitely in the van and took him back to her motel. "Why so glum, my dear? It's a happy solution and a happy occasion."

"Yeah, well, what kind of marriage can it be? She keeps looking and being like that forever, with no kind of funny powers at all, and she becomes a thing—a sex slave, and he'll need her 'cause he can't do it with anybody else. They'll have to always live in hiding in someplace like Africa or Brazil, afraid that every shadow will contain the Dark Man. Some kind of life."

"I talked to him at length on the telephone. He doesn't see her that way any more. He's in love. He's willing to pay the price."

"Yeah, sure. She can make you do or feel or believe anything—for a while. But once it's done those spells won't work any more and he'll be stuck and so will she."

"You believe it's magic, then? Perhaps it is, but perhaps it isn't her kind of magic. Do you think she wants this, truly?"

"I don't know. She wants him, that's for sure, but she also wants Daddy. She never had one, but since she got paralyzed she's always had somebody to push her around, feed her, change her, do all that for her. I think she'd do most anything to have him as her old self, whole and white, if you know what I mean, for she hates the way she is and she hates the idea of being that way for the rest of her life. The only thing that makes it O.K. for her is that she gets Daddy and someone to be wholly dependent on for the rest of her life. She'll still need special care and he won't be able to live without her, if you know what I mean. No, I'm not real happy.''

''You'd prefer her dead, then?''

''I don't know. Sometimes I think it would be best for everybody. At least it would be only her and not two of them being screwed up. But, no, I really love her, Bishop. I don't want her dead.''

It was not to be a fancy sort of ceremony, if only because no one had much in the way of fancy things to wear. Whitely used an abbreviated Catholic service, which was very close to the rite of his own church, with Maria doing the basic translation. As the ceremony progressed, the wind whipped up outside and they could hear lightning and thunder, unusual for this area at this time of the year.

The service seemed to please Angelique. The clergyman pronounced them husband and wife and blessed them in the name of the Father, the Son, and the Holy Ghost, and it was over. Whitely seemed relaxed and pleased by it, but he was also ever mindful of the business at hand.

''I regret not having rings nor cake, but those can come later. I think now, though, we'd best end this tension. Bless you both. Maria—you may take me back to the motel now and I will see how much expense money Pip has lost in the casino.''

For Angelique, the moment was particularly emotional. When the priest had run through the ceremony, which she could follow by form though she couldn't understand the specific words and phrases, she'd felt a sense of distance, of unreality, but when he'd pronounced them married and blessed them, she'd felt a sudden inward rush and a concentration of spiritual power from him to the two of them and she knew that this choice was *right*.

For MacDonald, the whole thing had been calming somehow, had given him an inner peace he'd never really known before. There was nothing spiritual about it to him, but for now he really wanted her and he did not wish to think about tomorrow.

For a while they just stood there, then turned and hugged and kissed, and ran their hands soothingly over each other's bodies. Words were unnecessary. She had a tense excitement tingd with real fear inside her, and she wanted to prolong this moment.

As the storm raged on, the lights flickered several times, then went out entirely. They hardly noticed, as they began to undress each other. The room was in near darkness in spite of the early evening hour thanks to the blackout.

"Quite a touching performance," said the Dark Man.

They both jumped, and as they did the lights flickered again and came on, and for the first time Greg MacDonald was face to face with the Dark Man. That is, if face to face was the term for it, since the looming shape near the door was more the animated negative of a man without any features. It was eerie, like a cinematic special effect, but he cast a nebulous shadow on the wall and in his hand he held something not at all blacked out.

"This is a Hallenger S-27 automatic pistol," the Dark Man pointed out. "It carries a twenty shot capacity in two parallel magazines and, while not well balanced, can spray all twenty throughout this room in less than one second. I can also fire one individually, Mr. MacDonald. It may not kill you, but if it doesn't the spin on it will keep you hospitalized for months."

Damn! MacDonald swore to himself, everything except the specter in front of him fading from his mind. *Finally I'm face to face with the bastard and I don't even have my pants on!*

Angelique just stared at him in horror, her joy and commitment crumbling within her.

"How did you find us?" MacDonald asked the strange

enemy. He was trying to place the voice, but, while it might be electronically altered, it really didn't sound like anyone he'd ever met or known.

"It was extremely difficult, I admit," the dark one replied. "Frankly, we felt we had blown it. Your organization is far more efficient than we had dreamed or planned on, Mr. MacDonald. Of course, there were twin objects to the exercise. One was allowing Angelique to both sink into savagery and see what it was like to exist like that in the modern world. To dismantle the last of her civilized ego, as it were, showing the futility of flight and leading to this moment, where we demonstrate the futility of true escape. The second was the hope that she would lead us to parts of your organization, which we'd been otherwise unable to find or penetrate. Still, you led us a merry chase. When that seaplane vanished into thin air after leaving Ensenada air space, we were thrown into a panic. The odds were good after time passed that even if we found you, it would be too late for our ends. I'm very happy to see that it is not so. We would not have been so hesitant to act."

"I'll bet. And yet you *did* track us down, even to this place."

"Believe me, we did not and could not. When we missed you at the house and discovered no one left knew where you were going or even what direction, it was almost as bad. We had to sit, and wait, and keep the pressure on, and, sure enough, it broke. Oh, don't worry about our little Angelique here being kept in the dark, as it were. She understands what I say as well as you—although not what you say, sadly."

There was a sharp double knock on the motel room door that startled them but didn't faze the Dark Man. He reached over and turned the knob on the door, but MacDonald already had figured out who was there before Maria walked back in, looking quite wet and not at all happy about it. For

Angelique, though, it was a crushing blow, worse in a way than the appearance of the Dark Man.

She closed the door behind her and stood there next to the Dark Man, looking at the pair on the bed with a grim expression.

"Miss Iscariot, I believe," MacDonald said with a sneer. "If you were his all along, why wait until the last moment? Just rubbing it in?"

"I wasn't—his," she replied, sounding nervous and miserable. "I just—figured it all out—that's all. After I saw—her—in that parking lot, I realized just what she had become and what I had become. There's an eight hundred number you can call that will route your call to the Institute. You know that. After I called you, I thought and thought, and then I called it."

"Pretty lousy response time for you, Blob Boy, isn't it? It took you almost three hours to hit the house."

"A message routing problem of sorts. It took a while to get the information to the right people, round them up, and get them in the right place to act without official interference. Still, you acted with even more efficiency than we did. That cost us. Then we had to wait. Wait until our little Maria decided to call again—either the number or the house. She finally called the house this morning from here. After that, it was mostly a matter of timing."

Angelique stared at Maria, appalled. *"Why, my daughter? Why? After so much and after all we have been through. . . ."*

Maria answered slowly in English, but it was clear that Angelique could hear and understand whoever and whatever the Dark Man chose.

"Because I knew. They were either gonna kill you or lock you in like that forever, and I never figured on Greg actually going through with it. Even when he did, I thought about it. Like that, forever, always on the run, never being human—it was horrible, and you were dragging *him* down with you. I couldn't let that happen, but I couldn't let those cold blooded leeches blow you away, either. And for what? They said it'd only slow 'em down a little, not stop 'em. It was for *nothing*! So I called 'em. We made a deal, that's all, and you won't be stuck and neither will he and nobody will die.''

Angelique felt tears coming to her eyes. *"More will die because of what you did. To save one, or two, you may massacre millions!"*

"Yeah, well, I don't know those millions and they never did anything for me that didn't benefit them more. I know me, and I know you two.''

"And do you think he'll keep that deal now?" MacDonald asked her. "Why should he?''

"A proper point, and at this late stage rather beside the point," the Dark Man noted casually. "However, we keep our bargains when we can. I must say it's rather nice to finally see you in the flesh, Mr. MacDonald. I must confess I'm rather glad you escaped our rambling and crude friend, which I wouldn't have sent in the first place, and I was quite impressed that you managed an effective escape from the island. You are a courageous, resourceful, and most dangerous man, MacDonald.''

"I appreciate the flattery, but it seems that fighting gallantly isn't enough to win the war. I'd rather be less impressive, get some breaks, and win.''

"Breaks. Fate. Such silly words to avoid any act of faith, any compromise with materialistic principles. Scientists ignore what they can not explain away, or create new theories to explain away problems that are more difficult to believe than the supernatural. One theory now says that the universe was created spontaneously out of nothing, with no cause. Don't you find that a violation of rational science in the name of science? Don't you find that concept even more absurd to the rational mind than the idea of a creator's will? George Orwell once saw a ghost and described it in great detail, yet he dismissed it in the end as some sort of hallucination because, in spite of the scientific evidence of his own eyes and experience, it violated his world view. He could not accept it. Neither, really, can Maria, here—or you.''

"Spare me the lectures, eh?'' MacDonald snapped. "What comes next?''

"Next? The most vital part comes next, and it is up to Angelique. She must return to us, willingly, with a vow to submit to her destiny.''

"I will never do that!"

"Oh, really? Now, consider your position, my dear. You are coming, willingly or not. You know that. But if you come willingly, and submit to us, I will not use this exquisite piece of precision weaponry on Mr. MacDonald.'' The Dark Man moved closer to them, so close that MacDonald would be within reach of that pistol with one quick move. He didn't think—he just acted, and nothing happened. He was stuck to the bed, his muscles simply not obedient to his commands no matter how hard he tried. After a moment, he gave up, resigned to it.

"Go ahead and kill me,'' he invited the Dark Man. "I'm not exactly thrilled at the prospect, but it sure won't get you what you want out of her.''

"No!'' Maria almost screamed. "He's mine! You promised me!''

"Shut up, Maria. I said we delivered when we could. Do not make me angry. You have seen what I can do if I am angry.''

Maria calmed down, but continued to stare menacingly at the Dark Man.

"Now, then,'' the mysterious one continued, "what makes you think I would ever kill you? These tiny little cartridges pack a mean wallop. If I fire one exactly so, into a particular area at the base of your spine, you will be permanently and totally paralyzed below the waist.''

Angelique stiffened as if shot. *"No! You can't!"*

"That will be where the first shot goes, but it will not, I assure you, be fatal. We will see to that. Then we will ask Angelique again, and if she still refuses, the second shot will be *here,* in a particular area of the upper spinal column. Then you will be as Angelique was, with no hope of ever regaining any movement or even feeling."

Angelique was sobbing now. *"No, no, no!"*

"You can't do that! You *promised* me!" Maria screamed at him.

The Dark Man turned and made a gesture in Maria's direction, and she was rudely slammed up against the wall by some invisible force and held there. "I promised nothing of the sort," he told her. "I promised that you could have him after we were finished our business with Angelique. I said nothing about what condition he would be in. You're used to handling such cases. You'd have him all to yourself and he couldn't get away if he wanted to. I also promised I wouldn't kill him, and I won't. But, after the second shot, I will ask again. If the answer is still no, then there will be a third and final shot here, at an exact angle into the brain. He will be alive, and conscious, and all of his autonomic functions will remain, but he will be unable, ever, to move or take any other voluntary action. Ever. You know what that means for him, don't you, Angelique?"

"You monster!" she screamed at him, and struggled to move against him, but, like MacDonald, she found that she could not. The fury and hatred building up in her was enormous.

"Then, of course, we will go, and achieve our goals by other, longer, and more difficult means," the Dark Man concluded. "You must believe that I will do what I have said I will do, Angelique."

"You *bastard!*" Maria screamed at him, struggling to free herself. "May you rot in Hell forever!"

"Why, *this* is Hell," responded the Dark Man calmly. "nor am I out of it. I weary of you. I was willing to give you what we could, but I think now that you will always have unreasonable demands. I promised you your youth until you die, and I will not take the craven out and kill you now to keep that vow the easy way. The rewards can be great if you understand your place, but if you do not then Satan will look to the fine print. In your ego you thought that he would fall into your arms if she were removed. You may have your crack at him, should he be worth having when we finish this business, but we can not trust you and have no more need of you. We leave you here—eternally young!"

Maria suddenly cried out, and changed before their eyes. The Dark Man had kept the letter his word, but only exactly. Maria now shrank and shimmered, and when it was done she was the cutest pre-pubescent ten or eleven year old girl anyone had ever seen.

"Now remain that way until death," the Dark Man said coldly. "Sleep now—I am finished with you forever until your soul comes to me."

She sank to the floor, out cold.

The demonstration of sheer offhanded power both impressed and scared MacDonald, who was frightened enough already.

The Dark Man checked his pistol, then went and stood in back of the helpless Greg. "Now, Angelique, the first stage. I ask you if you will come with me voluntarily, with your vow that you will not resist the future. Leave attempts to stop us to others. They are impressively organized. They *might* yet pull it off. Tell me now, or I fire the first shot. After that, it is irrevocable to that point. You know you're going back anyway. What's the point?"

Angelique felt shocked, confused, and upset. The Dark Man knew her own weak spots better than she. At this moment, she might even take that terrible fate, lying unmoving in that horrible hospital, but it was not she who was faced with this. Not she, but Greg.

She had just accused Maria of condemning millions for the sake of two or three, and she'd meant it, but this was not the same. Maria had betrayed them, when they had beaten even the Dark Man and were free and clear and about to foul up his terrible plans for good. She had elected to bring the Dark Man here. But now he was here, and what he said was true. She was going back, whether she wished or not, and she knew that one way or another he could break her. He already had, to an extent.

"What will you do to him if I go now?" she asked, unaware that she was once again speaking nothing but a French-accented English.

MacDonald was startled, but found that he couldn't say a word. He had to be perfectly honest with himself. He still loved her, and he still hated the Dark Man and everything he stood for, but right now he voted for her to accept the offer. The Dark Man, however, didn't know that and wasn't taking any chances on him being noble to the end.

"If you go now, following all that I say, nothing. He will live, and I will place no curse upon him. I will leave him here, for us to perhaps meet, and contest, another day. He, too, is no longer relevant to us. He is relevant only to you."

"You won't kill him, then? Or do what you say anyway?"

"I will not. You have my word on that, and the devil is a gentleman in such bargains. He will remain, frozen, on this bed until we exit. Then he will be restored, free, with no restraints and no compulsions. I swear it. Only if he comes after me again will all bets be off. The next time, it will be on his head, not yours or mine."

"How do I know this is true? After what I have seen you do, how can I believe you on anything."

Believe him, believe him! MacDonald thought, growing more and more nervous. He could feel the cold barrel of the pistol in his back occasionally as the Dark Man made his points. *Take the deal, Angelique. I'll try and rescue you later!*

"A fair question," the Dark Man admitted. "There is no real way to prove it. You can call on your spirits, but they won't come now. You can call on God and the angels, but they won't come, either. I can't really help you decide, but I can't think of a good clinching argument, either. You will have to make up your own mind, but I grow increasingly impatient. I believe that in one minute I will demonstrate my power."

"No! Wait!" She needed time to think, and she wasn't being given any. This was all happening too quickly, too horribly. And then, all at once, she remembered the great, ancient angel who had communed with her. *You will be forced to make many choices,* it had said, *but the outcome, the final choice, is not in your hands but in another's.* Might that other be Greg? She wondered about it. If the final choice, if whether or not they succeeded or failed, was out of her hands and in the hands of others, then she had no right to cripple him just to prove a point.

"Time is up. Choose," said the Dark Man.

"I—I will go with you, you monster of evil," she told him. "I will play your games and, as you say, leave the fight now to others. I give up. I have no right to cost him his life or limb for my pride."

Greg MacDonald almost passed out with relief. *I owe you one, honey,* he thought, still worried and fearful but feeling a little better. *More than one. And I'll repay it.*

"A good decision. And I will in fact keep my part of the bargain. Now, rise and come with me, Angelique."

She did so, and together they walked to the door, then stopped.

"Turn and face me, Angelique," he ordered, and she did so.

"By the oaths and spirits which bind all and rule all, do you agree to come with me, without protest, without resistance? We do not ask that you convert, only that you no longer fight. Do you swear?"

She hesitated a moment and swallowed hard. "Yes. I swear."

There was a sudden roaring of the wind outside as if the storm had returned, and it seemed to MacDonald that it penetrated the room and made it chilly. It was gone in a second, and the Dark Man reached over, opened the door, then turned back to the man on the bed.

"Our one compromise is this, Mr. MacDonald," the Dark Man warned. "You do not really figure prominently in our plans from this point. If you come again, there will be no one to save you." And, with that, both he and Angelique stepped over the body of Maria, snoring on the floor, went out, and closed the door behind them.

He could feel the presence leave, feel will and strength coming back into his body. Suddenly he leaped up, ran to the closet and pulled out his rifle, then ran to the door and outside, almost tripping over Maria.

He shouldered his weapon and looked around, ready to kill even Angelique to save her from this fate, but there were no cars visible except the van and two others parked in front of rooms down the block.

There was a sudden, great flapping noise, as if some impossibly gigantic bird had launched itself into the air above him. He turned and looked up, and for a moment saw a shape there, a huge, dark, terrible shape of a creature that was more monstrous than he could ever imagine, rising with incredible speed into the night sky. Before he could react, it was gone in the clouds.

He lowered the rifle, cursed, and spat. He needed Bishop and Rook. He needed a drink. No, he needed a distillery. He suddenly was aware of the cold and chill and looked down.

Before any of that, he realized, he needed some pants—if he hadn't inadvertently locked the damned door behind him.

Poor Angelique! he thought sorrowfully. *What will they do to you now?*

13

A SMALL, DEVOUT BAND OF SCOUNDRELS

"Why is it," Bishop Whitely asked grumpily, "that it is impossible to get a decent coddled egg in any restaurant in this country?"

"Because they ran away from home and mother when they were too young and turned their back on culture," Lord Frawley responded. "On the other hand, why are the best restaurants in London run by foreigners?"

Gregory MacDonald smiled and shook his head, although he wasn't in much of a mood for smiling. These two old men acted like doddering British codgers most of the time, and it wasn't an act. It was just difficult to take them all that seriously, and they were at heart very serious men indeed.

"So he really said to you, 'Why this is Hell, nor am I out of it?' " the Bishop asked between bites of toast.

"Or something like that. Why? Is it important?"

"It's Goethe," Whitely responded. "*Faust*. It's what Mephistopheles tells Faust when they're discussing the bargain and the demon's pressed on just what Hell is like. He may have a point, too. This world *is* going to hell. You can see it, sense it, feel it."

"It's been going to hell since I was a boy," Lord Frawley noted. "It hasn't gotten there yet."

"Ah, but that's a relative thing. I've been studying the news since I've been here, and I've called in for correlations. Did you know, for example, that those grisly murders in San Francisco made page fourteen of the *Chronicle* and didn't even rate a mention in the national news or in other papers? Not long ago that would have been headline news. Even Tass would have covered it as evidence of how lawless and savage and decadent the West was. Now it's barely a mention. Single murders, ordinary ones, and most rapes don't even get a line any more. Now people take it upon themselves to drive into crowds and play 'smash the pedestrian' in many major cities. It's almost common. Serial killers used to rate big play—they're still talking about Jack the Ripper, after all. Now there are so many that the media is hard pressed to come up with macabre new nicknames for them. Assassinations and assassination attempts are so commonplace it's odd when there's a day without one. No, Pip, it's on the move."

"Modern times, that's all. It's the price we pay."

"No, there's a pattern. It's well distributed, and the incidents are almost geographically uniform and patterned out. The beast is loose. People are going mad in droves, and the rest of the population is increasingly terrified. Nowhere is safe. We're being primed with violence." Whitely paused a moment and looked over at Greg. "He didn't ask you who the King was?"

"No, that was the most insane part of it. He as much as said that they let her run loose at least partly to expose the organization, yet he didn't ask me a single question about it. It was as if it didn't matter any more."

"Perhaps it didn't. Perhaps he already knows all he needs to know and has other plans. Perhaps he needs an opposition. Indeed, he may just have known that you don't know who the King is."

"But that's just the point," MacDonald said, slowly drinking his coffee. "I *do* know. And I would have spilled it, I have to admit. I would have spilled *anything* at that point. Until now, I've never really believed that somebody could be pure evil, but I've met him now."

"Rubbish," Pip sneered. "Evil is a relative term related to goals. This fellow had all sorts of electronic gimmickry to use and to disguise himself, but did you feel that he was supernatural, somehow? Or was he in fact a human being?"

"Well, Hitler was a human being, so I suppose it's not too far off. Yes, I'd say he was human. He wears boots, anyway. I could tell by the sound when he walked out. He has that power—tremendous gobs of it—but you could tell he really hated to use it. He much preferred the pistol and the physical threats and torture. He was such an arrogant, totally self confident bastard that you wanted to strangle him, but he was a pro. He knew exactly what he was doing and what buttons to push."

"After all she's been through, though; to surrender that easily. . . ." Frawley muttered.

"But that's the point, isn't it?" the Bishop responded. "I mean, he set her up for alternate rises and falls. He gave her physical freedom, but took away looks and communications abilities. He let her run free, even gave her a taste of power and killing, knowing that she'd be forced to give that up and lock herself in just to foil them. Then he lets her run, gives her plenty of rope—too much, as he admitted, a price of that arrogance and self-confidence—but at the very moment of consummation he appears to first show her closest friend in the world to be a Judas and worse, then to taunt her not with any more horrible things to her but rather to him, once she's really committed herself for love. Considering her background, her extreme naivete, it's a wonder she didn't crumble before this."

"Many brave men and women are dead because they preferred it to crumbling," Frawley noted.

"But many more aren't. The threat of death is still the strongest one. Consider—ask a group of women what is the worst crime that they fear and nine out of ten will say rape right off. Yet the vast majority of women who have been raped are still alive and even healthy. Why? They were given only two choices—the rape, which was incredibly repugnant, or death.

That's the same principle the Dark Man uses. He finds the thing you fear the most, whether it's death or perhaps paralysis and total helplessness, as in Angelique's case, and he gives you two choices. Let your mind and body be raped at will by him, or choose what you truly fear the most. It's quite effective, and it's an old story. He's just far better than most at determining your worst fear."

"He's got a computer to analyze his victims for him," MacDonald pointed out. "Funny. He quoted Orwell, too. I thought that was about as appropriate as could be, under the circumstances."

"I'm quite a bit more interested in how our friend here explains what happened to Maria," the Bishop commented a bit smugly. "No odd laboratories, no big computer or giant radiation dishes, nothing. Here, in the middle of nowhere, the Dark Man is not only able to appear at will but also exercise those considerable powers of transmutation."

"I don't know the explanation, damn it," Lord Frawley growled. "I don't know how the process works, but it's self-evident that it does. With that sort of disguise, anyone could play Dark Man, even with the Dark Man broadcasting his voice via satellite. There's a logical explanation for what happened, if we only knew and understood the physics—I feel sure of that. Who knows what kind of transmitting and generating systems the corporation might now have all over the place, ready to be deployed as needed?

Still, it doesn't change the basic situation. He can do what he claims to, no matter if he hides behind satanist claptrap or really believes it. They can re-make and transform whole populations into slaves of any design, reward with youth and beauty or punish with age and infirmity at their whim. It's a terrible weapon."

"I still can't understand why he left me whole and unchanged," MacDonald put in. "I mean, he had me cold, and I represent a demonstrated and very real threat to him, if not the power to thwart his plans, at least the threat of doing damage that might be very inconvenient. If I'd had him at a similar disadvantage I know I wouldn't have let *him* go."

"Oh, I suspect that was for Angelique's benefit," the Bishop replied, sipping his tea. "She had to be reassured that you were whole and safe or the bargain would have been invalidated. If he'd done anything, he wouldn't have your paralysis as a threat to hold over her any more. I suspect he thinks he's put a sufficient scare into you at this point that he doesn't really worry about you that much. If anything, you're the price he paid for getting her complete cooperation."

"You know how that makes me feel. The question is— now what?"

"We must take direct action against the buggers, obviously," Lord Frawley stated flatly. "We must put them out of business."

"Yeah," MacDonald responded, "but that's easier said than done. It was tough enough getting *off* that island. Now you're telling me we have to get on it and do a lot of operations when their power's strongest there and they can even sic invisible monsters on you at will."

"Exactly so," Frawley agreed. "An air strike is out. We might get some buildings and lots of innocents but we wouldn't touch that computer—and it could bring massive defensive armaments to bear on any such attackers. A full sea landing, assuming we could convince some nation of the extreme danger and get their troops, would be just as bad and couldn't be hidden. A nuclear missile or bomb would do it, but even if we could get one it's unlikely we could deliver it without going through the sort of channels SAINT can control and counter. Actually, I might be able to use some of my old terrorist contacts to actually *get* a small and dirty bomb in a few weeks, but those little monsters still weigh a few hundred pounds and would have to be assembled on the spot by experts. How would we get it there and in? They have radiological monitors that are the best in the world to keep ships and boats with such things away, and a whole naval force to intercept. They'd take no chances—we'd be blown out of the water.''

MacDonald thought it over. ''Not necessarily. Remember, my primary job at Magellan before all this blew up was to test and if possible penetrate security at company installations. I only failed once, and that was in the middle east against an adversary who was clever and of whom I knew nothing. With Jureau gone, Ross is the top security man there and just the type to play ball with any of them. I know him well, and I know what types of things he'd employ. I beat their system once, and recommended how to plug the holes. What do you bet that they implemented that report?''

Frawley almost choked. ''Good Lord! You mean they are defending themselves on the standard level according to a plan *you* devised?''

''I'd almost bet on it. Oh, they'd modify it a good deal, and they have these powers that will have to be taken into account, but Ross is not very creative and he's also quite literal-minded. His ego, arrogance, and self confidence also fits in with that crowd now running things. And, if that's true, we have a built-in edge.''

''Indeed? What is that? I'd be delighted to find any edge for our side at this point.''

''I made my living by making fools of the professional

security men. If I failed again and again, I'd have been fired.
I had to succeed to prove my worth to the company.''

"Obviously."

"Well, I plugged the major leaks and openings, of course,
but I always left something else open or slightly flawed so
that if I ever was ordered to try the same place again I could
still beat the system. I figured three separate ways to get into
the Institute and picked the easiest last time. I succeeded,
then plugged those holes, but I made only token changes
against the other two ways, sufficient to foul up somebody
who didn't know they were there but easily bypassed by me.
Now, I can't *take* the installation, but I can get a small group
of experienced infiltrators in with equipment—even, possibly, your bomb.''

"Pip," Frawley was rubbing his hands in glee. "Why,
this is marvelous! Marvelous!'' He looked over at Whitely,
and stopped and frowned. "So what is wrong with you?''

"I fear you miss some of the implications of all this,"
replied the Bishop. "Blowing the island is not sufficient. We
must be absolutely certain that Sir Reginald, the bulk of his
followers, the Dark Man, and, I'm sorry to say, Angelique,
are there as well. It will kill everyone, the innocent along
with the guilty, the women and children of Port Kathleen as
well as the bastards up top.''

"I agree that innocents must suffer, but that's the only
way," Frawley replied. "Why, however, do we need all
those others there? I mean, certainly hitting that computer
should be sufficient.''

"No, hardly. You, of all people, should see why. First of
all, the *Revelations* of St. John of Patmos suggest that the
beast shall receive a mortal wound and then be miraculously
healed by the Antichrist. What if we nuke, as I believe it's
said, the whole thing, and then Angelique shows up in
Montreal, say, or London, and announces that while it's a
terrible tragedy it's no time to panic, they have a backup

computer or two on line right now and nothing's interrupted? We'd have delivered a mortal wound to the beast and to Magellan, and then she would heal it and use the incident to further her own power. No, we must have them all—all in the basket at one time. It's our only chance.''

''And when would that be that you could guarantee such a thing?'' Frawley asked him. ''It doesn't seem possible.''

''October thirty-first of this year, when they intend to consecrate Angelique and turn over the power to her, and, not coincidentally, I would think, a day after the final transfer of her inheritance and a day before the next scheduled meeting of Magellan's Board of Directors. They'll all be there on that night, and probably only on that night. Not before or after will they be in one basket.''

''I think you left out one important point in that plan, my Lord Bishop,'' MacDonald noted.

''Oh? What?''

''Whoever goes in, assuming they can plant that thing, will almost certainly be stuck there. We don't dare to just arm and leave it. Security will be extra tight that day and we can't leave the success of a bomb to chance or remote control. It must be hidden, assembled at the last possible minute, and then exploded. Anyone involved in that would be stuck there, too. It's a suicide mission you're talking about. Leaving is as hard or harder than getting in, particularly now, after two escapes. We couldn't afford to risk anyone leaving and getting caught. Everyone involved in this will die in the same atomic blast as they do. And they'll know as well as we do how likely that date is for an attack.''

The Bishop polished off the last of his breakfast. ''Well, my boy, perhaps it's not quite as drastic as you suggest, nor are we quite as defenseless against the magic as you might believe. However, let's float this by the King and see what happens. We'll need some good, dedicated people, solid planning, as much training as we can get, and intelligence if we're to carry any of it off, and time is of the essence."

"Yes," added Frawley skeptically. "We've got all of five weeks."

There was no more need for secrecy now, as they packed up rather leisurely and prepared to link up with others in their organization. Greg MacDonald went back into the motel room to confront Maria.

There was no question that she felt both bitter and angry, but she also left little doubt that she felt less the betrayer than the betrayed. She was certainly still recognizable, but she now stood about four one and weighed perhaps sixty-five pounds, with long light brown hair. She had a good figure, for a kid, but, of course, no breasts, pubic hair or other signs of puberty, and her voice was higher and sounded very child-like. The Dark Man had chosen a particularly cruel point at which to revert and then freeze her; the child-woman, stuck eternally just on the edge of physical ripening.

He tossed some clothing down on the bed, having gone into Carson City to run a number of errands before leaving. MacDonald had never taken pains choosing his own clothes, but he had a good eye for what fit other people. He'd gotten her a sleeveless tee shirt, some jeans, a light jacket, and sneakers. He hadn't bothered with underwear; he thought she'd rebel against panties with cartoon characters on them and she hardly needed a bra.

She put them on rather sullenly, then looked at herself in the mirror and frowned. Many people had fantasies of being children again, but he could read her thoughts just looking at her. *I'm going to be like this forever*. . . . Worse, she might look like that and be subject to the emotional extremes that were physiological at that point, but inside she was the mature and highly experienced woman in her mid-forties she'd been before. Finally, she turned to him and asked the big question.

"What happens to me now?"

"Up to you," he told her. "None of us have any real sense of love and responsibility towards you, you know. If it wasn't for you, the nightmare for many would be over. Now, if we didn't lose everything last night, it'll cost a lot of innocent lives to put it right. As far as I'm concerned, I'll stake you to a couple of hundred bucks and drop you at the Carson City bus station."

There was panic in her eyes and her expression, and she fought back tears. "You *can't* just leave me here! You *can't*!"

"Why not?"

"What am I supposed to *do*? Where can I go? I don't have anybody, you know that. To everybody else I'm just some kid who should be in sixth grade someplace, only I got no papers, no identity, no family, and I'll never grow *out* of the sixth grade! I can't even go back to the church. Who'd believe me?"

"Yeah, well, that's a problem, all right. What would *you* do?"

"Take me with you," she said, almost pleading. "I'll be good—honest. No more trouble. I'll do whatever I'm told. Just—don't leave me here."

"I wish I could count on that, but how can I? We trusted Angelique to you, and you ran at the first trouble and then called in the enemy. We bet our lives on your loyalty, and at the first sign of trouble you turned us in."

"I still think I did the right thing. You heard that old geezer in the van! How many people has he killed or ordered to be killed? He didn't even care about people—he was talking about messing up her body like she was some piece of rock or something. And they wouldn't have stopped looking for you two if you blew her cherry. They need her as a front no matter what. I saved her life, damn it!"

"No, you didn't, Maria. You probably made sure she'd

die. What choice have you left anybody now? She's target number one, and probably so well protected that they'll have to take out half a city to get her—but they'll get her. You turned her from a fugitive needing protection into the most dangerous person alive. Can't you ever understand that there's no perfect world, no perfect situations, no perfect choices except in the movies? And did you really think I'd just fall romantically into your arms when you did this to her, to me, to everybody? What conceit! What arrogance! You really *should* have stayed on their side."

And now she was in tears, and, particularly looking as she did, it was a heart-rending sight. It softened him just a bit inside, but he wouldn't permit it to show.

"How can we trust you, Maria? Blow any plans we have and they'd offer you the moon for the information. You'd crack in a minute."

"No, no! I won't! I swear it! No more dreams, no more illusions! I'll stay this way until the end of time. What would I get out of *them* now? Lots of promises, but I got promises this time, too. No, all I want do now is get even. It's all I got."

He thought about it a moment. It was true she couldn't be trusted, but it was also true that she had roamed that island for weeks as one of the enemy. She alone might know where some of the traps were, and what new things had been added. She knew who was who. This information, supplementing his own, might be very valuable.

"All right," he told her. "You come along—for now. But one step out of line, one little thing done wrong, one look crosseyed at anything, and if you don't know too much you'll be dumped on a street corner with nothing in some city somewhere and that'll be that. If you know too much by that time, then it'll be *your* body they find someplace, and you won't go quick and easy. Understand?"

She practically threw herself at him, crying uncontrollably. "Oh, yes, yes! I'll be good. I swear it. . . ."

The model was a good one: a complete, detailed duplicate Allenby Island in miniature, measuring a good six feet by four feet and showing all the major details, including the town, road, Institute, and even the meadow and woods trails.

"Quite impressive for such short notice," Lord Frawley commented.

"It wasn't very hard. This one used to be in the lobby of the home offices of Magellan in Seattle," MacDonald told him. "It's not quite up to date, but it's useful."

"I won't ask how it wound up here," the older man said. "Here," in fact, was a luxury beach house on the far side of Aruba, well away from much of the built-up and tourist-dominated areas. "However, I've been going over the model with these aerial photographs from this year and I've noted changes where there shouldn't be any."

"Huh? How so?"

"This meadow—the evil place where all this devil rubbish centers—with this big hunk of obsidian in it. It's not very large, but the so-called altar stone on the model is shaped something like a primitive drawing of a sheep or deer. See the two little legs, the U shape between the curvature into this headlike protrusion? Now look at the photograph taken— let's see—May twentieth of this year. The meadow's the same, but the altar stone is a relatively straight line, like the flat of a ruler, with curvatures and slight protrusions on both sides. See?"

MacDonald frowned and examined the two carefully. He'd looked at this many times, but the fact was he'd always been looking for trails, roads, and new construction. The removal or planting of trees was important, but he'd never really paid any attention to the rock formations. Frawley was certainly correct in this, though. The altar stone *had* changed shape—if the model was accurate. "You're sure it's not just the model builder?"

"I'm certain. The early construction photos we have indicate the same shape as the model."

"Yeah, sure—but that's tons of obsidian! How could they switch or carve or do anything to it without messing up the meadow—and why?"

"Well, it wasn't carved. The mass now is larger than the mass at the start. Perhaps a side view would be more illuminating. See, here, that the computer complex goes down six stories below the common with the antennas. That's roughly a hundred and twenty feet. Now extend that elevation out towards the down slope of the mountain, and you see that the meadow is almost exactly at the surface elevation you would be at if you extended this sixth level out to the south."

"Yeah, but the engineering to do something like that would be enormous. We'd have seen something."

"Not necessarily. Do you know anything about the geomorphology of volcanoes?"

"I'm a cop from Canada."

"All right. Well, it's not necessary to build one if you understand that the island is honeycombed with natural lava tubes. When the old mountain blew its cork, lava rushed through, cutting its own way through cracks and weaknesses in the rock. The outside was cooler and the flow was fast, so it more or less built its own pipe. This sort of lava is common in Hawaii, quite rare in the Caribbean, but it was true of our old mountain here. Now, masses of obsidian are formed when lava reaches the surface in such a state that it cools rapidly, too rapidly to form crystals and become true rock. It's a glob of glass. It's my guess that there was a first eruption, the tube was born, but the lava from that cleared the tube entirely, leaving it a slightly crooked cannon, so to speak. Then there was a second eruption with a heavier, more plastic flow, possibly a small amount that shot down the tube and hit a rainstorm, or was blocked in some other way, and cooled immediately. The obsidian, the altar stone, is a plug for the tube which still exists.''

"There *are* some old caves on the island, but they're short and not much use and some of them are caved in or blocked off to prevent any accidents. None of 'em go anywhere that I know of.''

"Precisely. Now you know of one that does. I believe the chamber was opened up and then followed all the way to the plug. Then it was carefully excavated from the cave side, possibly with lasers or other high-heat diggers that wouldn't be good on solid rock but would be fine for obsidian. I have discovered that some such prototypical tools were in fact used during the construction stage. They removed the plug in this manner, taking the remains out via the tunnel, and then replaced it with something that looked natural, probably during the construction although not in the official blueprints. That explains not only the shape change, but why the replacement is larger. They had to lose some of the surroundings during the operation. I think you'll find long cables running from the power plant to the tunnel and through it to this stone or whatever it is. There's your device—computer controlled, computer activated—for all the mumbo jumbo of special effects, specters in the air, and the rest.''

MacDonald was fascinated. "Then it *is* high tech, somehow. But these caves, these lava tubes, interest me more and more now. If they could do this with one of them, maybe they have a whole warren under there. No wonder they could hide so much in such tight quarters! I wish we had a way of knowing where those tubes were, though.''

"We do,'' Frawley replied, and took out a set of rolled-up maps. "Remember, before this was anything it was a station of the Royal Geographic Society during its most active period.'' He took first one map, then another, then another, examining each for a moment, then said, "Ah! Here we are! The summit area before any major construction."

They were copies of what were less maps than blueprints of the mountain from the eighteen eighties, but they clearly showed all the known tubes, including a few that had crater openings. There was clearly one leading inward from the crater's low point, although no exit point was indicated.

"I think I'm going to go talk to Maria again," MacDonald told him, and walked out.

He walked out on the patio and found Bishop Whitely there, reading his Bible but dressed only in a pair of swimming trunks, a Panama hat, and sun glasses. Maria was out on the beach, doing something in the sand.

"Ah, my boy," said the Bishop, putting down his book. "Have you and Pip solved the whole thing for us?"

"Not quite. Uh—how is she today?"

"Mixed," the Bishop replied gravely. "She's right on the edge, Greg. Right on the edge. Do you know what she's doing out there? Building a sand castle. She's got her hair in pigtails, and earlier she asked me if we'd buy her a dog to play with her. She's put on a fairly thick southern American accent and let her grammar go to pot. When she's like this she wants to be called Missy—apparently a family nickname from when she was this age."

"You mean she's becoming what she looks like?" That worried him.

"I only wish that were true. It would be easier to deal with. No, my boy, she's splitting in two. When she's Missy she doesn't ask questions or take on airs, she just acts her physical age and that's that. When she has to be Maria, though—when she's forced to be—the change is quite remarkable. We took her on a shopping spree, so to speak, and the two sides were never more evident in what she bought or how it's used."

"I need to ask her questions about the island. How do I get Maria to come out."

He sighed, stood up, and stretched. "You go back in to your little war games there. I'll fetch her, but give her half an hour to get cleaned up. Be warned, though—Maria totally blocks out the idea that she's in a child's body. She doesn't see herself that way, but rather as she was."

"She's going 'round the bend, then. How dependable will she be?"

"Well, that's a matter of opinion. I don't think it's schizophrenia, if that's what you mean. I think it's deliberate, if not totally conscious. It is her way of coping."

Greg nodded worriedly and went back in to Frawley. "O.K.," he said, so we have the caves to deal with, and we have to assume they can get from here to there, maybe several places, without being seen. That just complicates the problem. Still, they wouldn't have let me get all the way to the power plant when I 'invaded' the place if they thought that access posed a security threat. I mean, they could have stopped me without blowing their cover."

"I agree. Now, that power plant—it is a small experimental fusion reactor, totally self contained?"

"Yeah, that's true. Not very cost efficient in that form, but it allows a totally independent power supply to be fed to the computer and the grids. It's used only for that, though. The power for the basic Institute is still generated by burning oil, which comes in by tanker every six weeks. It seemed wasteful to build a whole pipeline from Port Kathleen up the mountain, so instead a shorter line was installed here, at the base of the cliffs in back of the Institute. A small pumping station takes off the oil and stores it in these two tanks here, at sea level, then pumps it up to the Institute's tanks as needed along this nearly vertical pipeline."

"Uh huh. And the pipeline only goes up two thirds of the

way up the sheer cliffs on the north side, I see. That means the tanks themselves are on level six."

"Right. There's a ladder along both sides of the pipe, just in case, but it ends at that point and there's no access to Level Six from the cliffs. The pipe goes in through a hole only big enough for it, and the wall and tanks are on the other side, perhaps a foot or two, whatever was required for stability."

"Monitors?"

"Well, the basic tank and pumping station is unmanned but heavily guarded electronically. Additionally, there are six all-weather cameras, two of them infra-red types, mounted at various points along the ladders, and sound monitoring gear at various other points. If necessary, they can send a lethal voltage right through those ladders, and they're usually carrying a non-lethal charge to begin with to discourage anyone and also to keep away the birds and other critters that might accidentally set off their alarms."

"It sounds pretty formidable. That's the way you did it last time, though?"

He nodded. "It's the most vulnerable area of the island. I picked a new moon and had a small storm to help, so there was some electrical interference for them to contend with anyway. I wish we had somebody who could arrange a storm this time, since we're locked in to the dates." He sounded sad and wistful saying that, remembering someone who *could* arrange such a storm at will. "I'm pretty sure that they'll have a patrol boat anchored at the dock, too. No, I wouldn't come up the back side, but of the two remaining routes the least chancy—and it's still a dilly—is to come up the west face from this little cove here." He pointed to it on the model. "I'm sure they have no monitoring down there simply because it's where I put in for the day when I escaped, and they never caught me."

"Uh huh. Less of a climb, but still a deuced ordeal, and no ladders."

"It's a bad climb, that's for sure—almost a sheer drop, and complicated by this small but spectacular waterfall here. But it gives some shelter to people below, if we can get a boat in that far past the patrols and radar network, and if one man, a good, experienced climber, could get up there and anchor something. He'd take up a rope, then we'd attach that rope to a good rope or woven synthetic line ladder. With enough people up, we could use the same network to rig a primitive hoist and bring up the equipment."

"We'd be sitting ducks up there until it was all done," Frawley noted. "And the ladder would have to go before we moved anywhere."

"Agreed, but the sitting duck stage in unavoidable no matter how we come in, and as for the ladder—well, you only wanted a one way trip, didn't you?"

Frawley sighed. "Yes. Quite so. All right—now we're up with all the equipment. Now what? Isn't there a network of security sensors about the cameras strung here and there?"

"Yes. It's called the grid, but it's been there for some time. There are only a couple of cameras up there, in that region, both with heavy duty power packs, since you can't really run power lines. Their outputs run up to small microwave transmitters sticking out of the treetops, where the signal is beamed back to security and SAINT. King's base assures me that the latest satellite photos still show only those two—one here at the waterfall, the other covering the remaining cabin and pump, where they kept Angelique. That was one extra reason for putting her there. There are a few battery powered microphones as well, including a couple whose existence I'm going to assume since *I* would put them there—one here at the lookout, for example, which is how they knew Angelique was going to escape. Until now, I wasn't really sure how their output got back, since they're not tied into the transmitters for the cameras, but I think I'll get the answer in a few minutes, for I just saw the Bishop waving out the back window. Excuse me.''

He went into the living room and stopped dead in his tracks.

"Hi," said Maria softly.

He hadn't even known they made dresses like that in such a small size. She was apparently wearing falsies, and a clinging, smooth satiny dress of dark green material that was split most of the way on both sides. She had let her hair down, applied heavy makeup including eye shadow, rouge, and lipstick, and clip-on dangling earrings. She was even wearing a pair of matching high-heeled shoes in her tiny size. She looked more like a midget whore than a ten year old, he thought, even to the moves, except for the fingernails. Missy, it appeared, bit hers. He remembered the Bishop's caution that she either believed, or pretended, that she was fully adult in this phase, and although he didn't need *this* kind of adult he did indeed need that adult's memory.

He cleared his throat nervously. "Dressing for a night on the town?"

"No, I just wanted to see if you liked it. You don't know just how long it's been since I dressed like this."

"It's—stunning. But I only need the answers to some questions now, things I hope you can tell me."

"Go ahead, Greg. Anything you want."

Uh, yeah, he thought nervously. He felt like he was in a kiddie porn movie, even though he knew better. "Are there caves underneath the Institute that the Dark Man and his people use?"

She looked surprised, "Uh, yeah, sure. A few."

"Any that start up there or near there and come out elsewhere on the island?"

"Sure. One, anyway. It goes from the chemistry building— what is it, the Carrington Building?—basement over and down almost to the cabin where they kept Angelique. It's how we got all the supplies to her and got in and out without trampling down the forest. No lights—you had to use like miner's hàts and big lanterns—but it's smooth and easy. We'd bring the stuff on a hand truck and then it was only twenty feet or so to the cabin. They had it disguised and all at the cabin end. I don't think even Angelique ever found it or knew it was there. They said the old man—Sir Robert, I guess—used it to go from the cabin to the Institute when they were building, but it was bricked up on both ends when they tore the bulk of the cabins down. They just un-bricked it, I guess. It don't look like much from the outside.''

He nodded absently. ''I want you to take some diagrams of the island and show me every cave you know. Then I want to sit down with you and talk security.''

She stared at him. ''You're going back, aren't you? You're *really* going back!''

''Well, somebody is. Not necessarily me.''

''To kill Angelique?''

''We don't even think she's on the island right now, although it's hard to tell for sure. Let's say we're sending in some folks to try and blow that computer if we can.''

''You can't. You can't get near it without it knowing, and you can't even put its lights out without going through it. Nobody goes in or out of there without the mark, and it's something you can't fake. Strictly for the true believers and put on down there by the Dark Man or somebody.''

Bishop Whitely entered, still wearing his bathing suit. ''Did I hear something about a mark?''

''Yes, sir. It's a crazy looking thing, kind of a six written three times, in three sizes, one a little bigger than another and encircling the smaller one, then encircled itself by the biggest one.''

''Indeed. The number of the beast, or one of them. I expected that. How and where is it worn?''

"The forehead, mostly, but occasionally on the wrist. You can't see it most of the time, although they say that ones with it can always see it on others who have it. You could see it in the meadow, though. Real slick and professional, like a purplish tatto, only printed on."

"Makes sense," the Bishop responded. "Now, will you go in and show old Pip whatever it is Greg wants you to? I want to talk to him alone for a minute."

She looked disappointedly at Greg, but he nodded and she complied. When she was in the back room and the door was shut, the Bishop took him over to the patio doors and then out onto the patio itself. "Sit down, my boy."

He took a chair, and waited for the old man to begin.

"You know, I've been thinking about who should go on this little mission, considering what has to be done. I overheard you talk of caves under the island and it's changed the whole nature of the game, I think."

"Oh? How?" As of now, they had been going with a small sailboat handled by but three men. Two would assist in assembling the bomb and arming it, but would then get away in a small dinghy if they could for pickup at sea. He was, however, already thinking along new and more somber lines as was the Bishop.

"I've always been frightened of the bomb," said the Lord Bishop, "and I've even been involved in disarmament rallies. It kept me popular at Oxford and made my peers in the church think I wasn't *all* Tory. But this thing, this bomb, has to be right and it has to be effective. It's not going to vaporize the island any more than even Hiroshima, devastated as it was, was vaporized, particularly not when placed at the bottom of a cliff."

"We already knew that. Lord Frawley and I were just discussing how to get the bomb and man up top."

"All right—but just how effective will it be, I wonder? What of these caves and lower levels? It'll sear and huff and puff on the surface, but what about below? Will it kill SAINT when SAINT is so well insulated? Will those in the tunnels, with their great powers, be able to ride it out and then survive?''

"Well, the best place would be right in the common, and that's out of the question," Greg told him. "The second best would be over at the meadow, and I think that's no more likely. I think, though, that Lord Frawley is considering planting it in another cave that enters the Institute at that level. Most of the blast will still be surface, but enough will go up that tube that it should blow the Institute from the bottom up. Nothing is certain. We don't have the kind of bomb that will do it in, period, although such bombs exist. We haven't the means to steal it, we haven't time to build it, and nobody with one is going to give it to us. I would think an A-bomb about a third the size of what did in the Japanese should be enough.''

"But is it, really? If we explode something as terrible as an atomic bomb and then the computer and Angelique some-how emerge after-well, it would do their job nicely and fulfill the prophecy.''

"What are you getting at?''

"Two teams. One for the bomb, another for the Institute. An attack launched, let's say, no more than an hour before our bomb goes off. Blow up what we can, kill whoever we can, God forgive me, get as far as we can. In particular, blow the suites, the library, whatever and wherever key people are likely to be. They're expecting something. Let's give it to them.''

"A diversion?''

"Yes, indeed. That, and more. Real damage, as far and as far down as we can get.''

"But Security—''

"—Will be preoccupied and harried during that period. This is a chance to act boldly, audaciously, decisively—as they do. To give them a taste of their own medicine and their own fears. Who knows who we might get strictly at random? Sir Reginald? The Dark Man?"

"Angelique," said Greg hollowly.

"What can I say except that we will save her immortal soul by doing so? Don't fear death quite so much, my friend. Angelique didn't, which is why the Dark Man found something far more terrible. Greater love has no man but to lay down his life for his friend. Even greater, I think, for strangers. Is living in the fascistic Orwellian world they will create for the West better than death or is it merely a slower, more miserable, more prolonged death horror? Knowing that their inevitable goal is a massive nuclear exchange with the East? Even the most conservative of governments and the most paranoid do not want nuclear war today even as they build bigger and better weapons. *They want it*, and if you want it and gain control you shall have it."

"It could backfire and tip our hand to no profit," he said. "We might not get anybody important or insure anything, but alert them. They'll put everything on hold and scour the island."

"Pip is rigging a dead man switch for the triggering mechanism. If it sounds as if anyone is even coming close ahead of the deadline it will be triggered, and if they shoot him, as is most likely no matter what powers we talk about, he releases the switch and it blows. No, his period of danger is between set-up and detonation time."

"You're talking like you expect to be there."

He sighed. "My boy, I have *always* expected to be there. I am seventy-two, but I climbed a mountain in Wales as late as last year. My heart and mind are sound and I'm in excellent shape. Now Pip, of course, will be the trigger man for the bomb."

"Now wait a minute!"

"No, no, hear me out! He knows what he's doing. He's an

expert and he's designed this thing. There's none else nearly as qualified. What you don't know is that he's got a cancer. A bad one, in the brain and inoperable, with a good deal of it running around his body and settling elsewhere. He is in constant pain, and had methodically prepared for his own suicide before it grew so bad and he so weak that he'd be in bed. He doesn't believe in God or the afterlife, but he does believe in miracles and this is his. His whole life he's sent young men and women out to die, or ordered the deaths of others. His whole life has been spent in the dark corners. He never married, and he lives only for that, but it was taken away several years ago in a scandal involving some of his superiors as well as a strong and unrealistic idealistic streak on the part of the last Labour government. The very existence of the bomb we're using is an act of treason, since it's one of many that he and several colleagues saved and hid with RAF connivance when the stages of Britain's unilateral nuclear disarmament policy were announced by the Prime Minister. That's how he got it.''

MacDonald was stunned. ''I—I didn't know.''

''You see, it's his one last act, his one spectacular way out. He'll save the world, and, more important, *he'll do it personally,* not sit back and order others to do so.''

''But we're talking about a climb up a sheer rock face of almost four hundred and fifty meters! He can't possibly make it!''

''He'll make it because he wants to more than he wants anything else in the world.''

''But—you! You were just telling me how healthy you were!''

''I am indeed. For me it is a different thing. I might live another ten or twenty mostly useless years watching everything fall apart. I might go tomorrow, of course—only God knows that for sure. But, my boy, I have spent my entire life in the service of God and His holy Church. I have fought a lifelong, devoted war in His name—and I've been losing. All my life I've wondered, after every failure, every setback, why God called me to this profession. I've felt like Job. Call it madness if you wish, or conceit, but I feel that all of that was preparation for this. I am called to do battle with Satan himself. No greater glory could a man of my faith ask. More, I'm the only one that understands them as they really are, and, as a result, I'm the only one who can fight them on spiritual grounds. No one, but no one, will deny me this. If I am forbidden to go, I will get a boat and sail right into Port Kathleen myself. I know—I'm sounding less like a doddering old fool and more like a fanatic."

"Yes," MacDonald agreed, not at all reticent to say so.

"Well and good, my boy, because no matter what their high-tech pyrotechnics and black magical parlor tricks, *so are they*. *So are they*."

MacDonald sat back and sighed. "I need a drink," he said. "That and a change of subject for the moment."

"The first is easily remedied. The pitcher there has sangria and there are two glasses sitting inside each other next to your chair. As for the second—what do you think of Maria now?"

He poured one and took a good swallow. It tasted fine, and he had no idea of the power of it, although he knew that the Bishop liked his drinks strong. "I—I don't know. It's really sad, somehow."

"Why? With all that paraphernalia, she feels like the woman she is inside, and she needs to be. Without it, she's a defenseless little kid with no future, so she might as well *be* that kid."

"Well, what else can she do?"

"No matter what she looks like, she's another Angelique. She's really a mature woman and she desperately needs to be treated like one in all respects. Most of all, she needs to be trusted again, particularly by you. She is as in love with you now as she was before all this. She needs your trust and your love, and she'll follow you anywhere, even die for you.''

"Well, she may have to adjust otherwise. You and I know, Bishop, that if this thing is to be pulled off I'm going to have to be there. I'm going to have to be the one to keep everybody else from tripping sound alarms and getting on camera. Nobody else, except maybe Maria, has the—*wait* a minute! You aren't suggesting that she go along?''

"I'm suggesting that she be told nothing or even have intimated to her anything about the bomb. Pip will be secure, and so will I. That other team, however, is valuable. I think she ought to be offered a chance to participate, to redeem herself, with the full understanding that she is going to die up there.''

"You'd put that much trust in her—after all this?''

"I would. Treat her as she wants to be treated. Give her everything she wants—and I say this as a man of God, I hope. In the end, it will come down to Maria or you. You can supervise—and survive to continue the fight if we all fail. You don't have to go, Greg—if she does. I'll take the responsibility.''

He sat back and sighed. *Damn!* "Who else are you including in your suicide pact?''

"No more than two or three others. King's base has already got them picked, if they agree. They'll be here drifting in, one at a time, starting tomorrow.''

"More geriatric wonders?''

"No. But each has their own reasons for wanting to do this, and they all know it's certain death. They'll do.''

He stared for a moment at the old man. "You're some strange kind of priest,'' he said at last.

"Yes, I know. It's been my own cross to bear.''

MacDonald sat back and finished the drink. He didn't care how strong it was; he needed something stronger. "Look—I never bargained for all this. If I hadn't been handy and convenient when they polished off Sir Robert, I wouldn't even know any of this was happening. I don't mind risking my life, but suicide is not part of my make-up.''

"Pip intends to commit suicide and yet make his death count for something. The others—they have their reasons, I think, but they aren't suicidal any more than I am. Not even Jesus wanted to go to the cross in the end. You're far too young to remember the Second World War, but none of our brave lads wanted to die. Still, when you stand there and see your own capital burning, when you hear the screams of trapped women and children and can do nothing to save them from the roaring fires, when you see the horrors of the concentration camp, the ovens, the piles of bones, the gold melted from the fillings of victims, you know that if you do not face down evil, no matter what the cost to you, you deserve just what you see. You are most fortunate, my boy. God has mercifully given you a supporting role in which sacrifice is not a requirement. No one is blaming you. If this cup could be taken from my hands I would relinquish it, but it can not. Now—go. We have much to do, and the clock is ticking.''

MacDonald got up and walked slowly back into the house where Maria was waiting to be led like a lamb to the slaughter, if only he would act his part.

14

BEST LAID PLANS . . .

Bishop Whitely introduced them as Shadrach, Meshach, and Abednego, but their nationalities were, respectively, Sikh, Lebanese, and Nigerian. Most surprising to MacDonald was the fact that the Lebanese was a Christian and a woman. The Nigerian was a Moslem, and Sikh's flowing beard and turban marked not only his nationality but his faith as well.

They sat around the living room in the warm, comfortable island resort nation of Aruba and MacDonald could not think of a less likely looking group in a more incongruous place. He wished he knew why these three, particularly the darkly attractive woman, had volunteered for such a mission, knowing only that it was against some great evil and would cost them their lives. With them, too, were Whitely, Frawley, and Maria.

"We have only ten days to work this all out," Frawley told them. "There can be only a small amount of practice, and I'm sure that they have agents here and possibly already know that we are gathered together. There's no way to keep it secret here, I fear, but I believe they will allow us to keep going. It's in character for them to let the enemy try, so when he fails he will know it. You should know that because there is, I believe, not the slightest chance of any of us coming out of this alive, win or lose. Still, the armies of the world are at *their* beck and call, not ours. Only a very small, expert force, will be able to get onto that island and do damage. I say this because this is your last chance to back out. Replacements are still possible, but not after this afternoon. After this, you will know too much. After this, anyone who backs out, or hesitates, will be killed. There is no other way around it. The enemy can hear and see far more than we can, though they lack, I hope, the details of the plan. Therefore, anyone who still wishes to back out now should do so at this time. I will ask you one at a time. Shadrach?"

"It is my moral imperative to go, for I understand the nature of the enemy you fight," said the Sikh, in Indian-accented English. "I wish you to understand that the Indian government years ago wiped out my entire family in their *pogrom,* yet I did not lose my faith. It sustained me, as I sought to discover the reason for such events. It is because of this, I feel, that I was spared. I am ready to join them, but my death must have meaning. I will go."

The Bishop and the Rook nodded absently to themselves. "Very well," said Frawley, "you are in and welcome. We need you desperately, for you are our mountaineer. The bravery and greatness of your people's fighting skills are well known and taken for granted. Meshach?"

This was the dark Lebanese woman. "I will go. Since they butchered my children I have been nothing but a madwoman, a killing machine, but it is endless. It will be good to have meaning, to have an end."

"Excellent. One of your experience will be invaluable. Abednego?"

The dark Nigerian in tennis whites shrugged. "It seems we are in a confessional stage. I leave that to the others. I am a professional without ties whom Allah has called to this purpose. I will do the job. The rest is in the hands of Allah.''

Frawley nodded. "My Lord Bishop, I'm not too keen on taking you along on this, although I understand that some were not too keen on me so I have to reserve judgment. You are determined?"

Bishop Whitely nodded soberly. "I am."

"All right, then. You all know, or should know, that is unlikely that I will see another Chrismas, nor do I want to. It's a good thing this is in ten days, for if it were thirty, as much as we need the time, I might not be able to manage it. I will manage it now, though. And that leaves us with our two younger folks here. I ask the newcomers not to judge the young lady. She is older, I suspect, than the three of you and a victim of their powers.''

Maria smiled, welcoming that. She had dressed informally for this, but had kept her made up face and manner.

MacDonald had swallowed both his pride and his inhibitions and had spent most of the previous evening with her, mostly, as Whitely had suggested, making her feel like an adult woman. Nothing serious—he'd arranged a candlelight dinner for the two of them at a small private beach house, including champagne, and they had just talked and then walked on the beach, discussing everything but the situation at hand or her own limitations, and he'd found, just as he had with Angelique, that it was possible for him to remember who and what she really was and look beyond the physical. Ultimately, when they had returned to the house, he had told her that they were going back, and soon, and that they needed guides for the island itself.

"You're going with them?" she'd asked him.

"I may have to. There's no one else who knows the island as well in our group."

"And—it's one way, isn't it? They'll either kill or capture everybody in the end no matter how much damage you do.''

"Yes," he'd admitted.

"Then I'll be the guide. I'm small, light, and I know the places you never found. I—appreciate tonight, more than you can ever know, but I don't have any future. I have nothing to live for, really, and I'd love to get back at them. You—they'll be looking for you, expecting you. What they'll do to you will make what they did to Angelique and me seem like nothing. You can have a future."

"But you'll die."

She'd whirled and faced him. "Don't you see? All my life I've made the wrong choices. All my life I've messed up everything and everyone I've come in contact with. It's my last chance. I want a chance as my instructors in the convent put it, to redeem myself. This is it. I can wipe the slate clean if I do this right. Besides—who knows if I die or not? Anything's possible the way this thing's been going."

He hadn't been able at that point to really go through with it. He just wasn't that much of a heel. "Don't think you have to for me."

"No, if they'll let me, I'm going. Oh, I know why you're doing all this, but that's O.K. You're the only one who'll ever treat me like this, though, so I'm going to enjoy it and pretend it's all real as long as it lasts, but I'm not just going for you. I've *got* to go—for myself."

"As you may know, Miss, I'm not too keen on having you along," Frawley was saying. "It's neither a matter of age or size or any sort of gallantry. I simply do not consider you reliable under pressure. Still, I have been overruled on this, and I accept it, but you must understand this. I do not believe in the life beyond and I do not believe we are dealing with anything not somehow explainable by science, but if you betray us or fail us in the slightest way at all, I will come out of my grave, if need be, to make certain that you will do no more harm."

key building housing the important people and containing direct access to the library and computer complex below. The primary objective is to reach and, if possible, blow the computer and/or its power plant. To give you an edge, we're going to first lower a time bomb to the pipe at the rear and blow it. That explosion might ignite the oil tanks. In any case it will cut the general power and cause a hell of a bang, drawing security and everyone else to that point, outside and in.

"With any luck, the most dangerous players will already be at the meadow area or in the cave leading to it. We feel they will send a few people back, but mostly try and continue down there, figuring that their security people can handle it. There may well still be innocents in the Lodge, but you can't tell who's who and it's certain death to try. Anyone who comes upon you must be killed, as quickly and as silently as possible, with no hesitation. Man, woman, child, dog—I don't care what. If you're discovered, do what damage you can and blow what you can. If you're fatally down, there will be a way to blow whatever you're carrying all at once."

The understood the plan.

"Bishop, your main job, if you think you can handle it, is to carry and place as many charges as possible at the antennas in the common. You'll be exposed there, but you should wait until all hell breaks loose in the Lodge, as it inevitably will, and everyone rushes there. There are seven small enclosed boxes that simply have to be placed on the concrete pads and a trigger switch thrown on each. Their combined weight is about fifty pounds. Not much, but forty five seconds after each switch is thrown they will go with enough force to wreck or possibly topple those antennas, putting SAINT off the air."

"I think I can manage that," the Bishop said. "I've carried heavier packs than this. But what of the eighth outlet

at the meadow? If they can't put it out for good, it will still
have at least a local outlet.''

"We'll have to forget it and hope that Lord Frawley's blast
does the trick,'' MacDonald replied. ''It'll be well defended
and will have those of greatest power there, making it next to
impossible to get near. If you somehow can, then all the
better—take out whoever you can. After the dishes are blown,
you're on your own.''

"Don't fret about me, old boy. I can think of quite a lot of
mischief to do in the—what?—half hour or so until Pip's
thing blows. Don't fret.''

"What about me? What am I supposed to do?'' Maria
asked him. ''I can't carry much weight, and one of those
automatic popguns would probably knock me over.''

"Your first objective will be in getting them in and settled
at the first assembly point,'' MacDonald told her. ''Then
you'll have to do some reconnoitering. You're small and
light and you know the place well. That night, you'll get the
team up to the Lodge. After that—you're on your own.''

"Why don't Maria and I blow the oil line first?'' the
Bishop suggested. ''She can come with me and assist on the
common, and, after that, she might be able to get me down
to that meadow.'' Unspoken, of course, was that she would
be under someone's watchful eye after things broke loose
who would see that she didn't then try and renew old
friendships.

"Maria?''

She nodded.

"O.K., then. We'll start now with a cross-section of the
Lodge itself. . . .''

Over the next week, they practiced and rehearsed over and
over again. Shadrach, the Sikh, was unhappy that the rope
and ladder assembly, which arrived on the fourth day, couldn't
really be tested, but it was understood that they were probably being watched and, even if they were undiscovered,

finding a suitable cliff in the region and climbing it would be sure to attract unwanted attention. They were, however, able to rig up a forty-foot rope off an inland cliff area and try climbing it at night. It was only a fraction of the distance they would have to go, but it helped.

The three professionals had no trouble with it, nor did MacDonald or the Bishop. Frawley had considerable problems, but he made it, and swore he'd make it no matter how long it was. Maria, too, had extremely sore arms after it, but since both would have a rope ladder affair they felt certain they could get up there if they had to—which they did.

Treating Maria as one of the team helped her ego enormously, and MacDonald continued to pay real attention to her in the evenings, giving her rubdowns and being gentle with her. He still didn't agree with her actions back in California, but he understood them, he thought, and that made her betrayal a little easier to take.

They had gradually adjusted their schedules forward, sleeping much of the day and up all night, and the time passed all too quickly. They weren't ready, it was clear. They needed more time, more information, more practical exercises—but they weren't going to get any of them. The thirtieth came, and MacDonald and Maria sat on the beach and watched the dawn. For the first time, all of them, including him and her, felt the finality that was approaching quickly.

"Greg?" she asked nervously. "Do you think there's a God? A real heaven and hell?"

He sighed. "I don't know, and that's honest enough. Frawley's a brilliant man, and he's convinced there's nothing but the laws of science. The Bishop's every bit his equal, I think, and he's just as convinced that God, heaven, hell, and the rest of it exists. Me, I've always just sort of felt there was a God I guess, but I can't tell you who or what God is. Take that trio in there. They all are believers and all believe in one God. The woman's a Catholic and her view is pretty close to

the Bishop's, although I think she doubts and has doubted
since they blew her kids away in a random shooting spree.
The Nigerian is a firm believer in his God as the only one,
and in some ways his god's the same as the Christian one.
The Sikh has a lot of Hindu stuff in his religion, even some
reincarnation I think, but he's still convinced that his god's
the same one the others have. The Hindus and the Buddhists
and the like have different ideas and many gods, but they
may have a little of the truth. There's no way to know
without being there.''

"I know. I never thought of it much until I went into the
convent, even though I was forced to be a good church goer
all the time I was growing up. For all its complicated rituals
and beliefs, Catholicism is an easy religion, really. It doesn't
demand a whole hell of a lot. Go to church every Sunday and
on certain other days, take communion, confess your sins,
say some prayers or do other penance, then go out and sin all
over again. It's an easy thing to fall into, particularly when
the Church makes sure you get all the basics, but deep down
I never was able to swallow it whole.''

"Do *you* believe in heaven and hell?" he asked her.

"I don't know. I think that there's *got* to be a hell, just so
people like the Dark Man and Sir Reginald and folks like that
will get it. When you see some good people corrupted, when
you see a kid who just happened to be in the way lying there
beside his bike bleeding to death. . . . There's got to be a
hell someplace. I'm not so sure about heaven, though. In a
way, you have to go along with the Dark Man. If *this* isn't
hell, then the blood of all those innocents, the babies who die
blameless, all the horror with no purpose—it just isn't any
kind of place a good and merciful and just god would allow
to happen. Oh, I heard all the arguments—all the priests with
their high-sounding long-winded explanations of just about
everything—but I can't buy it. Even the Bishop can go on for

hours, but the Dark Man makes more sense. Either God *is* crazy, or He isn't what we think at all.''

"Yeah, well, maybe it's just one of those things our brains can't solve, even with these super computers.''

"I like to think maybe Frawley's right,'' she said, ''but I can't. I've seen babies being born, and I look around and see how complicated it all is and I just can't believe that it came from nothing. I just kind of think sometime that we're just higher animals in His playground, though, that He never really listens or cares about us except maybe the way a farmer cares about his cows or sheep or pigs. I look back on my life and I'm just going to pretend we're just animals, anyway. No inhibitions, no thinking, no caring. Think *you* could pretend, just for a little bit?''

He held her close. ''What do you mean?'' he asked her softly.

"I want you to pretend that you love me, for just this morning. I want you to pretend that I look like I did back on that oil rig. Just this one last time I want to be kissed all over and do the kissing like we meant it. I want to be naked and feel somebody inside me, going off, exploding there. I want to be loved real hard one last time.''

He felt a tear in his eyes, and he'd seldom felt that before. *He* would come back, but to an empty house. . . . What the hell could he do but what she wanted and what he wanted to give her?

It looked like a small recreational sailing vessel of the kind seen by the hundreds in the Caribbean. They had not reached it directly, but had left in twos and threes by various means throughout the afternoon and rendezvoused shortly before midnight at a staging point off the Venezuelan coast about thirty miles from the island.

All their supplies and equipment had already been placed on board, and the ship was crewed by three silent young men supplied by King's base. All but the Nigerian blacked their faces and exposed skin; the African chuckled at their efforts and did an unflattering critique. Of the group, only he and the Bishop seemed not the least bit sullen or worried. Everyone else, including Frawley, seemed to be in a state of high nervous tension.

Under their black clothing, each wore a cross on a chain that had been blessed by the Bishop at a private mass he conducted just for them. Even the Sikh, the Moslem, and Frawley wore them, because, while *they* weren't Christian, the enemy was following a Christian script. They might not mean anything at all against the Dark Man or any other, but there was a slight psychological advantage they didn't want to miss.

The moon was a mere crescent sliver, hardly giving any light at all, and as they sailed they ran into choppier seas and heavier clouds, and the night grew black as pitch.

"Perhaps this is our first sign of divine help," the Bishop noted, looking at the darkness.

"If, of course, we make it into the lagoon without cracking up and make it up that cliff wall by braille," Frawley muttered.

"We'll make it in, sir," one of the crew whispered to him. "We've snuck in and out of there three times already without once being detected, and two nights ago it was just about this bad."

MacDonald was confident, too, at least of that much. "I kind of expected a cloud cover for tomorrow night, but it looks like they're starting early to make it look more natural. I think that tomorrow there's going to be a hell of a rainstorm everywhere around here for twenty or thirty miles except right on the island itself. They don't want anybody seeing what they're doing up there."

The Bishop shrugged. "Whether by heaven or hell, it helps us and hinders them. I glanced at their little radar in there. There are so many false blips from wind and thermals and waves that it looks like a riot of light green. I doubt if anyone could pick us out of it from the surface, and the cover makes it unlikely that we could be picked out by infra-red satellite for a day or two at least, if then."

"You act pretty confident of success," Frawley grumbled.

"I am confident only of what God wills, and I don't know His will in this matter. I am confident only that we are the anointed ones to do this job, and that if we did not at least try He would allow the end to come. I am confident that, starting tomorrow, we will at least know some of the answers."

MacDonald worked his way back to Maria, who was just sitting there, staring out at the blackness. "Butterflies?" he asked her.

"That and a lot of soreness. I feel like somebody ran a broom handle straight through me and out the ass end."

He felt embarrassed. "Sorry."

"No, no! Don't *ever* be sorry! I must have done it ten thousand times and that was the first time it ever really counted, ever really *meant* something."

He was touched. "That doesn't sound like an animal talking."

"No, not an animal. You know, it's crazy, but after forty five years I think I finally just grew up."

He took her tiny hand and squeezed it.

"That thing Frawley's got," she whispered, her voice barely audible. "It's an A-bomb or something like it, isn't it? You're gonna blow the whole island tomorrow."

"Yes," he replied, deciding it wasn't worth hiding any more. "Something like it."

"All those people. . . ."

"No, it's not as bad as we thought. It turns out they've evacuated the whole town except for a staff. Took them off in small groups over the past several weeks. Where, we don't know, but definitely incommunicado until November, when I guess they'll be brought back. They're using the town to put up a bunch of visitors. The choppers have been coming in and out for days now. It's a good bet that there will be nobody on that island we don't know about who's an innocent party, anyway.''

She sighed. ''That makes me feel a little better. You know, it's funny. I'm not really scared of them any more. No matter what, I'm not really scared of the Dark Man or any of them. I'm just scared of that cliff and that rope ladder. I don't know if I can make it.''

''You'll make it,'' he told her. ''Still, you can back out now. I have to go up and help haul up the stuff and get it in place.''

''I'll make it,'' she told him flatly. ''Somehow, I'll make it.''

There was mostly silence for the rest of the trip.

They didn't realize they were there until suddenly large rocks loomed on either side. Nobody but the crew had seen the marker and warning lights both at sea level and up above.

The man who was code-named Shadrach had studied the photographs and geological reports of this area for nine days, but this was still the first time he'd seen and felt it. The rock was heavy, black, and basalt-like; rich, dark lava from ancient flows atop compacted ash, then more basalt, and so forth. He liked the feel of it.

The rock wall was not sheer, although it looked it and they talked as if it was. Actually there was a slight slope and a great many irregularities in it, and there was even random vegetation growing out of cracks and crevices all along, thicker at the top and bottom.

The Punjabi mountain man basically used pitons, counting on the constant noise from the nearby waterfall to mask any strong hammer sounds. He was quick, and expert, and seemed to go up the wall without them in places like a human fly, although it was clear that he was using unseen footholds here and there in the rock.

He was soon out of sight, going rapidly upwards beyond their field of view. Only once, though, did he seem to slip, and a piton came down, bounced off the rock wall once, and splashed into the water very near the boat, making everyone jump and go for their guns.

They waited nervously, and it seemed like they were going to be trapped in the blackness forever. Shadrach had asked for an hour and it took him exactly fifty-seven minutes. They knew this because suddenly the long rope that was attached to him and which lay coiled in a free-spinning roller on the deck suddenly began to move much faster, and soon the first part of the rope ladder was going up. They watched, and waited, until finally the whole of the ladder was unfurled and the bottom of it stood there, waiting.

MacDonald hadn't wanted any part of that night ascent, but he'd climbed a lot of mountains in his time and so he was first up the new entrance to Allenby Island, stopping every so often to drive two hooks into the mountain, one on each side of the ladder, and so loosely secure it in a dozen or so places. It would not do to have it nailed to the wall, but these few connections, even though they might provide some problems for those coming after, gave the thing some stability.

Climbing it, he decided, was pretty easy if you were in any condition at all and took it easy. He did find, near the top, that they'd slightly underestimated the height and that the last twenty feet or so were accomplished by walking up the rope and through some irritating brush, but at the top he felt a strong hand take his and Sadrach pulled him over the top.

"Nothing to it," the Sikh whispered.

"If you say so," he responded, and sat for a few moments.

Next up, to their surprise, was the Bishop, puffing a little but not seeming to have much of a problem. Then came the Lebanese woman, code named Meshach, and the Nigerian.

To their great surprise, the Nigerian was actually carrying Maria on his back as if she were nothing at all.

"Had to do it," he whispered. "She'd never had made it any other way."

It was several minutes more until Frawley made it, sounding horrible and looking almost too ill to move. The man was nasty, ill-tempered, and callous towards everyone and everything not exactly his way, but there was no denying his will power or his guts.

"I'll be all right," he gasped, lying on his back and sounding as if he were going to die. "I'll last another twenty-four hours."

Now the Sikh was back down the ladder in a flash, unsecuring it except at top and bottom, then risking a single tiny signal with his flashlight.

The two at the top and MacDonald busily undid the packs they'd come up with, and the Canadian and the Bishop quickly assembled a basic military ranger winch as the Lebanese and the Nigerian picked up sub-machine guns and established a guard post.

It took almost four hours to winch and haul all the equipment up; an hour longer than the plan called for, but barely within tolerable limits.

The winch was now disassembled and repacked into one large backpack, and it was time to separate. MacDonald looked at the pack, which he was to carry back down, and then the company, just shadows in the near blackness.

They strapped the pack onto his back and he looked at them and he had a strange feeling of unreality about the moment. Somehow he could clearly see the Bishop, Frawley, and Maria standing there, looking back at him. He wanted to say something, anything, but no words would come.

He went over to the rope and grabbed hold, and for some reason he just couldn't move. He just stood there, frozen, in a very stupid position.

Shadrach came over to him. "You go now! We need the dark and we must be away!"

He tried again, and his muscles just wouldn't obey, almost like it was back in the motel with the Dark Man. For a moment he wondered if they'd been spotted after all, if some spell now held him, but he knew that it was not the case. Finally, realizing that the clock was ticking and that all their lives depended on keeping as much of a schedule as possible, he got back up and sighed and took off the backpack. "This may be the stupidest thing any North American has done since he stepped across the line at the Alamo, but I'm staying, too."

Maria gave a little gasp and whispered, "No. You don't have to." The Bishop, however, gave a soft, wry smile.

"Yeah. I know I'm going to regret this, but I have to. Shad, can you get this pack back down?"

The Sikh picked it up and put it on expertly. "Don't leave without me," he said lightly. "I'll be back."

And, with that, he vanished down the mountainside.

It cost another twenty-seven minutes for the round trip, but he was soon back. "They think you are crazy, but they want to leave," he told MacDonald.

"I guess I am," he sighed, then helped untie the rope from its tree base. They winched in the ladder, then cut the rope and backed out. Three short flashes on a light, and those up top let the rope itself go. It fell all the way, coiling and snaking, and crashed into the water below. Expert eyes, aided by infra-red viewers, checked and moved back in, untangling the rope from a few places where it had hung itself up on vegetation, then let it sink to the bottom of the small inlet. With that, they moved out and made ready to get as far away as possible from Allenby Island.

Only when the rope went over the side did MacDonald feel the crushing implications of what he'd done, and the finality of it. Frawley had managed a sitting position and seemed to

be recovering, although he had never looked so frail. He
stared at MacDonald in disgust. "Why?" he croaked.

"I really don't know," he responded. "That's a fact. I
really don't know. . . ."

MacDonald made their first priority locating and disabling
the basic electronic monitoring gear in the area. Using the
rushing water of the creek to mask sounds, he located two
microphones and one camera pretty much where he thought
they'd be. As long as Ross was in charge of security, he felt
confident that he could almost exactly predict placement and
type of equipment and so far he was justified.

Locating the wires, they patched in a small extra loop with
alligator clips and then removed a section of wire well away
from the microphones themselves. A tiny tape recorder with
a continuous loop tape and a battery life of at least thirty-six
hours was used to record just what the mikes should have
been hearing. Then it was patched into the line and the mike
was disconnected. This was done with both, which allowed
them to move about fairly freely within the heavily overgrown area. The two cameras they would simply have to
avoid; although some thought was given to doing the same
thing with videotape, the inability of such a tape to reflect
changing shadows, weather conditions, and night and day
pretty much ruled that out.

Because of her experience with Angelique in the same
area, Maria was able to guide them around in the under-
growth and around the cabin area, which they all avoided.
There were both sound and visual monitors inside and out on
the cabin and they had no wish to get near the place. The
stream had provided them with full canteens of water, and
that and dried foods would have to do.

MacDonald had always identified this area as one of the
most vulnerable on the island, and so far he'd seen nothing to
indicate that they had made any real changes.

Still, it was daylight before they had everything in place. The lava tube entrance was easily identified, but they elected to set up a small camp above it, giving them first look and helping them to avoid any messy complications, should anyone come out. MacDonald used the monitoring gear to check for any electronic listeners or motion sensors, and found none in the immediate area although every time he pointed it towards the cave the needle went off the scale. He'd known from the beginning that a nice direct way in was impossible, but he still felt some disappointment.

Frawley seemed newly energized by the mere fact that he had made it up the cliff and that they were finally on the island. He spent some time working with his heavy equipment, which took three of them to lift and carry. The object inside was imposing, but looked more like a piece of very bad plumbing than a bomb. MacDonald was certain that there would be a security sweep with human agents down the tube after dark, and it was decided that until those agents arrived and had done their work the bomb wouldn't be moved down and in front of the cave where it would do the most blast damage. Still, Frawley had the thing armed and activated by mid-morning, but not with the dead man's switch. It was agreed that if they were discovered at any time before their own deadline, he would blow it where it was.

Setting up a guard schedule, they settled back for the long wait and tried to get some rest. It wasn't easy, though. MacDonald settled back and tried to keep his mind on the job, telling himself it was just another security test, but he couldn't really do it.

Maria came over to him. "Well, I hope you're satisfied," she said, keeping her voice to a whisper as they all did.

"Don't start in on me," he responded wearily. "I'm here and that's that. I know it's stupid and idiotic and all that, but there was just no way I could go back when everything I've spent the last six months on is here. I can't make myself

believe it's a last stand, anyway, but if you all came in and
then nothing happened, I'd always wonder what happened
and whether I could have made a difference. I guess maybe
dying here beat the idea of living with that. Maybe I just
want to see, for once, what's under that Dark Man disguise if
I can. Or maybe I just flipped out. Crazy, eh?''

"Crazy, yeah, but—I'm glad you're here even if it is a
dead end. Oh, I don't want to die, and I don't want you
dead, either, but I'm still glad. I'm not gonna screw this one
up, I swear it.''

They settled back together and dozed fitfully.

It was still light, though, when they awoke, although the
sun was waning now and they knew it would go down
rapidly in this latitude. There had been occasional warnings
from the sentries, and once or twice somebody had come
down the path towards the cabin although they couldn't see
who, but they'd left fairly quickly and apparently without
seeing any signs of the invaders. The day had remained
cloudy, with a few drizzles, and the weather had just maintained the feeling of impending doom.

All day long, though, helicopters, some heavy, came in
and landed at the heliport, and they heard an occasional boat
whistle as well. The island, it appeared, was filling up for the
occasion.

Maria was itching to go off on her own and see just what
was going on, but Frawley would have none of it. The last
time they'd let her go off on her own she'd called in the
enemy, and he was taking no chances. He didn't care who
was coming. Whoever they were, they wouldn't matter after
eleven-thirty that night.

Finally they heard hollow voices ahead of them, just as the
light was beginning to fade, and they froze as the brush
moved back from the tunnel entrance and two men emerged.
MacDonald stared and recognized both of them. It was Ross,
puffing away on a cigarette, with one of his toadies in

security. Clearly the big man was doing all the last minute checks personally.

". . . Cramming so many people in that meadow it'll look like a bunch of sardines," Ross was saying.

"Well, what can you do?" the other man responded. "You see who some of those guys *are*? Jeez! We already *run* the god-damned world!"

"A real United Nations," Ross agreed. "Sort of gives you a lump to see what progress they're makin' towards world peace. Some of them are at war with each other right now."

They laughed at that.

"You go over to the falls and out to the lookout, I'll check out the cabin," Ross ordered his aide.

"Uh-oh," MacDonald whispered. "If anybody's monitoring those mikes and doesn't hear footsteps, we could be in trouble." He knew it was a risk, but one they had to take.

It was getting dark fast, though, and the aide was back quickly, holding a large lantern-type electric flashlight. Far too quickly to have made the whole rounds and done a careful check. MacDonald relaxed. That was Ross, all right.

"Anything?" he heard the security chief call.

"Naw, nothin' much," the aide replied. "Ain't nobody gonna wander around here much anyway."

"O.K., all secure at this end. Go back up and take a sweep team around both sides of the Institute. I'm going down to the meadow."

"Suits me," said the other, as they approached and then re-entered the tube. "I don't even want to be near that place tonight. . . ."

Their voices faded away into the mountains.

There was a collective letting out of breaths, and they relaxed a little more. "Give them a half hour to be busy elsewhere," MacDonald whispered, "then we'll go down and plant my Lord and his big box where it'll do the most damage."

Ross hadn't even bothered replacing the thick brush camouflage over the tube mouth, so they took advantage of that. Getting the bomb down there was far easier than getting it to where it had rested for the day had been, although there was more nervousness because it was now assembled and armed. They dug the old man in as best they could, then watched as he rigged the dead man's switch and set the timer, then rigged it to himself. They then used the camouflage to mask him and the bomb from view, and it looked pretty good when they were through.

"We have an extra man," the Nigerian pointed out. "Want to leave someone here as guard?"

"No, he'll be more good up there," Frawley rasped. "What could a guard do here? If they find me, I blow. If they shoot me from behind, or strangle me, I blow."

"And if you get a sneezing fit you blow," said the Bishop glumly. "Still, I agree that a sentinel here is a waste. Anyone who can get close enough to prevent him from releasing the switch would take out a sentry as well." He sighed. "Pip, you old rascal, good luck and god speed. I'm almost looking forward to seeing your reaction on the other side when all your lifelong beliefs are shattered."

Frawley's right hand was on the dead man, but he put up his left and the two squeezed hands firmly.

"I still believe we're going to be snuffed out like a candle," the old man said, "but I'm prepared to be pleasantly surprised. "Besides, even if you *are* right, I'll have the last laugh. I'm sure no candidate for heaven, but I'm going out fighting Hell." He paused a moment, and all humor faded. "Goodbye, Alfie."

"*Au revoir,* Pip."

There was no easy way to break off, and that did it.

They huddled together up top and checked their watches. "We have two and a half hours to attack time," MacDonald told them. "Maria, I want to get up as close to the Institute on this side as possible without exposing ourselves. Remember—don't let them take you. You've all got poison capsules. Use them if you have to. Get ready to move out!''

The Bishop's pack was particularly heavy, containing the eight small bombs, but he managed it pretty well for a man his age. Clearly he was in top shape. The rest clipped preloaded magazines of ammunition on their belts as well as both gunpowder and concussion grenades. Maria, barefoot by her own choice, wore one of those tight children's dance outfits in black and a small belt around her waist. She took two grenades and clipped them on the belt, and a small pistol. It wouldn't do much damage in a fight, but it offered her some means of defense against the conventional opposition expected. The Dark Man and those with his powers, it was hoped, would be far too occupied in the meadow.

The sweep Ross had ordered was almost completed by the time they got up close enough to see. They had been slow, methodical, and thorough, but also talkative and using bright flashlights. Clearly they were not expecting any trouble and were pretty confident of their own security.

The place was brightly floodlit, and there were people and little electric carts going to and fro, but there didn't seem to be any sentries. The common area was covered by cameras, though, which were linked to security although not directly to SAINT. There were, however, among the people going about, men in uniforms, some with rifles. Their presence was welcomed rather than feared by those watching from the bush.

"You said something about audacity, Bishop," MacDonald recalled. "Well, there's how we do it. Just walk in the front door from both sides like you own the place. SAINT has some ground to air and ground to ground missiles for staving off an air attack or sea landing, but they depend on people and their own gadgets up here. Once inside, act like you own the place until you get as far as you can. Then shoot anything that moves. SAINT does control the lights and air conditioning in there, so expect things to go dark fast.''

They slipped down the infra-red goggles and the scene took on an eerie glow. The lighted areas became difficult to look at, while the dark ones now stood out in bizarre if recognizable relief.

They moved carefully around the Institute until they were almost at the cliff's edge themselves. Here they would be exposed and up against a tall wire fence with barbs on the top. There were not, however, motion sensors on the fence, nor was it electrified. It was merely simply a way of discouraging anyone from getting too close and preventing them from falling off the cliff. MacDonald had recommended both motion sensing and electrification, but they'd had too much trouble with birds on the former and the latter was still on the drawing boards.

They took up guard positions, depending mostly on the darkness to conceal them, as there really wasn't any cover to speak of back here. There was a road in back leading to a rear entrance where the garbage would be left for cart pickup, but they couldn't make much use of it. It was covered both by a camera and by an automatic locking push-bar mechanism which sounded an alarm when opened. Also, entry there would put them at the farthest point from access to the lower floors.

They went to the fence, and MacDonald quickly cut a hole in it with wire cutters. He risked a slight noise by hammering a stake into the ground, around which a rope was tied. They removed one of the Bishop's small square bomb boxes and lowered it over the side, MacDonald hanging out and seeing that it went down next to the big pipe but not touching the ladder or the pipe itself. He could see all the way down, and it appeared that there was a small gunboat docked at the oil storage pier as he'd expected. All the lights down there were on.

"Cart coming!" somebody hissed, and he took the risk, letting go the bomb, and got back in. There really wasn't much he could do to hide the fence hole or stake, but they'd kept it in the dark and as small as possible. The cart actually rounded the corner before he was completely clear, but the small headlight wasn't aimed straight ahead but downwards in front and the spotlight was being casually trained back and forth. He made it to the base of the building and lay flat and quiet. The Lebanese woman and the Nigerian had removed forty-five caliber automatics with silencers and waited tensely further up.

The cart went by so close that they could almost smell the breath of the two men riding there, one driving, the other handling the spotlight. Both had weapons, but not in their hands.

They passed right by the fence hole and for a heart-stopping second the beam actually swept the damaged area, but the cart went on. When it's routine and no trouble is expected, MacDonald knew, people, even trained people, often see what they expect to see. Had their presence been suspected, that same sweep would have resulted in immediate exposure.

He moved back towards the Bishop and Maria.

"A close one," breathed the clergyman.

"Not so bad. I'd fire them for incompetence. O.K.—here's where we split. You, my Lord, and Maria get to the bushes on the near side here, where you can see the antennas and wait for our first boom. Good luck."

The Bishop shook his hand, and Maria kissed him, and he was off. He followed the cart down the road, linking up with the Sikh and making their way to the edge of the Lodge and then across to the next building. Taking up decent hiding places, they removed and clipped on their infra-red goggles. They expected a power outage, but as they'd have to be seen to get in, they didn't want anything obvious distinguishing themselves from the rest before they struck. The other pair did the same on the other side. Now the waiting game began anew.

The security patrols continued their random but perfunctory activities. Clearly they were ready for trouble, but they hardly expected anything to happen up here. The action was in the meadow and apparently also in other areas of the island. The helicopters no longer came and went now, and the traffic in and around the common had virtually ceased except for a couple of armed sentries at each entrance looking pretty bored. A fog had rolled in, partly shrouding the Institute and giving the whole thing a ghostly air appropriate to the moment.

From down the mountain somewhere, they could hear the voices of a great many people, and there was the sound of not very uniform chanting and other such activities. The words couldn't be made out, but clearly the preliminaries before the main event had begun.

The bomb blew slightly early, at 10:27, shocking and scaring them almost as much as it did the people in the area of the Institute. For a moment, everything and everybody seemed to freeze, then the sentries and security personnel started running towards the back of the Lodge, weapons at the ready, and they could hear the rear alarm as the kitchen access doors were opened.

For a moment it looked as if they had achieved only a big bang, but suddenly there was a secondary explosion far more powerful than the first, and a tremendous roar lit up the northern skies. This was followed a few seconds later by an earthquake-like rumbling beneath their feet, and then a section of cliff blew out in back as the Lodge storage tanks caught and burst, blowing not up but outwards. The floodlights on the common blinked and went out, as did all the lights in the Institute buildings. They heard the anguished screams of people dying and people on fire, and probably people going right off that cliff and straight down.

They moved, sub-machine guns at the ready, and ran out into full view and then quickly up the steps to the Lodge's deck and inside the door. The other pair had been ahead of them.

They all immediately pulled down or put back on their infra-red goggles and proceeded along their set paths. Mac-Donald and the Sikh went down immediately to the library. Dim emergency lighting had come on, switched there by the computer from its own power supplies, but now they were in the domain of SAINT itself. The terminals in the library were all on and their flat screens were glowing.

They heard more muffled explosions upstairs. The other team was checking out and cleaning out the upper areas if possible, guarding their rear. It had been agreed that until they were clearly discovered and exposed, they would use the grenades exclusively. With all the explosions and fire about, they might be taken for secondary blow-ups from the big blast.

"Hello, Greg," said the smooth, cultured English voice of the computer from one of the terminals. "I must say I'm not surprised to see you here."

He and the Sikh whirled, but there wasn't anything to shoot at really.

"It's sealed the doors!" MacDonald told Shad. "They aren't blast-proof up here, though. Let's blow 'em! Don't touch the terminals, though!"

"I must say, Greg," the computer continued, "that I'm most impressed with you and most angry at Mr. Ross. He will suffer for all this damage. However, you can't win, you know."

They got back as the door blew, then settled back on one hinge. They got up and pushed it out of the way and then continued on down.

The Sikh led the way, and they found the door at the bottom stuck open and went in. This level, the third, was the central control room area for the computer and security complex. Not caring now, they fired around in both directions, mowing down the dozen or so men and women struggling to get a handle on the damage done by the initial blast.

Access to SAINT was now just one floor below, but it would be hard to get down there. The doors down from this point were thick and blast-proof and could be operated only by the computer. They were also of the sliding type with a full-height locking mechanism, and solid as a rock. This was the point where they knew they might be stuck and where they might not pass, as SAINT was hardly going to open the doors for them and they couldn't bring enough firepower to really blast through doors that would take an anti-tank missile. Frankly, they were a bit surprised to have gotten this far this easily.

As they were trying to figure out some sort of plan, almost incredibly one of the doors opened and two figures stepped out, talking angrily. One was dressed in the reds of the computer technicians, but the other was dressed from head to toe entirely in black, including a black mask covering his entire face. His voice gave the last clue.

"Some people are going to wish they were dead before this is over," growled the Dark Man, without his eerie electronic protection.

They didn't hesitate. Almost at the point where the pair saw that they were not alone, both MacDonald and Shadrach opened fire. The force of the machine gun blasts cut through both men, knocking them back against the wall. The two invaders approached the door and the two limp forms carefully, but the door remained open. The Sikh, again, led the way, and as he approached the Dark Man he frowned. "No blood," he said. "The other is covered in blood. . . ."

He stooped down, carefully, reaching out to remove the

mask. The Dark Man did not bleed, but his black uniform was riddled with holes.

Suddenly the black-clad figure reached out with lightning speed, pushing at the Sikh and throwing him into the air as if he were a child's toy. MacDonald pulled the trigger on his weapon, but it wouldn't fire. The Dark Man was on his feet now, and chuckling softly.

Although he would have sworn he'd never actually use it up to a moment before, he found himself popping a poison pill into his mouth and crushing it between his teeth.

"I hope you like licorice," the Dark Man said, sounding vastly amused. "It is not only appropriate, it is the first flavor that popped into my mind."

The sweet, distinctive taste in his mouth left no doubt that the pill was not as advertised, but MacDonald did not feel relieved.

Suddenly the Sikh gave a terrible cry in his own tongue and leaped from a desk straight at the Dark Man.

"Go to your God, Sikh!" said the inhuman man, and sparks flew from his gloved hands and enveloped Shad in mid-air. He shimmered and disappeared, leaving not a trace of himself or his weapon to fall to the floor.

MacDonald took advantage of the distraction to hurl himself forward onto the Dark Man, knocking him down on the floor. Caught off-balance and unaware, the black clad man fell and was partly pinned by MacDonald, who was working in one fluid motion. He reached up and grabbed the tight black stocking mask over the face and yanked hard enough to pull it completely off.

Greg MacDonald screamed, then got quickly up and backed away from the Dark Man, who was slowly getting to his feet.

It was a horrible face, beyond a dead man's face, the face of one who had laid in the ground far too long. Much of the skull was showing, and what skin remained was peeling and flaking in rotten bloated masses. One lidless eye was hanging partly out of its socket, the other in, huge, bloodshot, and staring. Unkempt hair grew where skin still adhered to skull, and it was matted and mixed in with the rotting flesh. There was suddenly a stench in the room, a stench of meat left too long in the sun.

It was an impossible face, a face that held a grim, fixed expression and one that was such a horror that he could not bear to look at it, although he couldn't bear to turn away.

"I told you I didn't wear this mask to hide my identity," said the Dark Man through rotting lips. "It *disturbs* some people to look upon it."

"Noooo . . .!" MacDonald screamed. "You can't be! You can't exist! You belong in the grave!"

"Others agree, but after tonight the power will lie elsewhere anyway. I see my face has a strong effect on you. Would you like one just like it? You might have problems getting kissed after that. . . ."

"That's quite enough, Geoffrey," said a calm British voice behind MacDonald. "You have quite enough to do and time is running out. It's past eleven, you know."

MacDonald turned, thankful to have a reason to tear his gaze away from that horrible thing, and saw Sir Reginald Truscott-Smythe standing behind him with a quick-firing scatter gun much like the one the Dark Man had wielded in the motel room.

"The others?" the Dark Man asked.

"We killed the two upstairs, although they took a frightful toll, and they apparently planted bombs along the antenna array. Four are knocked out and the other three are off kilter. W're off the air right now, but we should be able to jury-rig something in three or four hours at worst."

The Dark Man reached down, found his mask, and fitted it back over his terrible head. "Very well. I hesitate to leave MacDonald here, though. He is a most resourceful man."

"You've deactivated all his weaponry and explosives?"

"Of course. Tell you what—sit down, MacDonald, in that chair over there."

MacDonald sighed and did as instructed. With everything else blown so far, he had to cling to the fact that they hadn't found them all yet, and they still had a big shock coming.

The Dark Man came over and touched a point on his neck. He felt a coldness, like a dagger of ice, go in, and when the creature's finger was withdrawn he had no feeling, no control or sense of movement below the neck.

"Geoffrey—it's eleven twenty," Sir Reginald said nervously.

Ten minutes, MacDonald thought anxiously. *Just ten more minutes . . . .*

"All right—I'll go. Have a nice chat, if you wish. I'm sure that Mr. MacDonald can be brought around to our point of view, one way or the other, at our leisure. He would be a wonderful replacement for Ross. Treat him well. After all, he *is* married to our Angelique. . . ."

With that, the Dark Man vanished, this time by walking back through the door.

Sir Reginald put down the pistol and took a seat himself. He looked both nervous and very, very tired.

"Reggie—what *is* that thing? You called him Geoffrey."

"He's my brother," the computer genius responded.

"Your brother hanged himself almost nine years ago."

"Yes, yes. I know. Oh, god! I'm so tired and sick of all this mess!"

MacDonald frowned, recovering a bit from the Dark Man's visage although it was never far from his mind. "Hey— aren't you the one behind all this?"

"Well, yes, in a way I suppose. You see, I was working up at Cheltenham on the defense computer system at the time. Geoff had been dead about a year, and until those books arrived I'd quite forgotten about it all."

"Then you weren't in any cult?"

"No, I had little use for such stuff, then or now, I'm

afraid. But, you see, shortly after the books arrived, I went down for a visit to Geoff's grave. I'd put it off—it's a silly custom—but when the books came I thought about him and just decided to go. I was there, at the grave, which had already been seeded with grass and overgrown, when I noticed some odd symbols at the bottom of the headstone. I kneeled down to get a better look and—'' his voice trembled and broke rather suddenly''—these two arms, these strong, terrible arms reached up from the grave had held me. I—I screamed, broke free, and ran, but *he* followed me, somehow. He was there, outside the windows of my house, in the shadows even in the high security area at Cheltenham and I couldn't do anything. I thought I was losing my mind. Finally I confronted him, and he told me what he wanted me to do.''

"Eight years. . . . Then he *couldn't* be a creation of SAINT.''

"No, nor anything else in this rational world. The project here was already under way, and he told me I'd get an invitation to supervise its final stages once construction was complete—and I did. He also sent a number of people to me; bright, young people with solid computer backgrounds who were none the less involved in cults of one kind or another. We designed many of the proprietary chips and circuits at Cheltenham for SAINT, and they were there, offering suggestions that were far beyond their possible knowledge, and *he* was there, too, in the shadows. The innovations he and they offered were brilliant, far beyond the capability of anyone I had ever known, even the Japanese geniuses on their projects.''

"And you never tried to fight them? Never tried to foul them up? You just went along?''

"I—I'm not as strong a man as you might think. How do you fight someone like Geoff? How do you rationalize it? You tried—and see where it's gotten you. And as a man of science, a man whose whole heart and soul was in computers, to be fed those incredible new designs, those whole new and revolutionary ways of doing things—it put me on top. It was the sort of knowledge a man of science would sell his soul for.''

"And that's what you did.''

"I suppose you could say so.''

"Reggie—what are they doing out there tonight?''

"Something revolutionary. Something that many of those new circuits were designed to handle, and something that fulfills almost an ultimate dream.''

"Eh?''

"The fusion of human and computer. To actually link someone directly to the machine so that the two are essentially one. The human mind can never hold or comprehend the power, speed, and data of a computer, but imagine having all that at your command, instantly, when and if needed. To get any fact, do any computation—instantly. To control any computer-controlled device as needed.''

"Angelique. You mean Angelique, don't you?''

"Yes.''

"But it's not possible, Reggie! I say that having looked into the face of a living corpse and surviving a bout with a monster that could not exist. You said it yourself. The brain would fill up.''

"No, we licked that. Even the personality shell will reside within the computer, not the brain. Only the autonomic functions, the lizard brain and the mammalian brain, will remain. The rest will be a blank slate, able to hold whatever data is needed. The transfer is at the speed of light. There is no need to hold anything permanently there.''

"Good lord! You mean she'll look like Angelique, sound like Angelique, but she'll really be nothing more than an extension of SAINT, a living robot.''

"It's a bit more than that. I would gladly do it myself if I were permitted.''

"Uh—Reggie? What time is it? How long until this happens?"

The Englishman looked at his watch. "It's eleven thirty-five now. No more than twenty-five minutes."

MacDonald's heart sank to its lowest depths. *Eleven thirty-five. . . . We should all have been radioactive dust five minutes ago.*

15

THE MESSIAH CHOICE

"When is this all taking place, Reggie?" MacDonald asked him. "The witching hour of midnight?" He was still amazed at being alive, and amazed, too that being alive now disturbed him so much.

"Oh, that's rubbish. They have all their leaders here, you know—kings of African tribes and Himalayan principalities, ministers from many countries, all that. They'll give them a real show before the climax, from their point of view. They have until the crack of dawn, as I understand it. *His* power wanes in the daylight."

"But not SAINT."

"No, not SAINT."

"How come you're not down there watching it all, or running around fixing up our damage?"

"I'm very tired, and stick of all this, frankly. They are taking the scientific breakthrough of the century, perhaps for thousands of years, and turning it into a mumbo-jumbo circus. As for SAINT—the sort of work you are talking about is heavy stuff, best done by the staff. When it's ready to be operational again, I'll have to check it all out I suppose."

"Why?"

"What? What do you mean by that?"

"Exactly that. Has it occurred to you, Reggie, that you're not really one of *them?* They needed you as the front to get their stuff installed in the computer, and they needed you up to now as insurance. But once they have this done, once SAINT and Angelique are one, the computer will be in complete control and you'll be like the revolutionary that puts the dictator in power. His friends know how to wage a revolt and topple a government, and they have expectations when their man is in. So, the first thing the dictator does is wipe out his friends who put him there—if he wants to survive himself. It's called a purge, Reggie."

Sir Reginald nervously took a cigarette from a silver case and lit it. It took him two tries. "That's ridiculous. Oh, I admit I've been used, but I've gotten a lot out of it as well. They still need me. No one but me could have located that diabolical erasure program Sir Robert snuck in with a mass of accounting data. Not even SAINT could remember or find it—but I did."

"And you totally deactivated it just in case we killed Angelique while she was in our hands. Clever. Now it fears nothing. As soon as it enters into Angelique, it'll have only one human being, one in the whole world, it actually fears, because there will be only one man it doesn't own who can harm it. You, Reggie. I don't think I'm going to live to see that dawn, but by god you aren't, either. When it's sure, if it works, you'll be the first item on its agenda. You're the ultimate sucker. You sold your soul for knowledge, but they always leave loopholes, don't they, eh? They always have an out. The very knowledge you gave them is the very same knowledge that they can't afford to have loose any more. Your only hope is that the project fails. The possibility of that is the only reason you're still alive now."

"You think I'm stupid?" he snapped. "Do you take me

for a dunce? *I* figured that out long ago! That's why the erasure program is still there. Oh, I deactivated it all right, but I left in a code I could give to have it be carried out anyway. They know it's there—I told them, truthfully, that we'd have to shut down half of its core memory to get it out—but they don't know that it's not dead.'' He looked smug. ''Now what do you think of *that*?''

''Well, Reggie, I'm impressed—but can't SAINT hear and see in this room, too? Didn't you just tell him how he could die? And didn't you just say that the only man who knew that code was you?'' MacDonald pressed, sensing an opening he never expected and pushing it for all it was worth with the one weapon left to him. ''Any chance you had of surviving before just went out the window.''

Sir Reginald suddenly got up and looked around nervously. All was quiet in the eerie emergency lighting, although there were dead bodies all over. MacDonald could see it in his face, though, and in the way he looked around, that the computer genius was suddenly more terrified than tired.

''I'm afraid he's right, Sir Reginald,'' said the smooth, unhurried voice of the computer from a wall speaker. ''The truth is, up to now no decision had been made on you. Call me—sentimental, if you will. Now, though, I fear Mr. MacDonald has done you in, although in so doing he has done me an inadvertent service.''

Sir Reginald picked up the pistol with its two strange clips. ''SAINT! I *created* you!'' he shouted, his voice echoing against the walls. ''No one else could have done so! I—I did *more* than create you! I *loved* you!''

''You did indeed create the machine,'' SAINT admitted, ''but it was only a shell itself, a receptacle for what was to come. Still, in an odd way, I did love you, too. Just wait there. In a moment it will all be over, and you will be with me forever.''

''Reggie! You don't have to stand there and die like a

dog!'' MacDonald shouted, cursing his inability to move. There was the sound of footsteps coming down the stairs from above. ''Damn it, man! Think logically! If there's hell and a return from the grave, then there's God in heaven, too! You still have a chance, Reggie! *Give the damned code!*''

Two red-clad men appeared, bearing rifles. Sir Reginald shot both of them with the pistol, which gave a sound like a short burp, and they went down for good. He turned and looked frantically around. ''I—I can't! I need a terminal! It can block the rest by simply preventing the code from reaching its banks through the audible sensors!''

He looked around as the sound of more footsteps approached, and made for the door down to SAINT itself. The terminals both upstairs and on this level were totally under SAINT's own electronic controls, but downstairs there was a direct input terminal, one which SAINT couldn't foul up or shut down without shutting down part of itself.

SAINT tried to slide shut the door, but it hung up on the body of the technician who'd been with the Dark Man and didn't have the living corpse's immunity to bullets. Neither did Reggie, though, and bullets flew and pinged off the walls as he slipped through and ran down the stairs to the next level two at a time.

''Reggie loved Daddy!'' Sir Reginald screamed as he ran. ''Daddy hates Geoff!'' They were simple words, key words, but he'd been right. The computer shut down its speaker inputs at the first words. The only hope he had now was the direct input terminal in the small glass-enclosed booth just outside of SAINT itself. But in shutting down its sensors, the computer had also shut itself off from direct help in its own survival. It had to rely on human help.

There! He was within sight of it, breathing hard. The glass booth with the one unstoppable entry into SAINT. He reached it! He reached the door, an old-fashioned door with a simple knob latch, and started to open it.

Bullets from men and women in red uniforms both on his level and from below cut through him, splattering the glass exterior with blood, although they did not penetrate the special protective glass of the walls. He took so many shots in his body that before he hit the ground he almost looked as bad as his brother.

MacDonald just sat there, unable to do anything, hearing the muffled sound of the shots below. Suddenly four big men came up from the fourth level and over to him.

"He didn't make it," one said casually. "Come on. They've decided you're part of the show. The boss wants you down there."

"I can't resist, but I can't move, either," he pointed out, cursing under his breath. *So close! Each damned time it's so close and no cigar!*

One big man took him under his arms, the other by the feet, and together they carried him through the door and down not one but two more flights, to the fifty level, where SAINT's refrigeration and small fusion plant were located. The place was quiet and antiseptic, but as they carried him down to the far end of the huge chamber he saw a small crew working on patching a gaping hole through which outside air was rushing in and he grinned. "A little more air conditioning than you want, eh?"

"Shut up or I'll cut your tongue out," snapped the big man forward of him. He shut up.

MacDonald was surprised to find one of the small electric carts at the end of the room, and he quickly saw why it might be there. One whole section of wall seemed to have swung outwards and away, revealing an enormous tunnel. The tunnel was lighted with four bright strips going its entire length, and also down it ran thick cables that apparently had been hidden by the wall, coming down as they did through holes drilled in the rock. So Frawley had been right about one thing.

They dumped him unceremoniously in the back of the cart
and the big man started down the tunnel. To MacDonald's
surprise, it opened into a fairly large chamber that might have
covered the entire base of the meadow. In the center was the
huge mass of obsidian that was below ground, going from
ceiling to floor and possibly beyond. It was not the cold
glassy black it should have been, though; all the cables
terminated, it seemed, directly into it, and the whole rock or
whatever it was hummed and glowed with an eerie light that
filled the entire rock structure. It seemed almost like something alive.

Men and women in brown saffron robes took him from the
cart and stripped him naked. He could see that on their
foreheads was a symbol that seemed to pulse like strange
protruding veins. The six inside the six inside the six. Somebody stuck a gag in his mouth and then they began to rub his
whole body with some sort of oil. He couldn't feel a thing
except on his face, where it felt like vaseline. Innterestingly,
the one thing they left on him was the chain from which hung
the Bishop's cross.

They took him back to the center rock formation now,
lifted him up to his feet, and pressed his entire body hard
against it. He felt a tingling, then some vertigo, and then a
sudden blackness for just a moment. Then he was outside, in
the open air, and he knew just where he was if not how he
got there. His head rested on the top of the high point of the
altar stone, and he looked both out and down.

The small cup-shaped depression at the low end was filled
with red liquid, almost certainly blood. The whole "stone"
or whatever it was seemed drenched in it. In back of the
stone and running its entire length they had erected a narrow
wooden stage-like platform, and there were people on it as
well as several enormous idols, each a stylized demonic
creature with gaping mouth and goat-like horns and vaguely
saurian appearance. Each had some sort of incense or another

sweet smelling material burning in their laps, but it gave off far more odor than smoke. Fires lit inside made the eyes and mouths burn and glow.

On either side of the central and largest idol were hung, upside down, the bodies of the Lebanese woman and the Nigerian. They had been stripped and then hung up by their feet like deer carcasses, and their bullet-ridden bodies twisted slowly as if their dull, unseeing eyes might take in the entire scene.

The audience, or congregation, numbered at least a hundred and fifty, which was more than anyone could have imagined being packed into the area of the meadow in front of the stage and stone. Many wore various kinds of robes and costumes, including leopard's head headdresses and demonic-looking helmets; others wore more traditional dress, from business suits to Middle Eastern garb, flowing white robes and headgear suitable for the desert. They represented all races and habitable continents, and they were the leaders of this new wave, the evil within. Not the presidents and prime ministers, not necessarily the princes and kings, but those who were behind the seats of power, giving advice and manipulating information.

In front of the altar stone, between him and the congregation, a group of naked women whose bodies were painted with all sorts of designs and colors danced a frantic, insane dance that seemed both sexually obscene and somehow animalistic and violent to the chanting of what was, at least to him, an off-stage choir and the frantic beat of drums. He recognized most of them with a start, as the women who'd been Angelique's staff, some of the wives of the most distinguished permanent administrative staff of the Institute, and others who were young, sensual, and overendowed who might well be ones he'd known now showing off the rewards of converting to the opposition. All had that same throbbing, pulsating symbol on their foreheads.

The Dark Man came over, and knelt down beside his head. No matter that he was both covered and using his electronic distortion disguise, MacDonald tried to shrink from his loathsome touch but could not.

"I thought you deserved a front row seat for the climax of the show." the Dark Man said to him in a low tone. "Rituals are just good show business but the masses seem to expect them. I will restore feeling to your body, but don't try and get up. You can't, and the pain will be great and they'll eat it up. Look at them. Look at their faces and their eyes. They can hardly wait until they have the power to do this themselves—and they will. Just relax and enjoy it and don't worry. Killing is not for the likes of you."

That was what he was afraid of. Still, he felt feeling return to his lower parts, and he found himself able to move his arms and hands a bit. They felt stiff and sore. He did try to rise just a little, though, and the pain in his back was instantly excruciating. He relaxed, and it slowly ebbed away. He wasn't going anywhere, and he knew it.

The revelry stopped suddenly, and for a moment there was dead silence. The women took places as a sort of honor guard on either side of the stone. At last the Dark Man broke the silence, sounding less like a cult leader than a master of ceremonies at a night club.

"Ladies and gentlemen," he said, his voice echoing through the meadow and beyond in ghostly fashion, "it is time to pause a moment and consider the basic things for which we stand and the threats we still must face. Here I present a man who several times has come within minutes, perhaps seconds, of destroying all that we have worked so hard to build for our lord and master Lucifer, Angel of Earth, the highest sane creature of the nether realm. Look you here to your right on the platform, and see what he almost accomplished!"

MacDonald struggled to see for himself, and his gasp was audible in the dead silence. On the platform was, unmistakably, the bomb Lord Frawley had been supposed to set off long ago now.

"An atomic device," the Dark Man explained, causing a stir and ripples through the crowd. "It would have scoured this island clean of life above, and set us back decades at the moment of our ultimate triumph. Oh, don't worry, it's fully deactivated now, its heart removed, as it were, but it sits here as testimony that we can not fail!

"Consider," he continued, his voice rising and falling for emphasis, "that this device was situated so that it would do the most damage, and attached to a dead man's switch. We did not find it in time! When we did find it, after the attack above, we found it with, of all things, a dead man. An old man, dead perhaps of a heart attack, his death so sudden, so abrupt, *that his fingers locked around the trigger so it could not fire!* There was a timing device, too, but for some reason he had either not connected it or disconnected it. I suppose he wanted to do it himself." This caused even more of a nervous stir in the crowd as they realized how close they had come.

Damn Frawley, MacDonald thought in disgust. *The climb was too much for his weakened body, but he had to be in full control, a self-centered egomaniac to the end!*

The Dark Man laughed in triumph. "But consider, my friends, how this is *our* time and that we are protected by our Lord even from such as this!" he went on. "Consider the miracles here represented! Our Lord Lucifer crept into his mind and made him disconnect the timer, then struck him with a blow that kept us all safe from harm and our cause totally intact. None can touch us! Our threats are revealed to us by our very enemies, and our Lord watches over where we can not!"

There was a sudden, apparently spontaneous reaction in the crowd. Most dropped to their knees and began to chant, "Blessed be Lucifer, also called Satan, Lord of Earth and the

Underworld, wise protector of the universe. May we draw
from him our strength and never waiver or fail him in our
duty.'' It was said in a babel of languages, but one of the
women closest to him was an English speaker and he made
out the words from her.

The Dark Man turned and pointed to MacDonald. ''Behold
the man behind it all, whom the enemies of our Lord set
against us! Do not be fooled by his position now! He is a
most formidable and worthy opponent, a brave challenger
who almost succeeded despite a notable lack of help from his
god.''

There were some snickers at that from the crowd.

''What is your price, MacDonald?'' the Dark Man asked,
his voice soft, his tone rhetorical. ''Not your life, for you
brought that thing here and remained. Not your love, for you
made no protest when you could and would have taken her
life tonight as well if you could. Not terror, not the dark and
the horrible things that lurk in every shadow, for you have
faced down a demon and looked into the face of death. Yet,
what is it I see in your eyes now? Not terror, no, but
something even more foreign to the truly godly. I see hate
there. Burning, festering, blistering hate. It feeds upon you.
It eats your soul. *It turns you, inside, into me!* And that, my
friends, is the ultimate power. Not magic, not sorcery, not
witchcraft, but rather this—that your actions, your deeds, *our*
actions and deeds, turn our enemies into ourselves! The more
they fight, the more they become ours.'' His voice rose with
the litany. ''Christian! Jew! Moslem! Hindu! Buddhist! Taoist!
Animist!'' Suddenly his tone lowered. ''Patriot,'' he added,
then walked back and stood directly over MacDonald.

''So, you see, we cannot lose,'' the Dark Man continued.
''Either in fighting us they become like us, or like the
martyrs of many religions they do nothing and do not resist.
The days of Buddha, Jesus, and Mohammed are done because they are bankrupt. More evil has been done by men in

their name than has been done in the name of our Lord whom they blame. What sort of prophet, what sort of god, is worth following if the result is a world where even the most starry-eyed idealists would murder a whole population of innocents in the name of the greater good? Let us be done with them. Let them join Zeus, and Jupiter, and the worship of emperors on the ash heap. We are the predatory animals given mastery over a world of brutality. Let us stop fighting our natures, our urges, our inclinations. Let us not agonize and recriminate. We were created the highest of animals, then cursed by god to always fight our unconquerable basic nature. Let us begin here to pull down this world and this mad god and build a new one based upon what we are. Let us banish the very concept of sin, and become like gods.

"For that's what God fears, my friends. That, knowing all, we can make him *irrelevant*!" He suddenly stopped and stared down at MacDonald. "But you would deny the animal, wouldn't you? *Mind* over matter. Very well, then. I will show true power, mind over matter, and make a small sacrifice of that which is animal. That we will return to our master."

MacDonald steeled himself, feeling real fear now, knowing what that terror from beyond the grave could do with the flick of a hand.

He felt the Dark Man's gloved hand around his genitals and he started to cry out in horror, but suddenly the pain there was so enormous that he shrieked in agony instead.

The Dark Man held up the object for all to see, then turned and fed it into the mouth of the largest idol, which suddenly flamed with extraordinary brightness. "*Now* he may serve the bride of our lord!" the Dark Man cried triumphantly, and the crowd and the choir began chanting frantically.

MacDonald passed out from shock and pain, but, unfortunately, he came to rather quickly.

*　　*　　*

When he awoke, he was still stuck, lying on the stone, but the lights were now dimmed and the scenery had changed. A group of hooded and robed people, male and female, now stood before the idols chanting in some impossible tongue, eliciting a response in the same tongue from the congregation at intervals. The Dark Man was out of view, if still in the assemblage.

It was impossible for him to tell just how long he'd been out, but it was still totally dark and he guessed it couldn't have been very long. He felt no more pain, only an itchy tingling in his groin. He managed to move a hand to the area, and felt only a small lump below which was a hole. Not a vaginal sort of hole, just a cavity about large enough to insert a finger. So it hadn't been a nightmare or an induced hallucination. He wanted to cry, but not even tears would come. The proceedings seeming like a dream to him. They'd been right, he realized. Angelique, Maria. . . . They'd been right. Everyone has a price, a fear, a secret horror which, if realized, makes even death seem pleasurable. The Dark Man had finally found his own personal demon, his own most secret terror, and had done it; done it with the knowledge that his victim knew that with the demonic mastery over form, it did not have to be permanent—but only the Dark Man could replace it.

But this was the Dark Man's swan song, he remembered. Tonight the power would be transferred, transferred and multiplied an infinite amount—or at least six to the sixth to the sixth power. Is that what they had in mind for him? A husband as chaste as she?

He was broken and he knew it. He just couldn't fight them any more. He had tried, tried harder than any could expect of a man, and he'd failed, as they all had failed, and he'd paid a price as dear to him as the innocents before him had paid. At least Frawley and the three mercenaries had been lucky. They were dead. He had no idea where Maria and the Bishop were, but they sure as hell couldn't get off this island.

The chanting hit a crescendo, and suddenly all the lighting went out. Then, slowly, the meadow itself began to glow, and varicolored lights of some kind of living energy traced complex designs on the grass. There was silence, but in the distance thunder could be heard, thunder all around, and there seemed a swirl of clouds overhead, as if the sky itself were alive and they were in the eye of some terrible hurricane.

A figure now appeared on the stage behind, just in front of the great central idol. The figure of a girl, radiant and fresh, dressed in some transparent white silky garment and nothing else. She knelt before the idol, then arose, turned, and looked out at the congregation. The choir and the women and then the congregation started in another rythmic chant. As they did so, she seemed illuminated, the perfection of her body showing and shining through the flimsy white dress. Her large eyes were open wide, but she seemed to be staring off in the distance, oblivious to the crowd, as if fixed on something only she could see. Her expression was fixed and yet relaxed, but there was no smile, or frown, or other hint to reveal her inner thoughts, if indeed she had any.

"*Angelique,*" MacDonald whispered, for it was she, and not the primitive she had been reduced to, but the true Angelique, skin fair, eyes greenish, with light, reddish-brown hair flowing down past her shoulders.

And now, above the soft chanting, he heard the Dark Man's voice.

"In the name of Satan Mekratrig, Lord of the Earth; in the name of Lucifuge Rofocale, Emperor and Supreme Ruler of the Underworld, I charge the Princes of the Throne of Dis to come forward and attend this most sacred rite," uttered the voice of the Dark Man, booming over the meadow and perhaps the whole of the island.

And, out of the air, there began to materialize—shapes.

They were so bizarre and the effect so fascinating that for a moment even MacDonald could do nothing but stare.

First came Ashtoreth, a great, dark shape outlined in fire, astride a great winged horse; then came Mammon, then Theutus, Asmodeus, Abbadon, and Incubus, and lastly Leviathan, rising majestically in the center upon a great throne. They were grand and awesome and, most incredibly, they were not visions of horror nor demonic nightmares but creatures of tremendous beauty and power and grace. They floated eerily above the meadow, then took their places in a line behind the stage.

A thought, a line from someplace, came unbidden to his mind. *How great must Heaven be, if such wonderful and majestic angels can still be so great and beautiful and wondrous after their fall from grace. . . .*

And now the very sky was lit with swirling cloudlike forms, and there seemed in the clouds, reflecting the various colors on the grass below, to be great faces, faces of other creatures. Faces of demons, and faces of goat-like creatures with eyes of fire, and faces of creatures so bizarre that man had no words to describe them and no similes he could use.

And the faces spoke as they swirled around the island, in a great single voice, saying, "Blessed are the Princes of Hell, for they shall be restored. Blessed are those who serve, for they shall be given the keys to the universe, and heaven and hell, which are outside the universe."

"In the name of all those who would serve thee unto final victory, we humbly beseech the Lord of the Earth, the Lord of Hell, the Lord of our creation and the true master of mankind who was created in his image, I ask you to appear and to anoint thy vessel for the trials and tribulations to come," called the Dark Man, and MacDonald, barely able to turn his eyes from the creatures lined up behind the stage, saw that the speaker was now standing at the other end of the altar stone, just beyond the pool of blood.

"In the name of the candlestick throne, which is yours to claim, we plead with thee to appear to us," the Dark Man continued.

And now there was a sudden collective gasp and sigh from the crowd, and they all turned and looked towards the Institute. The look on their faces was as if they had beheld the face and form of God Himself; total, complete, abject worship and subjugation. They fell upon the ground, and on each other, because there was so little room.

MacDonald could see a glow from that direction, but was unable to turn and see for himself what all, even the Princes, were seeing.

Angelique, too, turned now, and for the first time there was an expression on her face, a softening, as if all doubts and fears were swept away by one glance at whatever it was that hovered over the Institute, and there was even the trace of a smile on her lips.

"Behold, the Master claims his bride, and anoints her Queen of Earth," said the Dark Man.

Now MacDonald felt a sudden gathering of heat, and overhead he saw reach out just a tiny corner, just a fraction of what they were seeing, and he was still awe struck. A finger, but a finger of incredible size, glowing with a power and strength and greatness so incredible that it could only be thought *glorious*. There was total silence, and everyone lay flat, as the finger reached for Angelique.

"IN THE NAME OF THE LORD GOD JEHOVAH, CREATOR OF THE UNIVERSE AND OF LUCIFER HIMSELF, I COMMAND THIS TO HALT! I AM FILLED OF THE HOLY GHOST, AGAINST WHICH NOT EVEN HELL MAY STAND!"

The voice was so loud, so commanding, and such an obvious departure from the script that there was a frozen moment of silence. Even the finger seemed to pause in midair.

MacDonald stared, and saw a strange figure in one of the hooded robes standing between him and the Dark Man on the altar stone, facing Angelique. He turned and discarded the robe, throwing it on the ground, and they saw that it was just a man, a very old man with flowing white hair and still a few bits of black on his face, but dressed in the robe of a Bishop.

Alfred Whitely had a strong, determined look in his eye and a steely expression. He alone among the whole crowd seemed not the least bit awed or impressed by the display to date. The robe looked a little rumpled; he must have taken it in his pack and changed after blowing the antennas.

In his left hand he clutched his old, worn red Bible; in his right he held up a large golden cross that seemed to shine of its own accord.

Whitely ignored the Dark Man, only a few feet from him, and turned instead towards the vision whose finger alone MacDonald could glimpse.

"IT IS NOT YET TIME! BEGONE UNTIL THE BOOK OF LIFE IS FILLED!" the Bishop commanded in a tone and with authority so strong it dwarfed even the Dark Man. He suddenly and quite spryly leaped up onto the stage itself and put himself between the finger and Angelique.

The Dark Man became very confused. He attempted to throw his power and energy at the old man and absolutely nothing happened. Frustrated, he screamed at someone out of sight beyond MacDonald's head, "You men! He's just a doddering old fanatic! Shoot him! *Shoot him!*"

"*NO!*" came a voice that seemed louder than thunder and greater than any human voice could be.

There was a sudden short burst, and three bullets tore into Whitely from the front, knocking him back into Angelique. He smiled, pulled himself back up, and placed a bloody hand on her white dress which was already somewhat spattered. Angelique looked confused, blank, unable to react at all.

The Bishop was mortally wounded, yet he took a pain-wracked step forward, holding out the cross with his right hand, then another, until he was at the great extended finger. Nobody seemed able to move or do anything but watch.

"*I'm not afraid of you, Lucifuge Rofocale,*" said the Bishop weakly, but determinedly. "*I think* you *are afraid of me!*"

Whitely touched the cross to the extended finger, and there was suddenly a tremendous, almost blinding flash of energy. For a moment, it seemed to engulf the Bishop, and then reach beyond him into the ground itself below the stage.

There was a tremendous, mournful howl of pain and outrage from the creature with which he'd joined, a cry so terrible that the very ground shook and the island trembled.

There was a sudden panic, and screams and yells from the assembled multitudes, but MacDonald couldn't take his eyes off Angelique.

The altar stone shook, and the Dark Man fell off the bottom end, but somehow MacDonald stayed on as if stuck to it. The stage trembled as well, and the idols fell backwards and tumbled off with a crash. Suddenly a small form darted onto the stage, dressed in black, and pushed Angelique down onto the altar stone just as the stage itself collapsed. The tiny figure removed something from around its neck and put it over Angelique's head, then looked up at him.

"Maria," he croaked.

The entire island was shaking as if it were about to fracture itself apart, and trees began to topple. There was a strong odor of rotten eggs, and then from the ground all around plumes of steam erupted with great fury.

Maria came up to him and he heard her even above the roar. "Tough shit, Greg, but I told you not to come. The old boy was right after all, huh? I'd like to stay, but maybe I can make it off this sucker before it blows. If not, I sure paid back my dues!" She kissed him and jumped off the rock and started running into the trees.

Angelique lay there, half in the pool of blood, eyes closed, as the whole island continued to shake. He wanted to get to her, to try and get them both off, but he still couldn't move.

All around now there seemed a great fog of white, yet in the white there seemed to be shapes, strange shapes not unlike those of the cloud and the Princes, yet somehow different, brighter, *cleaner*. They were solid, humanoid, yet they seemed to grow out of the clouds and be yet a part of them. None was still long enough for him to get a clear view, but he knew they were all around.

There were the sounds of people screaming in pain and panic, screams which seemed to be progressively stilled.

And still he and Angelique were stuck to that damned rock!

He sensed a presence behind him and perhaps a bit above him, but he couldn't turn his head to see who or what it was. He couldn't be sure, but he thought he heard a clear, joyous voice, one that was very familiar.

"*Without a willingness to sacrifice, mankind is not worth saving from Hell or from himself,*" something whispered in what sounded very much like Whitely's voice. "*Without shedding of blood there is no remission of sin. Take care, son. We've won the battle, but the war goes on.*"

"My Lord Bishop!" he croaked, and reached out a hand to the air, but there was nothing, nothing there at all.

And now a tremendous blast of heat and flame roared down from the top of the mountain and engulfed not only the pair on the altar stone but also the whole of the island, and he could see the entire jungle ablaze before he passed out from its effects, this time for a very long time.

16

SCIENCE AND SORCERY

He slept the sleep of peaceful dreams. The nightmares were there, but every time they would intrude something gentler intervened and forced them away.

And yet, he finally did awake, although the awakening was tempered by drugs and seemed in its own way a dream. He opened his mouth as if to say something, but nothing came forth but a harsh croak.

"Don't try to say anything," said a woman's voice gently. He tried to focus his eyes, and saw that it was a nurse. "Just relax and take it easy. You are in the intensive care unit of St. Ignatius Hospital in Port of Spain. You've been here for quite a number of weeks now. We thought we were going to lose you."

"*Ange—lique?*" he managed, although it hurt him even through the drugs and pain killers.

"They found a woman with you, but she's as bad off as you are, if not worse. You just relax now and try not to think. It will take a long time to get you well."

He didn't try any more right then; even that effort had taken all his strength. Yet—how could he stop thinking? Wondering?

Am I—whole or—disfigured? How badly were we burned by whatever it was? Will we both look like the Dark Man?

These thoughts drifted in and out with his consciousness.

The improvement was very gradual, but as the days passed he found himself being able to remain awake and alert for longer periods of time, and to manage a few simple questions. Very slowly, he was able to get the whole story from the outside world's point of view, although they would tell him little about his own condition or that of Angelique. Their very evasiveness on it made him nervous and queasy. He was on a bed but all but his head was inside a form-fitting plastic device that was helping repairs and healing and minimizing infection. He couldn't really see or tell what was there, and when they opened it it was like being behind the wheel of a car when the hood was raised—his view was blocked.

After perhaps a hundred thousand years of dormancy, early in the morning of November first, without any prior warning, the ancient volcano that was Allenby Island had blown its top and erupted with tremendous force. The ash cloud reached around the world, and there were still particles in the upper atmosphere that colored the sunsets and might well for years to come. Actually, there was probably a single early warning, since the telecommunications network had gone off the air a few hours earlier, but a bad storm in the area prevented anyone from coming in by sea or air, and security people on the island, by short wave, had assured everyone that the communications break was caused when a freak explosion of oil storage tanks now under control created a power shortage.

After, there had been a flow of lava, thin and runny like water, very wide but not very deep, and it had run down and spread out so that it blanketed the whole of the island and flowed swiftly to the sea. The Institute, having been built almost entirely within the main crater, was completely consumed, and the flows burned away almost all the jungle and forest and came down to the sea through the town of Port Kathleen, which had been fortuitously evacuated a few weeks before. Not a single structure remained, although here and there were the blasted remains of trees.

No human being could possibly have survived such a blast and such a flow, and no survivors were expected. There had been a top secret meeting in progress involving a great number of important politicians and influential leaders from all over the world, the reason for the evacuation, but they and their entire staffs were lost, of course.

It was over within hours, and finally the superheated steam and gasses rose and created a torrential downpour that helped cool the mass. It wasn't until November third, though, that the first volcanologist could get to the scene and survey it by helicopter. They were making a swing around to look at a particularly odd formation jutting up from the blackness when they saw two badly burned figures on the thing. They assumed, of course, that both were dead, but managed to land experts who could remove the bodies. It was a shock to find that, impossibly, incredibly, both still had weak but definite life signs.

The mere fact of their survival could not be explained, and the fact that both did not die but actually responded to treatment was considered as much if not more of a miracle.

After emergency aid, they had been placed in special tanks created to transport bad burn victims and taken to the closest burn-specialized hospital, which was St. Ignatius. There they had been suspended in larger tanks, getting their air and food from tubes, while specialized solutions helped heal their burns and promote new skin growth.

All of their treatment involved revolutionary new and in some cases experimental ways of treating victims of burns and dehydration, and he was told that, even if they had survived the volcanic fury, an impossibility that had happened, and had survived the transport as well, they would have died within days in the hospital had it been even a year earlier. There was also the fact that the best specialists were immediately flown in, and money was no object.

The next day, the money walked in the door. The King, without whose help all along it would have been impossible to get as far as they did, looked simultaneously grim and overjoyed.

"I couldn't stay away any longer," said Alan Kimmel Bonner, President and Chief Operating Officer of Magellan. "You aren't supposed to have any visitors yet, but you'd be surprised what money and influence can do."

"I saw it—on the island," he said weakly.

"Well, yes. But even when they found out that their fight was a civil war with other elements of the company, they were so overconfident that they ignored us."

"You want a debriefing?"

"That'll wait. I already know the main facts, even the specific ones."

"But the Bishop—the Dark Man. . . ."

Bonner sighed. "Yeah, I know. I'll get your side when you're ready. I don't really need it right now, except for the record."

"If—you know—then you—can tell me," MacDonald managed. "Was it truly the devil? I've got to know!"

"Easy! Take it easy! Officially, and totally classified and buried, that is, it was a mad computer of a generation that maybe we weren't ready to handle yet programmed by even madder individuals. How the magic worked we may never know—but someday we might—but certainly the computer, working with people on the inside and possibly partly on its own, solved the basic matter to energy conversion problem and could somehow project that power wherever and whenever it was needed. Officially, and only for certain people very high in the company, the thing channeled all its reserves into a monstrous image, a fluid, plastic sort of energy, in the air above the institute. It reached down, then, to connect itself to Angelique, and instead the Bishop got in the way. We don't know for sure, but the official theory is that he was trailing something, perhaps a wire, all the way off the stage and onto the ground. When he stuck the cross into the field, the thing was grounded, and it discharged and shorted. Either that or it was partly touching that stone or whatever, to which it was connected, and it created a ground loop. Either way, the energy was forced back on itself, and so great was the power involved that it quite literally melted the rock beneath the Institute down to a depth where it reactivated the volcano. That do it?''

"The Dark Man—an animated corpse. Sir Reginald said he predated SAINT. Said it was his dead brother. . . .''

"Well, we checked that out. For the record, Geoffrey is still in his grave. It was hell to get clearances on that, but I just had to know. We know from Angelique that they were masters at mind control as well as transmutation. There's no doubt that Sir Reginald believed everything he told you, but there's some question as to whether or not those memories were implanted later and back dated to fit the facts. As for the corpse, well, the thing could create a giant lizard to order, in energy first and then solid as need be. If it could do that, why not something that looked like an animated corpse? The ancients had a word for it. *Homunculus.* Laboratory created intelligence. The bright boys think it was the proto-type for what it eventually wanted to do with Angelique— create a human extension for itself.''

MacDonald stared at him. "Do *you* believe that?''

The corporate president looked uncomfortable. Finally he said, "I don't know. I'd *like* to believe it, but there are just a few too many things that can only be explained by stretching the laws of probability beyond their limits. If you ask me if we had a mad computer on our hands, I'd say yes. If you ask me if it went mad because of the madness of its creator, I'd say yes. But if you ask me if there wasn't something else, something lurking there, waiting, taking advantage of all this and moving in to seize control—well, it's pretty unscientific, but I could feel it, and so could you. There was something there that came down and heightened the madness of the world beyond even its normal insanity levels, who pushed and probed and saw an opportunity and reached out to take it. It wasn't something new, but something very old, something usually forgotten or rationalized away until it strikes. We beat it in the past, and we beat it this time, but the opportunities our age gives it means we have to keep up the watch and the fight."

"The Bishop—he thought it all would fail from the beginning. He always planned right from the start to do exactly what he did."

Bonner nodded. "Yes. He and the girl. No disrespect to you and the others, but he had more guts than any human being I could imagine."

"Not guts, sir. Faith. He told me that fighting the ultimate evil required sacrifice. That only by sacrifice could we show God that we were deserving of being saved. He saw the key to the spread of the evil. We all had our price. Mostly it's a threat to life, but in Angelique's case it was the fear of total incapacity for a lifetime at first, then *my* life became the price. Sir Reginald was bought with the lure of the ultimate knowledge and understanding of his life's work and passion. For the others, like the leaders and politicians in the meadow and most of the Institute management and security staffs, it was the even older price—the promise of sheer power, the same thing that seduced the German leaders in the last war." He sighed. "I wasn't immune, either, although I kidded myself that I was. Right at the end they found it, and I forfeited my right to really end this thing. In the end, they couldn't find the Bishop's price, though; they never found a weak spot, and that's what did them in. They didn't find it because of his rock solid faith in his God, even to knowing that God well enough to understand that no materialist threat, no Frawley with his equations and his bomb, could stop them. Only an act of total faith could do so. He looked in the eye something that caused everyone else there to bow down before it merely because they looked on it, and he walked up and spit in its eye before them all.''

Bonner nodded slowly and said, ''Yeah.''

''What about Magellan? Has it survived the loss of its computer heart?''

Bonner chuckled. ''Sure. There was never any question of that. Data was always backed up to three remote units every time it was sent or received. It's not as efficient, but the company goes on, as even Sir Robert knew it would when he put that erase program in SAINT.''

MacDonald started. ''You mean there are three more SAINTs?''

''No, no. Although the Japanese have several that are somewhat SAINT-like, we don't, and even they lack whatever it was that was added to those circuits by Sir Reginald. But, some day, there's going to be another SAINT, or even worse. Nothing is more certain than that you can not uninvent something once it's been invented. Eventually, when we've sanitized and rationalized the data as much as possible, we'll issue a big public report on SAINT's perversion and madness in the hopes that it will be guarded against in the future, but we can only warn.''

''There aren't many nuclear power plants any more,'' MacDonald pointed out. ''It scared too many people.''

''Uh-uh. If you think that, you're deluding yourself. Nuclear power died because it became too expensive. Fusion remains in small laboratory and prototype units for the same reason. It's not the same with computers. SAINT was no larger than the average bedroom in a one room apartment. Not too many years ago, to get that kind of power and storage would have filled up half the world with chips and circuits. This is a technology that gets cheaper every day, and all it really takes is time and enough money to put together folks smart enough to build it.''

"Then—it was all for nothing? All of it? The next time it'll be a dozen SAINTs, or a hundred?''

"Perhaps. We set them back, that's all, like we always have so far. We took out key leaders and some of the best minds likely to serve that sort of cause, but we didn't take out the enemy. Violence is down. Random, insane violence is way down, and even the official kind—wars and very violent movements—is back to its old slow bloodletting levels, for the moment. Our own forefathers bought our generation with their blood and their lives. You, Angelique, Bishop Whitely, Lord Frawley, and the others bought the next generation, but they, too, will have to fight or lose. It's a hell of a system, and lord how it costs, but it's the way things are run around here and we're stuck with it.''

The President of Magellan got up and looked like he was preparing to leave. "You know," he said, "you'll always be on the payroll. Not much salary, but your expense account is higher than mine. A plane is waiting for me. I have to go. You remember, though—anything you want, anything you need, is no problem. You just tell us. It's the least we can do.''

"What I want and need is beyond even Magellan's capacity, I'm afraid," MacDonald said sadly.

Bonner stared at him for a moment, then scratched his chin and said, "You can't be a businessman or a politician, and I'm both, and ever expect a pat hand. Happily ever aftering is for fairy tales. This was more of a—morality play. In a fairy tale, the brave company endures many trials and terrors to fight the dragon holding captive the princess, and when they slay it, finally, the prince and princess go riding off into the sunset. Now the poet sees the struggle as the thing and the fight as really inconsequential. Folks like me look at it and say that if the damned monster was so easily disposed of, he probably wasn't what he was cracked up to be in the first place. No, the old mythologies, for all their monsters and gods had a much better view of the way the world is run. In them, the fight was as important as the struggle, the threat as horrible as its name, and when the dragon fought it fought well and gave the prince and princess terrible wounds. They kill it, but their wounds are severe and never really heal. There's always been a high cost to anything worthwhile. Saving the kingdom which could not save itself has to be first priority, but somebody's got to pay."

MacDonald looked at him glumly, but said nothing.

"It seems to me that you accept the cost, and by the wounds remember the evil but also remember the accomplishment they bought and paid for. You take what you have left, and you do the best you can, out of respect for those who got you through. Somebody cared enough to make sure that both you and Angelique were so coated with some kind of goo that you managed to survive the heat of the eruption itself. Somebody also got that cross over Angelique's head when it might have saved them, instead. Seems to me that your lives were bought with an even heavier price. Seems to me you lost sight of that girl in that wheelchair, all paralyzed from neck to toe, who you were attracted to because she wanted to get on with life and do what she could rather than sink into what she couldn't do. Maybe you ought to think about that."

MacDonald smiled, and wished he could grab the man's hand. He was emotionally touched by the speech, which struck at the very heart of his own dark thoughts and fears. Instead, all he said was, "I didn't know you were a philosopher and a poet, sir. Thanks."

"I'm not," replied Bonner, reaching for the door. "I'm a

businessman and a politician. I steal only from the very best.'' And, with that, he left.

They noted an improvement in his attitude after that, a deep down decision that maybe he did want to live after all. A day later, they sent in Dr. St. Cyr, the King's Rook in their guerrilla organization inside the company. The Jamaican professor was as kind and strong as always.

"The kinds of medical wizards they have on your case are like no others in the world,'' he told MacDonald, "but, like most experts, their bedside manner leaves a lot to be desired. They've got psychiatrists and psychologists all over the place, and if you want them they're available, but it was thought that you just needed some plain talk from somebody you knew.''

"I appreciate that,'' responded the man in the plastic case. "All I've wanted all along is some plain talk and a little truth, like when I'm going to be out of this thing and out of here.''

St. Cyr sighed. "All right. First, let's talk injuries. You know some, but I'll give you the litany.'' And a litany it was—of broken bones, severe external burns, weakened and scorched lungs, and the like. "All of those have responded well to treatment, and the artificial skin has taken to you like a glove. It's bonded so well you'll never know which is which, and in a few years normal wear and tear will cause it to be unnoticeably replaced with your own. You'll need exercise and a physiotherapy program, since your muscles are nothing right now, but six months from now you'll even have all your hair back, at least on your head, or so they tell me. It's snow white—I can see the fuzz—but it's growing out rather well.''

He nodded. "And when does this start?''

"Tomorrow, if you're willing. All things considered, even if we accept the miracle of your survival, you should be horribly crippled and disfigured. You aren't. With therapy and some time you'll look and be able to do pretty much what you always did—with one exception."

He'd known it, but he'd still dreaded it being spoken.

"I know you suspected, but couldn't tell for sure with all that automatic apparatus clamped on down there. This isn't easy to say, but the Dark Man took what you thought he took, and it's still beyond medical science or anything short of what blew in that volcano to restore it to you."

"I—knew. Doctor Bonner as much as told me."

"All right. When they were operating down there, they had to make some decisions very fast. They found enough tissue from the scrotum stuffed in there to graft some of this incredible artificial skin to match. They couldn't ask you, naturally, so they went ahead and formed a vagina and a clitoris like they do for trans-sexuals. It's an old procedure. But so far they've been maintaining your normal male hormone levels. The whole area has formed and mended well, but they have to have a decision before starting any program of rehabilitation with you. You can still attain orgasm, but not in the old way. They can construct a living prosthesis there out of the artificial stuff, but there would be no feeling in it and there's no prostate left. Or they can change the hormones and introduce permanent peptides into your brain that would turn you physically and probably emotionally but not genetically female."

"Huh? What do you mean, 'emotionally?' "

"My boy, they know enough about neural receptors now that they could introduce a substance that would make you fall madly in love for life with the next person you saw."

The idea frightened him. *The next battlefield for the enemy?* he wondered. The idea frightened him even more than SAINT.

"Let me think about it. See myself as I am. But—what about Angelique? They wouldn't tell me anything at all except she was recovering and they refuse to let me see her."

"You will. She's needed more help than you, not so much

for the outside as for the inside. When *she* thinks she's ready, you'll meet her.'' He paused for a moment. ''This isn't the worst of it, though.''

He grew suddenly concerned. ''What?''

''Nine hundred and thirty one men, women and children were evacuated to make way for their doings and held pretty much incommunicado at an old French army base in Guyana leased for the purpose. They're not prisoners any more, and it's been impossible to keep the press away from them. Bonner has managed a very smooth, scientific line complete with the mad computer warnings, but there's a worldwide hue and cry against all large computers. Magellan will survive, but only because it does so little business directly with the public and so much vital to governments, but the whole story is coming out and being splashed across the newspapers and television stations of the world. Even Tass, which is showing how huge capitalistic monoliths, in the name of profits, let such a thing happen beyond the control of weak western governments. Naturally, you and Angelique could hardly be kept out of it. An old associate of yours who calls himself 'Red' has already sold the story of you and he being chased by a monstrous thing to Hollywood for a good sum.''

''Well, I guess it was inevitable. Doctor Bonner was setting things up when he was here, I guess. He knew they couldn't keep a lid on it. So what's the problem?''

St. Cyr sighed. ''Well, money and muscle has kept them out of this hospital, although they've tried, but this isn't a country where secrets are easily kept and this is a pretty large hospital. It's one thing for you to have your private agony, a wound of war, but it's not private now. It's an enormous story, you know. Everyone who reads or watches television knows what happened to you, and also knows Angelique's problems. The *Enquirer* even paid a bundle to interview your ex-wife on what she thought of it and what kind of lover you used to be. The same goes for Angelique, of course, but it's a different sort of case there.''

The implications of it all hit him now, and he groaned. There would be no anonymity, no privacy, ever. Even when it had cooled down and become old news, everyone he'd come in contact with would know. *"Hey, what's it feel like to be castrated?" "Hey, when you gonna grow breasts?" "Oh, I like being out with a celebrity. You're the only guy I feel really safe with."* Jesus!

''The company will provide good security, but sooner or later you're going to have to face this. I thought you ought to understand, before making your decision.''

He sighed. ''What would *you* do?''

''Well, I can't comment, and at my age it wouldn't make much difference, but it's far easier to be one thing than neither, socially. With hormone, peptide, and plastic surgery you would appear normal and fit into society as one thing. A change of name and location, a false background, and you would be able to have a private life. Even without the change, you'd be ten minutes of old news then instead of a continuing. . . .''

''Freak. Yeah, I know. *Shit!*'' Normal, huh? To them, perhaps, but not to himself.

It was several days of exercising before he could manage even to stand with a walker, and he couldn't go far, but he did manage to look at himself, naked, in a full-length mirror. St. Cyr had been right—aside from what appeared to be a permanent new dark reddish complexion and white hair, whatever damage had been done to him had been so skillfully rapaired he could hardly believe how little he'd changed. He looked at himself, and tried to imagine himself as a woman, and failed miserably. All he could do was look at it all and cry.

But he knew he'd always be Gregory MacDonald, not

Georgette or whatever, until he died, and he so told his physicians.

The therapists were excellent, and he was on solids in a week and walking where he pleased within the month, although it would still be some time before he was absolutely right. He could, in fact, go to outpatient soon, although the truth was he had no idea where the hell he was to go now that it was over.

Father Dobbs paid him a visit near the end of the eighth week after he'd been freed of his devices. He'd been busy filling out forms and writing official reports and it had taken up a lot of his time and taken his mind off things.   .

He was glad to see King's Bishop, even if the title elevated him a notch, but he knew that Dobbs had not come all the way down to Port of Spain just to see him.

After the usual pleasantries and small talk and comments on how fit he looked, the priest got around to the point. "She wants to see you, my boy. She wants to see you very much, and the doctors think that it will be the best thing for her."

He was instantly excited, but he came down fast. "Does she—know about me?"

"No. We thought you should be the one to tell her. It's a hurdle you've already faced, and she must now."

He nodded. "How is she?"

"Well, she is as fit as she will ever be. There is no trace of the old paralysis, but she had extensive internal injuries. One of the bullets that struck the Bishop passed through into her right hand at an odd angle, and she's got only limited control of the hand and she's lost two middle fingers on it. Her scars aren't disfiguring, but they dwarf yours. She broke bones in her hip and pelvic region when she fell—repairable, but because of the time lost she'll always walk a bit stiffly. She claims that these are small prices to pay for having full muscular control, but we know it's bothering her. Of course, she'll need continuing physical therapy and medication for a while, as will you.''

"And her hair's white, too? I been thinking of a dye job now that I have enough to matter, but I've let it slide.''

Dobbs sighed. "No. Uh—she wasn't quite as fortunate as you. She was on the lower end of the stone and got more of the heat blast. She has no hair at all, and they say that none will ever grow there. They've tried transplants from others and some artificial business, but none of it took. She's done small eyebrows with a liner or somesuch, but she won't abide a wig. She says it's part of her penance and she wants to be seen just like that.''

He nodded. "That sounds normal. Does she remember anything?''

"All of it, until that last night. They put her into some sort of trance state. She has occasional visions, but nothing more, and the visions are disjointed and distorted and make little sense. She knows what happened, though. The only clear thoughts she has is someone pushing her onto the rock and then the screams and the heat, and she says that, during that time, Bishop Whitely came and talked to her. You can see the state she's in.''

"Well, maybe," he responded, remembering his own visitation.

"She's been burdened by tremendous guilt, as if everything that happened and everyone who died was on her own head. It's taken a lot of work on the part of psychiatrists here, all Jesuits, of course, to get her back this far. She's always been a mystic of sorts, and while she's quite normal in most ways, she's the Angelique who's been through all this. She puts on a brave front, but deep down she's scared to death.''

"When do we go?''

"As soon as you get dressed.''

He put on an old pair of jeans and a tee shirt, rejecting the

hospital garb for such an occasion, and followed Dobbs.
They had kept her in the opposite end of the wing from him.

A middle aged man in the black suit and clerical collar of
his profession met them and shook hands with MacDonald.
"I'm Father LaMarche, from Montreal," he said. "Glad to
meet you. I've heard quite a lot about you." He paused a
moment. "She wants to see you alone. I concure, but I think
we ought to have an understanding first."

"Go ahead."

"She considers herself married to you. Even though it was
by an Anglican cleric and wasn't consummated or legally
registered, you'll never convince her that anything Bishop
Whitely did wasn't with God's will. He must have been quite
a man."

He nodded. "He was. Uh—you know it'll never *be*
consummated?"

"Yes, but break it to her gently. I don't know what it will
do to her, and she's come so very far." He hesitated a
moment. "Her theology has also become, shall we say,
radically unorthodox, despite her background and my best
efforts. Be prepared there, too."

He nodded. "My theology's gone a little around the bend,
too, Father. Don't worry. Can I see her now?"

"Yes, go on in. Just—take it slow. Be gentle."

He could never be otherwise with Angelique.

They had cleared out a small visitor's room for them. It
was glass enclosed and looked out on the beach and the sea.
It had a number of plants and several padded chairs and one
sofa. She stood there, wearing a silk robe of blue which had
a hood to cover all of her head but her face. She was looking
out at the sea, but she turned when he entered and he saw her
face, the same beautiful face he'd seen on her when they had
first met so long ago on Allenby Island. Her eyelashes, at
least, had grown out, and she had put on lipstick and drawn

fine brow lines with an eyebrow pencil that looked quite natural and attractive.

She smiled when she saw him. "Hello," she said, her voice the same as it had been. "You look just as I expected you would. They told me you'd grown white hair. I think it looks very nice."

He returned the smile but did not approach her. "Then I won't dye it."

"You like the robe? I seem to have gotten a taste for silk somehow, and I have the money to get what I want."

"You sure do," he responded, trying to be light. "All I got was an unlimited expense account."

There was a certain tension on both their parts, each not sure how to really break their own secrets with the other.

"All that I have is yours," she told him, "if you want it. This is a Commonwealth country. We could make it legal at a magistrate in no time. But you must—see me—first." She pulled back the hood and undid the robe, letting it fall to the floor.

She had never stood more naked than she did there. The total absence of hair, particularly on her head, produced a startling effect, but she did not look like some horror. She had the head for it, and while she looked quite different, she was still somehow sensual and erotic. Her body was the same fine one she'd had before, although not the perfection it had been. Clearly she had been eating well. Still, her injuries were far more apparent that his. In spite of the unmarked face and good figure, she'd never be a photographer's model.

"You've put on weight," he noted softly.

She smiled, and the smile turned into a laugh, and she ran to him and hugged him and he hugged her back. She was overjoyed at his reaction, but she suddenly sensed a coolness in him, in his less than total embrace, and stepped back.

"Something is the matter. Something you are not telling me."

"You lost your hair. I lost something—else." Since it was public exposure time, he felt he might as well get it over with and undid his pants and let them fall to the floor.

She stood back and stared, and her jaw dropped a little. The physicians had done a perfect job. Aside from the growth of some pubic hair, which he hadn't expected, his looked just like hers.

"Then—then it wasn't a dream," she whispered. "They really did it."

He nodded and bent down and pulled his pants back up. "They really did."

"Does it—work?"

"If you're asking if I can get pregnant, the answer's no. Otherwise, they tell me I'd feel just what you would."

"You haven't—tried it?"

"No. I'm Greg, and I'll stay Greg."

Suddenly she started to laugh. Concerned, he went over to her. "You all right? I know it's a shock, but it was a shock to me, too."

"No, no! I am just thinking that after all this, somehow we are both now virgins!"

He had to smile at that, no matter what the internal anguish.

She stopped, seeing that it hurt him, and hugged and kissed him, then picked up her robe once more and donned it, this time leaving the hood down. "I am sorry. Truly so," she told him sincerely. "We two are not as far apart as all that. Much of me, inside, is now plastic. I, too, am barren."

He looked at her, and found more pity for her than for him. He still was in pretty good shape and he'd had half a lifetime whole and free. She had never had that kind of chance. She had mobility and money now, but she would never know normalcy

Up until now, she'd been open, confident, more extro- verted than she'd ever been, but now she seemed small and weak once more. "I need you, Greg. I really do. My money will bring me fair weather friends and leeches, who will say that they adore me until I am out of the room and they can laugh behind my back, but nothing else. They say you can leave any time? Be an out-patient almost anywhere?''

He stared at her. ''Yeah, sure. I just haven't had any place to go, and I couldn't leave without seeing you.''

''Very well, then. I have all this money, and money talks. I am selling Magellan to a group headed by Doctor Bonner for a pittance. A mere four hundred million dollars—American, not Canadian—in a massive trust fund with the other inheritance. Half of it I will donate to various religious charities and to medical research. I do not know yet what I will do with the rest. But, I think if I wish to go, they cannot stop me.''

''I'll go along with that. Where are you going?''

''*We* are going. First we are going to a magistrate who will waive all the technicalities because of who I am, and with whom you will not discuss your—injury. Then we are going to the finest hotel in Port of Spain and taking the grandest suite they offer.''

''Huh? Why—what?''

''You *idiot!* Did you think that would *matter*? Did I fall in love with your *organ* or with *you*? Once I was confused and silly on this matter, but I have learned so much about myself and the world now. Did not the Bishop, like the God he served, love us all far more than we deserve to be loved? And is it not love that makes us more than the animals the Dark Man claimed we were? It is lust that is from the animal. It is love which is the part of us that is from God.''

He wanted to do it, wanted to very badly, but he couldn't bring himself to inflict it on her, particularly as the years went by.

''It—it just isn't going to work, Angelique. I *do* have lusts, and I'm going to have a hard time dealing with them, even harder if I am always with you. Besides, I have no stomach for the rich life. I'd just get fat and lazy and vegetate, while you would want and deserve the glamor of the world. And eventually you would want what I can't give you, and I'd want it, too. What would we do in that honeymoon suite? Have some kind of two way dildo sent up from the local sex shop?''

She stopped and frowned. "What is this 'dildo?' ''

He told her, and she laughed again. "That sounds interesting. By all means we must try it!'' Suddenly the laugh faded, and she grew almost somber. I think you truly do not love me, then. Is it the money? I will give it *all* away. I have never had need of it before. *Oui.* I will give it away. We will start clean. And if your pride demands it, I will stay home and be the good little wife and clean and mend.''

"No, my pride doesn't demand that. I just—can't—see how it'll work out.''

"Then I give it all away anyway. I return to Quebec and take my vows. Without you, without your support, your friendship, your love, the rest is meaningless.''

He grabbed her suddenly. "You're really serious?''

"I am more than serious. I will do it. I will marry either you or Christ within the week.''

He sighed. "I guess you'll have to marry me, then. But keep some of the money. We're going to need competent security for the rest of our lives, I'm afraid, and that costs. Besides, if I ever needed to find a job, I couldn't pass the physical.''

She smiled broadly and threw her arms around him.

"Come, Gregory MacDonald! I will show you how serious I am, and how much you failed to learn through all this!''

Many on the staff and otherwise did not approve of it, but her chief psychiatrist thought it was the best thing for both of them and helped. When you're rich, what you want comes to you, including a magistrate and a pre-filled out marriage license and all the rest. Arrangements were also quickly made to sneak them past the waiting press and off to a private, well secured resort for the very rich on an isolated stretch of the Grand Cayman Islands. There, in a luxury condominium overlooking the ocean, unobtrusively protected by a security system and staff he himself designed, they were finally able to feel a measure of peace and relaxation.

MacDonald pretty much was along for the ride. He was washed up as a lover and even as a good socialist, yet he found himself surprisingly happy. He remembered his files, and his ex-wife's own evaluation, that he was the ultimate egocentric personality, and he realized with a start that he had changed far more than physically. He was no longer the sun, but a world in orbit around a different sun, that of Angelique. For the first time, he needed someone else to give him purpose and meaning, and it wasn't a terrible condition at all.

And now a three-quarters moon was rising above a darkened sea, and as they stood hand in hand at the doors to the balcony of the luxury suite, they held hands and comtemplated their first really private moments together after all of this. In a sense, he'd been dreading, even putting off this moment, when they were alone together.

"Are you happy, my darling?" she asked him.

"Yes, in a crazy kind of way, I think I am. Something dear was taken from my body, but, the funny thing is, something else was added in my head, something that had always been missing but I hadn't known it before. For the first time, I care about the victims."

"What?"

"Don't ask me to explain it. I can't. I think Bishop Whitely understood it, though. I think that's what he was trying to tell me at the end."

"He—came to you on the rock?"

"Yes. And you, too, I understand. You want to tell me what he said?"

"He said—love, and faith, and sacrifice were costs, but that they were why, up to now, we'd always won. He said that someone who kept love in their heart and faith in God and man would find any sacrifice a mere trifle. He said that I was saved by faith and sacrifice, and that I had now to carry on the love against which Hell itself could not stand, and that if I looked within myself there was no problem I could not overcome."

He kissed her, and that, at least, was the same, and he even felt a tingling sensation in the right area of the groin. She removed his clothing slowly, and then her own, and they embraced again, and hands felt each other's strangely identical parts. The room was dark, except for the light from the moon and a few street lamps below.

And, suddenly, Angelique knew exactly what to do and how to do it.

She closed her eyes and whispered, not to him, "*Unab sequabab ciemi!*"

There was a sudden rush of warm air all about them, although the balcony door was mostly closed and the room was air conditioned. He felt the sudden presence of *others* in the air of the room and all around, but there was nothing he could see or sense, and he stiffened, not knowing quite what to expect.

"*Father of all, angel of nature, spirits of Earth, Air, Fire, and Water, harken, for the Mother has found her perfect lover,*" she continued in the strange languare of the Hapharsi. "*Let that lover be filled with the soul of the he-lion and the bull, that I may be serviced and have release!*" It wasn't real, it couldn't *be* real, but it sure *felt* real, and if anything, even bigger and better than it was. He felt a sudden surge of pure animal energy, and he made love to her in the way he wanted to through half the night.

And yet, when they awoke, late in the afternoon, they both were as they had been. There was no mistaking the reason for the radiance of her expression and the softness of her manner, and he, too, felt satisfied, and remembered it all clearly. He was *sure* that, somehow, he'd made love to her, as a whole man, over and over, for a longer and more satisfying period than he ever had before with a woman, and that all had been—well, *normal*.

She kissed him playfully. "Do you still worry, my love?"

"Yeah. Am I going nuts—or what?"

"Magic isn't good, or evil, it just *is*," she told him. "Like everything else in this world, it can be good or evil depending on who uses it and for what purpose. That goes for spells, and—computers."

"Yeah, but—"

"Don't start with the 'buts,' my love. The magic doesn't work as well with 'buts.' And don't be so afraid. There's nothing to fear. They made me a Hapharsi *Mu'uhquah* for their own evil ends, but make me one they did. It doesn't matter what I look like or who I am—it's there, particularly in the dark. The ancient priestesses, to preserve their virginity and thus their power, took female lovers, but most of them still craved, at least occasionally, what they could not have. Sometimes as the male, sometimes as the female, they had it better and more often than the tribe. That's why they never succumbed to temptations of the bisexual flesh."

"Then—it was an illusion?" He'd known it, but it had been so good, so *real*.

She shook her head in disgust. "After all we have been through, you and I, you can worry about what is real and what is illusion? The world is a magic place, my darling, if you wish it to be, if you believe that it is. Who is to say where reality ends and illusion begins? Who *cares*?"

Who cares indeed? "You know, I can still get that change-over. Go all the way. I think that's what St. Cyr meant. It doesn't matter to me any more what I look like, but I'd be perceived as normal by others. Me like that and you with a wig and we could go places and do things without a whole army of security people.''

''Oh, no. I will not give you a chance to be a *voyeur* in the ladies' rooms of the world. I think you are perfect just the way you are, and I would be content right now if this, right here, went on forever. We have earned it. What I see in your eyes in more than enough of the world for me.''

He grabbed her, and held her close, and kissed her, and they were at it again without benefit of spells or special augmentation. She broke for air and laughed. ''We forgot the dildo.''

''Who cares?'' he retorted, and kissed her again.